PAPERCUTS

COLIN BATEMAN is an author, screenwriter and playwright. He is the creator of the BBC series *Murphy's Law* and was listed by the *Daily Telegraph* as one of the Top 50 crime writers of all time. Find out more at colinbateman.com

PAPERCUTS

A NOVEL IN EIGHT WEEKLY ISSUES

COLIN BATEMAN

HEAD ZEUS

First published in the UK in 2016 by Head of Zeus Ltd

This paperback edition first published in the UK in 2016
by Head of Zeus Ltd

9 7 5 3 1 2 4 6 8

A catalogue record for this book is available
from the British Library.

Paperback ISBN 9781784973803
Ebook ISBN 9781784974015

Typeset by Adrian McLaughlin
Printed in the UK by Clays Ltd, St Ives Plc

Head of Zeus Ltd
Clerkenwell House
45–47 Clerkenwell Green
London EC1R 0HT

WWW.HEADOFZEUS.COM

arts
council
of Northern Ireland

For Matthew and Isaac

Johnny Cash shot a man in Reno,
just to watch him die.
Rob Cullen bought curly kale in Tesco's,
just to watch it wither.

CHAPTER 1
THE DEAD AND THE QUICK

The way Rob heard it, Billy Maxwell choked on a Twix in the middle of an editorial meeting and they were so busy arguing about the unfair distribution of that week's stories that they didn't notice until he slid out of his chair onto the linoleum floor. When they asked if he was okay, they got a death rattle in response. They tried everything, but it was Billy's time. He was fat and fifty and opening the Twix was the most exercise he'd managed in years. Legend had it that Janine in Advertising was left to stand watch over him, like he was going somewhere, while everyone else ran about in a blind panic, and while she was there she unpeeled the untouched leg of the Twix from Billy's cooling hand and ate it. When he got to know her later, Rob realized that this was probably true. Janine was ruthless.

Now Rob was striding out of the George Best Airport staring around him like any other native lured reluctantly back for the first time in twenty years. On the plane some auld doll had said to him he wouldn't recognize the place and he thought, *Yes I fucking will*, but she was right, it was different, and not just shiny and new, there was something in the air, initially exhilarating but also somehow artificial, like Pine Fresh. The taxi driver was asking him if he was just here on business, but then caught a glimpse of him slipping into his black tie, gave him a nod, and said nothing else till they got to the church on the Donegal Road.

He had known Billy loved his football team, but not this much: the coffin coming in to the pumping Everton theme from *Z-Cars*, except they got the timing all wrong so that the hummable bit everyone knew was over by the time they were half-way down the aisle, leaving Billy to travel his last few feet to the weird, staccato jazzy bit that formed the latter part of the tune. Still, it would be another story to tell, and there were lots of stories about Billy and they all came out in the pub later. Rob knew some of the faces, older, more haggard, run to fat or emaciated, and he supposed his wasn't much different – less hair, more poundage – but he didn't know any of them well enough to chat about anything personal, which was a good thing.

In the early evening, a little the worse for wear and just about to make his exit, a pugnacious-looking fella, looking like he was in the same boat, caught his eye at the bar, nodded and said, 'Grand man, so he was.'

'Aye,' said Rob, 'taught me everything I know.'

'Really?' The fella moved closer. He was probably in his forties, a little heavy but with a good smile coming out of a neat beard. 'You in the business, too?'

'Aye, the *Guardian*,' Rob said.

'*Ballymena Guardian*?'

'No, the *Guardian*. London.'

'Really? Seriously? And you came all this way to…?'

'Like I say.'

2

Rob finished his pint and set it on the bar. Before he could turn to leave, the fella clicked his fingers and said, 'two more.'

The barman didn't look very impressed at being clicked at. Rob started to say that no, really, he had to be going, but he only had a cheap room waiting for him and he knew he'd only end up watching telly with a bit of a headache, and he might as well delay that misery for a while longer, so he accepted the pint and they stood and talked newspaper business. The fella's name was Gerry Black and he ran the weekly paper Billy Maxwell had been editing twelve miles down the road in Bangor before his confectionery-related demise. Rob remembered Billy as a take-no-prisoners sub on the daily *News Letter* at the tail end of the Troubles, and couldn't really picture him running a local paper in a comfortably middle-class and long-faded seaside resort. Gerry said his paper was the sort of place where old journalists came to die, and on this occasion, literally. Billy had actually started out on the same paper when he was a teenager before making a swift exit for Belfast. 'You either get out within three years, or you're there for life,' said Gerry. 'Nothing's changed.'

They were in the process of ordering their second pint when Rob noticed a blonde woman in a dark suit just along from them, staring hard at his drinking companion, one hand on the bar, fingers drumming. She drained a shot glass, then moved along to them. She was good-looking, maybe late twenties with a long thin nose. She was slightly the worse for drink herself, but then most of them were. Rob expected a showdown. It was the nature of funerals. And weddings. He turned to pick at the few remaining sandwiches sitting on a platter on the bar behind him as the woman said, 'Gerry. A word.'

'Ah now, Alix,' said Gerry. 'Let me get you a drink.'

'I don't want a drink, Gerry, I want paid.'

'Alix – this is hardly the time.'

He started to turn back to Rob, but the woman, Alix, all glare and flared nostrils, grabbed his arm.

'It's exactly the time! I'm sorry he's gone and all that, but I haven't been paid in a month and I'm starving.'

Rob, drink allowing him to think it might defuse the situation, lifted the platter and offered it to her. Alix gave him a look of utter disdain. He set it back down, though he couldn't help smiling. Actually, he thought it was a smile, but it was more of a smirk. He understood this because she pointed it out.

She said, 'What the bloody hell are you smirking at?'

Rob held up an apologetic hand and said, 'Nothing' through the tuna sandwich he had just squeezed into his mouth.

She probably would have had more to say to him if Gerry hadn't draped an arm around her shoulders and given her a squeeze. 'Alix, darling,' he said, with her stiffly against him for just a moment before she pushed his arm off, 'Alix, darling – it's not my fault. Billy was a great editor, but he couldn't manage for toffee. If he doesn't – didn't – send the paperwork through to me, then I can't, couldn't, process it – but it's not a problem. Just tell me how much it is and I swear to God I will sort it out.'

'When?'

'Now.' He pulled a chequebook out of his jacket and set it on the bar. He patted his pockets again and found a pen. 'Sorry – I've taken my eye off the ball a bit. Alix – your second name?'

She let out a sigh. 'Cross.'

He repeated her full name as he wrote it out. Then he said, 'And how much are we talking about?' When she told him he raised an eyebrow, but kept writing. He signed and dated the cheque and tore it out and handed it to her. She looked at it, and her eyes widened slightly. 'Just a little extra as well – call it a ... a bereavement bonus. Billy would have wanted it. He always spoke very highly of you.'

Alix took the cheque and blew on it before folding it carefully. 'I ... Sorry,' she said. 'Just—'

'It's fine. Now go and have another wee drink and then I'll see you bright and early tomorrow.'

It was a double-edged dispatch. She turned away without giving Rob a second glance. Gerry shook his head and said, 'She's trouble with ... a gorgeous ass.' He held his hands up and said, 'Sorry, you're not allowed to say that. I mean *arse*.'

He gave Rob a theatrical wink, and then did the clicking thing for more drinks. Rob had been having renewed thoughts about an exit strategy, but the pint was suddenly there before him and he was cut off at the pass again. And he didn't really mind talking newspapers because Gerry was lapping it all up, almost star-struck. Rob remembered when he was on a local, how easily impressed he'd been by anyone on a daily. He'd started there, too, different town, up the coast, but weekly papers were the same everywhere, or had been. Family-owned and -mismanaged.

It was early evening by then, and the after-work crowds had started to arrive, so they pounced on a vacated snug and kept nattering, and somehow three or four or maybe five more pints were consumed. Somewhere along the line Gerry said, 'I like you Rob. It's good to see someone do well for themselves. You must have liked Billy a lot, all the way back from the Big Smoke for a few pints and curly sandwiches.'

'Ah, it's not that far. And yes, he trained me up and then told me to get the hell out of Dodge. But the good old days, when journalism...' He gave Gerry the helpless hands and Gerry nodded but then looked suddenly thoughtful. He took another sip, then put his hands on the table, clasped, and rubbed the two thumbs together.

'Cards on the table?'

'Sure. Why not, aren't we old pals?'

Gerry smiled and said, 'My paper, the *Bangor Express*—'

Rob snorted involuntarily. 'That's what you call it? The *Bangor Express*?'

'Sure I do. What's wrong with that?'

'I've been to Bangor. There's not a lot of express about it.'

'It might surprise you.' Gerry raised an eyebrow. 'Or probably not. We've been around a hundred years, you know, never missed a week. That's some going. Now – cards?'

'Sorry, yes...'

'My paper – the aforementioned and much-derided *Bangor Express* – is, if you'll excuse my language, dying on its fucking feet. It's been in the family for ever, but we're losing money hand over fist. Tell you the truth, it's not my main interest. It never was. I'm into property. Correction, I *was* into property, the paper was always a bit of a side line, motored along quite nicely without much care and attention needed, and it has, or had, a bit of prestige about it, makes me sound more interesting that I'm a newspaper proprietor, a regular Rupert, than just doing up run-down properties and selling them on like any jumped-up brickie. But it's only when the property went tits up that I took a proper look and realized that actually it wasn't motoring on nicely at all but pissing money down the sink. So whether we're joining the late-lamented Billy underground around this week or next, I don't know. But I do know it can't go on the way it is.'

'Papers are going that way, Gerry. You're not the only one.'

'I know that. But I can't help thinking, there's something good there it's just – you know like that pond weed you get, that chokes off everything? Like that, or something. Something that needs to be teased out, nurtured, turned around.' He took another big drink. 'In fact, I have a plan.'

'Good to have a plan,' said Rob.

'Oh yes.' He took out his chequebook and slapped it on the table. 'So I'm going to write you a cheque for how much so that you'll pop down the coast with me, take a look at the set-up, and tell me if there's something worth saving or I cut my losses and get out? What do you say?'

'I'd say cut your losses and get out now.'

'Five hundred quid for a day's work.'

'You'd be pouring good money after bad. And I can't, honestly, I'm on the first flight in the morning.'

'Book another. Out of the thousand quid I'm going to give you.'

'No, Gerry, I appreciate the offer, but really. Have to get home. And besides, the *Guardian* is not the *Bangor Express* – different world. Find someone who knows about local papers. Probably in this bar, it's stuffed full of reporters who'll know more than I do.'

'I don't want anyone else. I want you.'

Rob burst into laughter. Gerry too.

'Ah, fuck it,' he said. 'Thought I'd give it a lash. Fair enough. If you can't, you can't. But I do believe it's your round.'

Rob bought the drinks.

Gerry bought some more.

About ten, they went for a kebab.

They got back into a different bar, later, with some band playing. They were doing Beatles covers, badly. Rob didn't actually remember going back to the hotel, or falling

7

asleep fully clothed on top of the bed, or throwing up in the middle of the night. He was aware it was morning because he'd forgotten to close the curtains and the rare Belfast sunlight was streaming in. His throat was raw, and he knew he'd started smoking again. He wanted coffee, but his head was too sore to move. His forehead felt odd, and it was only when he touched it that he realized it was because there was something stuck to it. A piece of paper. He peeled it off and struggled to focus on it. Eventually he came to realize that what he was holding in his hand was an Ulster Bank cheque for £1500 made out to his name and signed by one Gerry Black.

His head was busting, not just from the drink. It had been that way of late – there was a weight on him, on his shoulders, in his brain, in his heart, his soul, in the pit of his stomach. Avoiding it, displacing it, was an art form he had not yet mastered; nor, he suspected would he ever; that was the point of it. It wasn't one thing, it was several, within his power, without, depending on his mood, the time of day. He had been accused a lot of late of not being there; today, physically, he certainly wasn't, a geographical displacement that he'd leapt at, the funeral of a friend, or a former friend, of a colleague, of a mentor to whom actually he'd not given a thought in years. Billy had been all of those things, but Rob had never been one to look back, always forward. The backward glance was only caused by his accidentally stumbling on the news of Billy's death, but the jump to attend was not purely caused by the loss.

His head was not helped by the stop-start diesel racket of the train. Half an hour down the line from Botanic, sun was

8

blasting through the window so much that he switched to the shady side only to have a yammering kid and an endlessly patient or neglectful granny get on at Titanic Halt. And Rob was thinking, Titanic, what the fuck happened to Bridge End? Everywhere he looked, *Titanic*, a big sunk ship.

Rob had been to Bangor before, a few times. As a kid, a day out to the seaside, but then he remembered going one day with his folks and the seaside was gone, replaced by a monstrous concrete marina and they never went back after that. Once or twice as a journalist, one of those towns that had escaped the worst and even the least of the Troubles – three bombs in thirty years, a handful of shootings; hell, there were towns in Surrey that had had it worse, nearly. He got off the train and had a hot choco in the station and swallowed some pills and bought some mints and located the *Express* office half-way up the main street, Pizza Hut on one side, a Chinese herbalist on the other. He pushed through the door and a smiley woman on the desk left him standing there while she flicked through a bound file of papers. The decor was early seventies, no natural light, fluorescent beamers with dead insects inside dulling the glow, oil paintings on the wall with cobwebs hanging off them, stacks of papers, advertising department and salespeople at the front, behind them an open-plan editorial with what must have been Billy's office beyond. There was a partition wall, largely glass, and then typesetters in a bungalow, a variety of small presses for commercial jobbing but none remotely big enough to produce a newspaper. The girl on the desk finally noticed him and asked what he wanted, and when he asked for Gerry Black she looked at him suspiciously, and, he thought, defensively, and asked if he had an appointment and he said 'Sort of' because he was vague on the time he was expected, in fact he was vague about the latter half of the previous evening, but she nodded at him and was turning to fetch her boss when by chance he appeared at the bottom of the office and waved up, then ushered him through a waist-level swing door. 'Dead on time, chum,' he said. They turned right just before editorial, into a small kitchen where the troops were already mustered on mismatched plastic chairs, hugging mugs and looking nervous. Alix he remembered from the funeral, though she looked at him blankly; a young fella in a slightly-too-big-for-his-shoulders sports jacket; an older guy, older than Rob certainly, with a sour, suspicious look on his face, mostly bald, shirt and tie but corduroy trousers and soft shoes. Together with Billy, that made four to put out a newspaper, which was some going.

Gerry stopped him by a sink filled with unwashed coffee cups and stained with a ring of dried sediment around the rim and nodded at his team. He said, 'Look at your faces! I told you, it's nothing to be worried about – Rob, Rob Cullen is an old friend and he's here purely to give us the benefit of his experience, formerly as a top reporter across the pond and now as a senior management consultant ... just a wee bit of time and motion to see how we're doing, and what we can maybe do a wee bit better. Okay?'

The older guy nodded and said, 'Are you closing us down, Gerry?'

'Peter – no. Of course not. You don't kill a cash cow. You milk it.'

They all looked at him, variously hoping that he would or would not continue with the analogy, but Gerry deflected to Rob and said, 'You'll hardly know he's here. He'll work out of Billy's office for now.' He thumbed behind him. Peter started to say something but Gerry cut him off with, 'No, no decision yet – we've only just buried the guy, it would be ... unseemly to replace him so quickly. But thank you for leaving your CV on my desk.'

'I never...'

The younger reporter, Michael, turned away, trying to suppress a laugh. Alix prodded him with her finger and he burst out. He said, 'Sorry, but swear to God, it wasn't me. Wish I had thought of it...'

'And Peter's quite right,' said Gerry, 'the early bird might get the worm. Though, under the circumstances, worms are hardly an approp ... However, Rob, back to you, you've complete freedom to hoke and poke, but at the same time these guys are trying to put a paper together, and they've just lost their captain, so if it gets a little fraught, just...' He waved his hands randomly. 'You want coffee?'

Rob looked at the sink.

Alix said, 'Michael, your turn for the bun run.'

Michael said, 'I went yesterday.'

'We were at the funeral yesterday.'

'Day before.'

'What's your point?' said Peter. 'Cubs do the bun run. It's traditional.'

'Well, hopefully Rob will find that tradition has no place in the modern workplace,' said Gerry, removing change from his trouser pocket, 'but until he delivers his findings, I'll have a coconut slice and a cappuccino.' He went to pour his coins into Michael's hand, but the hand remained closed. Gerry added, 'Me being the owner of the paper, with ultimate power over hirings and firings.' Michael opened his fingers and accepted the money. Alix and Peter also gave him their orders. Michael looked at Rob and said, 'You?'

'Large coffee, black, like my men.'

They looked at him.

'Joke,' he added.

Whatever the opposite of a paper-free environment was, this was it. There was a requirement for journalists in the pre-digital age to hang on to their notebooks for a number of months, sometimes years, after they wrote their stories, in case any legal issue came up, so that they could refer back to their original notes and produce them if needs be. The *Express* had notebooks, press releases and the endless minutiae of a journalist's life stuffed everywhere and dating back not just months but decades. They were pathological hoarders. Billy's office might actually have been quite spacious if not for the teetering mountains of overflowing boxes, cupboards and stuffed filing cabinets. The desk where Rob was expected to sit still had crumbs of Twix that probably boasted the former editor's DNA. There was a diary with his copious but unreadable jottings open before him and a red felt pen with a chewed end. Rob was trying to interpret the photo bookings detailed in the diary and was so confused he picked it up and began to chew on it himself. When he realized, he almost gagged. He took a quick swallow of now-cold coffee and threw the pen in the bin.

Rob's head had subsided enough for him to get to work. He had not wanted this, but a grand and a half for a day's labour wasn't to be sniffed at. He would do it and do it properly. Senior management consultant might have been laying it on a bit thick, but certainly he'd long since moved on from the doubtful glamour of straight reporting, couldn't remember the last time he'd actually been out on a story. Organizing and leading a team, with one eye on the economics, that was where his career had taken him. He could do *this* with his eyes shut.

He started by going back to the counter and lifting out the bound files he'd seen on the way in. They went back about five years. He asked where the early years were and was told there were some in a strongroom, and the rest were held in the local library. The same girl reluctantly opened the strongroom. He asked her why they needed a strongroom at all and she said it probably didn't really qualify as one but they'd always called it that. They sometimes kept petty cash in there overnight, but mostly it was a suppository for office stationery. Rob said depository and immediately regretted it. She said 'Whatever' and pulled a flimsy-looking door with a metal bar across it open and pointed in at the files. They went back fifteen years. He carried out the oldest, set it on the counter and started to flick through it. He loved the smell of old newsprint. Local newspapers, he knew, were like community goldfish bowls. The same stories kept coming round, year after year after decade. The *Express* had been around for a hundred years without missing a single week, through two world wars and internecine strife that had driven much of the rest of the Province into anarchy. But comparing the papers of fifteen years past and the most recent issues – he could hardly tell the difference. The paper was composed to a basic template and he was pretty sure if he went to the library and checked the hundred-year-old issues there wouldn't be much between those ones either. Granted there was some ground given to colour photography in more recent years, but the stories themselves were almost identical – exhaustively verbatim reports of local courts, council and sporting events, composed on the thinking that, if everyone gets their name in the paper, then they will surely go out and buy a copy, rather than to any notion of writing a story whose length was judged by its news value. The photographs were wildly unimaginative – rarely more than a line of people standing looking fearfully at the camera, as if they were facing a firing squad. There were some attempts at action photos on the sports pages, but most of them were blurrily out of focus. The display advertising had hardly changed either – the same local stores, virtually nothing of a national nature. The biggest difference was in the classifieds – the earlier issues had pages and pages of what used to be known as penny-a-word adverts selling household bric-a-brac, but these had virtually disappeared, migrating wholesale to the internet and eBay – the paper had a website of its own, but it was basic and contained virtually no advertising. In short, the entire newspaper was little more than a relic of a bygone era. People, he thought, probably bought it because it was a tradition to buy it. The problem was, the people for whom it was a tradition were swiftly dying out. Their sons and daughters didn't have the time or patience to wade through the stories or the reams of advertisements that weren't relevant to them, and sales were down, year after year, after year. Rob was a newspaperman, had been all his life, and loved them. It was depressing when a paper like this limped along to its inevitable doom; it had simply failed to change with the times, and now it was far too late to do anything about it.

Despite this, Rob smiled to himself – it was just after 1 p.m. and his money more or less earned. He would do some more poking in the afternoon but essentially he knew what the paper needed. Closure or a proper kick in the arse. Although he didn't have much of an appetite after his night of drinking, he could have eaten something. But when he popped his head out of Billy's old office to see what Gerry or the rest would recommend for lunch he discovered that editorial was empty. In fact, not only was editorial empty, but the entire office. He was the only one left behind. The rats had left the sinking ship, leaving him in charge, with the front door open to all and sundry. He stood at the counter for a while, drumming his fingers, half-thinking it was some kind of wind-up and that at any moment they'd jump out and say boo. But the minutes ticked by, and nothing, nothing.

The phone went and he ignored it. Then another call, and another, and eventually he answered. Someone wanting to dictate a football-match report; Rob told him to email it, but the guy didn't have access to a computer so he started reading it out and Rob had to grab a pen and take it down, and the fella was so serious and verbose that he might well have been delivering the Gettysburg Address rather than an account of a scoreless bottom-of-the-league amateur football match. He'd no sooner finished that than someone from a hair salon rang, and asked for Janine, wanting to place an ad. Rob looked around him, found a rate card and gave her the rate, and she seemed surprised at the price, cheaper than she'd understood. Rob told her to call back after lunch to confirm. With nothing better to do, and with all the office computers on and nobody interested in hiding anything behind passwords, he sat at Janine's desk and started going through the circulation figures and how much was coming in from advertising, and it didn't take him long to find a pattern. He was looking at the numbers with something approaching disbelief when the front door opened and a young fella came in, not more than eighteen, hoodie, attitude, and asked for whoever was in charge. Rob gave him variations of coming back after lunch, but he didn't want to, could Rob not deal with it and Rob said he wasn't really supposed to but when the guy said something about he'd good photos of the robbery, he couldn't resist. He asked him what happened and the fella said he'd been hanging around outside the Mace/Post Office on Groomsport Road and two men in Hallowe'en masks had run in, and a couple of minutes later they'd come charging out with bags of coins. But one of the guys, the elastic on his mask had snapped and, in trying to keep it in place, he'd dropped his bag and the fucking coins had gone everywhere. The young fella had caught the whole thing on his phone, including the robber's face as he scrambled to get his mask back in place, and now he wanted to know how much the paper was going to pay him for his pictures. Rob looked at the pictures: they were brilliant. He could almost see the headline now: Caught red-handed. He loved the expression on the robber's face, the mixture of fear, adrenaline, panic and disbelief.

'Did you show this to the police?' Rob asked.

'Kiddin'?'

'It's really good, really, seriously good.'

'That's what I thought. There's others ... Look.'

He showed them. Just as good, maybe better.

'Are you a photographer? I mean, the composition—'

'Nah. So?'

'So?'

'So what were you thinking?'

'What was I thinking? I was thinking how good they are and how great they'll look on the front page with your name beside them.'

'I was thinking five hundred each, and no name because I don't want them coming round my house and doing the kneecaps.'

'Ah – right, I see. Yes, good call on the name. The money

– it's not my decision, but I'm pretty sure they don't pay for photos. It's just not that sort of a paper.'

He put his hand out to Rob, who was still holding the phone, and clicked his fingers. 'No problem – I'll take them to the *Telegraph*, or the BBC, they'll pay.'

Rob said, 'Yep they probably will. It's a pity though. This is your local paper.'

'Aye, and it's crap. My mate told me to come here first and I said it was a waste of time, and you know what? He was right, and he's not right often. See ya around.'

The fella gave him a wink and walked out of the office.

Rob stood at the counter. Should be no skin off his nose, but he wanted to grab the guy and wrest the phone from his hand. He wondered how long it had actually been since he'd handled something that actually constituted *news*, not a forecast or a spreadsheet. Rob swore to himself, and then pushed through the swing door and across the other side of the counter. He opened the front door and saw the fella just a few yards along, stopping to light a fag.

He said, 'Hold on.'

The boy exhaled and said, 'What?'

'What's your name?'

'What's it to you?'

'Nothing, it's just … I'm Rob.'

'So?'

'So, I want your photos, and I want them for nothing.'

'Aye, right. Why would I want to do that?'

'Because … because it's the right thing to do.'

'Really.'

'Really. It's the right thing to do, and you owe it to this place. These people.'

'Right. How'd you work that one out?'

Rob moved closer. The street was busy enough – an Asda a few doors down, and the all-you-can-eat buffet at Pizza Hut. He said, 'Look – I grew up in a town like this, pretty quiet most of the time, but every once in a while guys like your guy in the picture, they do something, something like a robbery, or they shoot someone, they do it because they can. That guy, he could just as easily have shot you if he'd seen you. He could have shot your sister if she'd been in there buying her groceries. Or her daughter, could have been caught in the crossfire. Or their getaway car, could have mown down your elderly parents just crossing the road. That fella in the picture, no one's going to find him, because he got away, he was wearing a mask, nobody but you and what you have in your phone knows what he looks like. But we put it in the paper, then someone's going to recognize him, he'll be taken off the streets and your sister, your niece, your mum and dad, they're all going to be safe. That's what a local paper does. It serves the community, it protects the community, it tells you who the bad guys are and stops them getting away with it. This paper, I happen to know it's going through a hard time, it really hasn't any money to pay you, and yes maybe you can get something for it up the road in Belfast, but this place, this *Express* is where your picture should be, you should give them it for nothing, because it's the right thing to do, it's your ... duty.'

The fella was nodding. He said, 'I don't have a sister.'

'I didn't—'

'And nice speech 'n all, but, like ... a load of bollocks, too. "A" for effort, mate, but no chance. *No chance.*'

He laughed, and walked off.

Rob stood, surprised at himself for coming over so evangelical, and thought maybe it had come from either being dehydrated or quite possibly he was still drunk from the night before. But then he heard a slow handclapping coming from behind and he turned to find the reporters, Alix, Michael and Peter, standing there, catching his performance on their way back from lunch, with sour-faced Peter giving the sarcastic applause and the other two providing a backing band of silent pity and mocking bemusement. Rob shrugged at them and said, 'I'm going for a sausage roll.' He stalked away, aware that the colour was up in his cheeks. As he walked he reminded himself about the money, the cheque in his pocket, and decided it was more than adequate compensation for half a day's work and looking a bit stupid in front of some bumpkin reporters he'd never have to see again.

Finding a sausage roll was harder than he had imagined. Bakeries and cafés had moved on. It was difficult to buy anything that didn't include sun-dried tomatoes. The closest he got was a panini stuffed with ham and cheese. He found a park just round the corner from the office. There was a duck pond that appeared only to have swans, a children's zoo with various tropical birds, and a wired-off enclosure that boasted a dozen or more pet bunnies and several discarded bottles of Buckfast. He sat on a green wooden bench opposite a small playground. Without the distraction of the *Express* he could feel the weight of home hard on him again, and it wasn't helped by the kids charging about screaming. There were lots of mothers standing guard, tossing him the occasional glance.

A woman sat down beside him, but he hardly noticed her until she nodded at the mums and said, 'Look at them, they don't know whether to shag you or shop you.'

He turned and saw that it was Alix. He said, 'Sorry, what?'

She said, 'You don't want to make it a regular habit, lone male watching kids at play. We write about them nearly every week. We've a lot of pedos.'

Rob said, 'Good to know.'

'We can see the park from upstairs in the office. I spotted you hanging around and thought I'd better come and say sorry. We haven't been very welcoming.'

'Really?'

'You hadn't noticed?'

'I'd noticed. I'm surprised you're apologizing.'

She smiled and said, 'Did you get some lunch?'

'Up to a point.'

'There's a café in Market Street we go to quite a lot. We should have invited you. We didn't because Michael thinks you're, like, a corporate raider or something. Asset stripper. The Liquidator. He has an overactive imagination, but he probably has some kind of a point. We know we're going down the drain. The question is, why are you really here?'

'Consultant.'

'That speech you made, didn't sound like a consultant's speech. I liked it.'

Rob shrugged. 'For all the good it did.'

Alix grinned widely as she produced her phone, tapped the screen and held it out so that he could see the photo of the robber the young buck had first shown him.

'How'd you manage that?'

'I'm a tenacious reporter, that's how. Also, I used to babysit him. Sean was only *this* high then, but you never forget the special ones. Always a wee bundle of energy. So I applied a bit of pressure and he caved, and for free too.'

'Well done,' said Rob.

She nodded, and sat back, and looked at the kids.

After a bit she said, 'So.'

'So.'

'So we should have been nicer. You're only doing your job and we should have invited you to lunch.'

He nodded.

'We kind of stick together, like a family. A dysfunctional family. A dysfunctional highly unpopular family. A dysfunctional, highly unpopular and poverty-stricken family. Well? Are you closing us down?'

Rob looked at her for what he intended to feel like a long time. Her green eyes flitted about, picking out every detail of his face and trying to decide if any of them represented a hint of their destiny or doom. Rob opened his mouth, as if to speak, but instead tapped the side of his nose. He gave her a smile and a wink and then stood and walked off.

He went back to the office, intent on telling Gerry his thoughts on the paper: really, he'd known what he was going to say twenty minutes after starting that morning, with only the complication of what was going on with the advertising still detaining him; but now it was time to finish up, break the bad news and get offside. He sat in Billy's office waiting for him to return, watching the journalists at work that never quite looked like work. He remembered that that was how it was when he'd started on his local paper, the work itself fairly mundane but the chat and banter great, and what Alix had said about them being a family, albeit a dysfunctional one. She was quite right, you got to know your colleagues ridiculously well on a small paper, but it was always something of a soap opera. On papers like the *Guardian* you worked your own patch and didn't share stories; they'd look at you like you were mental if you went round the office asking for an opinion, for advice. Here on the *Express* it was almost stream of consciousness; they just opened their mouths and jabbered their way through the day. Alix had been showing the young lad Sean's photo to Michael, and then Janine in Advertising, the girl on the desk, some of the printing staff, in case anyone recognized him; Peter came back in from a smoke break, took one look at it and said, 'Aye, I know him. That's Bobby McCartney's boy. Ahm ... Terry, I think. Aye, Terry, the oldest one.'

'Now that I look at it, I can see it,' said Alix. 'Clearly the apple doesn't fall far from the tree.'

Rob, passing, said, 'Who's Bobby McCartney?'

Peter pretended not to hear. Michael took his lead from Peter. Alix said, 'Agh, he's a pain in the neck, that's who he is.' She went back to her desk.

Peter said, 'We won't be using it, not yet at any rate.'

Alix turned in her chair. 'Too right we will. There's been half a dozen of these robberies, and we have him red-handed.'

Peter snorted and said, 'I think not. He hasn't been arrested, charged, anything.'

'He has a gun in his hand!'

'Do you know if it's a real gun? Or was he messing around with his ... his baby nephew or something and it's a toy—'

'The shop has just been robbed, we know that, he's just dropped half the proceeds!'

'Do we know that? Was he not maybe bending down to pick up the money and gun the real robber dropped?'

'Ah, for fuck sake, Peter, you know what it is.'

'Of course I know what it is. But until he's convicted in court we can't run it.'

'Right. Sure. You're just scared of his dad.'

'Who's his dad?' Rob asked again, 'Apart from a pain in the neck.'

Peter sighed.

Michael said, 'He used to be in the UVF years ago. Now he owns half the bars in town, and he sits on the local council. He likes to get his own way. He doesn't like us.'

'Janine?' Peter called. The advertising manager popped her head out of her office. She looked mid-forties, with died raven hair and a top that emphasized her cleavage. Rob suspected she was older than she looked. 'Tell me – you think we should run a pic of Bobby McCartney's son caught red-handed robbing a Mace?'

'Of course you should. If you want to be out of a job. He'll make a few calls and half our advertising will disappear. That's the truth of it.'

Peter raised an eyebrow at Alix. 'Plus he'll tie us up in injunctions we can't afford.'

Alix fixed him with a stern and steady look. 'Only if he finds out about it in advance.'

'What're you insinuating?'

'I'm not insinuating anything. I'm saying that you get a lot of stories out of him and he'll be expecting something in return.'

'You take that back.'

'Well, the proof will be in the pudding.'

'It gets out,' said Janine, 'he makes those calls, then we're sunk.'

'We're sunk already,' said Michael, 'just ask yer man.'

He nodded at Rob. They looked at him expectantly. Rob deflected by saying, 'On the *Guardian* we—'

Michael immediately mimicked, '*On the Guardian—*'

'It's where I work,' Rob said. 'You asked my advice.'

23

'I'm only saying,' said Michael, hurt that Rob had taken it thick.

'What would you do on the big paper in the big smoke? You'd run it, wouldn't you?'

'Yes, we would. It's a great news story and a brilliant photograph. And you have to stand up to bullies like ... what's his name...?'

'McCartney...'

'McCartney. Otherwise you'd never print anything. Big or small, you're first and foremost a newspaper.'

'See,' said Alix.

Janine pointed a finger at Rob. 'It easy for you to say, run it, but you don't have to slog around after ads when they've all been warned off.'

'Exactly,' said Peter, 'and you don't have to live here. We do. McCartney's hoods knocking seven shades of shite out of you'll soon change your mind. Different if he's charged and tried and convicted, then he can't complain.'

'I'm not saying it's easy. The *Guardian's* a powerful beast, it can stand up for itself. I know this is different. But sometimes you just have to ... do it.'

'Sometimes you just have to mind your own business,' said Pete, 'or concentrate on what is your own business, like time and motion and closing us down.'

Rob put his hands up and said, 'You asked' before walking between them back into his office.

He wasn't angry, or even mildly upset. It was none of his business. They could bicker away, for all he cared. He'd be out of there as soon as Gerry returned. He also knew how frustrating local-paper journalism could be. Daily papers, nationals, you wrote your story, you made sure you got it right, and then you really didn't care how it affected who you wrote about because the chances were they would never cross your path again; there was a splendid anonymity to it. But with local papers, as soon as you walked out your front door you were liable to bump into who you were just writing about, from puritan to pimp to pedo. You learned to deal with it. The best and only defence was the truth of your story. That was universal.

He spent another hour in the office. The door was open still, and the argument did not go away, but it became more about who had the right to spike the story, and therefore in essence a power struggle over who would eventually run the paper. Peter was the *de facto* deputy editor, but it seemed he'd never actually been appointed to the position or paid for it, which in effect made him just the senior reporter. Alix was also a senior reporter, but with only a tenth of Peter's experience. But she had youth on her side and he guessed that one step up her ladder of ambition would be to climb into Billy's biscuit-crumb-strewn chair. He guessed she would prove to be a dynamic and invigorating editor, which was exactly what the paper needed; but it was also a job for life, a job that aged you, that fatted out your arse; she should be out there seeing the world. Peter was dour and traditional and presumed he would get the job purely because he was next in line and that was the way it had always worked. He was more the 'job for life, don't care about the rest of the world' kind of guy. He would be a good, solid editor and wouldn't change a damn thing about the paper. Michael, an odd mix of cockiness and gauche inexperience, would still have to do the bun run, no matter who was in charge. Rob laughed to himself. Why was he even thinking about this? The paper was dying on its feet, and he was on one of the next flights home.

They were still going at it when Gerry arrived twenty minutes later; they covered themselves and the vacancy by switching back to their debate on the photo. Alix put it under his nose and he agreed that it was a great picture and Janine shouted from her office that if it was that good they should frame it and put it on the wall, not make her life difficult by sticking it on the front of the paper; Peter warned them again about what Bobby McCartney was capable of and Alix said they should print it huge and worry about next week next week. Gerry called for order, drew himself up and announced: 'At this point in time, there may not be a next week.' They looked shocked at that. He nodded at Peter and said, 'We've got how long?'

'We need to be at the plant at six.'

'Okay, then – put two front pages together, one with, one without, and I'll let you know. Now where's...' He looked about him and spotted Rob in the editor's chair. 'Ah ... do you want to...?' He indicated his own office.

Rob got up and followed him in. As he passed Michael's desk, Michael began to hum the death march.

Gerry's office was like the antidote to Billy's, but he said the only reason it was paper free was because he was never bloody there. 'Does that need to change, Rob? What are your thoughts about our wee paper which hasn't missed a week in a hundred years? Hitler couldn't stop us, the Ulster Workers' Council couldn't stop us and an INLA bomb couldn't stop us. What do you say?'

'I say you're losing money hand over fist.'

'Tell me something I don't know.'

'Your advertising woman is skimming off 20 per cent.'

'Fuck off!'

'You'd need to bring in a forensic accountant but, first look, that's about it.'

Gerry had moved in behind his desk and put his feet up, but now he moved them off and clasped his hands and leaned forward. 'Janine?' he said. 'Janine's been with us for years.'

'And she's probably been at it for years. She wouldn't by any chance do your accounting?'

'How did you ...?'

Rob raised an eyebrow.

Gerry sighed. 'She had some training when she was younger, and she's cheap.'

'No, Gerry, she's expensive.'

Gerry nodded sadly. 'She used to be my ... and sometimes is still my ... I wouldn't have thought in a million years that ... You're sure?'

'Like I say, get an expert in. But pretty much any idiot with an abacus could see it.'

'Okay. All right. So Janine's a bad 'un.'

'And the least of your worries.'

Gerry sighed. He got up and began to pace.

'I'm not an expert in advertising, Gerry, but when you dip in and out of recession, advertisers get choosy about where they spend their money – the paper's old and boring and clogged up with all kinds of shit people don't have the time to wade through these days, there's hardly any colour, doesn't look like it has ever known a designer and it's not in the least bit surprising circulation's in the shitter. It's not a good paper, Gerry. It's a bad paper.'

'I paid you £1500 to tell me it's a bad paper?'

'I tried to tell you that you were wasting your money.'

27

'You should have tried harder. But never mind that now – can she be saved?'

'If you throw enough money at it, of course you can prop anything up with cash, but the way papers are going, it would be good money after bad. And why would you want to?'

Gerry sighed again. He stopped by the glass panel that looked out over editorial. He shook his head. 'I don't have money to throw at it. What can I do without money? There'll be something down the back of my chairs, but not much. If I had some – what would I do with it? Where do I start?'

'Well – look, you're a local paper, but I think you need to make it more of a community paper, you need to get people involved, find out what they care about and then fight their causes, champion them. The radio, TV, they're not interested in what happens around the corner, most of what happens in a town like this is too small for them, but people still want to know, they just don't want to have to wade through seven shades of shite to find it. You have to make sure you're the first place they turn to if they want to find something out, that means proper news stories – at the minute every word anyone ever said in the history of the world seems to make it into print here. It's crap. Cut it. People won't wait a week for news, they need it regular, rolling, you need Facebook, Twitter, a proper website instead of one that looks like it's too much trouble. People want something they can't find elsewhere. The *Express* is a family-owned newspaper and has been for generations, that means that even with the best will in the world it just rolls along year after year and it never changes because this is the way it's always been done – but I guarantee you everyone in this building knows exactly what the problems are but they're either too scared to speak up or they're just happy with their nice easy life.'

Gerry was still looking out at his staff as they added the finishing touches to that week's paper.

Rob came up beside him and saw the grim look on his face. 'I know, it's not easy to hear,' he said. 'What it all boils down to? This paper needs its arse kicked. Hard. And repeatedly.'

Gerry shook his head. 'What I said about finding money down the back of my chairs? Well, I've been there, and I've spent it. You see Alix?' He nodded across at her, phone under her chin, talking earnestly to someone. 'Later today, maybe tomorrow, she's going to get a call from her friendly neighbourhood bank manager telling her that the cheque I wrote her at the funeral has bounced. I knew it then, and I still wrote it. Gave her a bloody bonus because I knew.'

Rob was staring at him. And then his hand went to his jacket pocket, and he pulled out the cheque Gerry had given him for his consultancy. 'You mean…?'

Gerry nodded. 'Aye,' he said. 'I'm sorry, but I'm a desperate man.'

'Desperate?' Rob repeated. 'You're not desperate. You're a fucking wanker.'

He tore the cheque in half, and then again, before throwing the pieces in Gerry's face and stalking out of his office. He stomped through editorial, not stopping even when Alix said hi to him and asked how it was going; he went through the swing door, with enough violence for the rest of them also to look up. As he pulled the main door Gerry came hurrying out of his office, flustered, pulling his jacket on and answered their confused expressions with: 'He wanted to sack the lot of you! I stood up for you! Keep at it!'

Rob continued on out.

In retrospect it was inevitable and predictable that Gerry would find him in the bar, it being just a few yards from the office and them both being the sort to enjoy a drink in times of stress or no stress. It was half hidden up a largely abandoned covered shopping arcade; from the chalkboard outside and posters within, he understood it was home to indie bands and cool teenagers with bumfluff beards by night, but in daylight it was mostly empty, with a solitary barman who asked him warily if he was in for something to eat and then looked relieved when he said no. He was just ordering a whiskey, straight, when Gerry came in and said, 'Make that two. And I'll get those.'

Rob said, 'Are you going to write a cheque for them?'

'Hey, if you'd didn't want me to find you, you wouldn't have come in here.'

'I chose the first bar I came to because I was in desperate need of a drink to kill the pain of being fucked over.'

'I didn't... Well...' Gerry sighed. He paid for the drinks and told the barman to keep the change.

'There is no change,' the barman said.

'Was I to know that?' Gerry gave him a helpless shrug, and before Rob could lift his glass he picked both of them up and moved them to a table further down.

Rob just looked at him.

Gerry took a seat and said, 'Well?'

Rob sighed. Then he joined him.

Gerry gave him a long look and said, 'Well, Rob Cullen. Rob Cullen of the *Guardian*. It's got a nice ring to it. *Cullen of the Guardian*, eh?'

'What do you want, Gerry?'

'What do *you* want, Rob?'

'What are you *talking* about?'

'Really, *Cullen of the Guardian*, who, as it turns out, probably isn't actually in that much of a hurry to get home?'

'Christ, get to the point.'

'You know, I'm not just a pretty face.' He raised an eyebrow.

Rob studied him, hard, and then knocked back his whiskey. He put the glass down hard and said, 'It's none of your fucking business.'

'Well, it could be.'

'What the fuck is that—?'

Gerry had a hand on his arm. 'Rob – Rob. Hear me out. Okay?'

Rob looked at him some more. Then kind of grunted.

'I'm a businessman, and generally a pretty good one, Rob, it's not my fault the property market has gone to shite. But if I want something, I know how to get it, and if I have an idea that something isn't quite right, and that might help me to get an advantage over someone or some rival or some other business, then I can't help but take it. It's the nature of me. So, Cullen *of the Guardian*, how is the *Guardian* treating you these days?' He let it sit there, but Rob said nothing. Instead he indicated to the barman for another drink. Gerry held up two fingers. 'So, Rob? Anything to say, anything to say about the fact that you're on gardening leave?'

'No, nothing.'

'I hoked and I poked, but really I didn't get much beyond the top soil. Gardening leave and you're not expected back any time soon. Do you want to tell me about it?'

'No, I fucking don't.'

Gerry held his hands up. 'Okay, all right, that's your prerogative. But I imagine – phone tapping, that's all the rage? Or insider dealing?' He wasn't fazed at all by Rob's lack of reaction to his prodding. In fact, he smiled. He said, 'And you know what? I don't care, because whatever problem they have with you is to my advantage.'

Rob sighed. 'How do you work that out?'

The drinks arrived. Rob paid for them. Gerry nodded his thanks and took a sip.

'It's like this, Rob,' Gerry said. 'We're both in a bit of a bind right now. And maybe it might do you some good to be away from there for a while, just until it's sorted, maybe it would suit you to be back here where people don't give a shit about all that phone-tapping malarkey—'

'I told you I—!'

'Okay, all right. Just saying. But my paper, the *Express*, I know it's a bit rubbish. But it has been around for a hundred years, it hasn't missed a week, it's in a big mostly prosperous town and there's no competition. And it is all I have left. Sure I can close it down, walk away and still be able to afford a Jet Ski, but that's not in my nature. My nature is to stay and fight, and I can do that, I really can, but I can't do it without an editor.' He took another sip from his glass. 'So what do you think?'

Rob laughed. 'So that's the grand plan?'

'It is grand. So what do you say?'

'Me? Back here ... doing...? I don't think so.'

'Rob – you told me yourself, you're management now, but I've seen how you operate, and the guys told me all about your little speech, so I know that inside there, beyond that corporate bullshit there's a good old-fashioned journalist champing at the bit to get out. I know it. And I know if Billy trained you, you must be good, and I'm thinking a man like you wouldn't take well to being put out to grass, even if it's only temporary. And that's what I'm offering you – temporary. Come back here for a few weeks, get us sorted out, and then go back if you want to. Come back here, Rob, save a newspaper, save the *Express*, these jobs. Think of it as a challenge. A well paid challenge, and if that business of the cheques is worrying you, don't let it, that was a blip, it happens in business. If you want, I'll pay you in cash. C'mon, what's the downside?'

Rob was shaking his head. But not necessarily in a negative fashion. It had more to do with disbelief, Gerry's chutzpah.

'Jesus, Gerry,' he said eventually, 'you don't half like the sound of your own voice.'

'Is that a yes?' Gerry asked.

'No it's not a fucking yes,' said Rob. 'It's a maybe.'

They returned to Gerry's office, saying nothing as they crossed editorial, though all eyes were upon them. Rob took a seat and Gerry paced, and the journalists followed him back and forth through the glass as he occasionally pointed an angry finger or let out a raucous laugh. They more or less stopped work, but the ensuing silence wasn't enough for them to pick up what was being talked about though they knew it was their fate; that didn't stop them straining their ears or pretending they had urgent business right up close to the door, but there was nothing doing. Then they were distracted by the office door opening and a big man in a big suit coming in, designer cut and stubble, glint of a stud earring and the ring of confidence of a toothpaste Saint. He slapped his big hand on the counter and demanded to speak to the editor. Every jack one of them knew him, and hated dealing with him. It was, to the best of their knowledge, the first time he'd set foot in their office, he preferred to do his business out on the streets. Peter was the first to react; he was already on his feet trying to eavesdrop on Gerry and Rob, so he merely took a few steps to his right so that he was out of sight of the counter and able to slip into the kitchen. He left the door open wide enough that he could hear but kept one hand on the handle so that he could lock it if things turned scary. When Bobby McCartney got angry, intimidation and violence often followed, occasionally in the shape of the two heavies who had entered the office with him. Big, silent types who were only silent because they didn't know too many words. They stood slightly behind and on either side of him, like stabilizers.

Alix turned from her computer to see why Peter Foster, as the self-proclaimed senior, hadn't answered, and then shook her head when she saw that he had vamoosed. She knew instinctively, but without any evidence, that the sleeked dick had tipped McCartney off. It didn't matter though, it was her story and her place to confront him, though as she approached the counter she wished that Billy was still alive; even if he didn't leave his office she would have felt his presence, that he had her back. Gerry she hadn't worked out yet.

She lied, 'Councillor McCartney – you got my message then?'

'Message? What message?'

'I sent you an email – doing a piece on the recent spate of armed robberies in the area, wondering if you'd care to comment, as one of our local councillors and certainly our most prominent business—?'

He shook his head, and then looked around the office. 'Who's in charge since Billy snuffed it?'

'No one yet, Councillor. We're just muddling along until—'

'I know what you have, and I want it.'

'What're ... what're you referring—?'

'The photograph you claim is of my son. I want it, I want an undertaking that it won't be used, and I want the negative destroyed.'

34

'Negative,' said Alix.

'You what?'

'Negative – you're so twentieth-century. Don't you know it's all digital—?'

McCartney slapped down hard on the counter, a belly flop of the hand. 'Stop shitting me. You know what I'm talking about and I want it sorted, now.'

Alix wasn't exactly sure what girding her loins entailed, but she suspected she was doing it already, instinctively. 'Councillor, we have a photograph of your son robbing a Spar. Would you like to comment?'

McCartney pointed at her. 'I've heard all about your so-called photograph. It's not my son. And if you even think about printing it, I'll have an injunction on you faster than you can toast Veda. I will sue you, and every single one of you, and the paper. Do you understand me?'

'Are you speaking on the record, Councillor?' Alix asked.

His eyes settled on her. Blue and steely cold.

'You're one of the Crosses, aren't you? Churchill Estate, no?'

She just looked at him.

He smirked. 'Thought as much. Bunch of wasters.' He looked beyond her. 'Where's Pete?'

'Pete's ... not available right now. Out on a job.'

Michael said, 'No, actually, I think he's still here.'

Alix rolled her eyes as Michael got up and hurried into the kitchen.

McCartney said, 'This place is such a shit hole.'

'Agreed,' said Alix.

His brow furrowed. 'Are you trying to be smart?'

Before she could answer, Michael reappeared, and a few moments later a sheepish-looking Peter stepped out of the

35

kitchen, clutching a cup of coffee and making an elaborate show of showing it to them by way of justifying his absence.

'Hey – Councillor, how's it going?' he said, coming up to the counter.

'I want that photo destroyed,' said Bobby McCartney.

'Well,' said Peter.

'Well the fuck what?'

'It's ... not mine to destroy, but I can assure you, whatever does appear in the paper – it will be fair and balanced.'

'Fair and balanced, me arse,' said McCartney, and indicated for his heavies to enter the office proper, though without giving them any further guidance as to whom they should threaten or what they should destroy. They moved towards the swing door.

Michael, who was closest to them, raised a hand as they came through and – though he was stick thin and they could have snapped him in two by breathing hard on him with extra strong mints – said, 'You shall not pass.'

The heavies looked at him with sympathy and pity, and passed. But before they got much further into the office they were confronted by two new arrivals, Gerry stepping out of his office with Rob just behind.

Gerry said 'What's all this?' in his disarming, jovial way.

Alix said, 'They want the photo. The councillor is embracing his electoral mandate to bully us.'

'You know what I want, Gerry,' said McCartney.

'Ah, Bobby,' said Gerry, 'didn't see you there. And you two – you're not allowed back here.'

The heavies stopped and looked to their boss for direction.

'I want the photo,' said McCartney, 'or I'll close you down. In a fortnight you'll be gone.'

'Excuse me,' said Gerry, 'but I'm not having you take the credit for running us into the ground, that's all mine.'

'Always a smart arse,' said Bobby, 'like the rest of your family, drunks and bankrupts the lot of you.'

'Always a sweet-talker,' said Gerry.

'If you want the photo,' said Rob, stepping up beside Gerry, 'call back at five and we'll give you a free copy of the paper. It'll be on the front page.'

'And who the fuck are you?' McCartney demanded.

'He's the new editor of the *Express*,' said Gerry.

'Since when?!' It was Peter, his mouth hanging open.

'Since about five minutes ago,' said Gerry. 'Now – Councillor, are you really going to have your over-fed friends cause damage in here? You are aware that we're journalists, and photographers, and we'll have it all over our website in minutes?'

'We have a website?' Michael asked.

'You wouldn't dare—'

'Bobby – do you not think you'd be better spending your time sorting your son out than hassling us?'

McCartney snorted. 'I'm not going to take parental advice from you, Gerry, with all your wee bastards running about!'

Gerry took a step forward, blood up, but Rob pushed him back before turning and pointing.

'Do you want to give us a statement for our story, Councillor?'

'No I do not.'

'Good. Then fuck off out of our office.'

McCartney looked a little bit stunned. Probably nobody had spoken to him like that since ever. He studied Rob for a *long* time, then a smirk slipped onto his face and he nodded slowly and said, 'Right, boys, let's go, let's not waste any more of our time on these guttersnipes. You?' He pointed at Rob. 'We're not finished. But this paper is.'

37

He turned and walked out of the office. His two heavies were left standing. They exchanged glances and then casually sauntered out through the swing door with a mildly embarrassed fixed-grin red-cheeked look about them, as if they'd innocently taken a wrong turn and were trying to cover it up by admiring the scenery.

As soon as they were gone, there was a bubble of disbelieving silence that was only pricked by Alix quoting, 'You shall not pass?' back at Michael. Everyone laughed, though mostly with relief. It also helped cover what they were all thinking, that they had a new boss, that the consultant had consulted himself into a job at least two of them had had their eye on. Gerry retreated to his office, taking Rob with him, without further explanation.

Peter looked at Alix and said, 'Bloody hell.'

Alix looked at Peter and said, 'Are they serious?'

Michael said, 'Cat, pigeons, all that.'

Blown up, covering most of the front page, it was an eye-catching, perfectly framed and focused photo: the panicked look, the gun, the mask, the money, it didn't need any words, though there were plenty delivered. Rob, though he wasn't really taking over until the following week, introduced them to his editing style by cutting huge swathes out of Alix's report, which shocked her a bit, but he explained and justified – though she sensed that that might be a one-off – that they would just have to adapt to a new style and not have their hands held. Alix had come up with the headline *Caught in the act* and Peter had reluctantly directed that it should be in huge bold type while still moaning about the risk of running it, not just to life and limb, but because it was exposing them

38

to legals: the boy hadn't been convicted, charged or even questioned. As Alix and Peter argued over it, and Michael stirred it a bit with smartish comments, Rob just came along, looked at the screen, reached past Peter and pushed a button, smiled at them all and returned to Gerry's office. The headline now read, *Caught in the act?* The question mark made all the difference. They agreed it was perfect now, but Peter and Alix still shook their heads, raging that they hadn't thought of something so bloody simple and obvious.

Michael said, 'And that's why he's getting the big bucks.'

Rob asked for a hundred quid from Gerry and explained what it was for; Gerry moaned a bit before reaching for his chequebook. Rob gave him the eye and Gerry took out his wallet instead and counted it out in cash. He told Rob to get a receipt. Rob took the money, thanked him and then said he needed to borrow his car as well. Gerry looked at him like he was mental, but very reluctantly handed over the keys. 'It's a Jag,' he said, '2005, it's not worth much but it's my pride and joy.'

'I've driven a big car before,' said Rob.

He had the address off Alix, and directions, though he took a few wrong turns. The estate sat on top of a hill overlooking the town; it was huge and mazy and samey. It was well tended, but that was the surface. This was Bobby McCartney territory, so it was little wonder that Sean McKee freaked when Rob knocked on the door. Rob was about to launch into a spiel about how great his photo was until he saw the state of Sean's face: all beaten, swollen, one eye closed and split lip.

Sean pulled him inside and said, 'Man, seriously uncool.' He peered out of the front window and asked him where his car was and Rob told him it was round the corner, out of sight, because he'd gotten a bit lost and actually stumbled on his house in the end as much by accident as anything.

Rob said, 'What happened?'

'What the fuck do you think?'

'Because—'

'Aye. And this is only because they're not completely sure it was me. Someone tipped them off, but I told them I didn't even have a camera and so they didn't fucking kneecap me. But, man, bad enough. So what do you want?'

Rob took out his wallet and counted out the hundred quid. 'Just by way of thanks,' said Rob. 'But it seems terribly inadequate now.'

Sean nodded, but took the money. 'No problem,' he said.

'You live here alone?' Rob asked.

'Nope, folks are out.'

Rob said, 'I really like the photo.'

'Gathered that.'

'Do you know who beat you up?'

'Of course I do.'

'Do you want us to do a story about it?'

'Of course I fucking don't. Are you mental?'

Rob sighed. 'I really like the photo,' he said again. Sean was about to snap something, but Rob held his hand up and said, 'And I want you to take some more. No – hear me out. I've been around a lot of people who think they're photographers, but they really don't have the eye—'

'I was in the right place at the right time, that's all,' said Sean.

'No, it's more than that. I'm sure of it. That's why I want you to work for the paper. Freelance. We're a community paper, we should have someone in the community taking photos.'

Sean laughed. 'Exactly how many beatings do you think this face can take before I start to lose my looks?'

'Yes, yes, that's a risk, of course it is, but once they know you're, like, gainfully employed by us, then they won't be so keen to pick on you, because we can pick right back.'

Sean snorted. 'I don't think so.'

Rob said, 'I'm serious, you'd be surprised by the power of the press, even a little diddly paper like ours. Give it a think, eh? Come down to the office, we'll get you sorted out with a proper camera. Sean – it could be a career if you stick at it, and if you want it, it's a way out of here.'

'I like it here,' said Sean.

'Then it's just a fabulous job.'

Sean said he would think about it. They shook hands. Rob said he hoped Sean's nose would be feeling better soon.

Rob stood outside, turned one way, then the other, trying to remember which way he'd come. He walked about twenty metres to his left, then doubled back and rounded a corner but still wasn't sure. He'd made a point of remembering the street he'd parked on, Westmoreland Drive, but knew he was lost already and so he decided to break the habit of a lifetime and stop the first person he saw coming towards him, for directions.

He was already smiling and about to say, 'Sorry to trouble you...' when he realized that the big fella coming towards him was one of Councillor McCartney's heavies who'd stood threateningly in the newspaper office just a couple of hours before.

The heavy said, 'Oh – hello.'

'Hi,' said Rob.

'I was just ... You don't happen to know where Westmoreland Drive is, do you?'

The heavy said, 'Aye – matter of fact, I've just come from there. Just go down that back entry there, along to the end and turn right, that's Westmoreland.'

'Excellent. Ah, thanks. Cheers.' He nodded, and walked on.

The heavy called after him. 'Ahm – mate?'

Rob stopped and turned, nervously.

'Ahm, all that earlier and … well, y'know, it's just business?'

'I understand,' said Rob.

'Gotta make a living.'

'Of course you do.'

They nodded at each other. Rob turned again.

The heavy said 'Have a good one' after him.

Rob raised a hand back at him, but kept walking. He had some reservations about entering the back alley – he glanced back to make sure the heavy wasn't following him with plans to mete out the kind of punishment Sean had suffered, but the fella was still walking away. It didn't mean there wasn't an ambush waiting. Rob put his head down, ducked into the entry and walked at speed along it, expecting at any moment to be set upon by thugs jumping over the back fences. It was only thirty or so metres long but it felt like ten times that. It was with considerable relief that he eventually emerged onto the relative safety of Westmoreland Drive and the close proximity of Gerry's car and the promise of escape.

It would have helped if there had been any wheels on the Jag, but no, they were gone. The windows were still there, but they were all smashed. The passenger door was open and there was a space where the radio and CD player used to be. The boot was open and the spare missing.

Rob took a deep, deep breath, and raised his phone.

He hadn't been home in twenty years, but really, nothing much had changed.

CHAPTER 2
THE RETURN OF THE NATIVE

When Alix Cross first applied for a job on the *Express* she thought it would help her cause by writing that although she was currently living in Belfast she was 'Bangor born and bread'. It was only when she came down for an interview and editor Billy confused her by quizzing her on her knowledge of local bakeries and she was clearly floundering that he put her out of her misery with a big laugh and pointed out her mistake, 'Born and bred, honey, b-r-e-d, not as in sliced pan.' He'd her CV printed out before him and he was nodding and said, 'You grew up in Kilcooley?' She'd nodded and a little cheekily said, 'You're surprised someone from Kilcooley went to university?' and he said, 'No, I'm surprised someone from Kilcooley went to school.' He had a point. It was a huge, sprawling estate, and it had a lot of problems, not the least of which were the successive generations of kids who managed to avoid getting any kind of education at all. The estate had been built in the seventies to house those forced to flee sectarian ghettos in Belfast, and it was a shock for the middle-class town to suddenly have to cope with an influx of tough-minded refugees who were no respecters of their nice, genteel ways. It was said that property prices went down overnight. Though she'd always wanted out of Kilcooley, Alix didn't have a problem with it. She hated the way it was controlled by ex-paramilitaries like Bobby McCartney, but it was still her home, she had family there, and memories, happy ones. Billy had said, 'Forget about your degree, what I want you to do is write three hundred words on why you want to be a journalist here in Bangor.' He sat her at a desk and a laptop and told her she had ten minutes. She spent the first minute thinking about how many other applicants had been set just this task, and how much bullshit they'd written, and she knew that that was exactly what she should do as well. She should write that she loved towns like Bangor, loved being part of a community, loved the huge variety of stories she would get to do on a local paper, that she loved meeting people, was interested in local history and sport. And though a lot of that was actually true, she convinced herself that she should write something completely different; that she shouldn't do exactly what every other candidate was sure to have done; she should be brave and bold. So she wrote: 'I need the money. And I've a Jack Russell to feed.' It was a lie, of course. There was no Jack Russell. She admitted as much when Billy called to offer her the job the next day. He laughed and said it was a good line. She said, 'Is that why you're offering me the job? Because I was 289 words short on my article.' Billy said, 'No, I'm offering it to you because the money is rubbish and nobody else applied.' She was never quite sure if he was serious, and now she would never know. That was two years ago. In the old days, Peter said, there was a three-year apprenticeship before you were considered a fully fledged reporter, but like so many other traditions and practices this had been quietly dropped. Now you were expected to hit the ground running. Peter, older and wiser, allegedly, never tired of reminding her that she was still technically a cub reporter. She never tired of telling him to bugger off.

During that two years she also discovered that the huge variety of local stories she'd been looking forward to covering – well, actually, there wasn't that much variety. The same situations and characters kept coming round. Aggravating councillors like McCartney, the thugs, drunks and dealers in the local court, the same complaints from do-gooders and religious nutters. So she really had to work to find stories that were out of the ordinary, that made her blood boil or gave her that rush of adrenaline; or, sometimes, they just fell into her lap, like when Roy and Ailsa, two of her best friends, came rushing into the office all tearful and upset and she rushed up to the counter wanting to know what was wrong, because God knows they'd been through enough.

Ailsa cried out, 'We saw him, we saw him! Can you believe it?'

Roy said, 'In the middle of fucking B&Q!'

'Mark Dillon!'

And then she knew. Mark Dillon had killed their daughter. It was as simple and as complicated as that. He'd been a drink driver, been convicted before but it hadn't made a damn bit of difference. His jeep had mounted a kerb, crushed the stroller with wee Peggy in it, broken Ailsa's leg though she'd hardly even noticed at the time. To make matters worse Dillon had pleaded not guilty to manslaughter, insisting on it all being played out in excruciating detail in court. He ended up getting six years – they knew he'd be out in three because of the cock-eyed way the legal system worked. Alix was surprised it had been that long already – the case dated back to before she was a reporter, but she'd been in court every day to support her friends. She remembered reading the reports in the paper and thinking how badly they reflected what had actually gone on in court. Later, when she joined the paper and checked back, she discovered it was Peter who'd been on court duty that week. Of course you didn't need to be a great prose stylist to be a journalist, but an accurate reflection of proceedings would have been a start. She'd raised it with Pete once she'd settled into her job, and he'd shaken his head, 'It was accurate, Alix – it's just that you remember it differently because you had a personal stake in it. Once you're a bit more experienced, you'll understand.' He was, she decided at the time, a patronizing gobshite, and she hadn't much changed her opinion since.

It took her a while to get them settled down enough to tell her properly. They'd been out shopping in the DIY store when they had almost literally bumped into him: they were pushing a trolley laden with paint, Dillon was stacking the shelves with tins of it. And for a few moments nobody had said anything, they'd just stared at each other, neither side quite believing what they were seeing. Then Roy recovered from his shock enough to advance on Dillon, and Dillon turned and ran through into a stockroom. Roy would have followed if another worker hadn't blocked his way; in fact he probably would have carried on after Dillon if Ailsa hadn't dragged him away. They told Alix they were furious not only because Dillon was out, but because no one had warned them, particularly as he was back living in town – Bangor wasn't that big, and sooner or later they were bound to bump into him. Unfortunately, in this case, it had been sooner. This had happened the day before and they'd immediately got on to the company about why they were employing someone like

46

Dillon, a killer; the company tried to be sympathetic but Roy had ended up slamming the phone down on them. He'd gone round that morning to try and confront Dillon again but there was no sign of him. He asked one of the workers, pretending to be Dillon's cousin, and was told he hadn't shown up for work. Alix listened to it all pour out of them, the anger, the frustration and the memories of Peggy. She had herself babysat Peggy, and remembered her as a placid, smiley wee thing. She didn't know how Ailsa, whom she'd known most of her life, had pulled through or if she would have been able to cope in a similar situation. Her friend had, she guessed, done what Ulsterwomen so often did: she'd put a brave face on it. And that face had now only crumbled because of a random and coincidental encounter in a DIY store.

Alix was thinking about what the best angle would be – every variation she came up with felt a bit tabloidy, and even though that was the shape of their paper these days, content-wise it wasn't really the kind of story that the *Express* had gone for in the past. Alix had briefly spoken to them at the counter, but then led them through to the small office kitchen and made them coffee and cheekily shared out the buns that had already been bought for their afternoon break. Then she left them for five minutes so she could get a steer from Rob. He'd come from the *Guardian*, and that was certainly a campaigning newspaper, so she hoped he would get behind the story; maybe they could appeal for public support to get the prison service or whoever it was that still held sway over Dillon – he was bound to be on licence, given his early release – to relocate him to a different town.

Alix hesitated outside her editor's office – she could see Rob and Gerry standing just inside the door, talking to Janine, their advertising manager. Then Janine turned and came out.

When she passed she kept her eyes down, but Alix could see a tear on her cheek.

Alix said, 'Do you want me to come back...?' to the two men, who were standing a little awkwardly, but Rob waved her in. Gerry gave him a nod and went after Janine. Alix stepped into the office and said, 'Is everything all—?'

'Yes, fine.' Rob sat back behind his desk. 'What can I do for you, Alix?'

Fine, Alix thought, usually means, *not fine*.

Janine was highly strung at the best of times, but not usually prone to tears.

Anyway, to the business at hand. She told him about Ailsa and Roy sitting in the kitchen, about the death of their toddler, how angry they were about Dillon being back in the neighbourhood, and what was the paper going to do about it.

She said, 'I mean, can you imagine what that's like – you're just out doing a bit of shopping, and next thing the man who murdered your daughter is standing there in front of you. Nightmare.'

'How old was she?' Rob asked.

She noticed that he had photos of his own two kids on his desk. 'Just turned three. Gorgeous.'

'And this guy Dillon was drunk?'

'Yeah, showing off with his mates, mounted the kerb, crushed her.'

'It's very sad, and meeting him like that ... just, I'm not sure there's a story here.'

'Killer released back into the community, and the bereaved family have to face him every day? Three years for a life? Where's the justice there?'

'Alix – it wasn't murder. It was manslaughter. And the justice was in the court. He was convicted and served his time. Look, it can't be pleasant, but if you go down that road, you start a witch-hunt. I do want this to be a campaigning newspaper, but we have to choose our campaigns carefully.'

'You're saying we can't do anything?'

'If he's just getting on with his life and he's not going out of his way to confront them, then we just have to accept it.'

Alix took a deep breath. 'Right. What am I supposed to say to them?'

'Just be nice. And blame it on me. I'll explain it to them if you want.'

Alix shook her head. 'No. It's okay.'

She went back into the kitchen and started to explain. Their disappointment was obvious, and more – an instant coolness towards her. She tried to explain that it wasn't her decision, and that this didn't have anything to do with their friendship, but they clearly didn't understand. It was black and white – either you were with them, or you were with Dillon. They left pretty quickly – vague promises of meeting up at some time in the future. Alix was torn – she was embarrassed and a little bit ashamed that she wasn't there for them.

As they were leaving they were joined by Janine, coat on, face wet. She didn't say anything. Alix watched her go, then, when the door swung shut again, turned to Michael and asked what was going on. He said, 'She's been suspended.'

Before she could ask what for Peter came out of Rob's office and Michael immediately re-focused on his work.

Peter said, 'What's up with you guys? They looked upset.'

'They *are* upset.' She nodded towards the editor's office. 'He won't touch them with a barge pole. He bleats on about us being a community paper, and he doesn't think the community will care about this?'

49

Peter lifted a newspaper from his desk and examined the front page. Without looking at her he said, 'Well, maybe there's more than one way to skin a cat,' then turned and walked towards the kitchen.

Rob was pissed off. He was only a few days into the job and already involved in a crisis that wouldn't have been any of his business on a paper like the *Guardian*. But on a Mickey Mouse operation like this? He was in it up to his neck. He didn't like to refer everything back to his former employer all the time, and he certainly didn't do it out loud, but he couldn't help himself. He'd been used to a certain level of profession-alism, there were disciplinary procedures and practices, and if Janine had been working there she would have been out on her ear. She'd been caught with her fingers in the till. Her siphoning-off of advertising money had contributed to the business nearly going down the plughole. And yet Gerry was *still* reluctant to fire her.

'She's worked here for years,' he said, 'and without her we would have gone under ages ago.'

'Gerry she's a thief, and she's admitted it. She's been ripping you off for years.'

'No, Rob – she hasn't. *They* have.'

'*They*!'

'Maybe you've been away for too long, Rob – but those protection guys, once they get their hooks into you…'

'There's no proof of any protection…'

'Well they hardly give you a receipt do they?!'

That was her argument – she'd been forced into it by para-militaries; they took a cut of everything she got by way of advertising, and it had been going on for years. Rob didn't believe her at all, and while her tears had been real enough, he didn't buy them either – she wasn't sorry, or being honest with them, she was just distraught because she'd been caught. There was also something about the way she spoke to Gerry that suggested that they were now or had once been more than just work colleagues, a familiarity, a touchy-feely vibe that fell just short of actually being touchy-feely. Rob didn't trust her at all. He wasn't really surprised, given the chaotic way the paper had been run, that she was able to get away with it for so long; a proper accountant would have sussed out what she was up to, years ago.

'Gerry, if we're going to rebuild this paper, we need to be able to trust everyone. Suspension isn't enough.'

Gerry took a deep breath. 'I know,' he said, 'I was just trying to soften the blow.'

'Well it's not – it's just prolonging the agony.'

Rob's phone rang. Before he answered it he raised an eyebrow at Gerry.

'Aye,' said Gerry. 'Well.' He walked out.

It was Michael on the phone, some woman calling about an article on badgers that was supposed to run last week but didn't. Badgers! Could he speak to her?

'Yes, Mrs McDermott,' he said into the phone, 'lovely to hear from you...'

'Don't you give me that, young man!'

Rob sighed. This definitely wasn't the *Guardian*.

Gerry knew he shouldn't, but he couldn't help himself. Janine had always bewitched him. And she'd always been there for him. She had admitted stealing from him, but he couldn't go along with what Rob was saying, that she was making up all the business with the protection money. He knew she was a smart operator. He knew that she had single-handedly kept the paper afloat for years, years when Gerry had barely been involved because of his other now-busted business interests. And he also knew her as a best friend, as an occasional lover, and looking back with the knowledge that she'd been at the mercy of, basically, gangsters, explained so much – the sadness that always seemed to lurk behind her eyes, the moods, the multiple break-ups they had endured, even the drinking. Gerry enjoyed a drink, multiple drinks, in fact; but Janine never seemed to have a wine glass out of her hand. He had tried to talk to her about it before but she'd always brushed him aside; now at least he knew, or thought he knew, why she'd sought refuge in the grape; all that time, through all their intimacies, she'd been carrying a secret she couldn't admit to. Trying to talk it out in front of the new editor hadn't been the right thing to do. After all, it was his paper, he should lay down the law. So now he found himself grabbing his coat and going after her. But before he could even get to the swing door they opened and two big guys in black crew necks came in. One of them had a clipboard in his hand. He said, 'I'm looking for Gerry Black.'

Gerry said, 'He's not here right now, can I take a message?'

The big guy looked at him doubtfully and said, 'We're here to reclaim...' and he looked down at his clipboard, '...six computers. A photocopier, two cameras ... various items of office furniture ... for non-payment of hire purchase...'

'I sent a cheque,' Gerry said quickly, aware that the staff were looking at him, and that just on the edge of his field of vision Rob was emerging from his office.

The big guy unclipped something and held it up. 'This cheque? It bounced.' He nodded at his equally big colleague and they began to move into the office.

Alix turned to Michael and said, 'Where's your *You shall not pass* now?'

Rob said, 'Problem, Gerry?'

Gerry said, 'No, no, no, no, no,' to Rob and then stood in the way of the bailiffs. 'And no, no, no, no, no to you as well. You can't be taking our gear – you'll never get your money back like that. Man, we're a small business, struggling to make our way, we need another chance.'

'We have our orders,' said the big man, 'and a court order.' He showed it.

Gerry wasn't for moving. 'Look, lads, fellas, I know what you're doing, turning the screws a wee bit, and great, it has indeed worked. Leave the computers, I've some cash in the car, c'mon downstairs with me and we'll sort this out. C'mon!'

Gerry nodded at the door behind them.

The big guy hesitated. He said, 'I'll need to check with the boss.'

'Absolutely.'

The big man raised a phone, and as he started to talk, Gerry began to subtly shepherd the two of them towards the door, and then through it. As the conversation continued out into the corridor, Gerry popped his head back in and hissed, 'Lock the door! If I'm not back in twenty minutes, alert the authorities.'

Alix looked back at Dillon's old court reports and saw that he was listed then as having no fixed abode; she thought there was a good chance that nothing had changed while he was inside, which meant that if he was back in town he was probably staying at a half-way house. She knew that the only one in town was one on Dufferin Avenue. Her plan was to call in, see if he was indeed there, and if he was, to see if she could get him talking. Sean, meanwhile, would be taking some surreptitious photographs. Or at least she hoped Sean would – he was very new to the job and, from the way he was studying his camera, not exactly aware of how it worked. They were just looking for a parking spot when Alix spotted Dillon – even though it had been three years since the court case, she'd attended every day of the trial and knew she would never forget his face. And he hadn't changed: still tall and lean, and with his trademark hair moussed up rockabilly style. He was just getting into a red Vauxhall. Alix turned the car at the end of the road and was back just in time to fall in directly behind Dillon as he turned left onto Main Street. She then followed him along the one-way system onto Seacliff Road. This coast road was one of her favourite drives, with Belfast Lough to her left, calm today, the sun shining and the footpath busy. About half a mile along Dillon parked outside the Jamaica Inn. Alix found a space which gave them a good view of the bar. There was a beer garden in front that was busy with customers enjoying a rare opportunity to eat and drink outside. Dillon, a newspaper tucked under one arm, moved up the steps into the garden and then entered the bar. A couple of minutes later he emerged with a pint in hand, looking about him for a table, but they were all taken. Instead of going back inside he chose to sit on a low wall overlooking the road and the sea beyond. He unfolded his paper and lit a cigarette.

'Without a bloody care in the world,' said Alix.

'Are you not going over to speak to him?'

'Not yet.'

Sean raised his camera and took some pictures.

Then he said, 'If you're scared of him, I can protect you.'

'That's reassuring.' Despite her sarcasm, she liked their

new young photographer. There wasn't much to him, but he had a confidence, a brashness she found reassuring. 'How're you liking the work, second week and all?'

Sean laughed. 'This isn't work,' he said, 'I was on a building site for six months, in winter. That's work. This is easy.'

To illustrate his point he took another photo.

They sat for another twenty minutes. Dillon got another pint.

Sean said, 'The thing is, I've got other photos to take, so I'm going to have to get moving soon.'

'Hold your horses,' said Alix, nodding forward.

Dillon had been joined on the wall by a woman with short black hair, wearing a low-cut top, shorts and sandals. It was a pleasant day, but it wasn't *that* pleasant. Most of the rest of the out-door diners were well happed up. It was Northern Ireland, one swallow didn't make a summer, or even an afternoon. They were sitting apart, so it didn't look like they knew each other, but when she took out a box of cigarettes Dillon immediately offered her a light, and they were clearly talking, the way smokers usually do.

Alix drummed her fingers. Dillon was enjoying his pints and his paper and his cigarettes and chatting – no, *flirting* – when he was responsible for the death of a beautiful toddler who would never get to do any of those things. And she could still hear bloody Rob Cullen telling her it wasn't a story.

Dillon drained his second pint – and then angled it at the young woman. She smiled. So he was buying her a drink. As he disappeared inside, Alix got out of the car. She didn't say a word to Sean, and didn't reply when he called after her. She stepped up into the beer garden. She stood in front of the girl, close enough that she looked up.

'Sorry,' Alix said, 'I know it's none of my business, but I couldn't help noticing you were talking to Mark Dillon – is he a friend of yours?'

'No problem, and no, I don't know him from Adam.'

'Oh right – well, just so you know, in case you'd any interest in him? He's out of prison on parole – he killed a child. A lovely wee girl. So I wouldn't be getting too close.'

Alix raised her eyebrows, and then quickly strode away, back to the car. She didn't know why the hell she'd done it, and didn't feel especially good about it. It was stupid and unprofessional, but she told herself she hadn't done it as a journalist – she'd done it as a human being.

Sean said, 'What was that about?'

'Nothing.'

She looked back across. There was now no sign of the woman. A few moments later Dillon emerged, carrying two drinks and crossed to the wall. He stood sipping his drink, waiting for her to return. Five minutes later, with still no sign of her, he drained his remaining half pint. The bar door opened again and he looked up hopefully, but when he saw it wasn't her he raised the second pint and downed it in one. He dragged the back of his hand across his lips and then stalked away across the road to his car.

Gerry was still recovering from the bailiffs when his phone rang and Janine's number lit up. He briefly considered not answering it – he was a businessman who'd been on the edge of bankruptcy for years, so he knew all about avoidance – and even though there was a possibility Rob was right, that she had been ripping him off, he found it very hard to be upset by it. He was a player, she was a player, and sometimes they played together. She hadn't a clue that he hadn't paid her National Insurance contributions in years. Or for any of his employees for that matter. So he answered it with a sympathetic, 'Janine – how are you?'

'Who did you tell?'

'Who did I tell what?'

'About me being suspended, and why?'

'No one, Janine – I mean, I had to say to the staff, because everyone's going to chip in on getting the advertising until we can replace ... but I didn't go into any detail, I didn't ...'

'They're watching me.'

'They what? Who are?'

'The guys, the boys, the men – the ones who've been getting the protection money, Gerry! They're outside now ...'

'Outside your apartment?'

'Yes!'

'Have they threatened you or tried to get—'

'No, not yet. But they're there. Oh, you could drive past and they'd just look like fellas chatting on a street corner, but I know them, I know their faces. Gerry, I'm scared. They're used to getting their money. And if they don't get it on time, they get angry. I've been there before Gerry, I tried to stop a dozen times and they don't like it.'

'Janine – are they there now, are you sure?'

'I'm frightened, Gerry. Hold on, I'll go back to ... I've the curtains closed ... No, no, they're away again. But they've heard something and they're letting me know they know where I live.'

'Janine, we've been friends, more than friends for a very long time, I'm not just going to let you go, no matter what you've done ...'

'I was forced to...!'

'I know ... I know ... Just ... try and keep your head down for a while, and I'll see what I can do from this end. All right, love?'

'Okay, Gerry. Sorry. Thank you. I know you will.'

When he set the phone down he looked up to see Rob standing in the doorway, arms folded, coat on.

'Janine?'

'Aye,' said Gerry. 'I don't know what I'm going to do about that bloody woman. Say what you like about her – she was very good at her job. I've been on the phone this last hour trying to sell advertising space and it's no, no, no ... I'm starting to think that maybe 80 per cent of something is better than 100 per cent of nothing.'

'No, Gerry, it can't work like that.'

Gerry sighed. 'So where are you off to?'

'Going to see that woman who does the badger column. We forgot to run it last week and she's spitting nails.'

'That sounds like her. Mary ... something?'

'Aye, Mary McDermott. I'm going to apologize, but also suggest maybe our paper isn't the right place for it. Encourage her to write a book or something.'

'Absolutely right,' said Gerry, 'we're an urban paper, we don't need some mad old biddy going on about thrushes and stoats and bloody badgers.' He got up from his desk and pulled his jacket on. 'I'm going to pop home myself, I'll walk down with you.'

They left the office, chatting away. As they stepped into the car park Rob took his keys out and then stopped. His brow furrowed. He looked about him.

'Something...?' Gerry asked.

'My ... car ... I could have sworn I parked it ... I *did* park it, right there. Bloody hell, Gerry, my car's been stolen.'

'Aye, well, it's a rough enough area.'

Rob's mouth dropped open a little. 'It what? What're you—?'

'Well, strictly speaking, it wasn't your car anyway.'

'Gerry?'

'Truth is, Rob, your car is being used right now. It's been borrowed. I'd a spare set of keys.'

'How do you mean, borrowed?'

'It's being used as security against a debt.'

'Gerry, Jesus – are you telling me it's been repossessed?'

'No, not at all – it'll be back in the morning. Swear to God. It's just a cash flow thing.'

'Gerry, I've personal stuff in the car. And how am I meant to get to the badger woman without it?'

'Everything will be safe and secure in a lock-up some-where. And there's a bus leaves…'

'Gerry!'

'Joking. Here…' He took his own keys out of his pocket and held them out to Rob. 'You take it. I trust you.'

Rob looked at the keys and smiled. 'You're lending me the Jag?'

'No, it's just a Jaguar key ring. I'm lending you Janine's…'

He nodded a few cars along. There was a tiny little smart car with the newspaper's logo splashed across it.

Rob said, 'Jesus Christ, Gerry.'

'Beggars can't be choosers,' said Gerry, and took out his own keys for the gleaming blue Jag parked a further three spaces along. 'Enjoy your trip.'

They followed him back to the half-way house, watched him park and then stand smoking on the doorstep with a young man they presumed was another resident. There was scaffolding around the outside of the building and some major-looking work being done to the roof.

Sean observed that it was a half-built, half-way house.

Alix just shook her head. Then she got out of the car. As she crossed the road, Dillon was just throwing down his cigarette and was about to follow his friend back inside. Alix called his name – his Christian name, and he turned, half smiling at the thought of a friend, but then he stopped and his brow furrowed as he looked at her.

'Who wants to know?'

'I work for the local paper, was wondering if I could have a word?'

'What about?'

'Well, a couple of things – I was wondering how you felt about coming face to face with the parents of the baby you killed? And then if you've anything to say about how you're out drinking and driving again?'

Colour came to his cheeks and he took a step towards her.

With perfect timing, Sean appeared at Alix's side. He said, 'Easy there, mate.'

Dillon looked from one to the other. 'What the fuck is this?'

'We have photos of you, drinking three pints and then driving – do you think that's what you should be doing, when you're on parole for—?'

'Oh piss off!'

Dillon spun on his heel and hurried up the steps and into the half-way house, slamming the door after him. Alix stepped up and rang the bell. Repeatedly.

Sean said, 'Alix … maybe you don't want to be—'

'He should answer the bloody questions!'

'Alix...'

The door flew open again, and they both took a step back.

But it wasn't Dillon, it was a shorter, chunkier man in a short-sleeved shirt and tie. He said, 'You're press? You're not allowed round here.'

'Actually,' said Alix, 'I think you'll find we're allowed anywhere.'

Even as she said it, she was aware of how self-important she sounded, but she couldn't help herself.

'You're not allowed to hassle the residents,' said the man. Now that she looked at him properly she saw that he had a name-badge on, reading, *Thomas Brady, Manager*.

'Yes, well,' said Alix, 'that may be, but we're doing a story whether he likes it or not and he has a right of reply. And the fact is, we know he's been out drink-driving and that's only going to get him into more bother – and that's not going to help the reputation of this place, is it?'

Thomas Brady shook his head 'Miss,' he said, 'I don't know who's rattled your cage, but there are ways of doing things, channels you can go through. If you were any sort of a reporter, you would know that. So if you don't mind?' Sean raised his camera to record the confrontation. Brady jabbed a finger at him. 'And I don't want my picture taken, all right?'

Sean took it anyway.

Brady scowled at him and turned back into the house.

As the door slammed for a second time, Sean said, 'Well, that went well.'

They returned to the car, Alix swearing to herself. On a good day, when she was focused, when she was professional, she could charm the fairies out of the trees. This wasn't a good day. As she started the engine she glanced back at the half-way house, and was pretty sure, if only for a fraction of a second, that she saw Dillon staring out at her from one of the bedrooms on the top floor.

The thing about local papers is that usually there's no problem finding a front-page story. There is always *something*, whether it's an act of criminality, something political, something about jobs or a fatal accident. No, the front page isn't generally the problem, or even the next few – it's filling the rest of the paper. There are pages and pages that require stories every single week and that can be difficult. It was a big enough town, but it wasn't Belfast, just a few miles up the road. It was a commuter town, there was never that much going on, and that meant that the editor couldn't just wait for stories to come to him, he had to get creative. In a local paper, that meant inviting contributions from readers, asking local experts in a dozen fields to write a weekly column, not because anyone was particularly interested in their material, but because it helped to fill the space around the adverts. If they were interesting, it was a bonus. The *Express* had a motoring column, a wine column, a bridge column, a camera-club column, five different Boys' Brigade columns; a dozen different sports were reported on not by a sports reporter but by the sportsmen themselves; there was a religious column shared out between the local ministers, there was a fashion column, a column written by a local 'disaffected youth' who did not seem that disaffected, or, indeed, youthful; there was a 'Green' page which was big on recycling (though in fact the paper it appeared in was not on recycled paper – too expensive); and there was the bloody badger column. It wasn't to be fair, entirely about badgers – it was also about art, and history, and botany, and interesting holidays the author had enjoyed; it was about food and classical music and the author's memories of Switzerland shortly after the Second World War, where she had attended boarding school. It was about everything, and nothing, and might actually have been salvageable if the author was a decent writer, but she clearly was not. She wrote, Rob thought, as if English was her second language. It read, Rob thought, as if it had been originally written in German, but had then been translated into English by someone who was not, in fact, English. It was stilted, formal and entirely lacking in humour. Rob didn't know why he was even driving out to see the stupid woman, in his stupid car, he should just have done it by email. But here he was, six miles outside Bangor, peering out of his rolled-down window, looking for Mary McDermott's house – looking for the numbers on gate posts which were few and far between along a winding country road. Eventually, as he squeezed past a tractor on a narrow corner, he asked the big farmer behind the wheel if he was anywhere near her house, and he shouted back that it was about a quarter of a mile along on the left. Rob gave him the thumbs-up. Gerry was right, they were an urban paper, with no significant sales outside of town – there was absolutely no reason to continue carrying Mary McDermott's tedious ramblings; he had been brought in to save the paper, and that meant re-inventing it, not being a slave to tradition. Mary McDermott could not continue to be published just because she always had been. She needed to make way.

Rob turned into the driveway – and then there was another quarter of mile up a lane hemmed in on both sides by tall, thick hedges that admitted little light. He finally emerged onto a large, paved courtyard that led to an immaculate and impressive-looking ranch-style house. There was a mud-spattered Land Rover parked in front, with a this-year's

Porsche right beside it. He already knew that Mary McDermott wasn't writing her column for the money, because there was none. But from the looks of this place she probably didn't need it anyway. It meant that she was writing the column not for financial gain, but for the love of it. Which would make his task even harder.

She was elderly, she was pleasant and she was genteel. She had a lounge filled with antique china, and oil paintings of wild animals. She had white hair that had a conditioning sheen. She insisted on providing a pot of tea and biscuits even though virtually the first thing Rob said was that he couldn't stay long. He asked if he could give her a hand and she said no, she was fine. He followed her into the kitchen nevertheless. There was a big black range with a pot of stew bubbling away on top. He said it smelled lovely and she offered him a bowl. He said no. She insisted. He gave in. He was actually starving. They sat at a long wooden table. It was lovely. He ate it too quickly, mainly because he wanted to get most of it down before the conversation turned to her column and her imminent sacking. In so doing, he burned the roof of his mouth. She got him ice-cold milk from the fridge to soothe it with. She was as nice as her stew. She told stories, he laughed, and genuinely; she remembered the old days on the farm, her experiences in war-torn Europe as a young girl. She was engaging and entertaining, neither of which pertained at all to her very dull newspaper column. She was half-way through one of her stories, this one about her pet badger – it had been orphaned and she had raised it from a cub and it now enjoyed the comforts of her home by day and went out with its badger mates at night – when she suddenly stopped, fixed Rob with a hard look and said, 'Mr Cullen – I know why you're here.'

Rob, like a rabbit caught in headlights, said, 'You ... do?'

'Yes. You want to kill me off.'

'I—'

'I appreciate that you've done me the courtesy of coming out to tell me, face to face. That is indeed the mark of a true gentleman. But still, that is why you are here.'

'Well, I, ahm, killing you off is a bit strong,' said Rob, valiantly trying to maintain eye contact, 'though I certainly do hope to discuss the column with you.'

'I expect you think that they're just the ramblings of a sad old woman.'

'No ... no! Not at all. It's just that with our re-design—'

'He tries it at least once a year.'

'Who ... What?'

'My nephew Gerry. Every time somebody new joins the paper, he sends them out here to fire me, because he hasn't the balls to do it himself.' Rob stared at her. She smiled back. She did not have the kind of face that you expected to hear the word *balls* issue from. She put down her spoon. 'And I'm sure that he didn't mention to you that I am one of the owners of the paper which he has so cleverly been running into the ground?' Rob shook his head. Mary shook her own. 'That boy was a bloody chancer from the day he was born. Now, would you like to meet my badger?'

Rob met the badger. It was fast asleep. He stroked it. Then it was back to work. Later in the afternoon he opened his office door and asked Alix if he could have a word. She nodded. As she got up she looked at Sean. Sean shrugged and said, 'I never said nothing.' She raised an eyebrow. Sean looked a bit flustered and then quickly handed her the best of the photographs he'd taken of Mark Dillon.

Rob moved to one side to allow Alix to pass. Gerry emerged from his office, and then hesitated as he saw Rob looking at him.

'The badger woman,' said Rob. 'Your auntie.'

'Did – did I not mention that?'

'Yeah, right. Well for your information, I didn't fire her. In fact, I'm giving her more space.'

'In God's name why?!'

'Because green is good, the environment is good, and kids love badgers. And also...'

'Yes...?'

'For badness.'

Rob smiled at him and retreated into his office. He was still smiling when he sat at his desk, so Alix smiled too.

'You've nothing to smile about,' Rob snapped. 'I had a call from a Tommy Brady. He runs a half-way house on Dufferin Avenue. But then you know that.'

'Ahm, yes, I do.'

'He's fuming.'

'I was only—'

'I told you to leave that story alone.'

'No, you told me there was no story.'

'And you know better?'

'Well, as a matter of fact...' She didn't mean it to be particularly cheeky, it just came out like that. She quickly handed one of the photos across – it showed Dillon drinking outside the Jamaica Inn. 'He had three pints, and then he was driving – well over the limit. It's like it all never happened, he can just do what he wants...'

'Three pints of what?' Rob asked.

'Well, beer, clearly...'

'Can you prove that? Or could it have been shandy? Or low-alcohol beer? Did you speak to the barman? Did you see his receipt? What do you really have? You have nothing, Alix, apart from a pissed-off manager of a half-way house who thinks you're hassling his charges." Rob took a deep breath and when he spoke again it was more quietly, but it still sounded like he was admonishing a child. 'Look, these houses have a hard enough time, nobody wants them in their back yard, so they have to keep a low profile, they don't need someone coming round threatening—'

'I wasn't threatening. And so what are we supposed to do, turn a blind eye to—?'

'Alix, we report the news, we don't make the news, okay? So just ... just drop it.'

She was glaring at him; couldn't help it.

'Okay,' he said, 'now I'm sure you've plenty of other stories to be getting on with.'

She nodded. He nodded. He returned his attention to his computer.

She got up and went to the door. She stopped. 'I was only trying to—'

'Leave it!'

But of course, she couldn't. She returned to her desk and brooded through the rest of the afternoon. She worked on other stories, but her heart wasn't in them. When she left the office, instead of going home, she drove straight to an off licence for a bottle of wine, and then on to Ailsa and Roy's house. When Ailsa opened the door she held the bottle up and said, 'I may not be much good to you as a journalist. But I can still be a good friend.'

Ailsa had looked quite hard-faced as she came down the hall, but now that the door was open and the wine was offered, she softened. She said, 'Ach, babe, there was no need. Come on in.'

They sat in the kitchen. It grew dark outside as they chatted about everything but what had happened in the newspaper office; at least, until the wine was downed, and then a second bottle worked through. Alix brought it up herself. She said she was sorry, that she'd tried everything but the new boss wouldn't budge. Her old boss, she said, he would definitely have done something, but not this new one.

'It's fine,' said Ailsa, 'and we know it's not your fault.'

Another glass necked and Alix said, 'Maybe you've seen the back of him anyway. I think seeing you two in B&Q scared the pants off him, I'm pretty sure he hasn't been back to work since, and as long as you avoid Dufferin Avenue, then maybe you won't have to see him ever again...'

'Dufferin? Why Dufferin?'

'That's where the half...' Some part of her stopped her finishing, though probably too late. It wasn't a state secret that there was a half-way house on Dufferin, but they didn't exactly publicize it. 'That's where they live the half of them – it's all bedsits and guest houses, isn't it? I expect that's where he is. Or Southwell Road, there's a lot of bedsits round there too. The dole office – they put the homeless up in Kilcooley as well I think. The important thing is to just try and forget about him. He's ... nothing...'

'He is nothing,' said Roy.

But Ailsa was looking tearful. Roy put his hand over his wife's and gave it a little squeeze.

Gerry got the call just after midnight. Janine's name lit up. Janine upset was one thing, but Janine upset and pissed in the middle of the night was something he couldn't cope with. So he let it go to voicemail, and wasn't even going to listen to it until the morning, but about an hour later, unable to sleep because it was nagging at him, he finally played it. She wasn't drunk. Her voice was shaky, but remarkably calm, considering she was calling from the hospital; she'd been beaten up. Gerry drove straight over. She was still in the casualty department, in a curtained-off bed. She looked a mess. One eye was closed, she had a busted tooth and her lip was split. He hugged her and she cried against him. When she settled a bit she told him she'd been set upon by some thug when she went for a bottle of wine at the off licence on the corner. She'd noticed him when she left her apartment, had passed him on the corner; they'd made eye contact; she'd looked away. She was quite relieved when she was walking back that he was no longer at the corner, but then he'd stepped out from behind a car and dragged her into an alley and thumped her half a dozen times. He hadn't stolen anything. He wasn't one of the alcoholics who normally hung around the offie, she knew them all by sight, and in fact they'd come running to help her when they heard her screams. The thug had run off. All through it he hadn't said a word. But she knew it was a warning, or a punishment; both, probably. Gerry said he was sorry, so sorry, that he hadn't believed her and she said, 'You didn't believe me?' and he quickly covered with, 'Of course I believed you. What I meant was Rob, Rob didn't believe you and he was very convincing. But I see now it's because he's spent so long in England and he doesn't really know how it is here. I hold my hand up, Janine, and admit I allowed myself to be swayed, but man, God, the evidence is here before my very eyes now, and as soon as Rob Cullen sees the face on you he'll be in no doubt either.' She said, 'Is my face that horrible?' and he said, no, it wasn't really, it was the swelling making it look so bad, not that it looked so bad, more sore than anything, is it very sore and she said yes. He asked if they'd given her painkillers and she said not yet; he said good and took out a wee flask of whiskey he'd brought and they sipped on that until she was given the all-clear to go about an hour later. He took her home and insisted on staying. He would sleep on the couch. She said, 'You're not normally so shy,' and he said, 'Your face isn't normally swollen up like a balloon.' She said, 'Sleep on the effing couch, then,' and stormed off to bed.

Rob Cullen got *his* the call at just after 3 a.m. A man was saying, 'Billy – Billy, is that you?'

Rob was still half asleep. 'Wha...?'

'Billy – big fire on Dufferin Avenue, thought you'd be interested.'

Rob had recovered enough to say, 'Who is this?'

'It's me, Fletch – remember, I do the darts notes? You told me if I ever saw anything exciting happening to be sure to call it in. It's just across the road. I called the fire brigade, then I called you.'

'Well, thanks, Fletch, much appreciated. Though I should tell you, I'm not Billy.'

'Oh – do you mean I've, like, a wrong number?'

'Right number, wrong person, but it's absolutely fine.'

When the office was closed, Rob had calls to editorial re-routed to his home phone.

'Can I speak to Billy?'

'Well, no, that would be difficult. But consider him informed.'

'Tell him he should get down here quick, there's about five fire engines.'

As soon as he hung up, Rob looked at the ceiling and said, 'Did you get that Billy?'

There was no response. Rob got up, pulled on a pair of jeans and a hoody and hurried downstairs. As he drove towards the centre of town he phoned Sean, but it went straight to voicemail.

Alix got *her* call five minutes later. She'd fallen asleep slightly tipsy while trying to get through *All the President's Men* for about the hundredth time. It was supposed to be *the* Bible for crusading journalists, but all the names just confused her. Her actual Bible was *The Odessa File* – it was a fast and exciting novel featuring a determined journalist tracking down Nazis. That was more like it. Although, it had to be said, she was unlikely to encounter many Nazis through the *Express*. She was still thinking about this as the phone continued to ring.

Focus.

She reached out and answered, groggy still and a little slurred – but snapped out of it as soon as Rob told her about the fire and where it was. She immediately felt sick to her stomach. She said, 'I can't drive, I've had too much to drink.'

Rob growled at her to get down anyway. Ten minutes later she climbed out of a taxi at Dufferin Avenue. The roof of the half-way house was on fire and there was smoke billowing out of the windows on the top floor. There were firemen everywhere, and crowds of onlookers; three ambulances were parked off to the right. She found Rob and asked if anyone was hurt or even still inside. He said he didn't know. He still sounded gruff. He moved forward and began to take photos with his phone. The police were there, but not enough of them to cordon off the scene properly, so Alix was able to get close enough to the ambulances to see Mark Dillon lying in the back of one, being attended to by paramedics. When they moved a little, she saw that he'd an oxygen mask on his face. Her back was poked suddenly and she turned to find Thomas Brady glowering at her. The half-way house manager's face was smudged black and he was wearing a shirt that was unevenly buttoned. He said, 'This is your fucking fault.'

'What're you talking about?'

'You think it's a coincidence, you poke your nose in and that very night someone firebombs us?'

'Firebomb?!'

'Yes, what the fuck did you think it was, spontaneous combustion? Someone poured petrol through our front door and set it alight.'

Technically, that wasn't a firebomb, but it wasn't the time or place.

She said, 'You can't say for sure that had anything to do with—'

'Is that right?! Is it?'

'Yes! I'm sorry that—'

'Well, here's what I can say for sure. You see that fella over there?' He pointed towards Mark Dillon. 'Not only did he raise the alarm, he went back in three or four times to get people out. He got me out. My room's on the top floor. Smoke rises. It was coming under my door. He had to kick my door in, and then he had to drag me down the hall and carry me down the stairs. He saved my fucking life. You want to write about Mark Dillon? How about instead of trying to stitch him up for having a drink you write about how he's a fucking hero?'

He waved a warning finger in her face, and then stormed away.

It was only then that she realized that Rob was standing beside her and must have heard the entire exchange, because he said, 'Now it's a story.'

Rob was barely into the office, bleary-eyed still, when Gerry came in and broke the news about Janine. Rob agreed it was terrible, and was on the verge of saying that nevertheless it hardly changed the fact that she'd been ripping the paper off for years, but he held back. It was, after all, still just a temporary job, he wasn't going to be spending the rest of his life on a tiny wee newspaper like the *Express*; as soon as the nonsense at the *Guardian* was cleared up he would be back there, or he'd pick up something else on another of the dailies; he had loads of experience, and, he hoped, a good reputation. He was picking up some cash here at home in Northern Ireland, he was giving something back to the community – he was like the Red Adair of local newspapers, an expert parachuted in to save and salvage, but then straight out again. The best he could do was give his advice and it was up to Gerry whether he took it or not. He was truly sorry that Janine had been beaten up, but – if you slept with sharks, sometimes you were going to get bitten. He didn't say this out loud either. Instead he made more sympathetic noises and then said he needed to be getting on with his work, but Gerry wasn't for shifting until Rob agreed that they should both go and visit her. Gerry said, 'We owe her that much.' Rob finally couldn't resist a comeback. 'Not as much as she owes us.' Gerry gave him a look, and Rob held his hands up and said sorry. He added, 'It'll have to be at lunchtime, it's all gone a bit mental with this fire.'

As it turned out, Sean had actually been at the fire, it was just that no one had spotted him. His pictures were fabulous. He had one black-and-white one of Mark Dillon being helped to the ambulance that looked like something out of the Second World War, his face black, his eyes wide, smoke and flames in the background. It was the kind of photo that won awards; it was the kind of photo that deserved to go national, international maybe. Rob was quite torn about it – his instincts were to send it out, let Sean and by association the paper, get the acclaim. But that would mean that, by the time they themselves were able to print it, it would essentially be old news, it would be familiar, and its impact would be lessened. His first duty should be to the paper he worked on, and after that it could do the rounds. He thought briefly about discussing it with Gerry, but he suspected the cash-strapped owner would immediately want to sell it, so he held his water. It was only for twenty-four hours. He was actually more concerned with getting a story that was worthy of the photo – Alix was struggling to get anything out of the hospital where Dillon was being treated, and the private company that ran the half-way house on behalf of the Prison Service said it was too busy trying to re-house its residents to be able to comment. Thomas Brady, previously vociferous, had clearly been warned to say nothing. Alix had included his quote, suitably censored for bad language, about Dillon being a hero, in her story, but it just wasn't enough. They needed more.

Lunchtime came and Gerry appeared in Rob's office, pulling his coat on.

Rob said, 'Do we have to?'

'Yes, we do.'

'I've—'

74

'Twenty minutes, that's all.'

Rob sighed and got up. As they walked down the stairs he said, 'Any sign of my car yet?'

'Mmmmmm,' said Gerry.

'Gerry ... I can't keep driving that bloody smart car around.'

'You're such a snob, Rob. People in the developing world would kill for such a car.'

'No,' said Rob, 'they wouldn't.'

They took Gerry's Jag. Rob asked why he hadn't volunteered the Jag as security ... surely it was worth a lot more than Rob's?

Gerry said, 'I didn't volunteer it because I volunteered yours instead. Because it's my company, they're all my cars, and it's all my debt.'

Rob said, 'Fair enough.' Half-way to Janine's he said, 'Though come to think of it you have something even more valuable you could have offered them.'

'Like what?'

'A performing badger.'

'Does it perform?'

'It rolls over and allows you to scratch its belly.'

Gerry nodded. He concentrated on the road for a bit. When they were drawing close to Janine's he said, 'I hate that fucking badger.'

Rob said, 'He speaks highly of you, too.'

Janine's apartment was in a swanky-looking complex off Maxwell Road. Rob raised an eyebrow and Gerry snapped, 'What?'

'I'm saying nothing,' said Rob.

They parked, and then Gerry reached back for a bouquet of flowers and a box of chocolates.

'Still saying nothing,' said Rob.

He found Janine's name on a panel with six others and pushed the intercom button.

'Hello?'

Gerry stepped up to it and said, 'It's me.'

'Oh good. I'll leave the front door open, honey. Come on in.'

Rob said nothing as the buzzer sounded. They entered the building and took the elevator to the third floor. As the doors opened, Rob put out his hand and said, 'After you, honey.'

Gerry scowled at him and said, 'We go back, okay?'

'None of my business,' said Rob.

'Exactly.'

The door was open. They went in: open-plan lounge and kitchen, big leather sofas and Janine standing in her dressing gown, sans make-up, her face swollen, her left eye totally closed, her skin blotchy. Gerry gave her a gentle hug and the flowers and she said, 'Och, they're lovely, so they are. 'Gerry had given Rob the chocolates to hand over and he did so, somewhat awkwardly. He barely knew her and didn't know whether to hug her or not, but she seemed to be in hugging mood. She came towards him with her arms out and he did what he had to do. She smelled of mandarin oranges and red wine. She sat them down and brought them tea. She opened the chocolates and cherry-picked the best of them.

'Did you get a decent look at him?' Rob asked.

'Just jump right in there,' said Gerry.

'It's fine, it's fine, and no, not really. It was dark, and although it felt like it went on for ever, I suppose it was really quite quick.' She got a little teary. 'So, no, I didn't see who it was, but then I know who's behind it, so what's the difference?'

'Who?' Rob asked.

'The hoods! The paramilitaries! They haven't gone away, you know!'

'I mean a name or a specific ... Someone the police will be able to arrest. What did they say?'

Janine's good eye flitted to Gerry. 'I didn't ... report it, yet.'

'Why not?' said Rob.

'Because what are they going to do?' said Gerry. 'She barely saw him. And even if they got him, he's not going to name names, is he? And if this is what they do when they're not getting their money, what're they going to do when they hear we've brought the police in?'

'Exactly,' said Janine. 'But I think – I think maybe that might be the end of it? Because now they know I can't pay them any more, and they've punished me, so what's the point in them carrying on with it? I was the weak spot, and they exploited it.' She took Gerry's hand and looked into his eyes and said, 'I'm sorry, Gerry, I should have told you, but I was scared. Will you ever forgive me?'

'Forgive? There's nothing to forgive! I don't know how you worked under all that pressure, it must have been awful. And I think you should take a few days to recover, and then start right back in with us on Monday morning. Isn't that right, Rob?'

'It ... I mean ... whatever you say.'

'Yes, absolutely,' said Gerry. 'Welcome back, Janine.'

'Oh, Gerry.'

'In fact, welcome home, Janine,' said Gerry.

Janine started to cry again.

When she finally stopped she apologized for making such a show of herself, and asked what they wanted for lunch. Rob said he couldn't stay. Gerry half-heartedly tried to persuade him. Janine thanked him profusely. Gerry offered to give him a lift back to the office, but he said he would walk, he didn't know the town that well but he was pretty sure it was only a fifteen-minute stroll.

Except, when he came out of Maxwell Park he turned right instead of left; it didn't make a huge amount of difference to his journey, maybe an extra ten minutes, but it was a happy accident because it brought him to the very end of Maxwell Road and he could see the Winemark off licence about a hundred metres away. Rob sauntered up and in. The woman behind the counter smiled at him and said what a nice day it was and could she be of any help and they had an offer on Australian wines. Rob said he wasn't in for any wine. He was with the *Express*. He wondered if she'd heard anything about what happened outside last night. She said no, though she had been working. He told her about the paper's advertising manager being beaten up just yards along and she said, 'Janine?'

'You know her?'

'Yes, of course, she's a regular – and I mean that in a good way. Lovely lady. She was attacked? I never heard anything – but then we're all double-glazed against the traffic, so a bomb could go off we wouldn't hear it. Oh dear. Is she okay?'

'A bit battered,' said Rob.

'And she was in last night, I served her.'

He thanked her anyway and turned for the door.

The woman called after him, 'Please tell her I was asking for her?'

'Will do,' said Rob.

'And is her boyfriend all right?'

'Boyfriend?'

'Aye, he was with her, he wasn't attacked too?'

'No, I ... Do you mean, Gerry?'

'Well, I really don't know his name. Big fella, not much in

78

the way of hair but he's like – you know, like a doorman or something? You know, like a bouncer? He looks like he could handle himself in a fight all right. He must have left before she was—?'

'Aye,' said Rob, 'I suppose he must have.'

As soon as Rob and Gerry left for lunch, Alix slipped out too. She was on a mission. Ailsa and Roy were supposed to be her friends – Ailsa more than Roy, because they went way back to primary school together – but she *knew* they were somehow connected to the fire at the half-way house. It was just too much of a coincidence that the very day she had accidentally mentioned where Mark Dillon was staying it was attacked by arsonists. She was determined to have it out with them – people could have been killed, and Thomas Brady very nearly had been. She'd spent the morning talking to the health board's press office trying to get an interview with Dillon, but he'd said no.

On the way there she faltered a little – the half-way house was, after all, a home for those who'd recently been released from prison; what if one of them was in fact an unreformed arsonist? Coincidences did happen, that's why they were called coincidences. She couldn't just burst in and accuse them.

Ailsa answered the door, all smiles and saying she wasn't long out of bed, then asking about Alix's hangover because her head was still killing her. Now that they were face to face across the kitchen table again, Alix realized how ridiculous she was being. She'd known Ailsa most of her life, she was incapable of hurting another human being. Ailsa poured coffee and brought out half a dozen cupcakes in a Tupperware box and they discussed why the hell they were called cupcakes when they were clearly just buns. Alix ate one and was starting on a second when she casually dropped in about the fire and Ailsa said, 'What fire?' and looked genuinely surprised. She got up and went to the bottom of the stairs and shouted, 'Roy – Alix is here! Did you hear about the fire?'

'What fire?' drifted down.

'At that place where Dillon is, Dufferin Avenue?'

'Didn't hear, but I hope it got the bastard.'

A minute later Roy appeared in the kitchen, wearing a T-shirt and tracksuit bottoms, with a towel draped over his shoulders and flecks of shaving foam still below one of his ears. He nodded at Alix and said, 'How serious?'

'Bad enough. Someone poured petrol through the letter box, whole place went up.'

'What about our guy?'

'He's fine. Actually – he turned out to be a bit of a hero.'

'Hero – what the fuck are you talking about?'

'Easy, Roy,' said Ailsa.

'Just what they're saying. He saved some people.'

'And is that what you're putting in your paper, that he's a hero?'

'I don't know what's going in, Roy.'

Roy crossed to the worktop and began to make himself a cup of coffee. Alix noticed for the first time that he was keeping his right hand in his tracksuit pocket. When he lifted the kettle he was somewhat awkward with it, and when he poured the boiling water it spilled out too fast and came up and over the brim of his mug. Alix glanced at Ailsa and saw that her friend was watching Roy too. When her eyes came back to Alix they flitted away again. Roy turned with the mug in his left hand and leaned against the sink, sipping at it and looking between his wife and Alix at some unknown spot. It was, suddenly, unbelievably awkward.

Alix studied the kitchen table. Ailsa was her friend, Roy was part of the package. She liked him all right, but didn't really know him that well. Billy, her former editor, had had a mantra based on forty years' experience in the newspaper business. 'You never know what goes on behind closed doors.' And she had begun to learn it herself. The most pleasant, charming and endearing people could be monsters at home; the outgoing, shy; the beautiful, plagued with self-doubt; the roughest, obsessed with needlepoint. Sometimes it ended with that nice Mrs Jones plunging an axe into her husband's head. Sometimes, Billy said, you never found out, but you always had to take it into account. Nobody ever showed 100 per cent of themselves. Anyone who did, you had to suspect there was another fifty per cent hidden away somewhere defying the laws of mathematics. Alix loved Ailsa, had spent weeks and months and years in her company, but she still would never really know what she was like once that front door shut, what she was really like with Roy. Roy himself was generally pleasant and had a good sense of humour, but according to Billy's dictum, he could just as easily be an arsonist, an arsonist with his hand thrust into his pocket because he had burned it while setting fire to a half-way house.

Eventually Alix broke the silence with a simple, 'Well.'

'Aye,' said Ailsa.

'Thing is,' said Alix, 'I think the editor will probably take me off the story anyway. He'll say I'm personally involved in it. And maybe that's for the best.'

'Is that because you think Dillon is a hero?' Roy asked.

'Roy, I can ... any reporter can only report the facts. As I understand it Dillon did save some lives. It doesn't mean you forget what he did before. Maybe he has turned his life around, I don't know. I mean – what he did was appalling, absolutely appalling, but what do you say then about someone who could pour petrol through the letter box of a building where a dozen people were sleeping, where a dozen people could have died? Aren't they just as bad?'

Roy shook his head. 'If you ask me, someone should have smoked those bastards out months ago. And actually, Alix – is that why you're here? Do you think we had something to do with the fire?'

'No, I—'

'Because if you are, you can just fuck off out of here and never come back.'

'Roy, please, there's no need for that,' said Ailsa.

'Well!'

'No, I'm not suggesting that, not at all,' though deep down, she knew she was, 'I just wanted to let you know about it, keep you up to date.'

Roy chewed on his bottom lip. Then he said, 'Okay. Well. Sorry. I'm just pissed off with him. It's not you.'

'It's fine, honestly.' She got up from the table and pulled her jacket on. Ailsa got up too. Alix leaned across and kissed her on the cheek. 'Sure I'll have youse round to my place soon for something to eat, eh?' Then she turned to Roy and put her hand out to him. 'Friends?' she said.

She waited for him to withdraw his hand from his pocket.

Roy nodded, then came forward and gave her a one-armed hug.

Alix hugged him back. When they parted, their eyes met, and he knew that she knew, and she knew that he knew she knew. When she looked at Ailsa it was just Ailsa, and she hoped that she really didn't know, but she knew now that she herself would never know unless she came straight out and asked them, and she just wasn't brave enough to do that. With strangers, yes, sure – but, with friends, impossible. The only thing she was really sure of was that their relationship had changed for ever, that, no matter what was said on the surface, she would never again be welcomed into their home.

Driving back to the office, she wondered if the job was making her cynical or if she'd always been that way. She realized that she felt happier now than when she'd made the outward journey – lighter, and more determined than ever to write her story, and write it properly. With that in mind she decided not to go straight back to the office. She'd been fobbed off all morning by the health board's press officer. She was going to get her story straight from the horse's mouth.

It was probably worth an article in itself – how easy it was to get into a hospital. All Alix had to say was that she was here to visit her brother and what ward was he on and she was told exactly where to go, wasn't even asked for ID. Mark Dillon was in an open ward, though with the curtains pulled around his bed. She hesitated before stepping through the slight gap, a little nervous, a little scared as to how he would react, aware that she was stepping outside the bounds of what she should be doing as a local newspaper reporter – but she was young, she was ambitious, she wanted to step up to the big leagues. Getting an exclusive (though in truth nobody else seemed to be clamouring for it) interview with the villain-turned-hero wasn't exactly tracking down Nazis, but it would be a step in the right direction.

She said, 'Mr Dillon?'

He was lying on top of the bedcovers. He'd an IV in his

83

arm. He had bandages on his hands and across his shoulders and the back of his neck. His eyes were red. He was reading the back page of a newspaper and said 'Yep?' without looking up, but when she said nothing he did and it took him a moment to place her. Then he said, 'What the...?' and looked about, a little panicked. His voice was ragged.

'Sorry – I just wondered if I could have a quick word.'

'About what?!'

'About everything, about the fire, about being back in town, about—'

'No! You've no right to come in here! Who the fuck do you think you—?'

'I'm just trying to write a story about...'

The curtain moved behind her. There was a red-faced nurse, 'Sorry – but what's going on here? Visiting time isn't for another—'

'I just wanted a quick word with—'

'She's a fucking reporter!'

'I'm sorry, but I'm afraid you're going to have to leave, you have to get permission before you can just—'

'I know but—'

'But nothing. Now, please...'

The nurse pulled the curtain back a little further to allow Alix to exit. Alix looked at Dillon and then quickly delved into her handbag and produced a card. 'Let me leave you this,' she said, setting it down on the table at the end of his bed, 'and if you want to talk you can—'

'I don't want your fucking card!'

'Please,' said the nurse.

'Going,' said Alix, her face burning.

She backed out through the curtain and began to walk away. She left the ward and was half-way down the corridor when the nurse called after her – 'Excuse me?'

She debated whether to stop – she was bound to want to report her for barging in on a patient, and that would undoubtedly get back to Rob. She stopped, and took a deep breath, and turned slowly. She was about to launch into another apology when the nurse said, 'He's changed his mind, he does want to talk to you. Shouldn't really allow it, but he is a bit of a hero, isn't he?' She turned on her heel and Alix fell in behind her. 'Just a few minutes, then? He's really not very well – smoke on the lungs. It's quite nasty.'

When she pulled the curtain back Dillon held his hands up and said, 'Sorry – look, I shouldn't have shouted at you. I'm just—'

'Of course you are. You've been in a fire. You're all burned.'

'No – not really. A few wee marks, that's all.'

'You're quite the hero, Mr Dillon.'

'*Mister* now, is it?'

'Well.'

'Is that what you're going to write?'

'It's what people are saying. Do you want to tell me what happened?'

'No, I really don't.'

'It's a good story, and we have to write it. Surely it's better to have your input? It might help rehabilitate you in the eyes of—'

'In the eyes of who, exactly? And who says I need *rehabilitated*?'

Alix moved to the end of his bed. 'Look, I'm not trying to cause you any trouble … but I have to report the news, and you saved people's lives in that fire, and we should celebrate that. But I can't write the story without saying why you were in the half-way house in the first place.'

'Why not?'

'Because we're a small town and people will know and if we don't mention it they'll think we're deliberately hiding it. And also, it's the right thing to do. We're just presenting the facts.'

Dillon was shaking his head. 'Sorry, look, if you put it in the paper it means everyone will be reminded of what happened. Even if you call me the greatest hero since Captain America, the one thing people are going to take away from it is that I once killed a baby. I could save ten thousand people in ten thousand fires but they'd still point at me and call me a baby killer. If you put my face in the paper, I'll never be able to walk down a street in this town and feel safe, never be able to sleep without thinking there's someone pouring petrol through the letter box, trying to kill me.'

'We don't know that that's what—'

'Of course it is! And you know something? I don't blame them.'

'Them?'

'Little Peggy's parents.'

'You don't know that they...'

'You forget, I met them, first day on a new job, face to face, and I saw how they were, the disbelief and the anger. If the dad had gotten hold of me there, I'm pretty sure he would have killed me. That, that ... bitterness doesn't go away. How can it? I killed their baby. If I could go back, if I could not drink, not show off to my mates in that stupid fucking souped-up car, don't you think I would? I am so sorry for what happened.'

'Why don't you tell them that? Maybe it would help.'

'You know something? I may be some kind of hero, but I'm not brave enough for that. Not in a million years.'

'So what are you going to do?'

'I don't know. I don't fucking know.'

There were tears in his eyes.

When she got back to the office and she started to write she couldn't quite settle on what she wanted to say. Dillon hadn't specifically said that what he was telling her was off the record, which meant that according to the arbitrary and meaningless ethics of journalism she was free to use it. She'd taken the precaution of recording their conversation on her phone. She hadn't hidden the phone, she had quite clearly had it in her hand, and even made a deliberate demonstration of pushing a button just as soon as she arrived back at his bed; if he had noticed, he hadn't commented. She was aware of the power that she had to slant the story whatever way she wanted. It was a question of how much prominence she gave to his previous conviction, how well she conveyed his sorrow, how she portrayed his undoubted heroism (and she managed later in the afternoon to speak to several other witnesses who confirmed what Dillon had done) and how much space she gave to the reactions of the still-grieving parents or if she even dared hint that they might somehow be connected to the fire.

In the end it was her new editor who solved her conundrum. The first part of the solution was him saying, 'I need the story, and I need it in the next half an hour because we're going to print.' The second part was him saying, when she quickly explained her quandary, 'Well, what's the story?' She started to launch into it, but he stopped her and said, 'Sell it to me in a headline.' She immediately said, almost without thinking, 'Fire hero is ex-prisoner'.

'There you go,' said Rob. 'Don't over-think it. Present the facts. People aren't stupid, they'll work it out for themselves.'

'But—'

'And now we have twenty-five minutes.'

'But what if I—'

'I'll fix it. That's my job.'

So she wrote it in ten minutes and sent it through. Five minutes later he called her in and nodded at his screen and said it was grand – dramatic, balanced and sympathetic. There was Sean's photo of Dillon in the back of the ambulance and her headline, *Fire hero is ex-prisoner.*

'Oh good. Do I get a gold star?'

'No, you get another story.'

She smiled and went back to her desk. Then she came straight back to his office and said, 'My friends aren't going to be happy with it. Dillon's not going to be happy with it.'

She nodded down at the screen, and then raised her hand and placed it across the top of Sean's photo, so that the upper part of Dillon's face was masked.

'This way,' she said, 'he'll be able to walk the streets and not many people will recognize him. Maybe he can get his life back together.'

'You think he deserves a second chance?'

'Maybe.'

'And everyone lives happily ever after?'

'Not exactly.'

'Well, it's a nice thought. But no. It's not our job to make people happy, Alix. We're here to report the news. And hopefully sell a few copies in the process. Good story, good photo, now on to the next one.'

Rob reached forward and pressed the send button.

CHAPTER 3
MR. TURNER'S PRIZE

His name was too good *not* to win the Turner Prize. It was a headline waiting to happen. He was, of course, already an acclaimed artist, but because he was called Richard Turner the critics and cynics, often one and the same thing, considered and concluded that he was halfway to being crowned already. He was on the shortlist, the announcement was a week away, and the local boy made good had chosen not to spend the last few days before it glad-handing around London but back home, opening a small retrospective in an old pal's gallery, a thank you for all his help on the way up. It would have been considered one of the hottest tickets in town in any town, but the fact that it was Bangor and the gallery only held a hundred people meant that they really were like gold dust. Or, at least, fairy dust.

It was a big thing for the town, but Rob was finding it hard to get excited. He'd worked in Manchester and London and seen plenty of big things and next big things and usually they turned out to be not that big or interesting at all, a mixture of hype and enthusiasm throwing up a kind of protective heat shield around works in which he was hard pressed to discern anything of value. Of course, it was all subjective. He didn't know much about art, but he knew what he disliked.

This evening he was one of the last to arrive at Easel. That's what the owner, Aiden Marten, called the gallery. Easel. Rob wondered why he didn't go the whole hog and call it Paint Brush. It was already nearly full. Rob had an earphone in. He'd only been in town for a few weeks so not everyone knew him yet, but those who did recognize him didn't try to engage him in chat because he looked like he was concentrating on whatever important information was coming through to him; they didn't know he was listening to the football commentary, and that he would much rather have been at home watching the game on the telly, with a carry-out from the Hong Kong Palace on his lap and a beer in his hand. Rob didn't make any attempt to dissuade them. If it looked like someone was about to approach, he put his finger to his ear and walked away muttering to himself. He didn't mind the wine, though. He had downed two or three glasses already. He wasn't a natural conversationalist, and he floundered at small talk with strangers in general and the kind of people who came to small private art galleries in particular. It wasn't because they were rich, because mostly they weren't, it was because they put on airs and graces the way they put on their make-up or after-shave; that is to say, generously. Case in point: Janine. She was on the far side of the room, war paint on, chatting, schmoozing, laughing too loudly, and all the while with a smug grin on her face that seemed to expand every time her eyes met Rob's. She had been back in work for two weeks. She had been as good as gold. She was getting more advertising than ever. And Rob knew she was laughing at all of them. She had stolen tens of thousands of pounds from the paper, come up with a frankly unbelievable story about being forced to pay protection money, and then persuaded someone to beat her up to back up her claim. At least, that was how Rob was seeing it. She was bad to the bone.

And then he saw Alix entering the gallery, with Sean and his camera trailing behind, and he found himself beaming at her. Alix looked – well, fabulous. She was a good-looking woman anyway, he'd thought that from the moment he first saw her at Billy Maxwell's funeral, plus she was smart and bolshie and sometimes a bit too convinced of her own abilities, but this night – something about her, the shape of her sky-blue summer dress, the heels, the eye-liner even, just everything, she just looked really lovely. He knew it was probably the wine, but he couldn't help thinking it, and smiling at the same time.

The first thing she said was, 'What're you looking so pleased about?'

'Me? No, not me,' he said, flustered, the colour rising in his cheeks. 'Just listening to the match, they've scored...' He pointed at his earphone, and then pulled it out.

'Who's they?'

'Tottingham,' he said.

'Tottingham?'

'I mean...'

But she'd already turned to snatch a glass of wine off a fast-moving teenage waiter. As she turned back to him Janine was just passing, probably in pursuit of the same waiter. But she took time to look Alix up and down and say, 'Very nice. Big date?'

'Absolutely not,' said Alix. 'Working.'

'Well, they're being very generous with the advertising. Be sure to give them a good review.'

Alix shook her head and said, 'It's not all about money, Janine.'

'Isn't it?' Janine laughed and continued her pursuit.

Alix gave Rob an exasperated look and said, 'She's probably promising them all kinds of favours. She just doesn't get that we need to maintain editorial integrity or whatever we do write has no kind of value ... I mean...'

'It's very early in the evening to be talking about editorial integrity, Alix.'

Alix laughed and took a long sip of her wine. 'Sorry,' she said. 'You're right, and she's probably just winding me up.'

'Probably,' said Rob.

'It took me for ever to get ready, then the car wouldn't start. Thought I was going to be late, got a taxi in the end ... Do you think I'm overdressed?'

'No ... not at all ... you look...' He waved his free hand. 'Suitably dressed.'

'Suitably dressed?'

'Nicely well dressed.'

'Nicely well dressed? You should do our fashion column, you're very perceptive.'

'Not really my field,' said Rob. He looked across the gallery. There was a microphone being set up on a small stage made out of a packing case. He hadn't spotted the artist yet. When he looked back to Alix she was studying one of the paintings on the wall beside him. It consisted entirely of alternating strips of black and white paint. 'So, what do you think?' he asked.

'I love it,' said Alix. 'I'm a big fan.'

'Really? It just looks like a zebra crossing to me.'

'That's because you're not looking at it properly.'

'I think you'll find that I am.'

'No, you're just looking at the surface.'

'The surface is all I can see.'

'You have to look between the lines. Literally, in this case.'

Rob made a show of trying to look between the lines by putting his face right up close.

'The only thing you're going to get out of doing that,' said Alix, 'is an epileptic fit.'

'Ah,' said Rob, 'a painting which should come with a health warning, now I see what you're getting—'

He was disturbed by a loud knocking sound coming from the speakers, and they turned to see that Richard Turner – the unmistakable Richard Turner, because his face had been everywhere this past few weeks – was on the small stage, wearing a white jacket, with nicely combed hair and a pair of what had to be designer glasses perched on the end of his thin, sharp nose, with another man, slightly taller, a little dishevelled-looking, standing beside him and now saying 'Testing, testing' into the mike.

'Aiden Murray,' Alix whispered in Rob's ear. 'He owns the gallery.'

Rob nodded. He wasn't thinking about Aiden Murray, but about Alix's perfume and how close she'd been to his ear. He gave a little shiver, and said to himself, 'Catch yourself on, Rob – no more wine for you.' And in support of that decision he drained the glass he had. Alix touched his arm. He turned. She had another glass for him. He smiled at her and took it and sipped. It would have seemed like bad manners not to.

'Ladies and gentlemen, if I could have your attention please,' Aiden Murray asked in a somewhat reedy voice. 'It gives me very great pleasure to welcome you all here tonight, and in particular to welcome an old friend of the gallery. Please give a big shout-out to the wonderful Mr Richard Turner.'

Aiden stepped to one side as Richard moved up to the microphone to the accompaniment of enthusiastic applause.

Rob gave Sean, who was standing drinking wine, a poke

in the back and said, 'Shouldn't you be…?' and nodded at his camera.

'Oh, shit,' said Sean. He looked around for somewhere to put his glass, but there was nowhere convenient, so he handed it to Rob before swinging his camera round and pressing forward.

'Thank you – it is indeed wonderful to be … home,' Richard Turner began. 'And it's a great comfort to me to see that so many of you have aged as badly as I have.' They laughed. 'Seriously.' They laughed some more. He was polished and professional and charismatic. 'It's a great pleasure to be back in town after so long – and all I can say is – what've you done with the auld place?'

More laughter. They were like putty in his hands until someone shouted out: 'Well, why don't you piss off back to London then, you thieving bastard?!'

A hundred heads swivelled to the back of the room. Most of them were actually looking in Rob's general direction, and probably thought it was him until a smaller man, middle-aged and with long grey hair in a ponytail and holding a glass of red wine, stepped out from behind him and shouted: 'You fuckin' fucker,' his words thick with drink. Rob felt a tug on his jacket and saw that Alix, possibly fearing some kind of violence, had grabbed hold of his sleeve.

'I'll have a glass of what he's drinking,' said Turner.

There was more laughter.

'Ah, fuck off', cut through it.

On the stage, Turner held his hand up to his eyes as if he was shielding them from a bright light as he peered at the drunk. His brow furrowed and then he smiled and gave his heckler the thumbs-up. 'Pat? Is that you? Sure haven't seen you in ages!' He put his hand over the mike, and nodded at the gallery owner

94

beside him, who stepped forward. Turner whispered something to him, nodded, then spoke into the mike again. 'Sure I'll see you later for a wee drink. Anyway, folks, it is wonderful to be home, and to see these paintings, mostly from early in my career, on display – Aiden here was such a great supporter of me way back in the day, but not just of me, of many, many local artists, many of you here tonight. Let's hear it for Aiden!'

Turner started to clap, and everyone joined in. As they did, two security men Rob hadn't previously noticed appeared and went to grab Pat the drunk. Pat saw them coming and tried to escape, but they caught hold of his arm and swung him round, and as they did his glass of wine went flying. Most of it sprayed across Rob and Alix. The security men finally got a proper grip on him and began to drag him away, leaving another flurry of swear words in his wake. Rob started to wipe the wine off his suit, although because it was black you couldn't really see any difference – but then he saw Alix staring aghast at her dress.

'Jesus, Jesus, Jesus. It looks like I've been shot or something.'

'No ... no ...' said Rob, trying to keep his face straight, 'you would hardly notice...'

Before she could respond, Alix's elbow was grasped from behind. She turned to find Richard Turner himself standing there.

'I'm really sorry about that,' he said.

'No ... no worries ... It's fine...' Alix put her hand out and Turner clasped it. 'It's really a pleasure to meet you ... I'm a big fan ... The exhibition ... It's fabulous...'

'I'm so pleased you like it.'

Turner nodded at Rob, and then he paused, and a look of vague recognition crossed his face. But before he could say anything, Aiden appeared beside him and said, 'Sorry,

Richard, but there are so many people who want to meet you. Lady Clandeboye is gagging to say hello…'

Turner raised an eyebrow at Alix, finally let go of her hand, and allowed himself to be led away, though not without another glance at Rob.

Alix immediately said, 'Do you know him?'

'I do believe I do, I just didn't realize it until right now. Our paths crossed briefly, years ago.'

'God, I opened my mouth and all this rubbish came out.'

'Nothing new there.' She made a face, but added a grin to it. A girl came past with another tray of wine glasses and they each grabbed one. 'Still, might be worth finding out what that was all about. The drunk fella.'

'Absolutely. I mean what kind of a nut job does something like that?' She began to examine her dress again, but then looked up suddenly. 'You mean I should do it now?'

'Strike while the iron is hot,' said Rob.

Alix, her usual enthusiasm bolstered by drink, gave him the thumbs-up, handed him her glass, and spun away. She staggered a little on her high heels, before disappearing into the crowd.

Rob looked at the two glasses of wine.

Ah well, he thought.

An hour later and the crowd had thinned to a handful. Sean was happy with his photos and away off to capture the climax of a darts final and Rob was outside with Alix. His apartment was within walking distance but he was waiting with her until her taxi came. Her house was also within walking distance, given a decent pair of shoes, but not in skyscraper heels. Alix had smuggled out a glass of wine and was still sipping.

'Is Turner gone yet?' Rob asked. 'I didn't see him come out. Maybe he went out the back way.'

Alix moved to the gallery window and went to put her head close so she could peer in, but misjudged it and her forehead banged off the glass. She fell back, cursing and laughing at the same time, lost her balance and began to topple over. Rob, only slightly more sober, caught her as she fell, and for a moment she was in his arms, and their faces were really close together, and their lips could easily have met. He held her there for a moment longer than was strictly necessary, and she wasn't objecting at all, and he might well have attempted something if the door beside them hadn't suddenly opened. Richard Turner stepped out. Alix's eyes were blissfully closed, but Rob's were open enough to see Turner giving him the thumbs-up. It did rather bring him to his senses, and caused him to withdraw enough of his support for Alix that she let out a cry and her eyes snapped open; she looked horrified as she flapped her arms and tried to regain her feet. Rob began to apologise for letting go of her, but Alix was suddenly focused on Turner. A taxi was just pulling up and the artist and the gallery owner were now stepping towards it. As Aiden opened the back door and ushered the artist in, Alix came rushing up.

'Mr Turner! Mr Turner ... it's me ... I spoke to you earlier, you said you'd talk to me once all the fuss had died down ... I work for the local paper?'

Aiden moved between Alix and the artist and said, 'And as I told you earlier – call the office and we'll try and set something up...'

'But I need it for tomorrow, if there's any way...'

Richard Turner's grinning face appeared by Aiden's midriff. 'Sorry, love,' he said, 'too late now. But you looked like you were busy anyway.' He gave her a wink and sat back. Aiden closed the door and stepped back as the taxi pulled away.

Alix glared after it.

Aiden shrugged and said, 'Artists, they're very temperamental,' and then moved past her back to his gallery.

Alix swore, and then looked about her, wondering where Rob had gone. She tottered across to the gallery door. There were three or four stragglers still finishing their wine, but no sign of Rob at all. Behind her, another taxi pulled up. She looked back into the gallery, shook her head, and then stomped across to the car and climbed in.

She was dying in the morning. Barely made it to work. Head going to explode. In the office kitchen she wolfed down pills from the medicine box while supercilious Pete asked if she'd had a good night and then said Sean had said that she and Rob seemed to be getting on like a house on fire. She said yeah, right. She got behind her desk and put her earphones in and pretended that she was transcribing an interview when actually she was listening to whale songs and desperately willing her head to improve. Rob kept one eye on her from his office. His memories of the previous night were kind of vague, but he definitely remembered the near-kiss and though he hadn't previously given a single thought to Alix that was anything other than strictly professional, he now found that every thought might be described as unprofessional. She had been drunker than he was; she probably wouldn't remember.

She remembered.

Once he had his own headache pills on board, Rob brought them all into his office for their morning editorial meeting. There was a strong smell of stale alcohol in the air. Alix looked a little red-eyed. The first thing Rob did was tell Michael he was sending him to the local library to do a feature.

'A feature on what?'

'The local library.'

'Yes, but what aspect of the local library? Are they launching a campaign or amnesty or something?'

'No. Just an ordinary feature. A day-in-the-life kind of thing.'

Michael sighed and said, 'It's hardly cutting edge.'

Peter said, 'You have to learn to walk before you can run.'

'At least I can walk, you're never out of the office.'

'Michael, it's not my job to go out and get the stories. And don't be so bloody ch—'

'Okay – all right,' said Rob. 'Michael – it's a challenge, of course it is, but you should embrace that. Make it interesting.'

Michael nodded, resigned. Rob smiled at him. Then he picked up one of Sean's photos from the gallery opening. He had once again shown his talent for being in the right place at the right time – it showed the drunk guy, Pat, in the act of throwing the wine; you could actually see the wine leaving the glass.

'Brilliant pic,' said Rob.

'I know,' said Sean.

'So you'll know his name, then?'

'Name? No, I—'

'Always get a name. It's worthless without a name.'

'But I thought you—'

'Did you check?'

'Uhm, no. But—'

'Just keep it in mind for next time. You can't always rely on someone else having the info you need. Peter . . . ?' Rob handed the photo over. 'You seem to know everyone in this neck of the woods. First name is Pat . . . ?'

'Pat Handley.'

'See? That's brilliant. Now, who's Pat Handley?'

'Don't *know* know him. One of those faces you see around. Bit of a dope-head from what I recall, but that's years ago. I think he teaches at the college. Art.'

'That would make sense. Any idea why he'd want to have a go at Richard Turner?'

'None at all. But I don't blame him.'

'How do you mean?'

'Ah, the likes of Richard Turner – once they get a wee bit of success, they forget where they come from. I'd be surprised if he's been back here once in the last decade.'

'Could you blame him,' said Alix, 'if that's the way people talk about him?'

'He seemed popular enough last night,' said Rob.

'Sure about that?' Peter asked. 'I've been to a hundred of those events over the years. I'm sure they were all smiling and clapping, but under their breath, they were sticking the knife in. I'll bet most of them were artists cursing his good fortune. It's the same with poetry launches, they all hate each other with a passion.'

'You are a very cynical man, Peter.' Peter shrugged, cynically. Rob nodded at Alix. 'Why don't you see if you can have a word with this Pat Handley, then. See what his problem is?'

'Would I not be better seeing Richard Turner and talking to him about being home and the Turner Prize rather than giving publicity to some drunk?'

'Do both.'

'I'll do the drunk, if you want,' said Michael.

'It's fine,' said Alix. 'Besides, you'll be having way too much fun in the library.'

Michael made a face.

Rob finished handing out the assignments and they began to file out of the office. Alix was at the back; she allowed the others to continue on out and then stepped back in. She said, without making proper eye contact, 'You okay? My head's still banging.'

'I was a bit rough earlier, but getting there. It was good fun.'

'Yes it was. You disappeared at the end.'

'No, you disappeared.'

'I what? No, I ... I was talking to Richard Turner, and when I turned round you were gone.'

'Ah – right. No – I saw you talking to him and popped in to use the toilet. I was only gone a minute, but when I came out you were gone.'

'Oh. Right. I thought ... and so I jumped in a taxi.'

'I see. Right. Well. Confusion all round, then.'

'Exactly. But yes, good fun. Too much wine, probably.'

'Ah, it's good to let your hair down.'

'Yes. Well. Exactly.'

'We were both pretty pissed.'

'Yes we were.'

'Anyway.'

'Yes.' She thumbed behind her. 'No rest for the wicked.'

'None at all. Paper to edit.'

They smiled awkwardly at each other. Alix returned to her desk. Rob wiped at the thin veil of sweat on his brow. It was probably the alcohol.

Michael was struggling to find anything remotely interesting. A library was a library. A big building with books. Bangor's Carnegie Library was housed in a large red-brick building that had been extended and modernised fairly recently, and was located on the edge of Ward Park, with a pond full of ducks immediately behind it. Michael would have been happier interviewing the ducks. He was talking to Maeve, a tedious woman, grey-haired, large glasses, quietly spoken, just as a librarian was supposed to look, who was telling him about the amnesty they held every year for people to return overdue books without being fined. He was trying to jazz it up. He said, 'It is just basically theft though, isn't it? If you borrow a book and don't bring it back, you're stealing it.'

'Well, we're trying to encourage people to come back, not brand them as thieves.'

'But if you keep losing books at the rate you say you are, couldn't you go out of business?'

'But it's not a business, that's the point, it's a public service. A certain amount of ... wastage is built into the, uhm, business model.'

'And do you never pursue them through the courts. Make an example?'

'No...'

'It seems like a huge waste of taxpayer's money.'

'Is that the angle you're going to take with this? Because it's not really what we discussed...'

'No, no ... not necessarily...'

Michael had some bold thoughts about doing exactly that. It was, he thought, ridiculous that the library could lose thousands of books a year, do nothing about it, and then complain about underfunding.

'What we're hoping for is a nice article about what we offer – a lot of people still tend to think of us as just somewhere to go and borrow a book. But we're so much more than that – we're a community service, we're an after-schools club,

a computer club, a crèche, we're really at the centre of everything.' She turned and indicated a long desk immediately
behind her. There was half a dozen surly-looking teenagers
gathered around a computer, and an elderly man studying a
large atlas. 'I mean, I think people would be lost without us.
Ask Mr Doyle here...' She nodded at the old man. 'Mr Doyle,
he's here every day. Aren't you, Mr Doyle?'

'What's that?'

She raised her voice. 'You're here every day, aren't you?
This is Michael, he's from the local paper. You're one of our
regulars, aren't you?'

'Yes. I'm a regular.'

'You'd be lost without us, wouldn't you, Mr Doyle?'

'Yes! Lost.'

'And why do you come here every day?' Michael asked.

'Nothing else to do,' said Mr Doyle.

'And what do you most enjoy about the library?'

'Oh – the books.' He nodded at Michael, and then returned
his attention to the atlas.

Hold the front page, Michael thought.

Alix, still being given the runaround by Richard Turner, found
it much easier to track Pat Handley down. He was at a desk
in a classroom on the third floor of the College of Further
Education at Castle Park, pushing papers into a briefcase;
his students were just filing out. There was a classroom assistant, a white-coated woman who looked to be in her fifties,
washing brushes in a sink at the back. Handley looked up as
Alix stepped into the room, nodded and said, 'You can leave it
over there.'

'Leave what?'

'Your folder,' he said, with a slight note of irritation.

'Sorry – I'm not a student. Though I'm gratified you think I'm young enough to be mistaken for one.'

He looked up, shook his head and said, 'We're a college, our students go from sixteen to ninety-one. It's not really a compliment.'

'Oh, well, I ...'

'Yes? I'm just leaving.'

Pat Handley was grey in the face. He looked angry already. Or still. Alix told him quickly who she was and asked if he'd like to comment or explain what happened at Easel the previous evening.

'I was pissed, it was nothing. So, no, not really.'

He lifted his briefcase and began to move towards the door.

'You said he was a thief. What did you mean?'

'What difference does it make? You're not going to say anything against him. So what's the point?'

He disappeared through the door. Alix stood where she was and blew air out of her cheeks. If she'd been the foot-in-the-door kind of journalist she occasionally dreamed of she would have been after him, demanding answers, but she couldn't bring herself to do it.

There was a bit of a laugh from behind. Alix turned to see the classroom assistant grinning at her. 'Don't take it personally,' she said, 'he's just got a bit of a gruff manner. I don't think he's even aware he does it. So what'd the silly sod get up to this time?'

'Ah, nothing much. Heckled Richard Turner. You know, the artist?'

'Of course I do. Ha! Fair play to him.'

'Are you another one thinks he's too big for his boots?'

'Richard? Nah, I don't mind him, I remember him when he was a student here under Pat.'

'Really? I didn't realize he—'

'Oh yes. He was an older student – there's not actually many years between them. But I know Pat's been dying to do something like that for years.'

'Really? How come?'

The classroom assistant stood deliberating for several moments, then gave a little shrug and said, 'Well, I can't see what harm it can do, as long as you don't write anything about me. Scout's honour?'

'Scout's honour.'

She led Alix to the back of the class, where there were several shelves filled with art books. She ran a finger along a dozen disparate spines before she stopped and pulled out a large volume with a garish cover.

'How much do you know about Richard Turner?'

'Well, I've a couple of his books in the house, a print on the wall.'

The classroom assistant began to flick through the book and then stopped on a double-page spread.

'Do you recognize this one?'

There were a lot of intersecting circles with what appeared to be different-coloured sperm trapped within. It was very bright and definitely grabbed your attention.

'I recognize the style,' said Alix, 'but I don't think I've ever...'

'It's one of Pat's actually. This is from the early nineties; back then it was Pat who had the growing reputation and Richard Turner was the eager student. Obviously I haven't been here *that* long, but you hear things from people who have, and the way it was told to me, when Turner's work started to get noticed Pat was quite proud of his successful student, but then people started to say to him that Turner was ripping off his style. Pat didn't really see it at first, but the more people said it the more he began to take it seriously. Eventually he confronted him about it, but Turner just laughed it off. He moved to the bright lights not long after, but I think it's been festering with Pat ever since. So maybe he got it out of his system last night.'

'Well, he got something out. It was quite a mouthful.'

'That's Pat – quick to anger. But actually, really? He's a lovely man at heart. Would do anything for you.'

'Good to know,' said Alix. She nodded down at the book. 'I don't know much about art, but on the face of it, it is quite similar to Turner's early work, wouldn't you say? I mean, do you think he stole Pat's style? Can you even do that?'

'Well, no, that's the point, and Pat should know that, and probably deep down he does. It's art – people nick things all the time, change them around, make them their own. Maybe he's too close to it. Or sometimes I think – well, it's more personal than that. I think because Turner was his student, and then when he got big he just forgot about him. I keep an eye on Turner myself, just interviews and stuff, awards and the like, and I've never once seen him thank his teacher, you know the way big shots usually do? Maybe Pat's more miffed about that. Anyway – work to do.'

Alix thanked her for her help and began to make her way out of the college. What she'd learned about Pat Handley was interesting enough, but at the end of the day it was little more than gossip. Pat was still just a drunk who'd abused a celebrity. Richard Turner being back on home turf was the real story. Now she just had to pin him down for an interview.

★

Michael thought it would be a good idea to try and interview some of the library's customers *before* they entered the building so that they wouldn't feel obliged to give a positive spin. He wanted someone to say something that wasn't worthy, he wanted someone to stir the pot and say, actually the place was badly run, or a waste of space or they should just admit it was a community centre and get rid of those boring books that took up so much space.

But he wasn't having much luck.

He said to one largish woman, returning an armload of books, and who said she was studying for a history A level: 'Would it not be easier to just Google everything?'

She said, 'I don't believe in the Internet.'

'How do you mean?'

'It's full of nothing but pornography and blasphemy.'

'You say that like it's a bad thing.'

He gave her a smile with it, but her face turned to thunder and she pushed on past him without another word.

Michael had more than enough information from the librarian anyway. It would just translate into one of the world's most boring articles. But at least he'd tried for something different. He started back to the office, choosing to walk through the park rather than along the more direct Hamilton Road. The gang of kids he'd seen in the library earlier was just in front of him, and they were right behind old Mr Doyle. A couple of them were mimicking the way he was shuffling along while the rest were laughing. As he watched, Mr Doyle turned suddenly and waved a black briar walking stick at them. Instead of being intimidated the kids moved even closer, daring the old man to strike out at them, which he duly did; they easily evaded his flailing stick while letting out wild whoops and cackles. As Michael drew closer he could hear them taunting and swearing at him. Mr Doyle was coming out with some choice language as well. Michael had hoped that his approach might have caused the gang to ease off on the old man, but they just kept at it.

Michael said, 'Hey, guys, come on...'

One of the kids snapped back, 'What the fuck's it got to do with you?'

The kid, Michael realized, was bigger than he was.

'Just ... leave him alone, okay?'

'Oh fuck off.'

But, actually, they did move on. They were just being teenagers, annoying, bolshie, provocative, but not necessarily evil. Michael knew all about it. He had been one just a few months ago. The gang was veering off to the left while Mr Doyle had already started towards the small bridge over the duck pond.

Michael called after him: 'Mr Doyle? You okay?'

Mr Doyle just kept walking. Michael was going in the same direction as the kids, but not wishing to push his luck, he paused to give them a bit more of a head start. In so doing he saw a book lying on the ground. He picked it up – a graphic novel with a half-naked super-heroine on the front. Michael briefly debated what to do. Then he hurried after the gang. He said, 'Hey...' and the fella who'd told him to fuck off spun back to him. Michael held up the book and said, 'I think you dropped this.'

The boy looked at it and shook his head. 'Not mine, mate.'

'Any of you...?'

They ignored him and started walking again.

Michael thought: *Well, what's the worst that could happen?*

And then he thought: *Well, a severe beating, but nothing ventured ...*

He drew level with them again. 'Look...' he said, 'I'm

doing a piece for the local paper about the library. If I don't use your names, could you tell me why you feel the need to steal books?'

The same guy: 'We didn't fucking take it, okay?'

Michael held the book up and said, 'It didn't just fall from the sky.'

A girl who didn't look more than twelve, jabbed a cigarette in the direction of Mr Doyle. 'Why don't you ask that old bastard? Why do youse always think it's us?'

Michael showed her the cover, and raised an eyebrow. 'Really?'

'Ah fuck off.'

And off they went.

Michael decided to take the other way back to the office.

Gerry was pissed off. Janine was pissed off. Together, they were pissed off. It had taken a while but Bobby McCartney's promise to cut off their advertising was now starting to bite. He was a local councillor, and a leading businessman, but he was also ex-paramilitary with a fearsome reputation and you crossed him at your peril. Gerry was just back from the bank.

Janine said, 'Not good?'

'Not good. I mean, they're a frickin' international bank, but I could swear McCartney's gotten to them as well. They basically said that the only differences between us and bloody falling-apart Greece, is that Greece has better cash-flow. And weather. Nothing at your end?'

Janine shook her head. 'Nope. They're finding all kinds of excuses, but it's him behind it, I can smell him a mile off.'

Gerry was at the office window, looking out at the car park. He was well behind on payments for his Jag. He knew it would be next to go. He said, 'Maybe I should sit down and talk with him, see if we can come to some sort of compromise. Extend the olive branch.'

'He would take that olive branch and stick it up your arse, Gerry. You know what he's like.'

'Well, what else can I do?! He's bleeding us dry, Janine!'

She came up beside him. '*You* shouldn't meet him. But maybe I should.'

'And what difference would that make? It's the paper he hates and what he thinks we did to his boy.'

'Well, let's put it this way – I have some leverage. We've ... broken bread together in the past.'

'Broken ... you mean you've...?'

'Oh yes.'

'But hasn't he been married to what's-her-name for years...?'

Janine raised an eyebrow. 'Well, it didn't stop us, Gerry, did it?'

'Well that was different.'

'How?'

'We were in love.'

'Really, Gerry? I thought we were in lust.'

'Yes, well, that too.' Gerry took a deep breath. 'Would you really do that? I mean, youse can't have finished well if he's doing this to us?'

'No, it was messy. But what harm can it do?'

Gerry gave his chin a theatrical rub. 'Well, if you really think. And you can be a bit of a charmer.'

'Look who's talking. Right, well, I'll give him a call.'

Janine gave him a wink and returned to her office. Gerry turned back to the window. He drummed his fingers on the sill. It was good to have Janine back and fighting for the paper, and that in some way suggested she hadn't been complicit in stealing money from him, that she really had been a victim of a protection racket. But he wasn't particularly comfortable with her going to meet Bobby McCartney, who was the sort of man who might have been behind the protection racket in the first place. However, it wasn't just that. It wasn't because McCartney was fearsome, and a bully, and had a history of violence. It was because they had once ... broken bread. Gerry didn't like the thought of that at all. He couldn't help picturing them together. He was jealous, of course, even if he wouldn't quite admit it to himself.

There were only a few hotels in the area. Alix phoned the Culloden first, because it was five-star, and the most expensive, but they denied any knowledge. She tried the Marine Court next, but same again. She tried the Salty Dog, which maybe wasn't quite a hotel, more of a pub-restaurant with some rooms above the bar. She asked if Richard Turner was staying there by any chance and the guy at the other end said no he wasn't, but he was currently having a pint at the bar. It was just about a small enough town for that kind of coincidence to happen. Alix said, 'Don't let him leave.'

The guy said, 'How am I supposed to ... ?'

She shot back with, 'I'll be there in five. Buy him one on me.'

She was there in less than five, it being just a very fast walk away from the office, even in heels. As she hurried along the side of the premises she could see him through the window, sitting on a stool at the bar, just finishing a Guinness. She was flushed with adrenaline both from the fast walk and the prospect of cornering Richard Turner, which resulted in her propelling herself through the revolving doors with just a little too much enthusiasm. She practically flew out of them; as she stepped onto the homely rug on the other side, her left heel dug into the shag of it and stuck, just for a moment, but enough to throw her off balance and cause her to stagger drunkenly forward towards the renowned artist. She stopped, she straightened and prepared to introduce herself again, but Turner cut her off with a big smile and a 'Jesus, you're always throwing yourself around the place'.

'Sorry, I...' She was all out of breath. 'I just wanted to catch you before ... I'm...'

'I know who you are, love.' Turner, in designer tweed and brown brogues, set his now-empty glass down and rubbed the back of his hand across his lips. 'And thanks for the pint, but I really have to be...'

'I was talking to your old teacher. Pat Handley.'

'Oh, for cryin', what's that old soak been saying now?'

He hadn't actually said anything. But Alix just gave a little shrug and said, 'I thought maybe you'd want to talk about it.'

'Not particularly, no.'

'He thinks you ripped off his work, back in the early days.'

'Does he now?'

'He did call you a thief the other night.'

Turner stood nodding at her. He bit on his lower lip. Eventually he said, 'Look, love, I don't really do interviews – kind of ruins the mystique, don't you know?'

'It would only take five...'

'No. But tell you what. Pat is actually an old friend and I'm just a bit rubbish about keeping in touch. It's been years, actually. So I don't even know where he lives. If you would be good enough to find that out for me, then maybe we can have a wee chat about me being back in town, the exhibition, that kind of thing. You don't want to get into all that theft business, that's just the drink talking, Pat knows fine well his work hardly influenced me at all. He was a fine teacher, but that's about it. My style, that comes from right in here.' Turner tapped his heart. And then his head. 'And in here. So do we have a deal?'

Bobby McCartney was already seated at a window table of the Hong Kong Palace as Janine approached. She waved at him and he raised his glass of wine in response. He stood as she was shown to the table and they kissed somewhat awkwardly, one on each cheek.

'Janine darling,' he said, 'it's so good to see you. Although I should warn you – the only thing I'm buying today is lunch.'

'Bobby – relax. I don't even want to talk business. How's Marie?'

McCartney looked at her over the top of his menu.

'Marie is fine, thank you.'

They exchanged small talk and gossip about mutual business acquaintances. They ordered food and before long a second bottle of wine. The food arrived and they began to eat, but very shortly Bobby put down his knife and fork.

'Okay, look Janine, I can't enjoy this until I know what you have up your sleeve.'

'Can't a girl invite an old friend to lunch without an ulterior motive?'

'No. Not you.'

Janine smiled. She put her own cutlery down and dabbed at her lips with a napkin. 'Okay, Bobby,' she said, 'I was going to wait for dessert, but have it your way. You've put the word out against us, just like you said you would. And I don't mind admitting that it's killing us.'

Bobby raised his hands in a helpless gesture. 'Janine – you put a photo of my son on the front page.

'He was caught in an armed robbery. We're a newspaper, Bobby. A community newspaper. Look – you love it here, don't you? This town. It's your ... what would you say ... power base?'

'If you insist.'

'And that's fine. Our power base is our readers. They have to be able to trust us. They have to know that we treat everyone equally. If they think we bury stuff just because it isn't convenient or it might embarrass someone, then we're sunk. If I do something wrong, it goes in the paper. If Gerry, if any of our reporters ... it all goes in, okay? We can't treat your boy any different. It was armed robbery. We can't ignore that. If you're worried about your own reputation – well, it was your boy that damaged it, not us. Not us.'

'Nice speech,' said Bobby, 'did you get someone to write it for you?'

'No, I made it up on the fly.'

'Well, my answer is this – no fucking way. Youse have gone out of your way to embarrass me. I know what my boy did was wrong, but at the end of the day he stole a few quid from a shop and yes he should be punished for it. That's what the courts are for. And I don't have a problem with you reporting it. But you go above and beyond. Big photo on the front page for everyone to see. There were other stories inside, other court cases, where people did things that were twice as bad as anything my Robbie did but you had to stick it on the front. Why?'

'Bobby – I'm not the editor, I don't make those decisions, but I'm expected to stand by them.'

'And so you are.'

'Yes, I am. And I'll tell you why. Because what goes on the front of the paper is always the biggest news story of the week. It can be anything, but in this particular case our photographer captured an armed robbery taking place. That doesn't happen every day, or month or year. Those other cases you're talking about, we only know about them because they've turned up in court. We weren't there. What Robbie did may not have been the biggest case of the week, but it was the most dramatic, and it was captured for all to see. We could not have not used it, Bobby. We're in the business of selling newspapers.'

'Not for long,' he said. He raised his glass to her, and took a sip, with what she would later describe to Gerry as a triumphantly smug look on his face.

Janine remained frustratingly unruffled. She slowly reached down and lifted her handbag. For a moment he thought she was going to walk out on him, but instead she took out a plain A4 manila envelope and passed it across to him. He saw then that it was not in fact plain, but that there was a date written in very small and neat handwriting on the front: *14 September 2006*. His eyes flitted up to Janine; now she was looking rather smug, and he didn't like it.

'Are you not going to open it?'

'What is it?' Bobby asked as he turned the envelope over in his hands.

'What do you think it is?'

His eyes narrowed suspiciously. 'That date. That's round-about when we were...'

'Yes, we were. And frequently, as I recall.'

'And this is...?'

'You're the one that was keen on the photographs. I don't think they flatter either of us.'

His throat had gone dry. 'You promised me you'd destroyed those.'

'Mmmmm,' said Janine.

His smug look had become a scowl. 'You sleeked bitch,' he murmured.

'Now Bobby, you weren't saying that at the time.'

'Well, that was before I got to know you.'

Janine raised an eyebrow. 'Is that really what you want to be saying, right now?'

Bobby sighed. He pushed the envelope back across the table to her, unopened, and rubbed at his brow.

'This is fucking blackmail,' he said.

'Yes,' said Janine.

He wagged a warning finger at her across the table. 'Have you *any* idea what I could have done to you? One call and you're—'

'But you're not going to make that call, are you, Bobby?'

He took a deep breath. His fingers drummed on the table. Then he spat out: 'No, dammit, Janine, I'm not.'

'I understand your pain, Bobby, but it's your son you should be sorting out, not us. So, these are my terms.'

'Your *terms*?!'

'Absolutely. I want every single advertiser you've scared away back by tomorrow. And I want ten more.'

'Ten more *what*?'

'Advertisers, Bobby. I want you to deliver to me ten full pages worth of advertising from new customers spread over the next couple of months.'

'Janine, Jesus Christ … that's, that's, that's…'

'Fair. And I want them paid for in cash.'

'Cash! Nobody pays in—'

Janine drummed her perfectly manicured nails on the

envelope. 'Cash. And we'll each take 10 per cent off the top for all the effort we've gone to. How does that suit?'

'That's... Janine... you mean you're ripping off your own—'

'Deal, Bobby?'

'It's fucking ... mental ...'

'It's business. Mental is what your wife will be when she sees you kissing my nipples on Facebook.'

Bobby's mouth dropped open. His eyes darted around the restaurant before settling back on his former lover. All he could think to say was, 'They don't allow nipples on Facebook.'

'Well, they haven't dealt with me yet. Now – deal or no deal?'

His head felt like it was going to explode, so about all he could manage was a short nod. But it was enough for Janine. She picked up the envelope and stood up. She gave him her smile, which he had always loved. 'Thanks for lunch, Bobby.'

As she turned to go he said, quickly, 'Janine?'

She stopped and looked down at him. He was in his fifties, but right there and then he felt like a fourteen-year-old schoolboy.

'Janine, I loved our time together. I don't suppose...?'

She laughed suddenly. 'Bobby, that shit has sailed.'

'Shit? You mean...'

'I know exactly what I mean.'

And with that she was away, striding purposefully across the restaurant, out the door and past the window, not glancing in at him once. Bobby watched her every inch of the way until she disappeared round the corner. Then he pushed his unfinished plate away and swore. Loudly.

Back at her car, her ridiculous smart car, Janine paused before getting in. She looked around, spotted a wheelie bin parked outside someone's house ready for collection and crossed to it. She took the envelope out of her bag, lifted the lid and dropped it in. If Bobby had followed her, if he'd retrieved the envelope and let out a whoop of triumph, it would quickly have died as soon as he pulled the photographs out. He would have found four pictures, all of them slightly out of focus, and all of them of a badger being petted by an old woman in a garden.

Negotiations of a different sort had also concluded on the other side of town. Alix was to find out Pat Handley's address and then she would drive Richard Turner there via a circuitous route that would allow them time to chat about the town he knew growing up. She would be part chauffeur, part interrogator.

The college wouldn't give out Pat Handley's address, and he was ex-directory, but there was a source of local knowledge even greater than a directory, or indeed, the Internet, and that was office-bound Pete. She had to go back and pick the car up anyway, so she left Turner with another pint and clip-clopped up the road again. Janine and Gerry were high-fiving each other in Gerry's office, Rob appeared to be reading a children's book in his, while Michael was at his desk, deeply immersed in a salacious-looking graphic novel. Pete was up to his oxters in his sub-editing and growled and groaned about being disturbed, but eventually he opened a drawer and took out a Filofax from a previous century and flicked through it until he found Pat Handley's home address. He quickly jotted it down on a sheet of A4, handed it to Alix and said, 'No charge.'

She gave him an odd look and said, 'Why would there be a charge?'

'It's from a song.'

'What song?'

'"*No Charge*". By Melba Montgomery. A big hit in the seventies. It's about...'

'Gotta fly,' said Alix, grabbing her keys and heading for the door.

Richard Turner was waiting outside the bar when she drove up. As he got in she apologized for taking so long and said he should have waited inside.

'Three pints before lunch? You'll be turning me into an alcoholic. Or back into one.' She glanced across and he said quickly, 'Oh yes.'

'Can I write that?'

'You can and will write whatever you want. But it's not a state secret. And it adds a little spice to an otherwise very boring life. I get up and I paint pictures, there's not much more than that to it.'

Alix laughed. She said, 'Sure you've been in and out of the tabloids for years.'

Turner laughed dismissively. 'Oh, it's all very managed. You'll notice, all the stories appear just about the time I'm having a big exhibition or there's an auction. It's all about building brand recognition.'

'That's, uhm, very mercenary, if you don't mind me saying.'

'No, I don't. You say mercenary, I say necessary. 'Tis the way of the world, unfortunately.'

He directed her out of the centre of town, up the High Donaghadee Road, and into Chippendale, and then Wellington Park, where he'd spent his first eleven years. He talked about how idyllic it was. He talked about the fields that used to surround the area, fields that had long since given way to suburban sprawl. He talked about staging mock Olympic Games in the summer, of marching with the bands, of building a bonfire on the Eleventh Night, of walking his pet Jack Russell for miles and Hallowe'en rhyming from the beginning of September. He passed a Mace shop on the corner of Windmill Road and let out a little cry of recognition. 'That used to be Rankin's shop. These two spinster sisters used to own it. Real old-fashioned grocery shop. Gosh, I can just picture them now.'

He actually looks a bit misty-eyed, Alix thought, though she realized that it might equally have been the three pints of Guinness.

As they headed back out along the High Donaghadee Road he said, 'So, your boyfriend? He looked kind of familiar.'

'Boy ... no ... not my boyfriend at all! He's my boss!'

'Really? Well you certainly looked ...'

'Not a bit of it. We were just messing. Too much wine, maybe.'

'Aye, well, been there. What do you call him?'

'Rob. Rob Cullen.'

'Rob Cullen! *That's* his name. I knew I recognized him!'

'Really? He sort of hinted he might have met you before, but didn't think you'd remember.'

'Aye, well it was a long time ago.'

'So how do youse know each other?'

'It's no great mystery. We both left this dump years ago, met on the Stranraer ferry. He ended up driving us down to London ... He should have said hello properly last night.'

'Maybe he was shy. You're the big man in the big picture these days. Literally.'

'Ah, don't know about that.'

'Of course you are. Turner Prize and all that.'

'I haven't won it yet, you know.'

'*Yet*,' said Alice.

'Well, it is inevitable,' he said, and gave her a wink.

They turned into Ashley Drive. Alix slowed down as she checked out the house numbers. 'It's number twelve, should be just...'

'Sure – pull in here. We can finish our chat before I go in.'

'Here? But...'

'Here's fine. I can dander the rest of the way myself.'

Alix put the car half-way up on the footpath and turned the engine off. She turned in her seat, picking up the phone she was using to record the interview to check it was still running, and then holding it in her hand as he talked on about his childhood memories, of going to Ballyholme Primary School, of his first art teacher Mrs Pow...

'Pow?'

'Pow. The most exotic name ever. Like something out of a Marvel comic. But that was her name. No idea of the provenance ... but she was great. Really inspirational.'

'As inspirational as Pat Handley?'

'Oh, easily.'

His eyes flitted suddenly to Number Twelve. It was a semi-detached house, with a somewhat overgrown hedge and a small red car in the drive. The front door was just closing and Pat was walking up the drive. Richard Turner immediately slithered down in his seat until half of his body was crushed into the foot-rest.

Alix stared at him with a mixture of surprise and disbelief. 'What're you—?'

'Get down!'

'Why on earth...?'

'Now!'

But Alix was restrained by her seat belt and the steering wheel, so the best she could do was to quickly pull down the sun visor and sit up a little straighter so that her face was mostly blocked from the view of the art teacher who'd now started walking in their direction.

She whispered, 'I thought you wanted to talk to—'

'Shhhhh!'

Pat's footsteps sounded by the passenger window, his shadow briefly crossed them, and then he was away.

Richard Turner slowly eased himself back up onto the seat. Alix pushed the visor back up – and then jumped as her window was suddenly knocked. She turned to see Sean smiling in at her, his camera dangling from his neck.

'Scare ya, did I?' he asked through the glass.

The window came down. 'Don't bloody do that!'

'Chill,' said Sean. He crouched down a little further so he could see Turner, then gave him the thumbs-up. 'Now, where do you want to take this pic?'

Turner got out of the car and stood for a moment watching Pat Handley as he reached the end of the road and then disappeared around the corner. Then he looked across the top of the car at Sean and said, 'I haven't time for a photo.'

'But...' Sean began.

Alix jumped out. 'The idea was to get one of you and Pat. You said that would be fine.'

'Well, I've changed my mind.'

'But—'

'Listen, love, we never agreed that, I said I'd have a chat if you found out where Pat lived and took me there. And here we are. So – listen, thanks for everything, and I can make my own way back.'

He gave Alix his latest wink, and then shut the car door and began to walk towards Number Twelve.

'But...!'

He ignored her and turned into the drive.

Sean was at her shoulder. 'I thought...'

'So did I.'

There was nothing she could do except give an exasperated sigh and get back into the car. Once inside, she drummed her fingers on the steering wheel, cursed under her breath, and then came to a quick decision. She looked back out of the window and said to Sean, 'You wait here. If I'm not back in five minutes, go on back to the office.'

She started the engine.

'I don't understand ... What're you doing?' Sean asked.

'I'm stirring things up,' said Alix.

Michael was on the phone to the librarian, desperately trying to get something else out of her, something even remotely newsworthy or mildly controversial or even vaguely interesting, because he'd written his article and it really was as dull as dishwater. He sensed she had plenty to say about the state of the library service, but knew that as a civil servant she wasn't free to speak out. As he chatted away, trying to soften her up but really getting nowhere, he randomly mentioned what had happened with old Mr Doyle and the librarian said that it was shocking, teenagers bullying an old man like that, before adding, purely as an afterthought, 'and him a war hero'. And that made Michael's ears prick up. She didn't know much more beyond the fact that she'd seen him parading on Poppy Day with a chest full of medals. He asked for his address. The librarian said she shouldn't really give it to him, what with the data-protection laws, but she did anyway – it was all in a good cause. Michael had explained to her his intention to write about what life was like for a war hero who loved nothing more than whiling away his days in his local library. But what he was actually after was how a war hero felt about being bullied – if he could encourage the old man into a bit of a rant about the behaviour of teenagers he was sure he could get a decent front-page story out of it, something that was generally lacking on his CV. Alix always seemed to get those stories. She was older, more experienced, but that didn't necessarily mean that she was a better writer or a more skilful journalist – she'd just gotten the breaks. Michael was waiting for his opportunity to shine, but it felt like it had been a long time coming. To be fair, he was just frustrated – old Billy Maxwell, the editor who'd hired him only shortly before his untimely death, had favoured Alix with the better stories, and now Rob Cullen seemed to be doing the same. Michael was convinced it wasn't only because she was senior to him; it was because she was a good-looking blonde.

Ward Park led onto Castle Park, and on the other side of Castle Park there was Church Street. Mr Doyle lived there in a small terraced house. Michael rang the doorbell and a dog barked from inside. He rang it again, and when there was still no sign of the old man he tried to peer through the window, but the venetian blinds were shut. As he returned to the door, a woman in a blue apron peered out from the next house and said, 'If you're looking for Joe he's probably down the library, he lives in that place.'

'Actually, I've just spoken to the librarian, he's not there.'

'Was it something you wanted to leave for him? I can pop it in later.'

'No, I … It doesn't really matter. I'll maybe call back.'

He was starting to turn away, but then the woman was out of her house and looking rather quizzically at her neighbour's door. 'You can hear barking?' Michael said he could. She said, 'He usually keeps Patch out in the back yard if he's not in. I wonder...' She rubbed a finger along her bottom lip. 'You know – he hasn't been that well of late. Blood pressure. Do you know – he leaves me a key, so I can feed Patch if he's not going to be back till late. Maybe if he's not answering the door and Patch is in the house, I should just check he's okay?'

The neighbour scurried back into her house and re-emerged half a minute later with key in hand. She quickly slotted it into the lock and opened the door. She called Mr Doyle's name, asked if everything was okay. Patch jumped around her ankles. She called again. She was in a small hall, with the door to the living room open beside her on the right and stairs directly ahead. Every step had a column of books sitting on it.

The neighbour called up the stairs. This time there was a sound – something between a weak groan and a cry. The woman, no spring chicken herself, immediately went thundering up the carpeted steps. Michael followed behind. She called out again and followed the sounds to a back bedroom. As Michael stepped onto a landing he could see the neighbour already crouching down beside Mr Doyle, who was lying on his back on the floor. She looked back at Michael, panic in her eyes and cried out to him to call an ambulance. Michael already had his phone out and was pressing the numbers. He stood just outside the door looking down at the old man – terribly pale and labouring for breath. The neighbour said, 'Do you know how to do mouth-to-mouth?' Michael shook his head. The woman said, 'I've only ever seen it on *Casualty*.' And then she took her top set of teeth out, slipped them into her apron pocket, and set to work.

★

125

Pat Handley was a fast walker. He was already almost up to Windmill Road when she finally spotted him, walking with his head down and with short but determined strides. She pulled in a little way in front of him and got out. He didn't notice her until she said his name and his head came up and his face registered first surprise and then the first flickering of anger.

'Are you following me?' he spat out as he continued towards her at the same pace. 'I told you I wasn't bloody interested in—'

'I've been talking to Richard Turner about you.'

'Do you think I care?'

If Alix hadn't stepped to one side she had no doubt that he would have barged straight into her. When she spoke again, she was already addressing his back.

'Mr Handley – I think he really wants to talk to you, but he's a bit nervous about how you might react. After last night.' He kept going. 'I know you think he copied your work.'

That finally stopped him. He shook his head, and then turned. 'Is that right? Really? You know what I think, do you?'

'No, I don't … but I think he wants to make amends. It would be a great story if we could get you two back together, get some nice photos too. And maybe it will get you some belated recognition for what you—'

'Do you think I need your approval? Or anyone's fucking approval?!'

'Please, Mr Handley, at least talk to him. He's only around the corner.'

'Whadyya mean, round the corner?!' He took a step towards her.

'He's come to see you.' She thumbed back towards the house. 'I just left him there. You came out of the house and

I think he got cold feet. But he's still there. I think maybe he was just going to leave you a wee note or—'

'Right, fuck!' Pat exploded. 'He's there now? The fucking weasel! Right, let's have this out right now! That your car?'

'Yes, but...'

'But nothing! Take me back this minute you can have all the fucking photographs you want!'

Alix had no idea what she had just engineered, but it was clearly going to be explosive. In the minute's run back to Pat's house he didn't say another word, but the closer they got the deeper shade of puce his face turned and the harder his foot drummed on the floor.

'The bugger!'

As they drew up, Pat had spotted Turner standing in his driveway talking to a slim middle-aged woman with short hair, wearing a denim skirt with dark leggings and a black cardigan. Alix presumed this was Pat's wife. She pulled the car up onto the kerb, but had barely stopped before Pat had his door open and was away. Turner had his back to him and was so engrossed in the conversation that he hadn't heard either the car arriving or the thundering footsteps of an art teacher in full charge. His wife, similarly engrossed, only noticed at the last moment. She let a shout out of 'Pat, no!' but it was too late. Pat barrelled into Turner's back and his forward thrust propelled them both across the narrow lawn beside them and over a small hedge into the garden next door. The wife screamed at them to stop. By the time Alix, swiftly joined by Sean and his camera, reached the hedge and looked over, Pat Handley and Richard Turner were wrestling for supremacy in a bed of pansies. Turner was tall and wiry with an expensive-looking haircut; Pat was squat and overweight with a short crop; neither was an athlete. They were puffing and blowing and launching blows that did not hit their target. Alix didn't know quite what to do, other than to nudge Sean to start taking photos rather than enjoy the spectacle. He gave her a stupid grin and began snapping away.

'Please do something!' the wife implored.

Sean shot off some more pics, before finally handing the camera to Alix and jumping over the hedge into the garden. He stood over the wrestling match for a moment, trying to decide on the best course of action. Then he grabbed Pat's foot and began to drag him off Turner and out of the flower bed. Pat, however, had a firm hold of Turner's shirt and wasn't for letting go. Sean took a tighter grasp, then gave him a good yank, which loosened his grip, and then another short sharp one that finally released the artist, who quickly flopped back down into the blue-and-yellow pansies. Sean dragged Pat further across the lawn before letting go of his leg. Pat immediately went to get up to renew hostilities, but Sean pushed him back down and wagged a warning fist at him. 'Quit it, okay?' Pat, gasping from the unfamiliar exertion, made no further move. Sean was barely out of his teens and not particularly large, but he looked fit and had the energy of youth. Pat sat where he was, fuming and glaring across at his enemy. Turner sat up and said, 'What the fuck was that about?' but Pat only growled in response. There was blood coming from Turner's nose and the knees of his expensive-looking suit trousers were muddy. His hair was all over the place. He slowly dragged himself back to his feet, puffing and blowing as much as Pat was. Pat also regained his feet, and they stood glaring at each other. Sean stood between them, shaking his head. 'Would youse both wise up?' he said.

The wife, rather than step over the hedge, was now coming down the neighbour's drive. She stopped in front of her husband. 'Pat,' she said, 'for goodness sake, he just came round to mend some bridges with you, and with me.' She turned to Turner. 'Richard, please – will you tell him once and for all ... nothing happened between us.'

Turner looked incredulous. 'Is that what this is about? Jesus Christ, Pat – of course it didn't, that's just ridiculous.'

But Pat wasn't buying it. He threw up his arms in disgust and yelled: 'Don't give me that, you fucking sleeked bastard! Youse two were shacked up in Scotland for three days – and nights!'

Alix was transfixed. So it wasn't about the paintings. It was ... a love triangle! She suddenly felt like she was watching a soap opera and not particularly enjoying it – while still being completely incapable of switching the channel.

Turner put a hand to his chest. 'Pat – nothing happened. Cathy – tell him.'

'Oh I've told him, over and over...'

'Listen to me Pat,' said Turner, 'please. She was crying the whole time. You were my best friend, I wouldn't do something like that. Youse had a row, she ran off, it happens. I just looked after her, mate, nothing happened!'

'Please, love,' said Cathy. She moved closer to her husband. She took his face in her hands. 'This has festered for thirty years. Richard was very kind to me, but I was never interested in him, it was always you, my love.'

She kissed him on the lips. She put her arms around him. He wrapped his arms around her, his muddy hands staining her shoulders. He closed his eyes. There were tears on his cheeks.

Sean slowly raised his camera.

It only took ten minutes for the ambulance to arrive. Mr Doyle appeared to be breathing more normally and there was a certain amount of colour back in his cheeks. His neighbour had her teeth back in. Michael asked if there was anything he could do, but there wasn't, and he felt uncomfortable hanging around in the bedroom looking down at the sick old man, so he said he would go downstairs and let the dog out the back.

The Jack Russell scampered ahead of him as he entered the lounge; but in pushing the door open he knocked over another teetering pile of books. As he moved into the room he realized that it was but one of many such teetering piles. There were books everywhere, covering almost every space, jammed onto shelves, on top of a sideboard, and spread across the entire floor, like a Manhattan cityscape of skyscrapers, but after an earthquake, with only the sturdiest surviving intact.

Mr Doyle – he loved his books. And he had eclectic tastes. Just at his feet there was a history of warfare in the seventeenth century, a Jamie Oliver cookbook and a hardback compendium of Agatha Christie short stories. As he began to thread his way towards the kitchen, his foot slipped on a glossy cover and he almost went over; but he righted himself, and then bent to pick up the offending tome. He saw that it was in fact a graphic novel belonging to the same series as the one dropped outside the library. When he opened the cover he saw the Carnegie logo and borrowing history stamped inside. It had last been taken out more than three years before. Michael set it down and lifted another book, a Swedish crime thriller, and opened it. It also had a library stamp inside. He checked another, and another, and then moved across the room, randomly picking up books and looking inside. They were indeed *all* library books. And there were probably five hundred of them in this room alone. When he entered the kitchen, it was hardly any different, books everywhere, with just a small corner left for the bowl of food that Patch was happily tucking into.

'He's a sneaky old bastard,' Michael told Rob as soon as he was back in the office, 'and a one-man bloody crime wave.'

'So, are they going to press charges?'

'Who knows? But probably not. Early days yet. It's, like, if you take one sachet of tomato sauce from McDonald's it's allowed – if you take two hundred it's theft, but what's the difference?'

Rob theatrically stroked his cheek. 'A philosophical question indeed,' he said, just as Alix appeared in the doorway. He beckoned her in, then told Michael to finish writing his story.

'With or without the phantom book thief?'

'With – but minus his name and any other identifying details. He is a war hero, after all, and no doubt there'll be some mitigating circumstances. If it gets to court, then we can run it properly. Anyway, it's a good way into it, Michael – well done. I honestly didn't think there was any hope of making it interesting.'

As he exited, Michael was glowing.

Alix sat down opposite Rob and gave him an expectant look. He kept her waiting. Her story on Richard Turner's triumphant homecoming was up on his screen. He clasped his hands in front of his face, and nodded at his computer.

'Mmmmm,' he said.

'*Mmmmm?*'

'You know something, Alix – this is a very smart piece, funny, vaguely ridiculous, and really quite moving. And they really didn't shake hands in the end?'

'Nope. But they went inside for a cup of tea, and nobody got thrown out through a window, so maybe it worked out okay. They didn't come out and make a grand statement either. It wasn't about the painting, just a misunderstanding about a girl.'

Rob smiled. 'Yes indeed. In fact, I should probably have guessed.'

'Oh – of course! He told me he recognized you. You gave them a lift to London, didn't you? All those years ago. So you know about it first-hand.'

'Absolutely.'

'God love her. There's been a few guys over the years I wanted to jump on a ferry to get away from, but she had the balls to do it. She must have been in some state. I suppose that's love for you.'

Rob laughed. 'Oh she was certainly in a state. In fact, as I recall, they were going at it like rabbits in the back seat.'

'They...? You mean Turner and—'

'Oh yes, all over each other for the best part of three hundred miles. I didn't know where to look.'

'But she said...'

'Of course she did.'

'Gosh.' Alix put her hand to her mouth. 'That's ... that's mad. So maybe ... he was just there to see the wife? Do you think I should re-write it to reflect—?'

'No, I don't, Alix,' said Rob. He paused then, and made a bit of a face. 'In fact, and I'm very sorry to tell you this, none of it is really any of our business.'

'But...'

'Which is why...' and he nodded at the screen, 'the half of this will have to go.'

'But you said it was smart and—'

'And it is, but we can't print it. It's private, it's personal, and legally a bit dubious.'

'But...'

'I know. Great piece, like I say, but we just can't. Sorry.'

Alix almost visibly deflated. She wasn't entirely convinced either. If she'd been working for a proper tabloid, she was pretty sure they would have splashed it all over the front page. Sean had some spectacular photos of the wrestling match in the flower beds, but now it looked as if Rob wasn't going to use those either. And the fact was that she wasn't working for a tabloid, her job wasn't to unmask the sordid past of a famous artist, or even to track down Nazis, it was to write a flattering profile of a local boy made good. She sighed. One day, maybe not too far in the future, she would be out of her small-minded, unexciting goldfish bowl of a provincial weekly. But until then...

'Do you want me to do it?' Rob asked. 'Or do you want to have another crack?'

'I'll do it.'

She stood up. Before she got to the door Rob said her name. When she turned, he was looking rather sheepishly at her.

'I just wanted to say – again, I think – I did enjoy the other night. At the gallery.'

'Yes, so did I.'

'Just thought I'd be clear...' He looked at his screen. He sucked on his bottom lip.

'Well, that's good,' said Alix. She thumbed behind her. 'Well, ahm, better get cracking on this.' But she didn't turn back. Instead she gave a little laugh. 'What is it they say – is it, never meet your heroes? Richard Turner, well, he turned out to be a bit of a prick. But – I think you knew that all along, didn't you?'

'Kind of,' said Rob, 'and maybe I'm one, too.'

'How do you mean?'

133

She didn't remember much about the wine-fuelled events in and around the gallery, but she definitely remembered the almost-kiss, her surprise that they'd come so close, and her vague sense of disappointment that they hadn't followed through. She thought he was talking about that, but no.

'Richard Turner and Pat's wife – I drove the pair of them those three hundred miles on the understanding we'd share the petrol. But when we finally got there, he confessed he'd no money left, but he had this portfolio of his work, so he pulled one of his paintings out and gave it to me instead. In fact I think it was an early version of that one we saw in the gallery.'

'Really? Seriously? But that must be worth—'

'—a small fortune? Yes, indeed.' Rob sat back in his chair and put his feet up on the desk, he clasped his hands behind his head and momentarily basked in the acknowledgement of his riches. But then he smiled at her and said, 'So it's a great pity that I threw it right back at him.'

'You did not!'

'Did too,' said Rob. 'As the saying goes, I don't know much about art, but I know what I like. And Richard Turner and his zebra crossing looked like a lot of crap to me then and still does now.'

'But what a heartbreaker,' said Alix.

'No regrets,' said Rob, 'sure, what would I do with all that money?'

'Yeah right,' said Alix. 'Anyway – if it's any consolation, he is a prick and you're not. But do be wary of prickish tendencies.'

She gave him a coy little wink and turned out of his office.

As he watched her go he thought that that was absolutely no way to talk to your boss. But he couldn't stop the smile from spreading across his face.

CHAPTER 4
HONG KONG PHOOEY

It is true to say that Rob did not settle easily into small-ish-town life. He was close to the sea, and there were parks with ducks near by and the High Street and shopping centres and familiar fast-food outlets and a cinema within a short drive, so everything was very convenient, but it wasn't what he was used to. If it wasn't exactly foreign, then neither was it familiar, or reassuring or inspiring. He was acclimatized to the variety and anonymity of metropolitan life. Though he was from this place, this province, he had lived longer in England; though all of those years in London and Manchester had hardly softened his accent, it had smoothed out his prejudices and his history and his culture. And even if he had lived largely behind a desk, or in the bosom of a malfunctioning family, he missed the possibilities of a big city, the opportunities, even if they were rarely grasped. He missed the galleries, the museums, the theatres and the gigs, even if he only occasionally partook. Here he rented a nice, modern apartment, with a view of a main road. His neighbours seemed pleasant and he woke to the sound of distant seagulls, not the incessant roar of traffic. But he was alone. The only one who actually sensed this was Janine at work; she saw him mooning over a picture of his kids and suggested he got a cat. He did not want a cat. This experience was temporary, cats were for life.

He had only been at the paper for a few weeks, and it ate up most of his waking hours; but there were always other hours to be filled. Instead of doing something, he mostly did nothing. He spent too long agonizing over groceries in the large super-market on the edge of town. Johnny Cash shot a man in Reno, just to watch him die; Rob Cullen bought curly kale in Tesco's, just to watch it wither. He could cook, but he had no desire to cook for one. By the end of his fourth week he was on first-name terms with the staff of the Hong Kong Palace.

Rob avoided the HKP at weekends because it was busy and he didn't want to look like a sad loner. During the week, when it was quieter, he didn't so much mind looking like one. He enjoyed a bit of banter with Anna, his regular waitress. Her English was pretty good and they would chat when things were quiet. When she discovered what he did for a living she convinced him to run a piece on the netball team she played for at the local college; they were looking for sponsorship to help them travel to away matches. Rob set up a photo and Sean took one that was a bit cheesecakey but attracted quite a lot of attention in a quiet news week; the sponsorship came through and Rob could have eaten for free the next time he was in, but he paid his way.

This night Anna was all smiles as she brought him his regular bottle of Tsingtao beer. He said, 'I'm guessing you won today?'

'We did! We're through to the finals in Scotland! First time!'

'Excellent,' said Rob. 'That's brilliant.'

He picked up his menu and began to study it.

'I do not know why you are reading the menu,' said Anna. 'Three nights a week, you have the same thing.'

Was it really three nights a week?

'Well, I might fancy a change. Let me see. Yes, indeed. I'll have the chicken fried rice with curry sauce.' Anna shook her head and began to turn away. 'Aren't you going to write it down?' he called after her.

'I already did. Ten minutes ago when you came in.'

He had a paperback book with him, he had his phone to browse the Internet, and he had a notebook and pen in case he had any ideas for the paper. He never really switched off. His curry arrived and he ate it slowly and methodically, all the while thinking about some kind of a fitness plan. If he ate like this three times a week for much longer his heart would probably explode. There were nine other diners: one party of six, one table of three. It was all very quiet. When he was done with his main course, he lingered over his second beer. A different waiter, a young man making a valiant attempt to grow a moustache, picked up his empty plate; Rob nodded his thanks and returned his attention to his book; but then he became aware that the waiter hadn't left; when he glanced up he saw that the young man in the white shirt and dicky bow was staring, transfixed, out of the window. Rob looked where he was looking and saw a police car parked across the street, with three cops standing beside it. A second police car pulled up, and then a third. At this point the waiter turned and charged towards the kitchen doors. A few moments after they swung closed, Rob heard raised voices; a few seconds after that, a man in a high-viz jacket barrelled through the front door, quickly followed by half a dozen cops. The high-viz man raised a laminated card and shouted: 'UK Border Agency, stand where you are!'

This was a bit pointless because there were only customers; the few other staff had melted away as quickly as Rob's waiter. More excited voices from the kitchen. The party of six kept eating. The high-viz man led the police across the restaurant and through the swing doors. As they swung back into place Rob heard plates smashing, yells; his young waiter with the attempted moustache came racing back out and was quite close to the front door before he was rugby-tackled by one of the cops. Two others then sat on him until he could be hand-cuffed. The owner, who went by the name of Mr Smith, but only because he said his Chinese name was too complicated for the locals to easily remember, a chatty, friendly man who'd been in the town for forty years and had a broader Belfast accent than Rob's, came and stood over the fallen waiter and let go with what might well have been a string of exple-tives aimed at the police but it was difficult for Rob to tell, what with them being in Mandarin. Two further staff were marched out of the kitchen while Mr Smith gave a running commentary and wrung his hands. The party of six called him over, drunkenly congratulated him on the entertainment, and asked if they could order more beer. The table of three sloped off, their meals eaten, without paying. Mr Smith let them go without a word. Rob finished his beer and gathered his belongings; he left money on the table; he was five days away from the next issue of the *Express*, so there was no urgency in interviewing anyone for a story, but he lingered outside and took some photos of the police activity, at least until he was warned off; he said he was press; a cop said he didn't give a damn who he was but to stop taking photos. It wasn't worth getting into a fight over. The arrested Chinese were in the back of a transit van; the cops were still moving in and out of the restaurant and being directed around by the guy from the

Border Agency, who appeared to be quite frustrated, perhaps disappointed at his meagre haul. Rob returned to his car. He'd only had two beers, and a large meal, so he supposed he was okay to drive but was a little wary because there were so many police around. As he patted his pockets for his keys he was distracted for a moment by a very slight movement to his left, just on the periphery of his vision; and at first he didn't realize what he was looking at; then he saw that it was a woman crouching by his car but facing away; he said 'Hey' and there was a sharp intake of breath and she turned towards him and in the orange gaze of the streetlight above he saw that it was his smiley netball-waitress friend Anna, and she looked terrified; she raised a finger to her lips and he nodded, but at the same time his right hand accidentally squeezed his keys in his pocket, pushing all of the buttons at the same time and inadvertently setting off the car alarm. The warning lights came flashing on and the alarm shrieked alarmingly, and everyone turned towards it. Anna leapt to her feet and sped right past him even as he said 'Sorry, sorry, sorry...' and the police took off in pursuit; she would probably have outrun them, but then two appeared from around the back of the restaurant and cut her off. Then they had her in handcuffs and were walking her past Rob towards the transit and he just stood there helplessly; she didn't look at him, and if she had she probably wouldn't have recognized him, she was crying so hard.

Rob hardly slept. He felt so bad about Anna. Next morning the first thing he raised at the editorial meeting was doing a story on the raid on the Hong Kong Palace. Alix, Peter, Sean and Michael were sitting before him; Gerry was leaning in the doorway, arms folded, listening in.

Gerry said, 'I make it a strict rule only to cover restaurants that advertise in the paper.' He turned and called across to

Janine, looking through a filing cabinet on the other side of the office. 'Hey, Jannie, does the Hong Kong Palace give us much business?'

'No,' said Janine, without looking round, 'not yet.'

'That's the spirit,' said Gerry. 'And anyway, I'm not entirely sure our readers are going to be the slightest bit interested in some illegal—'

'Could I just stop you there?' Rob asked.

'Yes, of course...'

'Well, first of all, it's not about whether the restaurant advertises, it's a news story. And second – you see that door beside you?'

Gerry looked at it. His brow furrowed. 'What about it?'

'Could you just read out loud what it says on it?'

'Ah. Yes. Ed-it-or ... very funny, Rob.'

'I'm not being funny. Could you close it on your way out?'

Gerry waved a warning finger at Rob. 'It's my paper, you know!' he cried, before pulling the door closed behind him.

Rob smiled after him, then turned to Alix: 'Do you want to get on to the Borders Agency, see what they have to say? I'll maybe have a talk with the guy who runs the restaurant, I kind of know him. Have a word with the college as well, one of the waitresses goes there, her name's Anna, I'll try and get a second name, but I know she plays on their netball team – the Aztecs? We carry their notes?' He nodded at Peter. Peter nodded back. 'Do you want to try them as well, Alix, see what they say about one of their star players getting arrested? Who's our contact, Pete?'

Pete said, 'I'll need to check. But before we go mad on this, if she's Chinese, and it's netball – can we just think about exactly who's going to be interested? If she was local, or she was, like, an Olympian or something, I could see the local—'

'It's human interest,' said Rob, 'so other human beings will be interested.'

'Not round here, they won't. Maybe human beings in China.'

'Peter, she lives here. It's a local story. She's come all the way over here to work, she's not taking anyone's job away and she just happens to be this terrific sportswoman who is bringing glory to her adopted town. So we are going to do this.'

'That's you put in your place,' said Alix.

Peter scowled at her.

'Alix, take Sean with you to the college, try and round the team up for some quotes, get a picture...'

'Sexy, page three kind of...?' Sean asked.

'No,' said Rob. 'Michael, you're for court?'

'Yup.'

'First time by yourself,' said Alix. 'Nervous?'

'Not in the slightest.'

'You should be, it's bedlam.'

'He'll be fine,' said Pete. 'I taught him everything I know.'

'That's what worries me,' said Alix.

Pete scowled again.

'You know,' said Alix, 'if you keep doing that, your face will stay that way. Oops, too late.'

Alix had only been back at her desk for a few moments when Pete stopped there and handed her a sheet of paper on which he had scrawled a name and a mobile phone number. 'The guy that drops in the netball notes, Patrick Donegan. I think he's the coach as well.'

'Thought it would be a woman. Could you not have said that in there?'

'It's just come back to me.'

Alix shook her head. She indicated Rob's office and said, 'You know, he's not the enemy.'

'Really?'

'No, he's just trying to do his job.'

'So you think he's here for the long haul, do you?'

'I think he's—'

'Oh, take your blinkers off, Alix. You don't switch from a national paper to the likes of this place purely for the love of the aul' sod. He's here because he has nowhere else to go, and he'll be off as soon as he gets a better offer. And as for exactly why he actually left the mighty *Guardian* – well, we don't really know that yet, do we? Maybe you should start thinking about that before you start throwing all of your eggs into one basket, eh?'

Alix shook her head. 'I'm not throwing any eggs into any basket, Pete, I'm just doing my work. Fact is, he's here, Gerry's satisfied with his reasons for being here, and that's good enough for me. Maybe if you weren't so green with envy, you might see that he's really not that bad, and he has a hell of a lot more imagination than Billy ever had.' She stood up and quickly pulled on her jacket. She swiped the note Peter had given her off the desk, waved it in his face and said, 'Thanks for this,' gave him a fake smile and headed for the door while indicating for Sean to join her.

As they walked out to the car she said, 'Have you ever met anyone grumpier than that fucking old misery?'

Sean said, 'Is that what you call a rhetorical question?'

She didn't answer.

She was still fuming. Pete was the kind of glass-half empty guy she despised. She knew journalists were supposed to be cynical, but she had always believed that that related to the stories they covered, not to how they related to each other.

But Pete never saw the life, or light or humour in anything.

As they drove to the college Alix said, 'He's a killjoy, a doubter and a back-stabber. He talks about everyone behind their back.'

'Like you're doing now?' Sean asked.

'Oh shut up.'

The timing of the netball team's next practice had been contained in their notes in the last issue of the paper, so Alix and Sean arrived just as the girls were gathering on the gymnasium court but before their coach turned up. They all expressed disappointment and concern, but didn't actually know a lot about Anna. Sean got them together for a photograph. He stood on a bench looking down at them and, bearing in mind what Rob had said, he instructed them to stop smiling. 'You're worried about your teammate, remember?'

One of the girls, Caitlin, said, 'We're only smiling because your zip is down.'

'Think I'm going to fall for that one?' said Sean.

'Up to you, but your cock's hanging out.'

The other girls creased up, and Sean had no alternative but to check.

'Oh very good,' he said. 'Now, c'mon, your best glum faces.'

As they tried their best to compose themselves the doors at the back opened and Alix saw a young man in a retro yellow tracksuit crossing the gym. As he saw the girls posing, he clapped his hands together and said, 'Come on, now! This is supposed to be a practice!'

The girls immediately dispersed and began to throw their netballs around. Alix put her best smile on and stepped forward with her hand out. 'Hi, hello,' she said. 'Mr Donegan? Alix Cross, I'm from the *Express*...?'

'Hi, yes, hello, we spoke on the phone. Patrick, please.'

He was, she thought, very handsome. And fit. 'And I told you we can't really talk about it – you'd need to call the school, and probably the Netball Association.'

'Yes, and of course I'll do that. But you must be really gutted, losing one of your players like—'

'Nice try.'

'I'm really not ... look, all I'm saying is that if we speak to them we'll just get a dry and dusty statement, but if I can actually get some quotes from you and the girls it'll make for something much more interesting, might even help get Anna back.' He pursed his lips. It wasn't exactly a no, so she pressed on. 'Could you not just tell me a little about her? How long she's been with the club, how you came to be working with her ... even off the record?'

'Tell you what,' he said, 'maybe if you buy me a fruit smoothie and a power bar I might be more inclined to say something.'

Twinkly eyes, too.

'What about a coffee and a doughnut?'

'Do I look like I eat doughnuts?'

A bit overconfident maybe, but that was no bad thing.

'No, you don't,' said Alix, 'but you've got smoothie written all over you.'

He grinned. She grinned. They grinned together.

Sometimes, she thought, this job has its bonuses.

Michael was still a cub reporter, though he bristled when Pete called him one. Pete told him that if he managed to complete his first solo magistrate's court without messing it up, he would give serious consideration to reducing the number of times he got the cub treatment.

The court sat once a week, on a Wednesday. Magistrates deal with relatively minor offences – thefts, burglaries, assaults, drunk and disorderly, and a lot of motoring cases. Though it's not written down anywhere, the job of the magistrate is basically to agree with whatever evidence the police present. His or her job is to find nearly every defendant guilty. If they're really not guilty the defendant can pursue it through a higher court. Very occasionally the magistrate will side with the defendant, but these cases are few and far between. Everyone accepts this: the Department of Public Prosecutions, the police, the defending solicitor, and even the soon-to-be guilty party usually comes round in the end.

The magistrate rarely hands out custodial sentences. If he does, usually they are suspended. He imposes community service, he fines and he chastises. The court is small and busy. In a weekly sitting the clerk of the court will rush the magistrate and the attending police and solicitors and soon-to-be-guilty parties and witnesses and relatives through the evidence; maybe seventy or eighty cases will be heard, often before lunch. There is so little room in the court and so many soon-to-be-guilty parties attending that there is no space for the public, for those who just want to listen to the proceedings. If someone is sentenced or fined, if someone admits to stealing women's knickers off a clothes line, pissing up a well lit alleyway or getting into a fight with a policeman, nobody in the town would know about it if it wasn't for the young cub reporter sitting with his back to the body of the court. Michael's job was to report the proceedings accurately and in detail. For most, the true punishment is not a fine or the suspension of a sentence, it is seeing their case reported in the paper. It's all about the public shame and the stick they have to take from family and friends.

Michael collects the summonses and charge sheets for the upcoming sitting on the day before and duly notes down the details of every case. If it seems interesting he flicks quickly through the statements if they are attached, just so that he has a broad idea of what is coming. Then, when he attends court the next day, he can concentrate on recording the evidence. The days when shorthand was absolutely essential for journalists are long gone, but Michael has his – one hundred words a minute and proud of it.

Michael is not a stranger to the court, he's been there maybe a dozen times before, usually with Pete, once or twice with Alix, following their lead, writing his own versions of the cases and then taking note as they picked holes in the results. But there were less holes each week. Last week there had only been a couple of minor mistakes, and now Rob, on Peter's advice, judged him good enough to cover the court by himself. Michael was anxious the way a driver is anxious when he passes his test but then drives the car for the first time without someone to watch over him. Qualified but nervous.

The morning session passed quickly. No surprises. His notes were neat and proficient and he knew he had a few good stories. There was a particularly vicious assault. There was a shoplifter who stole a packet of minced steak by slipping it down the front of his tracksuit and into his underwear; nothing unusual about that until the defending solicitor said the meat was fit for re-sale, which had the whole court groaning and laughing.

When they broke for lunch Michael bought a sandwich and sat on the sea wall opposite the old and crumbling courthouse building. It was a warm day with a nice breeze that rattled the yachts in the marina behind him. He bit into his

146

sandwich and put his face up to the sun and closed his eyes and chewed and enjoyed the heat.

'Hi – hello, sorry to trouble you?'

Michael opened his eyes, blinking, and saw that there was a girl of about his age standing in front of him. Her hair was dyed red, and short, and she was, he immediately decided, very pretty. Michael didn't know many girls, and had been out with even fewer. This unfamiliarity often caused him to blush. He blushed now.

She said, 'Sorry – didn't mean to disturb you, but I couldn't help but notice, you were in the court earlier?'

'Yuth,' said Michael, trying to swallow.

'Just, I didn't catch what they said about starting again after lunch – was it half one?'

'Two, I think,' said Michael.

'Oh right – that's better. I'll have time to grab something.'

'Absolutely,' said Michael, and he waved his sandwich for emphasis, which resulted in half of its contents sliding out and landing at the girl's feet.

She said, 'I was only asking a question, no need to throw it at me—'

'Sorry – sorry…'

She burst out laughing. Michael looked relieved. He smiled at her. She smiled back. She looked about her, and then sat on the wall beside him.

'It's nice to see the sun out,' she said.

'Aye.'

She nodded across at the court. 'I don't like it over there. Scary people, and I'm not just talking about the ones up on charges. Those lawyers, solicitors, whatever you call them, they're all very sure of themselves aren't they?' Michael nodded. He thought she was lovely. 'I saw you scribbling away at the front. You do the write-ups for the paper?' Michael nodded again. 'That must be pretty interesting? Plenty of head-the-balls, yeah? What was that guy with the mince down his trousers like?'

'It was funny,' said Michael.

She smiled up at the sun. Then she turned her full beam back on Michael. 'So, are you not going to ask?'

'Ask what?'

'What I'm doing in court? I could be an armed robber, or an international ... horse thief or a confidence trickster or something...'

'Well I'm ... pretty sure you're not.'

'Of course I'm not. But I was just wondering – you couldn't lend me twenty quid? Just to get some lunch? I left my bag at home and I'm bloody starving.'

'I ... uh ... I'm not sure if I have...'

'Stop! For goodness sakes! I'm only joking!'

She giggled. Michael joined in.

'Oh – right, yeah. Good one.' He looked about him, embarrassed, aware that his face was now lobster-red. 'So – ah, why are you here, then?'

'It's my brother Declan. The eejit. Walking home from the pub and some of his mates offered him a lift, so he jumps in. Before he knows what's happening, they crash the car and run off, and he gets nabbed by the cops.'

'Ah right – yes, I saw that on the list. Joyriding. There's, uhm, a lot of it about. You're here for moral support?'

'Aye – he's not a bad lad, y'know? It's more mum I'm worried about – she hasn't been at all well, this'll ... it won't help.' She shrugged and studied the ground. Michael wasn't sure, but he thought she looked as if she might burst into tears. 'Anyway,' she said suddenly, standing up, 'I'd better go

148

and get that lunch while I have the chance. Nice talking to you. I'm Shona, by the way.'

'Hello, Shona. Michael.'

She gave him a final smile and moved on. Michael felt warm all over. And a twinge of despair coursed through him because he hadn't said more to her.

Rob was used to the Chinese restaurant at night with its subdued lighting further muted by the red shades on the table lamps and the heavy red drapes. By day it all looked rather threadbare and run-down – not entirely unlike its owner, who was sitting opposite Rob at a window table. They had a Coke each.

'My father opened this restaurant forty years ago,' Mr Smith was saying, his face drawn, his hair tinged with grey, 'first in town, people didn't know what to make of it ... but now we're a...' He clicked his fingers, looking for the right word.

'Fixture,' said Rob.

'Fixture. Yes indeed. This is home. My children only ever speak English. They damn well don't want to work in a bloody Chinese restaurant, that's for sure. That's why I have to bring people in.'

'Illegals.'

'How do I know? They present papers, they look fine. Now three of them will be on plane home tomorrow.'

'Including Anna?'

'No, Anna, not yet anyway. She has a visa, but it is out of date. The community association has solicitors, this problem is not uncommon, so we will see.'

'And what about you, will you be punished for having them?'

'I will be fined. It is not the first time. So they will fine more, perhaps. Maybe I will be out of business.'

There was a small plate of fortune cookies wrapped in cellophane sitting beside the condiments. Rob lifted one and raised an eyebrow.

'Do you think it's worth . . . ?' he asked.

'No. They're bullshit, we buy them in bulk from a wholesaler in Newtownabbey. But feel free.'

Rob set it down again. He glanced up at movement outside, and saw Alix. She gave him a little wave as she moved to the door and came in. Rob introduced her to Mr Smith, who shook her hand but then said he'd better get back to work because he was short-staffed. He thanked Rob for calling in and hoped he could do something to help Anna. Rob promised to do his best.

Mr Smith began to check under the tables around them as he made his way to the kitchen, but was still within earshot as Alix slipped in opposite her editor and immediately said, 'This place is a bit of a dive in daylight.'

'Shhhhhhh. Jesus.'

Mr Smith pushed through the doors without looking back. Rob shook his head.

'Sorreee . . .' said Alix.

Rob gave a small sigh. 'How did it go with the netballers?' he asked.

'Mmmmm, not sure. I tried to sell them on launching a campaign to free your friend, but they weren't particularly interested. I called by the Chinese community association. They said they were looking at the case but couldn't comment and nearly had a fit when I mentioned a campaign. They're all the same, aren't they? So bloody PC. If it's not that it's data protection or they're frightened of being called a whistleblower or . . .'

'I don't recall mentioning a campaign.'

'It just came to me. It's one way to do the story, isn't it? Or maybe it's a rubbish idea.'

'Well, we'll see. Same story with the Border Agency?'

'Same again, PR guff. Nobody wants to rock the boat.'

'So...?'

'So... it's our job to rock the boat?'

'Well, a gentle shake mightn't do any harm. Mr Smith thinks he might be able to get me in to see her, where she's being held.'

'You?'

'Why not me?'

'You actually write a story?'

'I write stories all the time.'

'You re-write stories all the time. I'm not sure I've ever actually seen you write a story.'

'In all the four weeks I've been here.'

'Even so.'

'I'll have you know, I was a very fine reporter.'

'Even if you do say so. I'm happy to go in and talk to her.'

'No, I'll do it. It will do me good.'

'Okay. All right. How old did you say this girl is?'

'I don't know. She's at college but a bit older than your average ... why do you ask?'

'Just wondering.' Alix gave him a look and a smile.

'Oh, for goodness sake.'

'You forget, I've seen you work your moves.'

'You've ... you mean—'

'It's fine. We had a lot to drink. Don't worry about it.'

'I wasn't. At least not until—'

'Relax, Rob, I'm only winding you up.'

But she was giving him a coy look.

He nodded slowly. She was already leaning half-way across

the table to him, her arms folded. He folded his own and matched her position. Their heads were really quite close.

He said quietly, 'Do you want to know something?'

'Mmmm-hmmm?'

'I think it's time we ... got back to work.' He gave her a wink and pushed up out of his chair. 'Coming?' he asked as he began to walk away.

He was grinning to himself. But then he thought he heard her say 'You wish'. He couldn't help but burst into laughter. When he turned to her, she looked a bit flushed. 'I can't believe I said that,' she said. 'Said what?' Rob asked. 'Never you mind,' she answered, brushing past him.

Ten minutes later they were still laughing and joking and winding each other up when they entered the office and Rob stopped short so quickly that Alix stumbled into the back of him. Rob was staring across the office at a tall, striking and somewhat statuesque woman standing talking to Gerry. She was holding two toddlers by the hand. Alix apologized and asked what the matter was, but Rob ignored her. He pushed through the swing door into the office proper.

'Hello, hello, hello,' he said. The woman turned. She immediately let go of the toddlers' hands and they ran into Rob's arms. He lifted them up and peppered them with kisses. 'Daddy wasn't expecting to see you guys,' he said between hugs.

'We were able to get an earlier flight,' said the woman.

Her accent was English, and to Alix's ears, rather plummy. She was tall, broad-shouldered, almost Amazonian, and pretty with it. She wasn't even looking at her husband. Her eyes, which appeared large and very blue, were boring straight into Alix.

'Have you met everyone, then?' Rob asked.

'Gerry's been very patient with me...'

'My pleasure,' said Gerry.

'And this is Alix ... one of my reporters. Our reporters. Alix, this is my ... Rebecca.'

Rebecca put her hand out. Alix took it.

'Charmed, I'm sure,' said Alix.

Rebecca, not to mention Rob and Gerry, looked at her as if she was mentally impaired. It had just come out. She was trying to be funny, but it came out as take-the-piss-out-of-my-accent.

Rob tried to cover the embarrassment by jiggling the kids in Alix's direction and saying, 'And this is James, and this is Jenny, two little people we got from the circus.'

Rob then ushered Rebecca and the kids into his office as quickly as he could and closed the door. Pete, having missed it all, came out of the kitchen, and asked Alix where she was with the Chinamen story and she hissed at him that she was on it and hurried past him to make a coffee. Janine came up to her as she waited for the kettle to boil and said what a turn-up for the books that was. She knew Rob had kids but thought he was divorced. Maybe he was. But what a beautiful woman. Janine asked what her grip was like and Alix said, 'What?'

'Her handshake? Warm? Strong? Clammy?'

'I didn't really notice.'

'You can tell a lot by a handshake. She couldn't take her eyes off you, noticed that.'

'Maybe she's a lesbian,' said Alix.

'That must be it,' said Janine. She pointed a finger at Alix. 'Leave you to it. But chin up.'

And then she was away before Alix could ask her what she meant.

In his office, Rob installed the two kids on his swivel chair and quickly called up an old *Tom and Jerry* from YouTube. Rebecca stood looking out at the newsroom. Alix came in carrying a coffee and sat at a desk.

'She seems nice,' said Rebecca.

'What?' said Rob, looking up from the screen.

'The girl. You seem to get on very well.'

'Who, Alix? Yes, she is nice. But all strictly professional.'

'It's okay, Rob.'

'What's okay?'

'For you to meet someone else.'

'I haven't met someone else.'

'Okay. Whatever you say.' She moved back across to the desk, and stood with him, looking down at the screen. She stroked Jenny's hair. 'You're happy here?' she asked.

'It's fine. But it's temporary. Soon as the other stuff is sorted, I'm gone. You know that.' He smiled down at the toddlers, who had been immediately mesmerized by the antics of the cartoon mouse and cat. 'Thanks for bringing them.'

'They need to see their dad in the flesh.'

Rob ruffled Jimmy's hair. Jimmy pushed his hand away.

'They've grown,' Rob said.

'Rob, you Skype them three times a day.'

Rob raised his hands and held them about a foot apart. 'On Skype,' he said, 'they're about this size. Anyway – what about you, have you met someone?'

Rebecca looked at him for a little too long before she said, 'No, of course not.'

The court ended, finally, at about four. The last hour had been spent on a careless-driving case that was boring in the extreme and would make about a paragraph in the paper, but he'd had no choice but to sit through it and await the inevitable outcome. Guilty as charged. Michael was just crossing back on to Main Street when he heard a clip-clopping behind him and the lovely girl from before drew up alongside.

'Thought it was you!' Shona gasped. 'You move at some speed.'

'Well, y'know,' said Michael, 'stories to write.' But he slowed his pace.

'So tell me,' the girl said, 'how come you live here and I've never seen you around?'

'Ah, well, y'see – I've only recently moved down, when I got the job. I'm from Belfast really, Holywood Road.'

'Ah right, that's why – I mean, small town, even if you don't know everyone, you kind of recognize their faces. How're you finding it? Not a bad wee spot, is it?'

'Loving it,' said Michael.

'Really?'

'Well, mostly. Don't really know my way around properly yet.'

'Do you ever go to the Goat's Toe?'

'The wah ... ?'

'The Goat's Toe? It's a pub. They've great wee bands on most weekends.'

'Oh – right, yeah, I think I've been past it, never been in. I usually go home on weekends, you know, Belfast ...'

'One of my mates is having a party there on Saturday. I mean, it's open to the public and all. You should come down. I'll even buy you a pint.'

Michael could feel himself blushing again. He said, 'That would be really ... nice ...'

'Nice...' the girl laughed, 'is that the best I get? Sure your old granny is nice...'

'I didn't mean...'

She was laughing again. He laughed, too.

He was more than half-way back to the office, but he was debating continuing on past.

She said, 'That was a real drag in there, wasn't it? In the court? But my bro didn't do badly, did he? I mean, £75 fine, that's not so bad. Coulda been sent away.'

She stopped suddenly. Michael, surprised, took another few steps before he realized. She was standing, brow furrowed, looking worried and rather pale.

'Are you all—?'

'Yes – yes, fine. Really. Are you ... I mean, do you have to go back to work right away?'

'Well, I...'

'Do you fancy getting a coffee? That court really freaked me out.'

'Not a problem,' said Michael, 'that would be really ... nice...'

Rebecca, Alix decided, had thick ankles. Which matched her thick legs. Come to think of it, her back looked quite thick too, and slightly hunched.

Rob had walked Rebecca and the kids as far as the corner of the street and was now turning back towards the office. Alix kept her eyes down as she unlocked her car. She got in, closed the door and started the engine; then there was a tap on the window. Rob nodded in at her. She managed a quick smile as she brought the window down.

'Off anywhere nice?'

'Pete talked to a guy from the Border Agency, he's willing to meet for a coffee.'

'Excellent.'

'Yeah, well, it's off the record. I wanted to do it over the phone but he said he couldn't be sure I wasn't recording it, so it's face to face.'

'Well, I'm sure you'll get what you need.'

He nodded. She nodded.

She said, eventually, 'Your wife seems nice.'

'Up to a point, yes she is. Was just seeing them off. We're separated.'

'None of my business, Rob,' said Alix.

'No, I know … I mean … I'm just saying. It's not a secret.'

'Well, sorry.'

'Sorry?'

'Sorry you're separated. It can't be easy.'

'No. I mean, yes, it's the right thing, but hard … on the kids, and not seeing them.'

Alix nodded. 'Anyway…' she said, 'time and the Border Agency wait for no man, or woman…' She realized she was babbling, but couldn't help herself. 'Better hit the road.'

Rob stood back. 'Okay,' he said, 'don't take no prisoners.'

She blinked at him. 'Okay.'

Alix put the car into reverse and started to move back. Rob waved her off. She waved back. Her car was an automatic, so there was no clutch for her to rest her left foot on. Instead her whole leg jangled up and down, beating out a distress rhythm in Morse code, at least until she realized what she was doing.

'Ridiculous,' she said out loud.

She drove to the shopping centre on the edge of town. She met the Border Agency guy in a Costa Coffee. As arranged, she carried a folded copy of the *Express*; he was sitting right at the back, leaning back against the wall so that he had a clear view of everyone else in the restaurant and anyone else who came in. He looked nervous. Anxious. She crossed to his table and introduced herself; she asked if he wanted a coffee, but he indicated the full cup in front of him; she said she would pop up and get one for herself, and he looked pained at that. Alix went anyway. She had already deduced that this guy was a bit of a twat. They usually were, these government types, deluded as to their importance to the grand scheme of things. She would have her coffee. And buns. She came back with them and he gave her a look that said he didn't have all day, although being a civil servant meant that he probably did. She took out her notebook and asked him if he minded. He gave a slight shake of the head and said, 'No names.'

She said, 'Too late, I've already given you mine.'

He did not smile. He stirred sugar into his coffee. He said in a dull monotone: 'Anna Ng. Her visa ran out four months ago, and there probably wouldn't have been a problem renewing it back then, but after so long – we've been told to take a harder line.'

'It does seem very hard.'

'No, actually, all we're doing is enforcing the rules that are already there.'

'The raid on the restaurant – was that just a random check?'

His eyes shifted to the door and back. 'No, we were acting on specific information.'

'You mean a tip-off?' He nodded. 'Where does that sort of thing usually come from?'

'Usually from a member of the public, or perhaps a business rival.'

'So someone phones up and maybe says there's half a dozen illegals working in such-and-such a place…'

'Usually.' He hesitated then. He drummed his fingers on the table. 'Not in this case. The information we received was specifically about this girl. The other lads were a happy accident.' He reached into his jacket and removed a folded sheet of paper. He opened it, then scrutinized the clientele of the café. When he was satisfied nobody was watching he put the paper down on the table and then pushed it across to Alix. 'The caller was anonymous. But this is the number it was called in from.'

Alix could not help but look surprised. It was not what she had expected at all. She studied the number, then nodded across at her informant and said, 'Thanks, that's brilliant.'

She *said* it was brilliant, but she wasn't sure that it was. It wasn't the type of story she was planning on writing, and she wasn't sure what difference it made to Anna's situation. Perhaps if she worked for a tabloid or a daily newspaper she might have found some use for it, but as it was this was just the number for someone sneaky. The man from the Border Agency was already pulling his coat on. He said, 'Tell Pete that's us even, and not to call me again.'

He would have walked off without another word if Alix hadn't said, 'Excuse me – but what's going to happen to Anna?'

'That,' said the border agent, 'isn't my department. But usually – I'm not saying she won't be able to renew her visa, but she might have to go back to China to do it.'

'Is there anything we can do to help her?'

'Look – everything feeds down from the top. We just do what we're told. But they do respond to bad publicity, or maybe to politicians getting involved.' He gave her a quick nod and then was gone.

Alix sat with her bun and her coffee and looked at the piece of paper. It wasn't exactly WikiLeaks. She sighed. She folded it away. Then she looked at her bun. She took the smallest bite out of it. It had looked fabulous, and now it tasted fabulous. But she pushed the rest of it away. She didn't want to end up with thick ankles.

It was a weekly newspaper, but since Rob's arrival it now boasted a Facebook page, a Twitter feed and a website that did something more than just try to sell you a subscription. The content on the website was free; it showed a selection of the best stories from the previous week's paper, and also regular daily updates. Not everything that appeared in the paper was displayed on the website and vice versa. Nowadays a lot of the boring guff that the editor had felt obliged to print in the past turned up on the site instead – at least that way there was a public record but they didn't have to add expensive extra pages no one was really interested in to the paper. Rob thought it was a good idea to run edited versions of the court reports almost as soon as the petty sessions finished – if readers wanted to find out all of the salacious details, they would have to buy a hard copy. He knew from the stats that this was the most visited section of the site. So the pressure was on for Michael to get his reports out quickly. He worked methodically through them as soon as he got back to the office; he wrote good, clean, crisp copy and delivered it to Pete; Pete pointed out a couple of errors, but said Michael's first solo effort was reasonably good. This, from Pete, was like getting the Nobel Prize for Literature. Michael gave an appreciative nod, while inside his soul did a few cartwheels and a handstand. There was no hanging around either – twenty minutes after he delivered his final case, they were all up on the website. Thirty minutes later Pete took a phone call, and his face, dour and pale normally, grew more animated and puce the longer it went on. Whoever was on the other end wasn't giving him time to respond; he only managed a few *buts* and *honestly, madams* and *if you could just* before being mercilessly shut down. Michael tapped away on his next story, but couldn't resist a little smirk; it wasn't often he saw Pete on the back foot; rattled, even.

When he came off the call, Pete didn't say anything. He resumed his subbing. When it was coffee-break time he got up to go to the kitchen, but then said, 'Michael, could I have a word?'

Michael jumped up and bounced in after him, all right with the world and determined not to let old misery guts bring him down. Pete was leaning against the counter, arms folded, looking grim. He said, 'We've had a complaint.'

'We're always having complaints,' Michael said, moving across to pour himself a cup, 'people get annoyed by *everything...*'

'A complaint about one of your cases.'

And that stopped him. Suddenly alarm bells were going off. He was aware that his face was reddening.

'Mine?' he asked innocently, though he was also aware that it sounded a bit like a squeak.

'Some fella called Declan Connelly was done for joyriding this morning.'

'Yes, he was. He was fined, as I recall. Joyriding.'

'Indeed. Well, it seems he's just been round to the woman whose car he stole, who at considerable risk to herself called the police and appeared as a witness, and he started boasting that he'd fixed it so that his name wouldn't appear in our paper. I checked the story, Michael. There's a Declan Donnelly, not Connelly.'

'Shite,' said Michael, 'I'm sorry, Pete, I must have pressed D instead of C.'

'And you also accidentally gave him an entirely different address.'

'Oh – Christ. I'm sorry – I must have got him mixed up with someone else.'

'Really, Michael?'

There was sweat rolling down Michael's brow now. He avoided eye contact. He pretended to look about for the sugar to put in his coffee.

'Absolutely,' he said, 'and sorry. It's my first time and ... swear to God, it won't happen again.'

'I'm not sure he's the best person to swear to Michael, because he's less forgiving than I am. Y'see, Declan Connelly was boasting about it before the case even went live on our site.'

'That's not poss—'

'Michael.'

His eyes finally moved up to meet Peter's. 'It's not what...'

'The truth please.'

Michael put a hand to his forehead and rubbed at it. 'It ... Someone asked me to leave it out.'

'For Godsake, Michael...'

'I know, but they said their mum was seriously ill and if she saw it in the paper it would finish her off, and all I did was change it a wee tiny bit and the address is actually his sister's address and he stays there all the time and—'

'Michael!'

'I didn't think it would do any harm...'

'You didn't bloody think at all! Michael – it's a basic principal and you know it – every name goes in. Even if the boss gets done for speeding, it goes in. It's the only fair way. And if we start to leave things out, change the facts when

162

we feel like it, then people think we don't give a shit about the truth, then they'll stop believing anything we write. Do you understand?'

'Yes! I'm sorry. I didn't...'

'Just get out of my sight, Michael.' Michael stood there, shaking his head. 'I'm serious! Get out of here before I fucking clout you!'

Michael let out a loud sigh and moved to the door. He hesitated. 'Pete ... I really am sorry. What ... what're you going to do?'

'Me? Nothing. It's not really up to me, is it? It's up to Rob.'

'Rob? But, sure, you think he's a...'

'I know exactly what he is, Michael, and he still is. And no matter what I think of him, I care about this paper, and I care about its reputation, and I care about journalism. And you've crossed the line.'

Pete lifted his cup and brushed past Michael. He marched straight across to Rob's office; Michael felt like his heart and stomach had dropped out of him; he had been stupid, stupid, stupid, head turned by a pretty girl and now he was going to get sacked for it.

But Rob was still out.

Pete gave Michael a withering look and returned wordlessly to his desk. Michael sloped into his. There was no relief. It was only a delay in execution.

Because Rob was new in town, and didn't really know his way around yet, the Hong Kong Palace had become quite a comfort to him. But now, he realized, he could never go there again. It was part of a story, an important enough story in its own way, but even after it was printed and long forgotten by the readers, its very existence would create a barrier; if Mr Smith was unhappy with it, even if he was happy with it, it would alter their relationship. He would no longer be an anonymous customer. If they hated the story they would spit in his curry; if they loved it they would give him extra portions. He said all this on the phone to Alix that night. He had called to check how she was getting on and to fill her in on his meeting with Anna; he didn't stop to think that it was a conversation they could and perhaps should have had in work the next morning, at least until she'd already answered and immediately asked about Rebecca. He told her his wife was out with the kids with friends in Belfast; there was a little bit of coolness; but he kept talking and she slowly warmed up. When he told her about his reluctance to return to the Hong Kong Palace because of the story, that it would compromise his journalistic principles to dine there, she immediately said, 'That's bollocks. We had a court case about someone getting done for shoplifting in Tesco's last week – are you never doing your weekly shop there again?'

'I go to Sainsbury's,' said Rob.

'You know what I mean.'

'It just doesn't ... feel right.'

'That's because you're bringing your left-leaning wool-ly-minded arsey liberal principals from hoity-toity London and trying to apply them to our little home in the sticks. It's just not the same. We're a local paper. If you stop interacting with everyone we've ever written about you'll starve to death and your house will fall into disrepair.'

'So you've no firm opinion on my predicament.'

She laughed – good throaty laugh, he thought – and said, 'Sorry, I've had a glass of wine.'

'On a week night?'

'Those are the best nights.'

'Drinking alone isn't right.'

'Who says I'm drinking alone?'

'Uhm, good point.'

'I have a cat, you know.'

'Ah, that's okay, then.'

She said, 'So, tell me about your interview with Anna. How'd it go? Slip into the old routine easily enough?'

'Ah, sure, any idiot could conduct an interview.'

'Thanks very much.'

'I mean...'

'Just tell me, you eejit...'

'I really don't think you should be calling me—'

'Tell me!'

He laughed. He told her. Anna Ng had been very surprised to see him. She was being kept in a cell at the local police station. She had spoken to a solicitor appointed by the Chinese Community Association, she was tearful and apologetic and was beating herself up about her own stupidity in not getting her visa renewed. She didn't want Rob to make a fuss about her in the paper; it would be sorted out. Rob told her sometimes you have to make a fuss because otherwise you had no influence on your fate. He told her he would like to launch a campaign in the paper to free her.

'That's a good idea,' said Alix. 'And *my* idea.'

'I wasn't taking the credit...'

'I believe you were, but continue...'

'So she still wasn't keen, but I think I talked her round ... I got lots of stuff about her life back at home in Beijing, why she came here, what she thinks of the town, the college, her hopes for a career – she's studying law!'

'Oh, the irony...'

'Lots of good personal stuff anyway.'

'And when are you going to write it up?'

'Well, I thought I could give the facts to you and you could...'

'Hey – your story, you write it up!'

'I've a paper to—'

'Just do it and stop making excuses!'

Rob sighed. He said, 'So, was it a bit of a shock seeing my wife there?' He was on his own fourth glass of wine.

'Why would it be a shock?'

'No reason. Just wondering.'

'Do you mean because you hadn't actually mentioned that your wife from whom you are estranged was coming?'

'I—'

'There was no reason to. Your personal life is your own.'

'Yes, absolutely, but—'

'So. Enough. Anyway – better fly. My taxi will be here soon.'

'Taxi?'

'Oh yes, out on a date. Wish me luck.'

'Well—'

'That's it now! Talk to you tomorrow.'

The line went dead. Rob looked at his phone. He took a long drink of his wine. He had enjoyed talking to her. And now he was slightly annoyed. She had finished the conversation abruptly. That was his fault for dragging it back round to Rebecca. That wasn't smart. He wasn't convinced that she was actually going out on a date. She was just pissed off with him. In fact, he should phone her back and apologize. Or, no, he shouldn't do that at all. They had to work together. She was very pretty. It would be a disaster. Or wonderful. Maybe she wasn't interested at all. If she was interested, she wouldn't be going out on a date. Or maybe she wasn't going out on one.

Perhaps he should walk round to her house and check if she was still there. He could just knock on the door and say he was passing and thought he'd say hello.

That wouldn't be weird at all, your boss calling on you, late at night, half cut.

No, wise up, Rob, grow up, Rob.

With their big competition coming up, the Aztecs were practising every day. Patrick Donegan was pacing the edge of the court, shouting instructions, not looking very happy with their performance. Alix fell in beside him.

'You again,' he said.

'I have new and vital information.'

'Do you know how to beat a crack Scottish team that hasn't lost all year?'

'No, but I know how Anna got busted.'

He stopped and studied her. 'And what's that got to do with the price of fish?'

'Well, nothing for sure.' The number had been burning a hole in her handbag all night. She had tossed and turned trying to decide how to use it, while weighing up what Rob had told her about Anna. 'But I have a theory.'

'A theory. *Right.* Will that theory help us beat—?'

'Just hear me out. Someone called the authorities about Anna. From what I've learned about her, she basically has no life outside of her studies and her netball. Now – what if there was someone on the team who didn't like her, or who was actually being kept out of the team because of Anna?'

'That's just ridiculous.'

'No, think about it – who would have the most to gain by squealing on her?'

'I'm not even going to answer that. I know my girls, they just wouldn't ... I mean, they're together so much, they're like a big family.'

'Exactly. Families are always falling out.'

'No, that's balls. You've been watching way too many movies.'

'Do you not want her back?'

'Yes, of course I do.'

'Then is it not worth supporting our campaign?'

'What you're saying is that this so-called campaign is the lesser of two evils.'

'Remind me what the first evil is again?'

'Me buying into your nutty idea about someone in the team shopping her to the authorities. I mean, if Anna didn't know her visa had expired, then how on earth would one of her teammates know?'

'I don't know.'

'See?'

'Isn't it worth a try?'

'Isn't what worth a try?'

'Gathering the girls together once they're changed, then I call the number, see if any of their phones ring.'

'Jesus, you're like one of those conspiracy nutters. Are you sure you're a journalist? Do you have, like, ID or anything?'

He was laughing though, and so was Alix. He was very cute, she thought. He turned back to the game, shouting more encouragement, and then swore as Caitlin's attempt to net the ball from close range went badly awry. He glanced back at Alix, standing there smiling expectantly.

'Okay,' he said, 'let's discuss a campaign to get her out. We really do need her.'

'Excellent,' said Alix.

'Come back in twenty minutes when we're done here – I'll put it to the girls, see if they're willing to get on board.'

'Won't you have to check with the college, or the netball author—?'

'Once it's out there, they won't be able to do much about it. But one condition.'

'Uhuh?'

'You take me out for dinner.'

'I take *you* out?'

'I coach netball, it's not exactly Premier League football. Put it on expenses.'

'You clearly have no idea about working for a local newspaper.' She pretended to mull it over. 'How does a man end up coaching netball anyway?'

'Because we have no basketball team.'

'Okay. Maybe the more pertinent question then is – *why* do you coach it?'

'For the girls,' said Patrick.

Janine slipped outside for a fag and was surprised to find Pete there, cigarette in hand, pacing up and down, looking very pissed off. She said, 'Thought you were off them?'

'I am.'

He showed it to her – unlit.

'Fair play,' she said, lighting her own and taking a long drag. When she eventually exhaled she said, 'So, what's up with you and Michael? I heard youse having a barney.'

'Ah, nothing. He's young. He'll learn.'

'I didn't,' said Janine.

'Well, you were always a lost cause.'

'Thanks a bunch.' But she grinned, and inhaled. Pete was

what her mum would have called a funny-wonder. She had known him for years, and he had always displayed the same hangdog expression, now emphasized by the beginnings of a double chin and receding hair. She nodded across the car park as Rob came driving in in *her* smart car. It had been several weeks now, but they were still sharing the same vehicle. 'Here comes trouble,' she said.

'Fucking blow-in,' said Pete.

'Easy tiger,' said Janine.

As Rob came towards them, he made a show of tossing the keys to her, underarm like a child bowling at cricket; except they fell short. He apologized. She stepped forward and bent to retrieve them just as he did exactly the same, and their heads collided and they both reeled away clutching their brows.

Rob was full of genteel apologies.

Janine was swearing like a fucking trooper.

Pete finally lit his cigarette.

Five minutes later Michael looked up from his desk to see Rob and Pete come through the swing door and head straight into Rob's office. They began what appeared to be an animated conversation. Occasionally one or other of them came to the window and looked out at the newsroom. Michael wasn't sure if they were looking at him, but he made himself look busy, just in case. When they turned away again, he opened his desk drawer and examined the very few personal items within: some Tic Tacs, a half-eaten packet of Starburst, a graphic novel he had still not returned to the library and was somewhat embarrassed about taking out and reading when anyone else was around, and a copy of *Middlemarch* by George Eliot because he'd heard on the radio that it was the greatest novel ever written in the English language. He had been battling through it for more than a year. Or not battling, as the case generally was. Either way he would not even need a box to carry his possessions home when he was inevitably sacked, he would just put them in his coat pocket and slope out. Nobody would even notice him leaving.

Then Pete was standing in Rob's doorway, calling him in.

He walked across; his legs felt numb; his face was a mask of trepidation.

He loved his job, he didn't want to lose it. He immediately launched into, 'I just want to say that—'

'We're launching a campaign to save Anna Ng,' said Rob.

'Anna...?' He looked from Rob to Peter and back.

'Yes, absolutely – we're all going to work on it, see if we can get this poor girl out. It would break your heart to see her. I need you to work the phones, get on to every councillor, MLA, everyone you can think of ... This is a girl who is going to college by day, working every night, sending half her money home to China, paying for her own apartment and doing this country proud at a sport she only took up six months ago, and now we're trying to throw her out because she forgot to fill in a form...' Rob punched his fist enthusiastically into the palm of his hand. 'Do you get the picture?'

'I get the picture. But what ... about...?'

Pete moved beside him – and slipped an arm around his shoulders.

'Michael – we want you to use your initiative.'

'But what about...?'

'Just concentrate – one thing at a time, eh?'

Pete gave him a friendly squeeze and began to lead him out of the office, then right across the newsroom until he plonked him down at his desk. Michael, a little stunned, just looked up at him.

'You didn't...?'

'No. Now fucking prove you can do this properly. Okay?'

'Okay. And thank you.'

Half an hour later Janine came into the kitchen for coffee and saw Pete sitting at the table with his, leafing through a paper. She said, 'He's working like a fucking dervish in there.' Pete gave a smug nod but didn't look up.

The girls returned to the gym in dribs and drabs, the unity of their netball gear replaced with the sartorial inelegance of student fashion; they chatted happily and teased and flirted with Patrick. He returned it with expertise. Alix was looking forward to taking him out for dinner – it would be fun. But she wouldn't trust him as far as she could throw a netball. Which wasn't very far. She'd been rubbish at sport – apart from running; she could do that for ever. Now she sat on a bench just behind Patrick as the last of them trailed in.

Patrick started by praising them, their work ethic, how they were gelling together as a team, how he had high hopes for them at the championships in Scotland. He said, 'As we're all sadly aware, Anna isn't with us – she's languishing in a cell somewhere, her only crime is she forgot to have her visa renewed and now she's being threatened with deportation back to China. Now, I'll tell you what we're going to do – we're going to get behind a campaign to have her released. Not because she's a great netball player, though she is. Not because her presence will increase our chances of winning the championships. Though it will. But because she's a friend of ours. Because we have a laugh together. Because it's just wrong that she—'

Caitlin's phone began to ring. 'Sorry, sorry,' she said as

she opened her sports bag and began to search for it. 'Sorry.'

Patrick glanced back at Alix. She had her phone up and raised to her ear.

Caitlin found her phone and turned away to answer it with a whispered, 'Hello?'

Alix raised an eyebrow at Patrick, and then cut the line.

Caitlin turned back to her teammates. 'Sorry,' she said again.

Patrick continued to urge his players to get behind the campaign – not only would there be newspaper articles, there would be posters and publicity stunts and balloons would be released to represent whatever releasing balloons represented. The players began to throw in their own ideas – a 24-hour netball match, picketing the college to get it to support their student, shaving their heads ... They were enthusiastic and determined. And Caitlin as much as any of them. At the end Patrick confirmed the time of their next practice and then dismissed them. As they moved *en masse* towards the doors at the back of the gym, he called out to Caitlin and asked if he could have a word. She waved back, and then began a series of hugs and kisses with the other girls.

Alix said, 'How are we going to ... ?'

'We're not. I am. You shouldn't have done that. Now I need to speak to her alone.'

'But ...'

'But nothing. You can't prove anything, and I need to keep this team together. So, if you don't mind?'

Caitlin came skipping up, all smiles.

Alix held her hands up to Patrick. 'Okay. Understood. Does this get me out of dinner?'

'No,' said Patrick.

★

173

Rob thought the front page was looking pretty damn good. There was Sean's photo of the Aztecs, looking concerned, but also fit, and there was one he'd taken himself, on his phone, of Anna in custody, looking tear-stained and desperate. Michael had thrown himself into the story with surprising enthusiasm and had recruited a long list of politicians and minor local celebrities in support of the cause. Alix came rushing in, her end of the story to write and deadline approaching. She said through Rob's open door, 'I was right, it was one of her team-mates called it in.'

'Seriously?'

'Yup. She admitted it. Broke down. People do the daftest things. Wasn't even about the netball – she had her eyes on the coach and thought he was more interested in Anna, so thought she'd give her a bit of a fright by calling Immigration on her. But she had no idea her visa was up.'

'And she told you all this?'

Alix shook her head. 'Fraid not. It's all second hand.'

'Is she likely to tell you all this?'

'Sure. Just after hell freezes over.'

'So it's of no use to us at all?'

'No, but it is fabulous gossip.'

'Pity. Did the team not tear her to shreds?'

'They don't know – yet. The coach has just lost one of his star players, this would tear the rest of the team apart. So he's holding onto his water until we get Anna released and the championships are over, then he'll deal with it. Pity, but not much I can do about it.'

She'd come into the office by now and was looking down at the front page. She nodded her approval. Then she got to work. When her story arrived, within the hour, Rob worked at melding it together with Michael's, cutting, pasting, weaving, the best of both worlds. By four he had sent the finished pages to the printing works and by six the first bundle arrived back at the office. Thousands more were already being distributed to newsagents and supermarkets across the borough.

Rob always loved the moment when the first copies of the new paper arrived. He loved the smell of a freshly printed newspaper, the crispness of the pages and the blackness of the ink. He revelled in it when it was like this – an exclusive story put together by a talented team, with excellent photographs and a design that drew the reader in. And a story with an immediate impact. Within thirty minutes of the papers hitting the streets the calls of support began coming in, the Facebook page bulged with comment and debate, and other media outlets began calling for more details, which was always a sign that a story had hit the mark. This was why he loved journalism, and this was why he loved small-town papers – the chance to make an impact, the opportunity to change things. You could do the same on a larger, daily, national newspaper, but then you were always a small cog in a large machine; here he was ... the boss. He loved being the boss. He loved that the buck stopped *here*. Usually first in, mostly last to leave. This night he locked the door to the newsroom, then moved down the steps, set the alarm, switched the lights off and stepped outside. As he turned after locking the door behind him, he noticed Alix standing in the car park. She looked miserable.

'What's wrong?' he asked.

'Why does something have to be wrong?'

'Your face.'

She said, 'What's wrong with my face.'

'Nothing, apart from the misery written all over it.'

She let out a sigh. She looked on the verge of tears. 'I just got a call. They put Anna on a plane about an hour ago.'

'Jesus Christ!'

'Well, you could try him but I don't think he's got much sway with the Border Agency.'

'But how ... why would ... Didn't they think—?'

'Oh who knows? But a big fucking waste of time and we look like fucking eejits with it all over our front page and launching a fucking campaign when the fucking girl is on a slow boat to China already.'

'Fuck,' said Rob.

'Fuck, indeed.'

They stood, side by side, and sighed at the same time.

She said, 'Too late to change the front page? Could we not recall the papers and—'

'No. They're gone.'

'Bloody hell.'

'Yup.'

'Can they even do that?'

'They clearly have.'

'You don't think ... we might have caused this ... or at least made matters worse?'

'You mean by poking our noses in, asking questions, threatening a campaign? Yes, possibly.'

'But that would just make them mean and vindictive.'

'Possibly. But the truth is probably more mundane than that. They're just bureaucratic. And efficient. So at least that's a positive.'

Alix snorted.

Rob managed a smile. 'Listen, it's annoying, but it can't be helped. We did our job, same way as they did theirs. So don't beat yourself up about it.'

'Likewise,' said Alix.

Rob zipped up his jacket. He said, 'Can I give you a lift somewhere?'

'No, no – I'm fine.'

'Sure? It's no problem. I don't know if you fancy a dr—'

'Ah, here's my ride now...' said Alix, cutting in as a red and sporty Mini pulled into the car park at speed and stopped directly in front of her.

Rob saw a young man with short dark hair and gleaming teeth lean across, give a little wave, and then reach across to open the door for Alix. He appeared to be wearing a bright yellow tracksuit. Rob thought he recognized him from the photo of the netball team on their doomed front page.

Alix stepped forward, put one hand on the door, then glanced back at Rob. 'See you in the morning,' she said, and then climbed in before he could respond. She shut the door and the car immediately pulled away. Rob swore to himself. The Aztecs might not have gotten a result, but it looked as if Alix had.

Rob shook his head, swung his keys in his hand, and crossed to his car. His smart car.

He swore again.

CHAPTER 5
THE GOOD, THE BAD AND THE QUITE UGLY

Rob's crappy smart car car wouldn't start on Monday morning, so he gave Alix a call asking for a lift to work. She thought this was odd because Rob lived pretty close to the office and kept making noises about getting fitter, so she asked him why he didn't walk, or jog, even. He said it was raining outside. She said, 'Right enough, wouldn't want you to dissolve.' He said, 'If it's a problem, it's fine.' She said, 'No, it's not a problem.' He said, 'If you're not ready…' She said 'Always ready' and promised to be there in ten minutes, which would take some doing as she was half-way through a bowl of oats, her hair was up in a towel and she had the toenails of one foot freshly painted.

But she made it.

Of course she made it.

And a little spray of perfume before she left the car, just in case the one she'd applied before leaving the house had dissipated. She was wearing open-toed sandals, which she was already regretting. Not because it was still raining, but because she'd decided to go with the one-set-of-toes-painted look, which, in the fogginess of the new day she'd thought she might get away with, might almost pass as cool or anarchic, but which in the damp light of a street-lit morning just looked sloppy. She reasoned that Rob wouldn't notice, and put the nail varnish in her bag, planning to finish the job in the toilets once she got into the office. She was more preoccupied on the journey over with exactly why Rob had phoned her when, besides the fact that he could walk, if he was determined to get a lift, geographically both Michael and Pete lived closer to him. She thought maybe it was because he wanted to fill her in on why his wife, Rebecca of the fat arse, had turned up like that, or he needed a shoulder to cry on because she was probably the only woman – or man, for that matter – in the entire city he felt he could open up to. He was her boss, yes, but they were already pretty good friends. And there was that suggestion of a spark between them – hadn't they almost kissed outside that art gallery a few weeks back? Hadn't they felt awkward in the wake of it? That wasn't just because they'd been very drunk. Or, only partially. She didn't know how she felt about him. He was the boss. He was older. He wasn't particularly attractive, wasn't in any kind of shape – she had a sudden flashback to the netball coach – great snogger, six-pack to die for, vain as a supermodel, a three-times-a-night man, as sleek and reliable as a Ferrari, but you really don't want to be riding around in a Ferrari all the time, not when you've shopping to do in Sainsbury's, it was just impractical; Rob was much more like a ... like a ... she didn't really know her cars, but like a ... Land Rover, sturdy and dependable, maybe a little rusty; if you chipped away at it you might get it through the MOT, but irrespective of whether it was legal it would keep going for ever and still be sturdy enough to land on the beaches of Normandy to help rid Europe of Nazis. She was spraying perfume, smiling at the Nazis, final re-touch for her hair, while also thinking what a really, really bad idea it would be to even think about pursuing a relationship with Rob Cullen.

Alix parked beside Rob's ridiculous little car. She expected that he'd be sitting in it, waiting for her. But no. She pumped her horn. Nothing. She sent him a text. He immediately texted back saying he'd be down in five minutes, or you can come up and wait. Good sense told her to stay where she was, but purely out of journalistic curiosity she decided to take him up on his offer. She wanted to not only see where he lived, but how he lived. He was neat and efficient in his work, but he also always looked ever so slightly dishevelled, as if he lacked a mother to smooth his hair down and tuck in his shirt tails. She wanted to know if he lived in a typical bachelor pad with dishes piled high, air freshener instead of cleaning, a super-sized TV for the watching of football; or if it was pristine, because he'd nothing else to do in his life but clean, clean, clean. It was a relatively recently built apartment block; she read his name on the box outside and pressed his buzzer; he said, sixth floor, number 6D. The foyer was spic and span; the elevator glass recently polished; 6D towards the end of a corridor that gave a shock of electric static as soon as she stepped out onto the carpet. The door was open; she knocked on it anyway and he called 'Come on in'. And there he was, suit on, tea-towel over one shoulder, spoon-feeding his two children at a kitchen counter. One was in a high chair; one, somewhat precariously perched on a bar stool. His children had never entered her head. Not in a million years. She stood there with her mouth half open, flummoxed. She managed to say, 'Sorry, I didn't realize ... they were still—'

'Leaving today,' said Rob, while performing helicopter manoeuvres.

'Oh ... right ... and is your ex coming to—?'

'No, his ex is right here...'

Alix wanted the ground to open up and swallow her. Rebecca-of-the-fat-arse was standing in what had to be the bedroom doorway; she was wearing a shirt that looked a lot like the one Rob had worn to work yesterday, and, apparently, nothing else. She wasn't just standing in the doorway, she was leaning in it. She had her arms folded, and she had a smile that smacked of ... that just wanted to be smacked off.

Alix said, 'Oh – I didn't mean to intrude...'

'Not at all. I think it's great that Rob can call up his personal taxi service.'

Rebecca's eyes flitted up and down, giving her the once-over, and then she turned back into the bedroom.

Alix said *'Fuck'*, but under her breath.

Rob said *Sorry*, but miming it with an apologetic grimace.

'Run on, Rob,' Rebecca called from the bedroom. 'I'll take over in a moment.'

'Nearly done,' said Rob. He said to Alix, 'Do you want a wee cup of—'

'I'll wait in the car.'

She spun and was out of the door and down the corridor and into the elevator as fast as her heels would carry her; her face was burning. Personal taxi service. Personal fucking taxi service! She told herself, warned herself, to calm down. But who the *fuck* did Rebecca think she was?

His wife, said a wee voice.

Yes, but who the fuck is she to speak to me like that?

His wife, said a wee voice.

His wife who had fucking assessed her like she was a delivery from Argos. His wife with the big ass who she was virtually certain had spotted her oddly decorated toes and smirked and turned haughtily, dismissively, condescendingly away, with her still-big ass.

Alix slammed into the car and started the engine.

She was going to drive off.

The wee voice told her to catch a grip. What had happened, after all? She'd turned up to give her boss a lift to work. If Rob had had an ulterior motive, he certainly wouldn't have invited her up; he just wanted a lift. Had Rebecca really actually talked to her the way she'd imagined? Hadn't she just been joking, having fun? Had she actually looked at her one painted foot and scoffed?

While she was still weighing this up, Rob got into the car. He said, 'Sorry about that.'

Which Alix took to be confirmation that Rebecca-with-the-big-ass had been as nasty as she had imagined.

'None of my business,' said Alix.

They said nothing the rest of the way in. It wasn't far, and traffic was light, so it wasn't like it was a long journey, but still. She was fuming. Embarrassed. Belittled. Screw the painted nails, she had emergency comfortable shoes in her desk drawer. Nobody deserved to see her painted nails. She'd been looking for Nazis all her life. And now she'd found one. Rebecca was a big-assed Nazi.

When Alix got to work, first thing she did was go to the kitchen and put the kettle on. Major breaking news could wait until she had a coffee. Gerry and Janine were already in there. Gerry was standing over the open fridge and wondering who'd moved his cheese. Janine said she'd binned it because it was all blue-mouldy. Gerry said it was meant to be like that, and Janine said, 'Not bloody *Philadelphia*.'

Pete came and said it was a good movie.

Gerry just said, '*What*?'

'It was so sad,' said Janine.

'What was?' Gerry asked.

'*Philadelphia*,' said Janine. 'And it was blue-mouldy.'

'It was maturing nicely,' said Gerry.

'Tom Hanks certainly is,' said Janine. 'And it was rancid.'

'Just ... don't touch my stuff! I own this place!'

Gerry slammed the door and huffed off, though they were all aware that he was mostly only joking. Pete tried to engage Michael in chat about last night's football, but the boy seemed distracted. He asked if everything was okay and Michael said 'Sure', but unconvincingly. Michael took his cup and walked across to Rob's office. The door was open. Rob looked up from his computer and asked for five minutes to get himself sorted out for their morning editorial meeting. Michael said he wanted a quick chat before it, if he could. Rob, noting the serious look on his face, told him to come in and close the door. As soon as Michael sat down opposite him, he was up again and handing Rob an envelope. Rob took it wordlessly and began to open it up, but before he got there, Michael said, 'I've been offered a place at university. Newcastle. In England. Journalism.'

Rob said, 'That's brilliant.'

'I got it a couple of months ago, but with Mr Maxwell dying, and then you settling in, I've kind of been putting off telling ... It's just that I really like it here and I think, I hope, I'm doing okay, so I'm not entirely sure if I want to go or what benefit it would be to me.'

Rob took a quick look at the letter and then folded it back into the envelope. He handed it back across to his young cub reporter. He said, 'Michael – you're doing grand here.

Absolutely. You're part of the team. I should really be saying to you to stay, that jobs are hard enough to come by, and now you've got the foot in the door you should see it through, that you don't learn how to be a journalist by studying books and taking a degree, you learn about journalism by being a journalist, on the ground, knocking on those doors.'

'Yes, I kind of know that.'

'But at the same time, we're only a wee local paper, and there's a big wide world out there. I got out of here as soon as I could. I'd be a hypocrite to advise you not to grab this with both hands. But I'd be sorry to lose you.'

'I don't know what to do. My parents are keen for me to—'

There was a knock on the door.

Alix was there.

Rob began to say, 'If you'd just give us a couple of—'

But she already had the door open.

'I think you should talk to this guy,' she said.

'If you—'

'This fella's just walked in, says he's found a human skull.'

His name was Daniel Martin, and he said he'd found it 'round the Point'. The Point was the finger of rock pointing out to sea at the far end of the bay; it was all pretty wild ground out there, with a public right of way between the beach and the fields that was popular with dog-walkers and a pleasant enough stroll on a summer's day. Rob had walked it just the weekend before, and nearly got cut off by the tide. Janine had recommended it to him. She hadn't mentioned the tide. Part of him thought she hadn't mentioned it on purpose. When she asked him about his walk on the Monday he didn't say that he'd nearly drowned.

Walking to the counter, Alix said, 'I can't decide whether he's a time waster or he's genuine. He *seems* genuine.'

'The best time wasters always do,' said Rob.

Daniel Martin was in his late thirties, but had the kind of grizzled look of a much older man, a look that came not with being an out-doorsy kind of a guy, but from being a homeless alcoholic. He was flush-faced and wore his greying hair in a bushy ponytail. Rob shook his hand, and nearly had his own crushed in the process. He was quite relieved to get it back. He tried not to flex his fingers in case they were broken. As Rob said, 'Daniel, so what's the story?' his eyes flitted to Pete, who was just coming into the office. Pete clearly recognized Daniel, gave Rob a slight shake of the head, and almost tiptoed past him. Clearly he'd been caught with him before. For a moment Rob wondered if Alix had purposefully foisted the local nut on him in revenge for that morning's embarrassment at his apartment.

Daniel said, 'So I was in the farmer's field looking for magic mushrooms—'

Rob cut in with, 'For...'

'Aye, you have to get them first thing in the morning. That field's just perfect for them.' Rob looked at Alix. She was sporting what he could easily have interpreted as a mischievous grin. 'So anyhow, I was there first thing, not doing any harm to anyone, and next thing I know Farmer Giles was there with a bloody shotgun and a couple of his mates with him too, and I think maybe they thought I was out lamping—'

'Lamping?'

'Aye, lamp—'

'When you go hunting rabbits,' said Alix, for Rob's benefit, 'you blind them with a torch and—'

'That's it love,' said Daniel, 'but that's not my game, I

was just after the mushrooms, but they weren't the sort to stop and ask questions, so I took off and they came charging after me. I may not look it, but I'm fit enough, so I led them a merry chase...'

'A merry chase,' Rob said.

'I was across two fields, and then there's, like, a dip down and another field before the main road... you know where I mean?' Rob nodded, though he wasn't clear at all. 'Well I came to the slope and lost me footing there – still mostly dark, grass was wet, boots went from under me, and next thing I'm rolling down the hill right down into the bushes at the bottom and it's not a soft landing, I tell you that, bloody Farmer Giles has been using it as a dump, all sorts of crap down there, and I try to get to my feet but the ground gives from under me and I'm on my ear again. I put my hand out to stop my fall and when I look down – fucking hell, there's this, like, skull in my hand. A skull!'

'You're sure it was a skull?'

'Absolutely fucking certain...'

'But you didn't bring it with you...?'

'Well, it wasn't the first thing on my mind, mate, because Farmer fucking Giles right at that moment lets loose with his shotgun and nearly takes the arse off me, so I dropped the bastard and ran like billy-o. You see, I knew if I made it to the road then I'd be safe, they couldn't touch me, like crossing the state line in an old Western, you know what I mean?'

Rob nodded. Alix was still smiling.

Rob said, 'You're sure it was a human skull? Not like a sheep's skull?'

'Mate, I know the difference between a sheep and a human.'

'And you've told the police this?'

'No, the police and me, we don't agree. I wouldn't give them the skin off my custard. No I came to you because ... well, it's the right thing to do, isn't it? Someone lying dead out there, they deserve, like – proper burial and all that shit.'

Daniel nodded from Rob to Alix.

Rob said, 'Would you give us a minute?'

'Sure.'

Rob gave him a nod and indicated for Alix to join him in his office. As he closed the door behind her he said, 'Thanks a lot. That certainly needed my attention.'

'It's a *skull*. Skulls don't come along every day.'

'A skull found by someone on magic mushrooms.'

'He didn't say he was on them, he said he was looking for them. There's a difference. I mean, you have to dry them out and all that, don't you?'

'How would I know?!'

'I thought you'd be interested. I thought it might be a big story.'

There was a knock on the door behind Alix. Rob signalled for Pete to come in. When he closed the door he said, 'I take it youse are talking about Magic Martin?'

'Magic...?' Rob asked.

'That's what he's known as. The tragic old hippy.'

'Tragic as in...?'

'He's now a well-known expert on and supplier of magic mushrooms, but back when he was a teenager legend has it that he swallowed a handful of magic toadstools by mistake. Not quite the same thing, and highly toxic. Nearly killed the poor sod, and he hasn't been quite right in the head since. Though of course, the legend could all just be bollocks. Either way, he's in here a couple of times a year with crazy stories

– last time he'd photos of fairies out in the woods. I mean, he was deadly serious about it, just like he is out there, but it turned out some kids had photo-shopped them. Magic Martin is easily led, if you know what I mean. So, all I'm saying is, whatever he's selling, take it with a pinch of salt.'

'He's not selling anything,' said Alix.

'Not yet,' said Pete.

'You are a cynical man,' said Alix. She looked at Rob. 'So?'

'So it sounds like a wild-goose chase.'

But it was a Monday, things were quiet. Rob called Michael and Sean in and told them to take a run out to the Point with Magic Martin to see what they could find. He warned them that they weren't going on a picnic or a day trip. Alix looked a little disappointed not to be sent herself. He asked Pete, fount of all knowledge, if he'd come across this Farmer Giles and Pete looked at him like he was mental, and Alix snorted, and Rob said, '*What?*' Alix went out the door laughing, repeating, 'Farmer Giles.'

Rob said, '*What?*'

Alix called back, 'You were in England for too long. Farmer Giles!'

It was one of those damp grey days that the word mizzle was invented for. The wind off the bay was biting and the waves choppy. Access to the Point was via a narrow stretch of beach, and getting narrower all the time. They were in the car park, buffeted but protected.

'We could go the long way round,' Michael said.

'Where's your sense of adventure, man?' Sean asked.

'It's not that. They're not going to want me in uni if I'm drowned.'

'So you told him?'

'Aye.'

'How'd that go down?'

'Pretty well, actually.'

'Any clearer what you're doing, post-drowning, that is?'

'Still in two minds,' said Michael.

'Not unlike...' and Sean indicated Magic Martin in the back seat, who had his eyes closed and was mumbling away to himself. 'Two – minimum.'

Michael grinned. He took out his phone and started pressing buttons.

'I thought we were—?' Sean asked.

'We are, just as soon as I...' He typed something in. He hmmmmd. 'Okay,' he said, 'we should be fine ... Let's do it.'

He got out of the car and stood zipping his coat up.

Sean got out and looked over the top and said, 'Please tell me what you were looking at on your phone.'

'This. I have an app that shows me the tide times, high tides and the like.'

'Really?'

'Really. What's the problem?'

'Nothing beyond the fact that you need to get a life.'

Sean opened the back door and Magic Martin peered out. He said, 'It's raining.'

'It's spitting,' said Sean, 'and you need to show us where you found the skull.'

'I've explained exactly where it is. I'm not going out in that, and the tide's coming in.'

Sean looked towards the sea. 'Not according to Apple it's not, and in Apple we trust.'

'I'm fine where I am,' said Magic. 'And anyway, I don't want to get the hole shot off me again.'

Michael said, 'We can't force him.'

'We can force him out of the car.'

Michael sighed, looked along the beach, then shook his head. 'We'll want to interview him if we find the skull. Leave him where he is for now.'

'I'm not sure I like leaving him alone in the car.'

They both looked at him. Magic had taken out a joint and was just lighting up. He inhaled, then offered it around. Sean took a hit. Michael looked aghast.

'Sean, Jesus, we're working.'

'Oh relax, would you?' He handed the spliff back to Magic and said, 'Right, Daniel, we're off to look for your skull. But if you're staying here, I need to lock the car. No sudden movements, or you'll set the alarm off.'

Magic, eyes closed, head back, said, 'Do I look like I'm going to be making any sudden movements?'

Gerry wasn't convinced by Michael's letter. He said, 'Sure you know what they can do on computers these days. You're sure it wasn't faked, and all he's doing is angling for a pay rise? I can't afford a pay rise.'

'You probably can,' said Rob, 'and yes, I'm sure it wasn't faked. Michael hasn't that in him.'

'Sure about that? Never judge a book by its cover.'

'With Michael, I think you probably can. He's as honest as they come.'

'That's just what he wants you to think. Newcastle probably doesn't even do journalism.'

'I'm pretty sure it does. And I can't stop him going.'

Gerry sighed. 'I know that. It's the circle of life.' They were in Rob's office. Gerry lately seemed to spend as much of his time there as he did in his own. It was distracting, but there wasn't much Rob could do about it. He continued to study his screen. Gerry said, 'I was thinking.'

'Always a dangerous thing.'

'I was thinking, the paper's been through a tough time these last few months, maybe we could all do with going out for a bit of a drink after work, you know, rebuild team spirit.'

'I've been on those before, Gerry. They usually end in a fight.'

'Aye, maybe, but why don't we give it a go anyway? Nothing too formal, just a bit of a yarn.'

Rob spotted Alix passing his door and heading for the kitchen. He lifted his cup and moved out from behind his desk. Actually leaving his office and abandoning Gerry there was often the only way to get him out of it. Though sometimes, even if he went for lunch, Gerry was still there when he got back. Rob didn't even say anything, he just took his cup and walked out.

Alix was sitting at the kitchen table. She was studying her phone while the kettle boiled. Rob stood over the kettle and said, 'Get you one?'

'No, work away.'

'Biscuit?'

'I'm fine.'

'Sure? Wagon Wheel?'

'No, thanks.'

'They really are smaller than they used to be.'

She finally looked up from her phone. 'What?'

He was holding one up. 'They're smaller, much smaller than they were when I was growing up.'

'Well, maybe that's because you're much older than I am.'

'Ouch.'

She didn't smile. She concentrated on her phone. Rob poured his coffee. Then he poured her one. When he set it before her, she didn't react.

He said, 'Are you annoyed about not getting the skull story?'

'No.'

'Are you annoyed about what happened at my apartment this morning?'

'Why would I be annoyed about that?'

'Rebecca has a way of talking to people that sounds mean, but she really isn't. She's English.'

'She was fine. I don't know what you're talking about.'

'Okay,' said Rob.

He stood by the sink, sipping his coffee.

Alix tapped on her phone.

After a minute of silence she said, 'Do you think size matters?'

'Uhm,' said Rob. 'How do you mean?'

'I mean, have you ever heard anyone complaining?'

He shifted uncomfortably. 'Well, no.'

'I mean, bigger isn't necessarily better.'

'Well, that's a relief.'

'What?'

He gave an awkward little laugh.

'No, really, what do you mean?'

'Nothing, I...' He hurriedly took a sip of his coffee – too much, too hot, and immediately started coughing. 'Sorry, sorry...'

He had dribbled down his front. His face was flushed. Alix was looking at him, perplexed.

'Anyway,' he said, 'back to the grindstone...'

He started to walk away with his cup but, before he made

it to the door, Alix laughed suddenly.

'Rob?'

He stopped.

'You do know … you do know I was talking about Wagon Wheels?'

'Yes. Of course. Clearly.'

'I looked it up. The people that make them say they're only slightly smaller than they used to be. The problem is that, when you were a kid, your hand was much smaller, so the biscuits appeared really large. It's your hand that got bigger, not the biscuit that got smaller.'

'Okay, right.' He nodded at her. 'That's good to know.'

She held up her hands. 'Do you think I've got small hands?'

'I … really don't…'

'Or average-sized hands?'

'I don't…'

'There's nothing wrong with average, is there?'

'No, not at all.'

'I mean, you wouldn't want huge big hands like a giant, or wee tiny hands like a doll, would you?'

'I suppose not.' He cleared his throat. 'Are we still talking about Wagon Wheels?'

Alix nodded slowly. 'I'm not sure,' she said, and returned her attention to her phone.

Rob stepped out of the kitchen, aware that his shirt was stuck to his back.

Alix watched him go, and a small smile appeared on her lips. Or it might have been an averaged-sized smile. She was aware that she could be evil at times, but it wasn't a Nazi kind of evil, it was a good kind. She took a sip of her coffee, then got up and took a Wagon Wheel from the packet. She unwrapped it and held it up. It did appear smaller than she remembered. She bit into it anyway. She smiled. Rob's wife probably ate a whole packet of them at a time.

It was bleak, out there. They didn't even have proper raincoats and their shoes were smooth-soled town shoes not designed for long wet grass and gorse and climbing over barbed-wire fences with tufts of torn-out wool flapping in the wind, which meant they were damp and green-kneed and swearing a lot as they battled to remain upright. Sean led the way, taking care to protect his camera more than himself, with Michael following precisely in his footsteps as they tried to avoid the cowpats, like two fey soldiers crossing a minefield in enemy territory. When they got to where they supposed Magic Martin was talking about, they found a fly-tipping mess; torn black bin bags spilling their household rubbish, mountains of rubble, and soil, and broken furniture and ancient mattresses, all at the foot of a slope with an open farm gate at the top and a lane where cars had clearly stopped and dumped their loads. There were brambles growing up through it, and nettles, and glass underfoot. It stank.

Michael and Sean stood looking at it.

'There should be a law against it,' said Sean.

'There is. Doesn't seem to make much difference.'

'What're we supposed to do with this lot? Are you going to poke through it?'

Michael shook his head. 'We could be here for months.'

'Should have brought Magic with us.'

They both nodded at what appeared to be an impenetrable mess. The rain was picking up, and the wind with it.

'Bloody hell,' said Michael.

But before Sean could respond, there was a: 'Hey! What

do you think youse are doing?'

They turned to their left, where a man was just emerging from a small copse of trees. As he advanced towards them they both saw the twin barrels of a shotgun poking from under his poncho-style yellow windcheater. Michael quickly reached into his jacket, produced his laminated press card and held it up.

He said, 'Sorry to disturb – we're from the local paper.'

The man said, 'I don't care about that, you're on private property.'

'Sorry, no ... Yes, we are...'

'You tell him, Michael,' said Sean.

The man was wearing rain-speckled glasses and had a short goatee beard; as he drew closer, he pulled the poncho back to reveal the shotgun properly. He said, 'You're trespassing.'

'Sorry,' said Michael, aware that he had apologized for the third time, 'we didn't realize you ... and we're just following up a story ... Someone reported finding something, something here ... on this land. This is your land?'

'Yes, it is, if it's any of your business.'

'They found a skull,' said Sean.

'A human skull,' added Michael.

Sean gave him a look.

'Like fuck, they did,' said the man.

'Well, he swears—'

'I don't care what he swears. Human skull! Listen, this is my land. You shouldn't be on it. No one should be on it without my say-so. I've things to be doing, animals to look after, but I spend half my time chasing people off of it and I'm pissed off. Private property is private property. Just because it's near a beach, just because there's a public walk way over there, doesn't mean youse can roam across here. Private is private. And for your information – this is a farm, has been for hundreds of years, skulls turn up here all the time. Sheep skulls, cow skulls, wild cats and badgers. But not human skulls. Animal skulls. Did whoever it was take it with him? Do you have a photo? Why're the police not swarming round here if there's a human skull?'

'We haven't been able to establish … confirm if—'

'I thought not. Listen, youse look pretty young, maybe youse haven't been doing the job that long … You don't want to be listening to every looper who comes to you with some mad story. If it's not drunks and druggies it's lampers or thieves trying to get the lead off of the roofs of the out-buildings, so I've enough to be worrying about without youse asking me about bloody human skulls. So if youse don't mind…'

He waved the barrel of the gun up the incline to the road above.

Michael said, 'Fair enough. But we're parked the other way, do you mind if we hike back across—?'

'I do actually. Take the road.'

It would add half a mile to their walk back to the car.

The rain was getting heavier, and colder.

But the man had a shotgun.

It took them several attempts to get up the hill, two steps forward, slithering three steps back because of the sodden grass and their rubbish shoes. The farmer watched them the whole time, stone-faced, comment-free.

When they finally made it, and stepped through the gate and tramped away out of his sight, Sean said, 'What a fucking ball-bag.'

'Perfectly within his rights. But yes. What a fucking ball-bag.'

'And, all the while, Magic Martin smoking his lights out

in the back of our nice and warm and dry car. He's another ball-bag.'

'We're in a world of ball-bags,' said Michael.

'What a stupid ridiculous job this is.'

'It is daft. Some drugged-out nutter comes in and says he saw something unlikely, and we scamper off like obedient puppies. I mean, bloody hell, a human skull.'

'Bloody hell, why didn't he let us walk back across his fields?'

'Just being bad for badness sake.'

'He's a mean son of a bitch.'

'And a ball-bag.'

'Definitely a ball-bag. Strutting about with a shotgun like he owns the place.'

'He does own the place.'

'Good point. But even so. Who walks about with a shotgun? He shot at Magic Martin, and if you ask me he wasn't that far off shooting at us.'

'He's fucking nuts.'

'He fucking is.'

They walked on. A car roared past and splashed them. Sean yelled after it.

A little further on, Michael said, 'Why would he have a gun?'

'To shoot people like us.'

'Yes, but I mean, why? What's he got to be scared of, cattle rustlers?'

'Some people just like guns. Makes them feel big.'

'That may be – but he was there at dawn, chasing Magic away, and he's still there now, like he's on patrol, like he's protecting something.'

'Or he's just a ball-bag and a nut.'

'Even so.'

They walked on. Veterans now, they both instinctively moved to one side as another car roared through a large puddle, and avoided the splash.

But then Michael stopped abruptly. 'Fuck this,' he said.

'Fuck this what?'

'He's hiding something. He chased us off far too easily. We should have pressed him. I should have pressed him. You should have taken his picture.'

'I did.'

'You...'

'Absolutely. No flies on me, mate.'

'Right, well. Then I was fobbed off too easily. We're going to get the car, give your man a chance to disappear, then we're coming right back to check that dump out properly. C'mon.'

Michael started up again, marching forward with new determination.

Sean stared after him, then gave a shake of his head. 'Bloody hell, Michael – he's a ball-bag and you've just grown a pair. There's hope for you yet.'

As they walked, Michael called the fount of all knowledge and asked him to find out who owned the land in question. Pete said, 'I don't need to find out, I know. Name's Derek Galvin, bit of a rogue, bit of a wheeler-dealer, been up in court quite a few times over the years, doesn't actually do much in the way of farming these days – more into scrap metal, huge piles of old cars and the like everywhere. Council are on to him all the time to clean the place up but he pays no attention. Popular opinion has it he wants planning permission for houses so he can sell the land for a fortune, but he's smack in the middle of the green belt – so he thinks if he creates enough of an eyesore they'll grant the permission as the lesser of two evils. But he's got no chance. Not there. Why, what's he up to?'

'I don't really know, but he chased us off with a shotgun.'

'Aye, sounds like him.'

'We're just heading back there now, take another wee look.'

'Well, be careful. He's a law unto himself. And you wouldn't want him to go postal on you.'

'Will do.'

Michael had no idea what going postal meant. He was too young. But he suspected it wasn't anything good. He cut the line. They were just coming up on their car. They couldn't tell if Magic Martin was still inside because the windows were all smoked up. When they opened the door Magic was lying flat out, mumbling incoherently, but with a big smile on his face. 'Don't breathe in,' said Michael as he climbed behind the wheel.

Pete sat back, clasped his hands behind his head, and said, 'Aw.'

Alix glanced back. 'What?'

'The enthusiasm of youth.'

'Michael?'

'Michael. And Sean.'

'They'll grow out of it.'

'They will. Sad, though. When I first joined here, I was seventeen. Seventeen! Seventeen. I'd never peeled a potato or kissed a girl, but I was out doing courts in my first week.'

'Was this back when the paper was printed on parchment?'

'Funny. Three and a half days of hard work, and then a day

and a night of heavy drinking and recovery. Glorious. And speaking of which, looking forward to this thing tonight? Gerry's team-building?'

'Haven't decided if I'm going,' said Alix.

'I think it's compulsory.'

'Well, that will help with the team-building.'

'It does sound like a bit of a nightmare. But maybe a chance to get to know Rob better.'

'Yup.'

'Maybe a chance to tease things out of him.'

'You mean, like, who's his favourite? Because I'm pretty sure you're not even in the top—'

'I mean, like, what he's doing here. Why he left the glorious *Guardian*.'

'Maybe he just wanted out of the rat race.'

'Leaving his wife and kids, to come here? No, there's something deep and dark there. I tried Googling, but nothing came up. Maybe I shouldn't say this, but I've a few feelers in with guys I know in England, see if they can come up with any gossip.'

'You're right,' said Alix.

'Right about?'

'You shouldn't be saying that. It's none of your business.'

'It absolutely is. We have to work with him.'

'Oh, get a life, would you, Pete?'

She turned back to her computer.

Pete said, 'No smoke without fire.'

'There's no fucking smoke!'

'Maybe you just don't want to see it.'

'Maybe you could just try shutting your cake-hole for a while.'

'Lovely. You're such a lady.'

A silence descended.

After a while Pete said, 'You just watch this space.'

Alix just kept typing.

Now that they had a good idea of the lie of the land, Michael and Sean tried to get a more specific idea from Magic Martin as to where he'd found his skull. But Magic was pretty much out of it, so they decided to release him back into the wild. Then they drove out to the farm and got their first proper view of it from the road – it was, as Pete had described, a real eyesore, with abandoned and rusting cars littering the approach to a large but equally dilapidated-looking farm-house, with various barns and out-houses in similar disrepair visible beyond. Sean took some photos, then they drove back to the rubbish-strewn field and parked in the shelter of some overhanging trees about a hundred metres from the open gates, but on an incline that gave them a view of the trees from which Farmer Galvin had emerged to chase them off.

There was no sign of him now.

Michael told Sean to stay in the car and keep an eye on the trees, and the farm itself; if he saw any movement he was to flash his lights and Michael would flee. Sean would have preferred to join in the hunt, but he could see the wisdom of Michael's plan. He told his colleague, his friend, to be careful.

'This time he'll probably shoot first and ask questions later,' he warned. 'Or *Trespassers will be executed*.'

'Thanks for that,' said Michael.

He got out of the car, still damp and green-kneed from his earlier retreat, and hurried towards the open gates. This time he picked his way cautiously down the incline, seeking out footholds and testing them before giving his full trust and weight, and made it to the bottom without further mishap.

Then he began a careful, inch by inch, examination of the dump; he mostly used his feet to turn items over, to upend bin bags, to shift sheets of corrugated metal; after ten minutes the only item of interest he had discovered was a rat that scurried away as quickly as he himself scurried backwards. He – Michael – was pleased that Sean was secure in the car and therefore out of range of hearing the yelp he let out as he confronted the creature. It was at least a foot long. And would grow bigger in the telling.

Michael was just moving to a different part of the dump, closer to the trees, when he became aware of a beeping sound, and then a mechanical rumble. He had been facing away from the road, but now that he looked up, the first thing he saw was Sean flashing the lights, and then his attention was diverted to the open gates and the lorry just reversing into them. It stopped, and the metal bin on the back began to tilt up. He could see bricks and soil and rubble – and then as the angle increased it all began to tumble out and cascade down the hill towards him, an avalanche cloaked in dust.

Michael stumbled backwards, tripped over an old tyre, and then bounced back to his feet just as he was enveloped in the cloud. Something heavy cracked into the back of his legs but he managed to stay upright and kept moving away until he found refuge behind some sturdy-looking bushes. The bin finally emptied and its load began to settle at the foot of the incline. As the cloud dissipated, Michael peered up at the lorry, and saw that the driver had climbed out and was now talking to Farmer Galvin, who was still in his yellow windcheater, and still armed and dangerous. The driver climbed back into his cab and Galvin began to shut the gates. When he had bolted them he walked away along the inside of the hedge alongside the road; before he got as far as Sean's car the incline had decreased enough for him to slip down the bank and continue across the grass towards the trees and the path leading to his farmhouse. Michael waited until he had disappeared inside before he ventured out from behind the bush. He began to smack at his trousers and jacket, trying to get the dust off while studying the bricks and masonry and branches and mud that had just been tipped. He looked back up at the gate – the fact that it was now closed and locked suggested that it had been left open because Galvin was expecting the truck, which meant that at the very least the farmer was running an illegal dump, no doubt undercutting whatever rate the local council was charging. It was, he supposed, a story, if not particularly earth-shattering.

'You all right, mate?'

It was Sean, his head just visible over the hedge.

'Sure. I'm super. I look like a bloody zombie!'

'It suits you,' said Sean.

Michael was dirty and damp, and disappointed, and embarrassed. And he would have been quite happy to be any of those things if he had gotten something out of it, but there was no making a silk purse out of this sow's ear; he had come in search of a human skull and a major news story, but that dream had literally turned to dust; all he had discovered was some pretty minor fly-tipping. That was the reality of a small-town paper. He could very easily get stuck there, for ever. But at least he had a ticket out. A memory came to him, standing there in the rain and the wind, with his nostrils filled with masonry dust and his trousers sticking to him, of watching an old movie with his mum, a movie he had loved yet found incredibly sad. She had had to persuade him to watch it because it was in black and white, and he never, ever watched them, they were from the Dark Ages, but she had persisted and because it was Christmas he'd given in and sat through *It's a Wonderful Life* and what had really struck home with him had been the main character – George Bailey? – and the way his plan to see the world was endlessly frustrated by the dull realities of small-town life. It had all worked out for poor sappy George in the end – but only after years and years and years of stultifying frustration. Michael couldn't wait for years. He would go to Newcastle. He would graduate and work for a daily paper, become a foreign correspondent, see the world, or maybe go into television, radio, there were a million...

'Michael?'

'What?'

'What the fuck is that?'

Sean was leaning on the gate now and pointing towards the top of the landslide of rubble. Michael's brow furrowed as he zoomed in on where Sean was indicating; but he was looking at whatever it was from a different angle and couldn't quite make it out; something wiry and pointed.

'Michael...'

Sean was over the fence now, and cautiously approaching the summit of the rubbish. Michael, already in a mess, negotiated his way up the hill slightly faster, so that they converged on the object at just about the same time.

They both looked down at it.

It was, without doubt, even caked with soil, the skeletal frame of a human hand.

Michael said, 'Correct me if I'm wrong, but last time I checked, sheep don't have hands.'

'Holy shit.'

'Bingo,' said Michael.

As Sean took his photos, he said, 'Shouldn't we be calling the—?'

'Yep,' said Michael. 'But not yet.'

He looked about him, found an old blue plastic crate, upended it and then placed it over the hand to protect it from any disturbance.

He wiped off his own hands and said, 'Okay – if we move fast enough, we'll still be able to catch it.'

'It?'

'The lorry, Sean – the lorry. C'mon…'

Michael climbed onto the top of the gate, jumped down and hurried towards the car. Sean scrambled to catch up. As he drew level he said, 'Are you sure about this? Isn't it like a murder scene or something? What if we leave it and the farmer comes and moves—'

'It's not a murder scene.'

'How can you possibly know…?'

'Well, I don't – I'm guessing. Look – if Magic found a skull at dawn this morning, then it was probably dumped there just like the hand was, but sometime yesterday. The hand looks ancient, so even if it is a murder it was probably years ago. Common sense says the skull and the hand are connected and must come from the same site, and probably dumped in the landfill by the same truck or at least the same company. So, if we can follow the truck back to wherever it's come from, we'll have a much better idea of what's going on.'

They reached the car. Sean opened the driver's side door, but then paused before he clicked the lock on the passenger side. He looked across the top of the car at Michael and said, 'Gee whizz, Sherlock, you've got it all worked out.' Michael smiled back. 'Or you're talking a pile of shite and giving the farmer time to hide the evidence.'

Michael nodded. 'There's always that possibility.'

There wasn't much traffic to slow them down, but the same would be true of the lorry. It had maybe a five-minute start. Neither of them remembered any logos on it because they'd been concentrating on the actual dumping, but now as Sean drove he handed his camera to Michael and told him to scroll back through his pictures to see if there were any identifying marks. Sean had taken a lot of photos, but all necessarily from one angle: there was nothing on that side to indicate the lorry's origins; however, he had captured the licence plate. If they'd been cops they could have run the plates there and then – but they were able to access the next best thing, Pete, who knew everyone and had connections everywhere. Michael called it in. Pete asked for an explanation. Michael said, later. He didn't want to run the risk of Pete or more probably Rob telling him to report their discovery to the police immediately. He wanted to get the story first. He *needed* to get the story first.

'There!'

They were barely onto the ring road and there it was – labouring along at just under the speed limit, like a pensioner with cataracts. Michael fell in just a couple of cars back. When he glanced across, Sean was smiling at him. Michael smiled back, no words required. Another mile further along and the lorry turned off onto Millbank Road. Another few hundred metres and it arrived at a building site next to St Patrick's Church. According to the billboard that towered above the site, a shopping centre with luxury apartments was under construction with a completion date the following year. They couldn't quite tell how far advanced the building was because there was a wooden fence at least six foot tall surrounding the site.

Sean drummed his fingers on the steering wheel for a few seconds, then indicated and pulled across traffic into a car park in the grounds of St Patrick's. Millbank Road had a steadily rising gradient; with the church being slightly further up that road it meant that anyone standing in its grounds could, from a certain position, get a clear view over the fence surrounding the building site. Sean parked at the highest point and they both got out. They peered over the dry-stone wall that was the boundary of the church grounds and across the building site, which was basically a large muddy field with one small part dug out with trenches and pegged with wooden stakes, while closer to the wall there were diggers excavating and then dropping their loads into the back of a lorry, which, as they watched, was joined by the one they had just followed.

Sean took more photos. Michael turned and studied the church behind them. It was a former monastery that, more than a thousand years before, had served as a university, one of the largest in Europe, until repeated sackings by marauding Vikings took their toll and it gradually faded from significance. They had both attended events here in the course of their work. Funerals, charity auctions, gigs by visiting bands taking advantage of the church's ancient and marvellous acoustics. There was a brand-new hall behind the church in which Michael had recently endured a badly produced, poorly acted and over-long pantomime. He said as much in his review, and had then received at least a dozen calls from irate parents calling him every name under the sun. One furious mother had actually threatened to arrange to have his legs broken. Rob had allowed the review to appear in the paper as a lesson to him in small-town journalism – don't apply West End standards to amateur productions. 'We're here to celebrate their endeavours,' he'd said, 'not to tear them apart. It's not a news story, so look for the positive. Every time you mention that Jimmy did this or Katie did that, the parents rush out and buy multiple copies of the paper for all their relations. That works for us financially, plus the parents feel good about the paper and hopefully go out and buy one next week as well.' The minister, who had written the panto-mime, and directed it, was particularly vitriolic in his attack on the paper in general and Michael in particular. And now he was standing behind them, asking what they were doing on church property.

Michael said, 'Reverend Erskine, I hope you don't mind but—'

'I do mind. This is private property. And particularly where you are concerned, Michael Foster.'

'Ah,' said Michael.

'Yes, indeed.'

'Sorry about that – got a bit carried away.'

'Yes, you did. Apparently I can't direct traffic.'

'It was supposed to be a funny...'

'Not many of us were laughing.'

It was on the tip of his tongue to say, 'A bit like the panto...' But he held it and tried to change the subject. 'We just wanted a closer look at what they're building.'

'I'd rather you asked permission.'

'We didn't see anyone around,' said Sean. 'Oh – and I should drop round those pics of *Puss'n'Boots* – didn't they look great in the paper?'

Rev Erskine hesitated before giving the young photogra-pher a begrudging nod. With that he seemed to soften a little; he shook his head at Michael and stepped up beside them. He gazed out across the building site. 'They'll be at it for a year yet,' he said, 'so what's so interesting?'

'Well, some drug-addled—' Sean began, before Michael cut him off with, 'There's some issue with fly-tipping. May be nothing.'

'Well – they're a big enough company, I don't see why they'd be indulging in that kind of nonsense.'

'You have many dealings with them, Reverend Erskine?' Michael asked.

'Well, initially, yes, of course. There was some haggling, but since the deal went through, I'd say we've gotten along famously.'

'Deal? How do you mean exactly?'

The minister's brow furrowed. 'Do you never read your own paper?' Before Michael could answer he carried on: 'They bought the land from us. You covered it in quite a big way.'

'Oh, I—'

'How else do you think we could afford our lovely new hall? And a community centre to come. It's been a real windfall for us. You do know all about the new hall, don't you?'

'Well, yes, I—'

'You know, the hall where that calamitous, poorly directed hodgepodge of stale jokes was only recently presented?'

'Oh *that* new hall. Right enough.'

'Now – if you don't mind?'

Rev Erskine nodded across the car park towards the gates. Clearly he hadn't softened *that* much.

'Do you mind if I just get a few more pics?' Sean asked.

'I do, actually,' the minister replied stiffly. 'And next time, call our press office. I'm sure it won't be a problem, but there's a right way to do things.' He raised an impatient eyebrow.

'Fair enough,' said Michael.

They thanked him again and turned away, leaving Rev

Erskine looking out over the building site.

As they approached the car, Sean muttered, 'People are really frickin' touchy, aren't they?'

'You can say that again,' said Michael.

So he did.

Alix was at the office window, looking out at Rob on the corner outside, talking to Rebecca-of-the-huge-hips and their two children. She couldn't remember their names, though she was sure she'd been told. What's more, she didn't care. Janine came up beside her and tut-tutted. Alix asked what she was tut-tutting for and Janine said, 'The body language, it's not good.' Right enough, Rebecca-of-the-big-ass was leaning back against a car with her arms folded. Alix thought, 'It's a wonder it doesn't collapse under her,' but resisted the temptation to say it out loud. However, looking at Janine, seeing the slight smirk on her face, she guessed she was probably thinking the same thing. We're such bitches, she thought, but hey-ho. Then the little family idyll was interrupted as Sean and Michael swung into the car park and stopped briefly beside Rob. Words were exchanged, then Rob turned to kiss his kids; there was what Alix thought was an awkward hug with Rebecca-of-the-elephant-legs.

Alix was back at her desk as Rob, Sean and Michael entered editorial. Michael had a large book under his arm. Rob asked her and Pete to join them in his office. The two boys looked flushed with excitement. Rob cleared space on his desk and Michael opened the book up and set it down before them. He jabbed his finger at an illustration – an old map. Pete let out a bit of a sigh as he looked down at it – 'Is this something to do with the sheep skull?' he asked.

'Sheep skull? Bollocks to that,' said Sean.

'You better bring them up to speed,' said Rob.

As Michael breathlessly told them about the morning's events Rob smiled to himself – weekly newspaper reporting could be a bit of a drudge, so it was great to see the cub so excited about getting his clutches on a great story. He had them in stitches, too, talking about Magic Martin being out of his tree in the back of the car, and conveyed a real sense of menace when confronted by Farmer Galvin and his shotgun.

'So we followed the truck back to beside St Patrick's and we were just looking at this building site, you know where the new shopping centre's going up? Then Reverend Erskine appears and starts giving out about his panto...'

'It was shite,' said Sean, 'and I had to go three nights in a row.'

'...when he lets slip that the church used to own the land the shops are going up on, and it just struck a chord with me, so we went straight down to the library.'

'Your favourite place,' said Rob.

'It is now. Yer woman there loved the article I did, and when I explained what I was looking for she lent me this...' He tapped the book on the table. '...which isn't usually out on display or available to borrow because it's so old and valuable and anything with maps in kids tend to tear out or colour in ... and as soon as I saw this map I knew we'd hit the jackpot. You see this is a map of old Bangor *circa* 1890. Of course it's—'

'It's a graveyard!' said Sean, jabbing a finger at the map, 'and they're digging up bloody skeletons!'

Michael glared at him.

'Sorry,' said Sean, only a little embarrassed, 'but get to the point.'

'Right. Thanks for the advice.' Another shake of the head.

'We believe the developers, having purchased the land from the church, have discovered an old graveyard, which we can see clearly marked on the map here.'

'I hope it doesn't turn out like *Poltergeist*,' said Rob.

Pete nodded. The others looked at him.

Sean said, '*Wah?*'

'Doesn't matter,' said Rob, 'old movie reference ... Please continue...'

'Right, okay,' said Michael, 'so what we're thinking is that if a developer, builder, anyone, turns up human remains, then they are obliged to inform the authorities, and there has to be a full investigation, maybe even an inquest. That can take months, maybe even years, and with a big project like this clearly is, it could cost them hundreds of thousands of pounds, maybe cause them to lay off workers because of the delay. So what if instead they say nothing and come to an arrangement with Galvin to dump the evidence on his private property where there's less chance of someone stumbling across it?'

'Enter Magic Martin in search of mushrooms,' said Sean.

Rob was nodding, lips pursed. 'You haven't spoken to the developers about this yet?'

'Nope.'

'The church?'

'Nope.'

'And Galvin?'

'Nope, and when I do it'll be by phone. I've no desire to have my arse shot off.'

Rob nodded at Alix. 'Do you want to get on to Reverend Erskine, see if you can tease anything else out of him...?'

'But it's my—' Michael began.

'Yes of course it is,' said Rob, 'but given your pantomime past we might get more joy with Alix asking the questions.'

'Well, he said to go through the press office, so I could phone—'

'Yes, do that, but you know what they're like – you end up with the bland leading the bland.'

'Let me handle Erskine,' said Pete. 'I know him pretty well. Our wedding was there.'

'You're married?' Alix asked, though she did of course already know. 'Sure, who would have you?'

'I'll have you know,' said Pete, 'that I used to be quite the catch.'

'*Where?*'

Pete sneered up his top lip.

They discussed it for another while, with Rob keeping a close eye on Michael. He was contributing enthusiastically, but he could detect a little hiccup of fear that the story might indeed be taken away from him and put into more experienced hands. Rob had no intention of it but, with a big story and deadline approaching, both experience and teamwork were essential. Michael was still very much learning the ropes. But, as Rob dismissed them, he made sure to congratulate him on getting the story, and within earshot of the others. Michael glowed. Pete said, 'It's not done yet.' Sean pointed at himself and said, 'What about me?'

'Well done, you,' said Rob, 'though I haven't seen a single photo yet, so that may be premature.'

'You will,' said Sean, 'and they'll knock your socks off.'

He didn't lack for confidence, that one, Rob thought, returning to his desk and leaving them to get on with it. When he looked up again, Alix was in his doorway. She glanced behind her, then stepped into the office and half-closed the door. She asked him if everything was okay.

'As far as I'm aware,' he said, his brow furrowed, 'unless you know something...?'

She smiled and said, 'Sorry – couldn't help but see you outside with ... Rebecca ... and the kids...'

'Oh. Yes. Right. Fine. Just saying goodbye. On their way back to England.'

'Oh. I see.'

'Nursery school – places like gold dust. You don't take them, you lose them.'

'That'll be hard. Your kids.'

'It will.'

He nodded. She nodded. She turned and opened the door.

'Alix?'

'Yup?'

'Thanks.'

'Nothing to thank me for. Just if you were leaving, then there'd be a job going – you know what they say about the early bird?'

She continued on out.

Michael didn't get anywhere with the developers, who denied everything; the church press office promised to get back, but hadn't yet and that was two hours ago; even Pete couldn't track down a phone number for Farmer Galvin. Rob knew denial would be their default position, but that more than likely they'd be panicking. Sean brought his photos in and they were as good as ever. Rob spent a long time looking at the skeletal hand, poking out of the debris, as if it was clutching despairingly at life itself. He knew they were on something of a sticky wicket, because Michael and Sean had not only trespassed on private property, but had also themselves failed to alert the authorities about what they had discovered. They had the photo as evidence, of course, but it wasn't proof, it couldn't be examined forensically; for that, they would need the hand itself. Rob pondered that for a while – if they'd found the skull Magic Martin had claimed to have found and returned with that, then they could certainly have been blamed for disturbing a potential crime scene. But as they had actually witnessed the hand being dumped on Galvin's farm and knew it had come from the shopping-centre building site, then that was clearly a different situation. Galvin might or might not know about the human remains; but he was certainly complicit in the dumping. If Galvin, after discovering the reporters on his land, got curious or was tipped off by the developers, he would very quickly move to dispose of whatever human remains were now showing up. But whether to call the police to tell them now or secure the story?

Rob moved to his office door and asked Pete if he'd talked to Reverend Erskine. Pete said he was waiting for him to call back. Rob asked if he should give him a call. 'No,' said Pete, 'because he thinks you're the anti-Christ.'

'Because of *Puss'n'Boots*?'

'Exactly. You know he ranted and railed against you from the pulpit?'

'Really?'

'He told us all to stop buying the paper.'

'I hope you stood up for me. For us.'

'I hid behind my New Testament.'

'Good to know. And in fact, have sales dipped?'

'Nope. They've increased.'

'There you go. *Bangor Express*, bigger than Jesus. Why don't you take a run out and see him?'

'Me?'

215

'Sure. The personal connection might work. Eye to eye. Threaten to join the Presbyterians if he doesn't play ball.'

'Well I'm a bit snowed under with all the subbing. I'm sure he'll be back to me soon enough.'

'I'll handle the subbing.' Rob nodded at Michael, busy on another call. 'And, sure, take the young whippersnapper with you.'

'But Michael actually wrote the—'

'Yes, he did. It's a bridge-building exercise. Or bridge-burning, depending on how it goes.'

'Well, if you insist.' Pete reluctantly lifted his jacket off the back of his chair.

Alix swung round in her's. 'Did I hear that right? You're going out on a story?'

'Yes, it's not so—'

'How will your agoraphobia deal with that?'

'I haven't got—'

'Really? *Really*?'

'You're very funny, Alix. Hilarious. If only you put as much effort into your writing.'

'Ouch,' said Alix.

Michael came off the phone. He saw Pete with his jacket on and asked what was going on.

'He's going out on a story,' said Alix.

'What about the agoraphobia?' Michael asked.

Alix snorted. Michael gave her a wink.

Peter shook his head. 'Michael Foster,' he said, 'Pantomime Correspondent, for life.'

'Is that a threat?' Michael asked.

'Yes.'

'Bring it on,' said Michael.

But his face fell a bit when Pete told him he was to

accompany him to St Patrick's. He looked to Rob, still in the doorway, who confirmed it with a nod.

Pete said, 'Should we take Sean as well?'

Sean looked up from his computer. Rob shook his head. 'It'll look like a company day out if you turn up en masse. Besides, I've something else for you.'

Rob turned back into his office, indicating for Sean to follow.

Pete nodded at Michael. 'Right, let's get going. And tell you what? How about you let me do all the talking. Watch the master at work, eh?'

Peter walked ahead.

Michael said under his breath, 'Watch you lick Erskine's arse, more like.'

Alix sniggered.

'Did I say that out loud?' Michael asked.

'Yep,' said Alix, 'but maybe not loud enough.'

Pete could tell from Michael's sour face that he wasn't looking forward to seeing Reverend Erskine again. Pete told him to relax. 'What you have to remember about ministers, politicians, anyone who sticks their head above the parapet, is they usually like the sound of their own voices and they don't take well to criticism. Yer man Erskine is expected to get up in a pulpit every week and get on like he has a hotline to God. That tends to give you a big head. Just be pleasant to him. His bark is worse than his bite.'

'He's an ignorant old shit is what he is.'

'He's not so bad. And what do you mean, old? He's younger than I am.'

'I rest my case.'

Pete made a face.

They found Rev Erskine setting out chairs in the community hall or, as Michael muttered as their footsteps echoed on the polished wooden floor, at the scene of the crime.

Rev Erskine looked up as they approached, smiled at Pete and then his face visibly darkened as his gaze fell on Michael. 'Peter,' he said, 'and the critic. How's Fiona coming along?'

'Grand,' said Pete, 'really looking forward to her confirmation.'

'Sure about that? I don't think anyone really looks forward to their confirmation. So I take it you're here for professional reasons?'

'Yes, of course – but also to clear the air if we could, as far as young Michael here is concerned. He did rather go to town on *Puss'n'Boots*...'

Michael immediately cut in with, 'I was only giving my—'

'Michael?' Pete had his hand raised to quiet him. 'Please? Hear me out.'

It took a mighty effort to bite his tongue.

'Thank you,' said Pete. 'Reverend Erskine – Michael is entitled to his opinion, no one disputes that?' The minister hesitated before giving a brief nod. 'And let's face it – he was never going to enjoy *Puss'n'Boots*, no more than I would enjoy a ... a ... Metallica concert...'

'Metall—?' Rev Erskine began.

'Heavy metal band,' said Pete, 'and if I was forced to sit through one of their concerts and then write about it I'm sure I wouldn't hold back. But it's the job of the editor to decide the difference between fair comment and a hatchet job. In this case, the editor made a mistake, and I've spoken to him about it and he held up his hands and asked me to apologize to you, he shouldn't have allowed it through. He does hope no lasting damage has been done to our relationship, which has over the years been very good, and mutually beneficial.'

Michael was literally biting his tongue.

'Well,' said Rev Erskine, 'it wasn't so much me – I felt sorry for the kids, they put in so much effort ... but, but, if he sincerely ... and he holds up his ... and it doesn't happen again ... then, I'm sure we can ... work something out...'

'That would be great, and much appreciated, wouldn't it, Michael?'

'Yes,' said Michael, who could now literally taste blood in his mouth.

'Good. Excellent. Now ... an equally delicate matter. And let me say first, we're not trying to cause any trouble, but it's something that's been brought to us by a reader and we can't ignore it...'

'Is it the theft of lead from the church roof?'

'No, Reverend – I think we covered that a few weeks ago?'

'Aye, you did, fair enough. Although it worked more like an advertisement than a news story – they came back the next week and took what was left. Okay, Peter, it's not about the lead. I know that – it's about the bones...'

He drew the *bones* out, made it almost musical, but also scary. Hallowe'en bones.

'So you're aware of—?'

'Only what the press office has told me.'

'I didn't speak to—' said Michael.

'No, but you did call the developers, and they called our press office, and the press office called me. With instructions.'

'Instructions?' asked Peter.

'Instructions to say nothing. About the bones. But given our new state of brotherly love ... Look, Peter, what I will say is this – yes, there was a graveyard, dating right back to the old monastery. But it hadn't had any new customers in over two hundred years. When the land was sold, must be seven or eight years ago now, all of the remains were disinterred and transferred to a different site, all with the blessing of the bishop, the local council, the Department of the Environment, God knows who else, but there were a million pieces of paper that had to be signed. And I do believe it was fully reported in your paper at the time.'

'Why didn't they go ahead with the building back then?' Michael asked.

'I really don't know, but I imagine that's what developers do – buy up land so that they can develop it when the time or market is right.'

'But what if, when you were moving the graves, you missed some of them? What if...?'

'Sorry, Reverend,' said Pete, 'he's like a dog with a ... bone...'

'And that's not a problem, I'm all for enthusiasm, but in this case, young man, you're barking up the wrong tree. We're talking about many hundreds of years some of those coffins were in the ground, they degenerate, the ground shifts, I think it's inevitable that something might have been left behind.'

'Exactly!'

'I mean that we're talking about fragments.'

'Absolutely,' said Pete, 'not like entire skeletons and—'.

'Exactly. Frag—'

'Fragments?' said Michael, producing his phone and flourishing it as if he was suddenly revealing the crucial and damning evidence in a murder trial, 'You call this a fragment?'

Rev Erskine peered at the screen. His brow furrowed. He peered closer. Pete looked in too. His eyes flitted up to

Michael, confused. Michael squinted at the screen.

'And that's my cat. But this ... this is a hand. An entire hand. If there's an entire hand then—'

'Then somehow it got separated, perhaps washed away. But I can assure you – those poor people, our ancestors, were all treated with the dignity they deserved, and if by accident, and through no one's fault – some ... small parts were somehow left behind, then they will be equally well treated if and when they are brought to our attention. I'm sure this happens all the time with building projects that are close to populated areas, and I'm equally sure that respectable newspapers don't make such a song and dance about it. So let that be the end of it, eh?' Rev Erskine nodded at them, then glanced at his watch. 'Now, I've to get these chairs out in time for choir practice tonight. We would normally do it in the church, but with the lead gone and the slates falling off it's cosier in here ... I don't suppose you'd care to give me a hand?'

'Love to,' said Pete, 'but—'

'I know, stories to write, deadlines to meet! Never mind – I'm glad we had a chat, and I'm happy we've sorted everything out, I do so hate a frosty atmosphere. Though next time – maybe someone else for the panto, eh?'

He gave a little giggle, which to Michael sounded forced.

The minister put out his hand and Pete shook it enthusiastically. Michael, less so. His urge was to pretend to shake it and instead raise his thumb to his mouth and wave his fingers like a six-year-old might. But, of course, he didn't. He gave what he hoped was a good, firm, manly handshake. Rev Erskine nearly crushed his fingers.

As they left the hall, and satisfied that they were well out of earshot, Michael said, 'What a lot of crap.'

'How do you mean?'

'They've been caught out, and they're scrambling to cover their arses with niceness.'

'Michael, he's trying to help us, you, by not making us look like idiots by blowing this up into something it isn't.'

'You mean you actually fell for that shite?'

'I didn't fall for anything. There may be some bone fragments. It happens. We really shouldn't be making a big deal of it.'

'It's *absolutely* what we should be doing – church sells land to big business for profit without taking due care of the poor souls buried on its land. Great story!'

They were at the car. They glared at each other over the top of it.

'Well, we won't be running it.'

'Excuse me?'

'I'm sorry.' Pete drummed his fingers on the roof. 'Look, Michael, even if there is something in it, and I don't think there is, sometimes you have to remember who you are, and sometimes you have to look at the bigger picture.'

'You mean because I'm just a cub reporter I should listen to my elders and so-called betters?'

'No, I mean you should remember we're a community newspaper – here to serve that community, not to make things worse. If we run a story about bones being turned up, then that shopping centre could be held up for months, maybe even years. The developer might even decide it's not worth the effort and withdraw altogether. As it is, the project is bringing jobs, it's helping to regenerate the community, it's certainly been of huge benefit to the church – you want all that to disappear just so you can get your name on the front page of the paper?'

'It's not about that!'

'Isn't it?'

Pete opened the door and climbed in.

It was five minutes back to the office. Michael resolved to say nothing more, but he couldn't help himself.

'Did Rob really apologize for running my review?'

'No, of course he didn't. Does he ever apologize for anything?'

'Then why on earth did you—'

'Because it works. You tell them what they want to hear, suddenly they're co-operative, and they never dream of checking it out. Everyone's happy.'

'I'm not bloody happy!'

'Well, you,' Pete said with a wink, 'don't matter.'

Michael was still seething when they got back. He desperately wanted to rat Pete out to Rob, and was on the verge of saying something – he seemed eternally on the verge of saying something, and was very much aware of it – when Rob called them both into the office. Alix was already in there, together with Sean, who was looking pretty pleased with himself. There was a blue plastic crate upended on Rob's desk that Michael immediately recognized as the one he'd used to cover the skeletal hand before they'd left Galvin's farm. He immediately smiled – maybe he wouldn't have to say anything. Pete had gone along with Rev Erskine's dismissal of the photo of the hand, but actually seeing it in the office, up close and physical, would surely change his mind.

Rob said, 'So how did it go?'

'Grand,' said Pete, 'though not sure if there's a story there. Turns out the graves were moved five or six years ago, and we covered it at the time in the paper. Before your time, Rob, and I'd forgotten about it completely. Rev Erskine acknowledged the hand, and doesn't deny there's a possibility of other bone fragments and the like turning up...' Michael let out a sigh. '... but would appreciate it if you didn't make too much of a fuss because of the impact it could have on the shopping centre.'

Rob nodded. Alix *hmmmmd*.

'Well, that sounds like a lot of bollocks,' said Sean.

Rob said, 'To be fair, Reverend Erskine maybe isn't aware of the full extent of the problem.'

He gave Sean a nod. The photographer leaned forward and lifted the blue crate; Michael kept his eyes on Pete, waiting to see the face that the word crestfallen was created for.

Pete's eyes widened. He said, 'Fuck a duck.'

Michael snorted. He then looked at the crate himself and immediately said, 'Fuck a duck.'

Skulls.

Three of them.

Hollow-eyed – yet somehow staring.

'Fuck a fucking duck,' Michael added, for clarification.

The photo of the three skulls was mesmeric and frightening. Gerry peered at it for a long time and then said, 'I see the hunger strike was successful.' He glanced up at Rob and said, 'Bad taste?'

Rob ignored him. Janine was in the office with them. She ignored him as well.

'It's a moral conundrum,' said Rob, 'and it's only right that we talk it through.'

'I face moral conundrums every day,' said Gerry.

'I'm not sure I'm aware of the concept,' said Janine.

'Well,' Rob began, 'it's when—'

'She knows fine well,' said Gerry. 'She's asking how someone like herself, without morals, can possibly have a moral conundrum.'

'Business is cut-throat,' said Janine, 'we can't afford morals.'

'See?'

Rob shook his head. 'It boils down to this. We're a community paper. We've discovered an illegal act which, if we expose it, might also damage that community.'

'There will be at least fifteen stores in the shopping centre,' said Janine, 'all potential advertisers.'

'Exactly,' said Gerry, 'we have to be pragmatic.'

'On the other hand,' said Janine, 'it would be a big story, we'd sell more copies, we could possibly hike up the advertising rates on the back of it – a known quantity, a short-term gain, as opposed to an unknown quantity. The shopping centre is at least a year away, and there's no guaranteeing we'll be around to see it.'

'Thanks for the vote of confidence there, Janine,' said Gerry.

'You wanted pragmatic, you got pragmatic.'

Gerry rubbed his hands together. 'Oh, fuck it,' he said, 'run the bloody thing. We're a newspaper, and stories like this don't come along very often. I can't spend money I haven't got and from where we're standing the shopping centre might as well be a million years away. So go for it.'

Rob nodded.

Janine smiled at Gerry. 'Not like you,' she said. 'Usually you're sitting on the fence.'

'Aye, well,' said Gerry, 'my bum was getting numb. Rob, when I hired you, I promised you complete editorial freedom and I've not stopped you from printing anything yet. That's not going to change.'

'Appreciate it,' said Rob.

Gerry turned for the door. Janine went with him. But Gerry stopped then and turned back, a quizzical look on his face. 'You were going to run it anyway, weren't you?'

'Yes, of course. I just thought it would be polite to run it past you.'

Gerry shook his head. 'I still own this paper. That desk of yours, it's mine. Your chair – it belongs to me.'

'You might own my desk and chair,' said Rob, with a smile, 'but you'll never own my soul.'

'I don't want your fucking soul. Just sell me some papers. You still coming for drinks tonight?'

'Are you buying?'

Gerry laughed. 'Good one,' he said and walked out.

Janine nodded back at Rob. 'He's serious,' she said.

'I know,' said Rob.

Alix, Janine, Gerry and Pete were all going home first and meeting up in the bar later. Rob, behind on the subbing, worked on. He didn't mind – he could get more done without the reporters constantly knocking on his door, or the phone ringing incessantly with requests for photo bookings, though truth be told he wasn't much looking forward to Gerry's night out; it was both prescriptive and conscriptive, a social drinking experiment which was bound to backfire. It was after eight when he finally decided enough was enough. When he left his office he was surprised to find Michael was still at his desk. The rest of editorial was in darkness, but Michael had his desk-lamp on and was leaning back in his chair, shirt open, sleeves rolled up, slowly tapping the phone receiver against the tip of his chin and muttering to himself. He nearly toppled over backwards when Rob suddenly appeared beside him. He said 'Fuck!' and made a grab for the desk; he just managed to hold on and then right himself. He gave Rob an embarrassed grin and said, 'Sorry, didn't realize you were still here. And these guys are spooking me.'He reached up to the lamp and angled it so that it shone on the shelf beside his desk – the three skulls.

'Right enough,' said Rob. 'You should put them in a drawer or something.'

Michael shook his head. 'They're scary but also ... I don't know, they're also kind of ... inspiring? They're keeping an eye on me, anyway. Making sure I do this properly.'

'And are you?'

'I don't know. Obviously we have these guys, and the hand ... but it's not enough, is it? We need people to react but they're just saying nothing. If there was some way to date the skulls, find descendants or ... someone to get angry. But everywhere I turn it's a PR girl saying there's no story here, local councillors are the same, don't want to risk the shopping centre not happening or annoy Reverend Erskine, it's like a bloody conspiracy.'

'It's not a conspiracy,' said Rob, 'it's *Chinatown*.'

'It's wah...?'

Rob sighed. 'It's a movie. Like *Poltergeist*. But nothing like *Poltergeist*. Just go and see it, then you'll understand.'

'I haven't time for—'

'C'mon – enough for tonight. Did you forget about Gerry's party?'

'I think I'd be better—'

'No – and that's an order.' Rob slipped Michael's jacket off the back of his chair and held it out for him. Michael rose reluctantly. He nodded at the skulls. 'I should put them in the drawer, otherwise the cleaners will have a fit.'

The mop women came in in the early hours. Michael had never actually set eyes on them, or seen any evidence of their work. There were cobwebs everywhere.

Rob, who had, said, 'They'll more likely use them for ashtrays. C'mon.'

Rob locked up, and together they headed to Fury's in King Street. Gerry, Janine, Pete, Alix and Sean were standing rather awkwardly at the bar, drinks in hand. As they approached Gerry said, 'At last, now the party can get started.' Everyone nodded pessimistically. 'What'll you be having?'

Seven pints later, with some whiskey chasers, Rob could barely stand and Michael was off being sick in the toilets. The barman had called last orders and was shepherding them out. It was gone midnight. They staggered back to the office. Gerry let them in. He produced an ancient looking CD player and began to blast out Rory Gallagher and then Van Morrison. Janine found a bottle of vodka in her desk and a duty-free carton of Regal Kingsize. Gerry went to his desk and found a bottle of whiskey and a duty-free carton of Regal as well. Pete compared the price tags and language on the cigarettes and saw they'd been bought in the same airport shop in Tenerife, which he deduced meant Gerry and Janine had been on holiday together. Gerry said it wasn't a holiday, they were at a conference. It was purely business. 'Apart from the times we were screwing,' said Janine and cackled. 'Right enough,' said Gerry, 'there was a lot of screwing.' Rob opened up Michael's drawer and removed one of the skulls. He held it up and said, 'Alas, poor Yorick, I knew him well.' Sean said, 'Who the fuck is Yorick?' Rob said, 'Used to play inside right for Linfield.' Pete said, 'You got it wrong. The quote. You got it completely wrong.'

'I think not,' said Rob.

'I think so. It's not *I knew him well*. It's *I knew him, Horatio*.'

'Bollocks it is,' said Rob.

'It fucking is.'

'I don't know either of them,' said Michael. 'Yorick or Horatio.'

'Who's Horatio?' Sean asked.

'He played outside right,' said Rob.

Pete stumbled away, saying he had a book of quotations somewhere. Rob went to the toilet. When he came out, Janine was waiting for him. She pounced, locking her lips onto his with hooverish aggression. Rob managed to disentangle himself by pretending he was going to be sick. Alix saw the whole thing and was doubled over laughing. Janine reeled away. Rob told Alix it wasn't funny. Alix said it was hysterical. They got very close. Nose to nose.

'Are you planning something?' she asked.

'I don't know. Do I have planning permission?'

She said, 'The jury's out.'

He suggested they move round the corner into the morgue – the repository of all their old newspapers and notebooks and photographs – to discuss it further but she said, 'We are not having sex in the morgue!' and they started laughing again and moved even closer but then Pete came bounding round the corner with the skull in his hand, raising it high and crying out, 'Alas, poor Yorick. I knew him, Horatio!' and waving a piece of ragged paper he'd torn out of whatever book he'd found, and the moment was gone.

Gradually, gradually it wound down. The alcohol ran out and their drunken energy dissipated. Pete could hardly stand, so a taxi was called for him. Alix of all people helped him out to it. Then she looked back at the office, at Rob standing talking animatedly to Gerry. She sighed, and then climbed into the back of the cab beside Pete.

Rob didn't realize she was gone until about twenty minutes later when Gerry staggered off to the toilet, flushed with the drink but happy that his team-bonding exercise seemed to have gone so well. Rob saw that Michael was sitting at his computer. When he came up behind him, he saw that he had his story about the skulls up on his screen. Michael looked up at him and said, 'I don't know what to do. Pete's right, this is a community paper, we should be protecting jobs, but still, bloody hell – I've three human skulls in my drawer.' To prove it, he opened the drawer. 'I call them the Good, the Bad and the Ugly.'

Rob laughed. 'At last, a movie you've heard of!'

'How do you mean? What movie?'

Rob sighed. He nodded at the screen. 'It is a conundrum,' he said, 'but not one that you have to worry about. You just write the best story you can, and let me worry about whether we use it or not.'

Michael nodded gratefully. 'And when do you think you'll decide what—?'

Rob had raised his hand to quiet him. He also had his phone clamped to his ear. He said, 'Police, please.'

A moment later he said, 'Hello, yes – I want to report a murder.'

Michael's mouth dropped open.

'Yes,' said Rob, 'there's a body hidden on a building site next to St Pat's church in Bangor.'

And then he hung up.

'That,' he said, 'will put a cat amongst the pigeons, and guarantee that we've absolutely no excuse not to publish the story.'

Michael said, 'I can't believe you did that.'

'An anonymous phone call to set things in motion. That's why I get paid the big bucks,' said Rob.

'I heard that,' said Gerry, finally returning from the toilet, 'and it's a damned lie.'

'Ahm…?' said Michael. Rob looked at him. 'It wasn't exactly anonymous, if you called from your own phone, was it?'

Rob suddenly looked troubled.

'And that,' said Gerry, 'is exactly why I don't pay him the big bucks. Now, where the bloody hell am I going to get another drink from at this time of night?'

CHAPTER 6
THE EAGLE HAS CRASH LANDED

Rob was a hero. Absolutely no doubt about it. He saved a young woman's life. He gave her the kiss of life. 'Even if she didn't need it,' said Pete, and they all laughed as they scoffed the buns Alix bought to celebrate his selfless act.

The thing about journalism – about *reporting* – is that mostly you're reporting after the fact, you're not usually there when major news events occur, or even minor ones. But sometimes, sometimes, right place, right time. And occasionally you become part of the story. Rob was only there because he was doing something that he really should have delegated to one of his team. Someone, possibly angered at featuring in one of their stories, or maybe it was just a passing vandal, but anyway, someone had spray-painted the word 'tit' across the delivery van. It was in silver paint, and in large letters, and it was very noticeable. It had happened exactly a week ago, and Gerry kept promising to have it removed, but nothing seemed to happen. Rob wasn't exactly filled with confidence when Gerry said, 'Sure, there's no such thing as bad advertising,' while Janine rolled her eyes and said, 'That's bollocks.'

Sean, who used the van more than most, scooting around town to take his photographs, said that he would be in severe danger of biting off his own tongue if he had to put up with another week of people calling him a tit or, even worse, joked about him driving the tit-mobile. But still Gerry wouldn't come up with the petty cash to have it cleaned off, so Rob just threw up his hands and said he would get it done himself. He was pretty sure it wouldn't take long – one of those high-powered hoses would do the job, and didn't he pass a car wash every morning on the drive into work? He'd nip out in the van at lunchtime and get it done and then present the receipt to Gerry and demand that he immediately make good on it, and if he didn't come up with the cash he'd ... probably do nothing much. But it still needed to be done. The tit-mobile was becoming a laughing stock.

So at lunchtime, which was a sausage roll and a Mars Bar, both taken on the hoof, Rob drove over to the car wash, which was set up in the forecourt of a long-abandoned petrol station on Abbey Street. There was a somewhat tattered poster promising the world hanging across the entrance, and a largish wooden hut. When he drove up, a stubble-faced man in a shell suit came up to his window and said, 'All right, mate? What're you for?'

Rob said, 'Take a wild guess.'

The guy stood back, noticed the graffiti for the first time, gave a short nod and said, 'Fair enough.' He moved up to the 'tit' and ran his fingernail along the paint, before examining it. 'No bother,' he said. 'Eight quid.'

'Eight quid,' said Rob. 'And can I get a receipt?'

The man looked at him like he was a space cadet. 'It's a car wash – cash only, we don't exactly—'

Rob raised a hand. 'Don't worry about it,' he said, and gave a resigned sigh. The man came back to his window, and stood there with an expectant look on his face, confusing Rob for several moments; then he twigged and removed his wallet. He counted out eight pound coins and tipped them into the man's outstretched hand. His puffy fingers closed around them. He turned and let out a loud whistle – and immediately there was a rush of movement from the hut behind. Five ... no, six figures hurried across the weed-strewn forecourt. They looked to Rob to be of Indian or Pakistani origin: two adults and four children ranging from late teenage down to a wee tot who couldn't have been more than four. This youngest one turned, chamois leather in hand, and indicated for Rob to pull the van forward. Rob smiled indulgently and did as instructed. He then stepped out of the vehicle – they looked a little surprised by this, but they were also smiley and pleasant and set about the van enthusiastically. Rob was just starting to wonder if there was a story here – good as they seemed to be at their job, four of them were children, and the tiny one, that was bound to be breaking the law – when there was a shout from behind, and he turned – they all turned – towards it. There was a set of traffic lights about twenty metres along, and there was a car stuck on red sitting facing them. The passenger door was open and a young woman was sitting half in, half out; as they all watched she tried to get fully out, but was immediately pulled back in by the driver; there were more angry shouts before she finally managed to rip free of him. She sprang away from the vehicle and started to run across to the other side of the road while completely unaware that the lights had now changed. A blue Renault car, even though it hadn't had time to build up any speed, immediately thumped into her and she went down silently. But a high-pitched scream did come – from within the car. There was another girl in the back seat who tried to climb out but was quickly hauled back in by the driver. There was a squeal of tyres and the car sped away with the passenger door flapping open and the other girl pressed despairingly against the rear window.

So the kiss of life followed, required or not – the girl was conscious but confused. She was pretty in a starved kind of way, her blonde hair was lank and her eyes appeared large in her head. She spoke but the language wasn't familiar – Eastern European, most probably. The car-wash workers, with the exception of the boss in the shell suit, fussed around with the same enthusiasm and expertise; they had hot water, and a sponge to clean off the worst of the dirt of the road that speckled the cuts on her bare pink-white legs. They placed towels under her head and a Puffa jacket over her shivering body.

'And you didn't get the number plate?' Pete asked.

Rob shook his head. 'I was more concerned with—'

'But a blue Renault.'

'I think, yes.'

Alix said, 'It's bound to be in there – you must have seen it, but, like, subliminally. We may have to hypnotize you. Although goodness knows what else might come out.'

'Absolutely,' said Rob, 'let me just check our hypnotism budget. Oh – we appear to have overspent it this month. Maybe we'll just let the police—'

'You do realize,' said Michael, 'that you're supposed to compress the chest, not give the kiss of life. I've done a course and it's all changed.'

'I—'

'I bet if it had been some homeless drunk you wouldn't have been so quick to lock lips,' said Alix.

'We should get a pic of you for the front,' said Sean, 'you with the girl, thanking her hero...'

235

Rob finally held up his hand. 'Okay, enough. I'm not the story. Alix, if you weren't too busy buying buns, did you get a chance to talk to the police about it?'

'Oh yes.' She glanced down at the notebook in her hand. 'At the moment they still have it down as a traffic accident but are waiting to talk to the girl.'

'And the hospital?'

'They weren't for saying much either, patient rights, data protection, all that bollocks. However, my highly placed sources—'

'It's your sister who works there, isn't it?' said Pete.

'Shhhh,' said Alix. 'My highly placed sources say she has broken ribs, concussion, and is generally lucky to be alive. She's conscious, but not talking. I think maybe she's waiting for her hero to arrive with a bunch of flowers. It would certainly get me talking.'

'I can't just waltz in there and—'

'You're always telling us to be bold and—'

Rob sighed. 'Okay. I'll think about it. Sean? Did you get round to the car wash?'

'Aye, I did, said I wanted a photo of the family who helped with the girl, and the guy in charge told me to take a hike.'

'And did you take his photo, surreptitiously?'

'Of course I did.' Sean raised his iPad and placed it on the desk. They all stood over it.

Rob saw a pretty-damn-good photo of the guy in the shell suit looking directly at the camera, and somewhat angrily. He could also just make out the family in the background, busily washing a car. Rob jabbed a finger at the picture and said, 'This guy interests me. Let's find out who he is and—'

'It's Jimmy Crilly,' said Pete.

Rob shook his head. 'Is there anyone you don't know?'

'Probably not,' said Pete. 'I remember him from my court days, he was always up for something. Burglary, generally, stolen goods, fancies himself as a bit of a hard nut, but really pretty harmless. You're thinking the car wash is some kind of a scam or the family is being exploited...?'

'I really don't know. There was just something about it – I mean, a kid working there who's only out of his nappies.'

'Kids help out in a family business all the time.'

'Yes, I know, but I mean – would you say the same thing if he was covered in soot and being sent up chimneys?'

'At least he's cleaner at the car wash,' said Michael.

'Well, seeing as you're volunteering, Michael,' said Rob, 'maybe you'd like to find out what exactly is going on round there? Why the kids aren't in school, maybe?'

'I wasn't volunteering, I was only—'

'Too modest to put yourself forward, that's your problem. Luckily I can read the signs. Go for it, young man, go for it.' Rob clapped his hands together and then indicated the door. Michael's cheeks reddened somewhat as he got up. The others began to follow, the meeting over. Rob called Alix back and asked her if she knew the best place to buy flowers.

She said, 'That depends if they're for me or some other floozie.'

'The girl in the hospital.'

'Garage forecourt,' said Alix and gave him a wink.

She'd barely closed the door after her when it opened again and Gerry came in, tie loose, shirt collar open, two days of a beard and a bit red in the eyes.

'Oh-oh,' said Rob, 'here comes trouble.'

'And you're right there.'

Gerry came in and sat on the side of Rob's desk. He blew air out of his cheeks.

'What?' said Rob.

'Nothing.' He nodded to himself. Then: 'Nothing at all. Sales are up. Advertising is up. Everything is very rosy indeed.'

'That's good, then...'

'Yes, all good, apart from the fact that we're in dire financial straits.'

'But you—'

'And we are! But the bank plays by its own rules and it sees what it wants to see. We're going in the right direction, but not fast enough. We have to cut costs. They say that, for what we are, we are overstaffed.'

Rob took that in for a moment. Then: 'I presume you meant to say, understaffed.'

'I'm serious Rob. And what that means is—'

'No...'

'... is that somebody has to go...'

'Absolutely no...'

'... and that traditionally means: last in, first out.'

'No chance.'

'That would be Sean. But what we're paying him, it wouldn't make any difference.'

'Gerry, there's no—'

'Then it would be Michael – but I know he put university on hold because we encouraged him to, so that wouldn't be great.'

'Gerry, you're not listen—'

'So Alix, then. Although she's probably the best we—'

'I'm not getting rid of any—'

'Or Pete. He is a bit of a pain in the neck, we all know that. And expensive. But he's also a walking encyclopaedia of this town and we'd be lost without him.'

'Gerry, you can keep suggesting names, but it's not going

to happen. We're stretched as it is. We're trying to grow this bloody paper, not make it disappear up its own hole. Try cutting someone from advertising instead.'

'Ha!' Gerry scoffed dismissively, 'Janine is the advertising department – she wouldn't allow it. No, Rob, I know we're having a bit of a laugh here...'

'I'm not...'

'But I'm deadly serious. Someone has to go, and it has to be from editorial. You're the editor, so it's your call, okay? There.' Gerry got up from his desk. 'Job left in your capable hands. Will you let me know asap, these things are best done quickly and efficiently, eh?'

Gerry was up and out of the door so quickly that Rob couldn't be sure that he even heard him swearing after him. The second word was off. He would have made sure, and was already half-way out of his seat when his phone began to ring.

He let out a loud sigh. Duty, as ever, called.

Gerry was pacing in his office when Janine came in and closed the door. She said, 'What's up?'

'Nothing's up, why should anything be up?'

'Because I know you and something's up.'

'Well, nothing's up, I assure you.'

'And I just heard Rob telling you to fuck off, so something's up.'

'Well, I didn't hear anything. How come you heard something?'

'Because I'm not deaf,' said Janine, 'and also I'm an efficient lip reader.'

'Janine, there's—'

'Just tell me Gerry, it'll save a lot of time.'

'Janine, I swear to—'

Janine closed the door. Then she folded her arms and said, 'Out with it.'

Gerry thought later that she would have made a very fine detective, or possibly a Gestapo interrogator. She had the fact of the impending redundancy out of him in less than a minute.

'But you can't tell anyone,' he warned her, 'it wouldn't be fair.'

'Who am I going to tell?' Janine laughed as she skipped out of the door, armed and dangerous.

Michael didn't have half of her investigative skills, but managed to get by with a lot of Woody Allen-style *hmming* and *haaing* as he attempted to speak to the Indian – as it turned out – man at the car wash. He co-operated enough to say that his name was Navar, but after that the shutters came down. His family, and Michael was presuming it was his family, but nothing was for sure, was crammed into the flimsy-looking wooden hut behind him, picking at food laid out on what looked like a decorating table.

Michael said who he was and that he wanted to talk about the accident – it was his way in – but Navar said he'd spoken to the police already, and then urged him to leave, that he was on private property. He didn't appear particularly nervous or anxious, but firm and to the point. As Michael was being kicked out anyway, he decided to go for broke. He dropped his voice to a conspiratorial whisper and said, 'Listen, I see what's going on here, there's at least six members of your family working – four of them are kids. That looks to me like child exploitation. Maybe even slavery. If you're in trouble and you need help, we're a community paper it's our job to—'

Navar turned and shouted: 'Mr Crilly!'

Crilly, up to that point lurking unnoticed at the back of the hut, came barrelling out, not overly concerned at first because Michael looked so inoffensive, but then he clocked Sean, standing a little back, and put two and two together and snapped out, 'I already warned you once, now get the fu—'

And that was that, theoretically off with their tails between their legs but actually just more intrigued and determined. They retreated to the van and drove off, but actually just circled for a while before picking out a parking space that gave them a view of the car wash but also managed to mostly mask them from being themselves observed. Sean switched off the engine. Michael produced a can of Red Bull and a Mars Bar. Sean smiled and said, 'You look like you're in for the long haul.'

'We stay until we crack this case,' said Michael.

Sean nodded. Then he said, 'Yeah right. I've a list of photos as long as your arm to take this afternoon, so I'm here for twenty minutes max.'

'This is a big story, Sean, or it could be.'

'Then you can hang about in a shop doorway or disguise yourself as a tramp, but I'm away in nineteen minutes.'

Michael sighed.

Fifteen minutes later, Sean was just getting set to dump him. Michael had already picked out a fresh vantage point. They had observed a steady stream of vehicles coming and going – Crilly certainly seemed to be raking in the cash, and all the work he was doing was clicking his fingers for poor Navar and his young family to spring into action. Of course, that was how business worked – bosses and workers, but not if there were tiny kids involved. Michael felt an exposé coming on, or a campaign, something that might even put his name in lights. Almost on cue, Crilly came walking across the forecourt, spoke briefly with Navar, then stepped out onto the footpath and began walking towards the town centre, zipping up his tracksuit as he went.

'Okay,' said Michael, 'let's see where he's off to.'

'Michael – I've to be somewhere else. And in the opposite direction.'

'Just give me ten—'

'No, because if I'm late for the first one, then I'm late for the second one, and that turns to chaos further down the line.'

'Don't make me pull rank on you.'

'Like that could ever happen.'

'Well, what am I supposed to do, then? We only have one van.'

Sean pretended to give that serious thought, then pointed. 'See those things at the end of your legs? I believe they're called—'

'Funny,' said Michael and opened the passenger door.

'See ya later, alligator,' said Sean.

'Bog off,' said Michael.

A minute later he was about thirty metres behind Crilly, but it was still close enough to hear him whistling happily.

It was early afternoon before Rob found time to get to the hospital. He stopped on the way to pick up flowers from a petrol station, then decided it was a bad idea and left them in the car. Even if he had saved her life – and he was pretty sure he hadn't – he was still a reporter, and although he was anxious to know that she really was okay, he was still visiting in that capacity. He was curious and intrigued as to who she was, and why she had felt the need to spring so dramatically from the car that she didn't even think about the oncoming traffic; he wanted to know who the driver was, about the other girl. There was a story there that had to be teased out and for once he wasn't doling it out to one of his reporters; it was a chance to get his hands dirty again; and to find out if he missed it. He had to admit he quite liked getting other people to do the donkey work.

Times were supposed to have changed, and perhaps superficially they had, but Rob was still able to enter the main building, go up three floors and then walk into the correct ward completely unchallenged. But then he had to ask one of the nurses because three of the beds in the open ward had their curtains pulled completely round and he wasn't about to go poking his head around them. Of course he didn't know her name – yet – so the nurse treated him with suitable suspicion until he explained who he was. He was the guy who'd saved her life. He blushed as he said it, but it did the trick, because her face momentarily brightened into a smile. He said he just thought he'd check in on her to make sure she was okay and the nurse said 'Of course, but...' and glanced at the curtain closest to them. She drew Rob away into the main corridor and lowered her voice: 'I'll have to check with her. Marja's a nervous wee creature.'

The nurse disappeared behind the curtain, while Rob mouthed the name: *Marja, Marja* ...

He heard a hushed but nevertheless agitated exchange without quite being able to make out what was being said. Then the nurse came back and asked, with a little hint of embarrassment if he had any photo ID on him. Rob hesitated between his press card and his driver's licence, before going with the press card. The nurse took it from him without comment and returned behind the curtain. Another, briefer exchange, and then she was ushering him in.

Marja was lying on top of the bed; she smiled nervously at him; he started to explain who he was and she cut him off with, 'I remember. I remember everything.'

He could see bruising on her forehead, and down her bare left arm; each time she shifted on the bed she gave a little grimace. Her hair was dyed blonde with the black roots showing; it was also tangled and matted. She was free of make-up and naturally pretty, but there were dark rings under her eyes; her fingernails were brightly painted, but he could see the natural colour growing up from the quick. Her accent was indeed Eastern European, Czech as it turned out, but her English was good. She said she was here on holiday with friends and they had an argument and she jumped out of the car in a temper but didn't actually remember anything about getting knocked down until Rob was giving her the kiss of life.

Rob listened and nodded sympathetically, but he was also aware that she was avoiding eye contact, and that her story felt somehow rehearsed. She appeared nervous when footsteps sounded in the ward beyond the curtain; she was crumpling the top bed sheet in her fists so hard that the skeletal white-ness of her knuckles shone through her pallid skin.

Rob said, 'And have your friends been to see you?'

'No – not yet, their English is not so good. I think perhaps they do not know where I am.'

'They didn't hang around at the accident. Friends would…'

'We were having an argument. That happens with friends sometimes, no? I think they then panicked when I was knocked down…'

Rob said, 'Well – that's unfortunate. If you tell me where they're living I can certainly let them know where you—'

'No,' Marja cut in, 'you should not do that. They will be

worried, of course, but they will be working. I should not worry them. I will be home tomorrow, next day perhaps, they will see me then.'

'Where do you work, Marja? Do you want me to call them or anyone to—?'

'I am secretary, but – how you say, between jobs? No, there is no need. Mr . . . ?'

'Cullen. Rob Cullen.'

'Mr Cullen – thank you for seeing me. And for the kiss of life. But I will be fine now. Thank you very much.'

And that, clearly, was his cue to go. He had a dozen questions he wanted to ask, but he just stood there, nodding for what seemed like an eternity. He felt awkward, and somewhat small. He eventually summoned a reassuring smile, and said that he hoped she would be feeling better soon. Then he took one of his business cards from his wallet and left it on her bedside locker and backed away. He tramped unhappily back down the corridor and out to his car, frustrated that he hadn't really been able to get her talking and that she had dismissed him so easily, like a sparrow giving an eagle its marching orders. He was supposed to be the big experienced journalist, not a floundering cub reporter. He got into his car, but he didn't start the engine. Marja wanted to be left alone, but at the same time everything about her seemed to scream out the opposite. Her pinched face and large eyes gave an impression of abandonment and fear.

Rob called the office. Maybe if he didn't quite have the tools in his kit any more, he knew someone who would.

He explained the situation, before adding: 'I'm just not very good with—'

'Women,' Alix said.

'. . . teasing these kinds of stories out, it takes a more

sympathetic ... but thank you for that vote of...'

'Are you still there?'

'I'm in the car park.'

'Okay, I'll drive over.'

Twenty minutes later she was opening the passenger door and climbing in; he quickly jumped to move the garage-bought flowers from the seat.

'You shouldn't have bothered.'

'I didn't, I—'

'No, I really mean it, you shouldn't have bothered. I get paid for this.'

'Alix, I—'

'So basically you want me to go in there and offer her a shoulder to cry on.'

'I—'

'You want me to ruthlessly exploit a woman who has recently been mown down by a car so that you can get a story for your rubbishy local rag?'

'Yes, Alix.'

'Are you upset because she didn't throw her arms around you and pepper you with kisses for saving her life?'

'No, Alix ... Have you had one or two extra cappuccinos today?'

'Absolutely not. I'm just high on life.'

She climbed back out. She came round to his side. When the window came down she said, 'You know what Pete said?'

'She's not local, what's the point?'

'Exactly. And you know what I said?'

'No, but I can probably guess.'

Alix smiled. 'Why don't you go back to the office, let the real reporters get on with their job?' Then she wheeled away without waiting for a response.

Rob watched her walk towards the hospital entrance, and then quickly looked away when she glanced round to check if he was.

Michael, now abandoned by Sean, followed Crilly at a snail's pace as he lazily perused his way through the charity shops that in recent years seemed to have taken over much of Main Street. Crilly didn't actually buy anything, but rather looked as if he was just killing time. Eventually he turned onto Hamilton Road, and Michael fell in about twenty metres behind him. Crilly passed along the trees at the edge of Ward Park and then the new library and continued on as far as the dole office. He stopped outside the gates to finish off a cigarette, before throwing it down and disappearing inside. Michael took up a position on the other side of the road just down a bit from the entrance, leaning nonchalantly against a lamp post while ostensibly studying his phone, but actually preparing it to take a photo of Crilly when he emerged. Here was a man who was not only exploiting an Indian family to the extent that their children were forced to work to make ends meet, but was also clearly signing on the dole as well. This more than justified the time Michael had spent following him. He began to imagine variations of the headline Rob might put on the story, most of which involved the words *benefit cheat* and puns to do with the car wash. Ten minutes later Crilly came sauntering out, lit another fag and headed back towards Main Street. Michael fired off another couple of photographs as he passed on the other side of the road, then, satisfied with his morning's work, began to walk back to the office, all ready to impress Rob with his story of dogged journalistic persistence. He was just passing the library and approaching the entrance to the park when Crilly suddenly stepped out from behind a tree and grabbed him by his lapels. He marched him backwards until he was forced hard up against the same tree.

'What the fuck are you playing at?'

Michael, who could immediately smell cigarettes and alcohol, spluttered out: 'I ... I ... I'm not playing at—?'

'You're following me you little shit...'

'I'm really not...'

Crilly shoved him again. Michael's head bounced back off the bark. 'Just fucking tell me or I swear to God I'll—'

At that moment a woman pushing a pram came walking out of the park: she glanced over at them. Crilly immediately dropped his hands from Michael's jacket and stepped back. Michael should have taken advantage of her interest to call for help or to run, but he couldn't quite form the words or make his legs work. His heart was beating ninety to the dozen and he felt slightly groggy from striking the tree. All he could do was rub at the back of his head and mutter, 'Fucking hell...'

The woman walked on. Crilly stared after her, then, apparently satisfied, back to Michael. But his intensity was evaporating. His hands moved slowly to his own face until he was covering his nose and mouth; he swore into his cupped fingers. His hands came down again and he said, 'Sorry – I didn't mean ... I just get angry when ... You're the reporter, right? You were at the car wash earlier...?'

Michael nodded warily. He straightened his jacket.

'Just ... tell me why you're following me.'

'I ... wasn't following ... exactly ... I just wanted to grab a word ... waiting for the right ... opportunity...'

'About what?'

'The ... the ... the ... accident and—'

'I told youse about that...'

'And ... and ... we were ... concerned ... for the well-being of that family you have working for you. For the kids.'

'The ... are you joking?'

'No ... my ... my ... my editor wants to run a story about ... immigrant families being ... exploited by...' He cleared his throat. '... I mean employed by...'

Michael felt a little bad about trying to shift the blame to Rob. But it was more or less the truth. And also, he didn't want to be assaulted again.

But Crilly was shaking his head incredulously. 'Man,' he said, 'you've got to be fucking joking.' He jabbed a finger at Michael and then at his own face. 'But I'm telling you this, if you put my mug in your fucking paper, I'll find you, and I'll beat the fucking life out of you, okay? And you can quote me on that.'

Michael swallowed. He nodded. He would indeed quote him on it, but now wasn't the time to say so.

'Exploitation,' Crilly laughed suddenly, 'exploi-fucking-tation! Tell you what you should get ... a *fucking life*.'

He gave Michael another shove, before stalking away.

Michael stood where he was, trying to catch his breath for what felt like a very long time. At least until Crilly had completely disappeared and his own heart had stopped racing. He was a reporter, he wasn't supposed to respond to intimidation or provocation, and he hadn't. But he felt a little bit diminished for acting so meekly.

Rob was just starting to get worried about Alix – she'd been gone for two hours and wasn't answering her phone – when she came charging back into editorial, face flushed, hair flying. She barely paused to take her coat off before she came into his office and threw herself into the chair opposite.

'Bloody hell,' she said. 'I wasn't expecting that.'

'No one expects the Spanish Inquisition...' said Rob.

Alix's brow furrowed. 'You what...?'

'Nothing,' said Rob, with only a hint of despair. 'So what happened with—?'

'She's a hooker!'

'She—?'

'I've been all over the bloody place with her. Hold on. I need another coffee.' She was up and out of the chair again and back out of the office and into the kitchen.

Pete came and stood in the doorway. 'What's got her knickers in a twist?'

Rob shrugged. 'But take a pew, I think we're about to find out.'

Alix returned, sipping her coffee as she did. She gave Pete a look before taking her seat. 'Right,' she said, 'that's better already. Now, where was I?'

'She's a lady of the night,' said Rob.

'Who is?' Pete asked.

'My damsel in distress. Marja.'

'Not only that but she's...' Alix stopped herself. She held up a hand and said, 'Breathe ... breathe ... okay, I'll start at the very beginning.'

'It's a very good place to start,' said Rob, acutely aware from the blank look on Alix's face that she wasn't getting this reference either.

'Okay, whatever – I got to the hospital, okay? I went to the ward and there's a bit of a scene going on, some guy had walked in and she spotted him and locked herself in the toilets and was screaming blue murder and the nurses called the police but he took off before they arrived. Then she wouldn't come out for ages and wouldn't say anything to the cops when she was eventually persuaded out. She was in a dreadful state – really terrified.'

'And they let you stay?' Pete asked.

'Absolutely not, they chased me as well. I said who I was and they told me to call the press office. Then about ten minutes later I'm still there in the car park when she comes walking out, real slowly and there's a taxi waiting there and she goes up to it and speaks to the driver, but he shakes his head, and she just stands there like she doesn't know what to do next, so I guessed she had no money. I went up to her and asked if she was okay and she basically just collapsed in my arms, still clearly in a lot of pain but she says she can't stay in the hospital because 'he knows where I am' and can I help her? So I did. I gave her a lift to the Women's Aid place, in Castle Street, and along the way I said who I was and of course she remembered you and that made her a bit more trusting. I got her there and luckily they had a room and I hung around until she got settled in and I got talking to the staff and I've done some volunteering…'

'You have?' said Pete.

'Before I was working here, but they know me okay, and they said they see girls like Marja all the time, they answer adverts in Prague or Poland or Romania for nannies or hotel work and then when they arrive at the airport these guys take their passports and force them into sex work.'

'In Belfast,' said Pete.

'No,' said Alix, 'well, yes, in Belfast, but here too.'

'In our town?'

Alix's brow furrowed. 'Yes, of course.'

'In *Bangor*?'

'Yes. *Duh.*' Pete looked absolutely perplexed. 'Do you not think our wee town...?' Alix laughed suddenly. 'You really don't! Pete, for Godsake, you really think we're some sort of perfect wee chocolate-box town where nothing like this could ever happen?'

'Well I'm sure—'

'She's forced to work in a brothel! Right here in town, walking distance. And not just our town, every town.'

'I'm not convinced that's necessarily—'

'Oh for goodness sake – Rob, tell him, every town has its pimps and prostitutes and—'

'Oh absolutely,' said Rob, 'they're all over the place.' And then he became aware that he'd said it with a little too much enthusiasm, and that there was an involuntary colouring of his cheeks going on. 'Not that I...' he added hurriedly, which only served to make matters worse. He faked a cough, to help explain the colour, and it didn't work at all. He swore to himself. He'd covered plenty of down and dirty stories in his time in England and he was pretty sure he hadn't blushed once, but there was something about even talking about prostitution, and therefore sex, in front of Alix that his sub-conscious seemed to find deeply embarrassing. 'So,' he said, getting up from his desk and moving to the window and looking out, resting his hands on the windowsill and leaning down with a pose of studied nonchalance, 'what're we going to do about it? Her, I mean.'

'I was going to give her a couple of hours to settle in, calm down,' said Alix, 'and then see if she'd be willing to talk. I mean, she's going to have quite a story to tell, and if we can expose the people who are doing this...'

'Are you sure that's a good idea?' Pete asked. 'I mean, we're a small, community paper and if there is a … brothel … in town, do we really want to publicize the fact? Better just to hand it on to the police and let them deal with it. Or tip off one of the nationals and they can do a proper exposé. It's not really our thing, is it?'

Rob, calmer now, turned from the window in time to see Alix shaking her head. '*Our thing*,' she mimicked. 'Christ, Pete, you're so parochial.'

'And there's nothing wrong with that. People buy the paper for local news about local people, not—'

'*Local news for local people*. And this *is* local news.'

'No, it's a bunch of foreigners who come over here to make money and end up fighting amongst themselves.'

Alix swore.

Pete folded his arms. Then he sighed. 'I'm just listening to myself, and I'm thinking that I'm sounding somewhat to the right of Hitler. I don't mean it like that.' He nodded at Rob, back behind his desk. 'All I'm saying is, your predecessor had a very fixed idea of what our paper was – a family newspaper which old women and young children could read without ever getting offended or having to ask or answer awkward questions. He'll be turning in his grave if we start plastering hookers and brothels all over the front page. We shouldn't give them a platform.'

Rob nodded from one to the other. 'Well,' he said, 'let's see.'

'*Let's see*,' Alix repeated incredulously.

'Yes, let's just see.' He smiled. 'And before you climb onto your high horse, I happen to believe that anything that happens in this town is going to be of interest to our readers, and whatever we do report will be handled responsibly, so that old women will not suffer heart attacks and young children won't be corrupted. But we have no story yet. We have a road accident involving a foreign national. Get me the story, then I'll decide how we handle it. Deal?'

Alix looked at him for what felt like a long time, then nodded.

Pete, with a bit of a smirk on his face, turned back out of the office.

Alix glared after him. 'He *really* annoys me.'

'I know he can be—'

'And you're not much better.'

'Alix...'

'You should just tell him to *fuck off* or go edit the *Church Times* or something.'

'I'll bear that in mind.'

'*I'll bear that in mind.*'

Then she got up from her chair and went back to her desk, fuming quietly at Rob's lack of commitment while simultaneously being a little turned on by his rosy cheeks.

Wise up, she told herself, *concentrate*.

Michael was still annoyed with himself. He knew what Rob would say – you're not supposed to respond, you're supposed to report, you did the right thing – the trouble was it didn't *feel* like the right thing. Crilly was bigger and stronger than he was, for sure, but he still should have done *something*. Shoved him back, at the very least. Threatened him with the police. The trouble was that every time he imagined himself doing it, he sounded all high-pitched and whiney, like a little girl running to tell the teacher. He knew if he told Sean about it, he would take the piss out of him, and he certainly wouldn't be allowed to forget what had happened. To Sean it would just be a bit of a wind-up; but it would still hurt. There was also a story in *benefits cheat assaults reporter*, but it wasn't one he wanted to write. He didn't want to star in a story that would make him look like a coward. Rob would tell him to take the moral high ground. His revenge would be writing a good and powerful story about the exploitation of the Indian family by a local bully boy, and he knew he would do that, but he really didn't want to mention the assault or the fact that he'd been threatened. That was the thing about small towns – if you fell out with someone, you would inevitably bump into them at some point. Crilly was a hard man and he'd threatened to *beat the fucking life out of him*. Crilly knew Michael had been scared, and he could exploit that for ever.

No.

He would *not* let him get away with it.

Rob was right – even if he didn't know anything about it and therefore hadn't said a word – he would get his revenge in the only way he could. He would expose and condemn Crilly. He would make sure he went to prison. He wouldn't mention the assault or the threat in his story, because ultimately they were nothing really, he would suck it up and get on with his job. He couldn't let himself be intimidated, not if he wanted to make a proper career out of this, not if he wanted to get out of town, see the world and work in exotic but occasionally dangerous locations. Proper journalists probably got threatened all the time.

Suddenly full of vim and vigour again, Michael began to march right back to the car wash, although the closer he got the more his new determination to confront and expose began to evaporate. By the time he actually got there, he was content to take up his lurking position across the road. There was no rush, he told himself, no panic; sure, those Watergate reporters Alix was always talking about, hadn't they been calm and methodical? And they'd brought down a president – all he wanted to do was bring down some hood in a shell suit.

Michael was a little relieved that there was no sign of Crilly, just Navar and his family, hard at work. There weren't quite so many cars, most probably because the skies had darkened and it was beginning to rain. As it grew heavier, Michael lodged himself in a shop doorway and watched as Navar and his family took shelter in the wooden hut. Once or twice he saw little faces peering out and up at the sky. After another twenty minutes a decision was clearly made – the rain wasn't going to ease off, so enough for today. The kids came racing out to tidy up whatever portable equipment had been left outside, and it was quickly locked away in the hut. Then they raised two umbrellas and Navar led his family out of the forecourt and along the road towards the centre of town. They did not seem to notice the bedraggled reporter behind. Michael's plan was to follow them home so that he could expose the squalor they were presumably being forced to live in. That would speak volumes. They would probably all be crushed into one room. Perhaps Crilly was even their landlord, a double whammy of exploitation.

And Michael would indeed have followed them all the way home, but for the fact that half-way along Hamilton Road Navar produced a set of car keys, and the lights flashed on a huge and beaming white Toyota Land Cruiser, boasting that year's plates, and the whole family quickly scrambled inside. A moment later it pulled out, leaving a sodden reporter thinking exactly one thing: *this does not compute*. Michael knew a thing or two about cars. A brand-new Land Cruiser like that went for about seventy grand. A brand-new Land Cruiser costing £70k suggested neither exploitation nor squalor.

Christ, thought Michael, *their tips must be fucking stellar*.

Val, who ran the town's Women's Aid house, got Alix a cup of coffee in the kitchen, then went up to check on Marja. She came back and said, 'Give her ten minutes, she's just had a bit of a sleep, God knows she needed it. She wanted me to go out and get her vodka – that's how she's been getting through it all, what they make her do.'

Val was a big, pleasant woman with unruly hair and wide blue eyes. She was from Scotland originally but had married an oil worker from here. The oil worker had nearly killed her and she'd sought refuge with the charity, before becoming a volunteer and eventually the head of the local operation. Alix had interviewed her the year before, and Val had liked the story, even though legally they hadn't been able to print the half of it.

'Has she said how long she's been—?'

'Six months. Basically a prisoner all that time.'

'God…'

'I know … but she's here now, she's safe…'

'And this brothel, do you know anything about—?'

'Oh yeah, the guy who runs it – we know him well enough. As you know, we're supposed to be secret here, so husbands and lovers and parents can't come storming round, but a town like this, word gets out and so pretty much everyone knows where we are. That's why we've doors like bank vaults and cameras everywhere. But the guy – he's too smart to come here and cause a fuss, he knows eventually Marja's going to step outside, and sure as hell he'll be waiting. It's happened before and it'll happen again. The half of them get lured right back into it.'

'What about the police, do they not—?'

'Oh, they know all about him okay, but they're kind of stuck – most of the girls won't press charges because they've family back home, and all yer man has to do is threaten them, or even let it be known that they've been working as prostitutes, and that scares them into silence.'

'And can they not just find a way to send the guy back home instead – would that not solve the problem?'

'Honey – he is home.'

'How do you mean? I'd presumed he was, like, Czech or Polish or—'

'God, no, he's from here, just around the corner, in fact. I don't know exactly how it works, you'd need to talk to him and I don't think that's going to happen, but the girls keep turning up at the airport on a promise of work, so I'm presuming he has connections in these countries who recruit the girls, and then he's waiting when they get to this end. They arrive all bright and bubbly and they're given a lovely room and wined and dined by this charming guy who keeps promising their work is going to start soon, but somehow it never quite happens, and next thing they know he's presenting them with a bill for all the fun they've had, and the expense he went to flying them over and putting them up, and of course they haven't the money to pay him and the interest is piling up every day, but he's a good guy of course and tell you what, if you show one of my friends a good time I'll knock some of it off, and so the pressure's on and they do it to keep him sweet and because nobody is ever going to find out, but suddenly there's another friend, and another, and next thing you know they're queuing around the block and before very long they've gone from some lovely young girl who likes a bit of an adventure to a fully fledged hooker who's being held prisoner because he has her passport, and she still somehow owes him money, and he's plying her with vodka and speed and ecstasy and her life is a fucking nightmare and she wants to die. And that's why girls like Marja step in front of cars.'

Val was breathing heavily by the end of it. She cupped her untouched coffee in her hand and sighed. 'Sorry,' she said, 'once you get me started—'

'It's fine,' said Alix, 'goodness me, it's hard. But you think Marja did it deliberately, jumped in front of the car?'

'Absolutely. It was her only way out.'

'That's terrible.'

'It is terrible, and there's precious little we can do about it except try and provide somewhere safe for them.'

Alix sipped at her own coffee. 'Well,' she said, 'maybe there's something I can do about it. The paper, I mean.'

Val studied her for a moment, then gave her a sympathetic smile. 'Honey,' she said, 'don't get your hopes up. We've been down this road before.'

'You—'

'Maybe it was before your time, but I went to see your boss. And he didn't want to know.'

'Well, there's a new boss now.'

'And it won't make a blind bit of difference. Oh, he might make the right noises, but he'll always find an excuse not to do anything. There'll be a legal reason or he'll say it's not quite right for our paper or—'

'My boss isn't like that, he—'

'Honey, they're all like that. These are the men who queue up to use girls like Marja. They aren't all seedy low-life's who can't get it any other way. They're fathers and husbands and sons. They're your neighbour, your postman or your priest. They're men.'

Late afternoon and Rob had his feet up on his desk, work

ignored and studying the framed photo of his kids that he now kept in his top drawer. It had formerly enjoyed a place to the left of his computer, but after the first few days he'd found it too distracting. He missed them, every minute, every hour, every day, but they were out of reach and he could see no easy solution to that. It was easier, and it became a necessity, to put them away, in the drawer, rather than have to look at them, because he had a job to do and he had to focus, but he felt inconsolably guilty for doing it. Occasionally, usually towards the end of the day, he sneaked them out, like it was exercise time in prison and then he would glow with pride or feel sad or anxious depending on his mood before hurrying them back into their cell so that he wouldn't have to scratch at the wound by talking about them when someone like Alix came into his office.

Today she sat opposite him, looking a little anxious herself. He offered her one leg of the Twix he'd just opened, but she shook her head and said, 'Be careful, that's what done for your predecessor...'

'I think *what done* for Billy Maxwell was old age and a chronic heart condition, but I'll take it on board. Starting tomorrow.' He bit into the biscuit. 'You don't know what you're missing,' he said as he chewed. 'So what's up with you? Did you see her?'

'I saw her.' She nodded glumly.

'*And*?'

'And she's in pieces, God love her, but she gave me|everything, from her home life in the Czech Republic, how she was recruited, how she was forced into prostitution, who forced her, how he operates, even the names of some of the men who regularly use her.'

'*Excellent*. But I sense a *but* coming on.'

'*But* she won't let me use any of it – at least not while her friend is still being forced to … you know … You may have seen her friend, she was in the back of the car when she jumped out…?'

'Mmmm, I'd a brief—'

'Anyway, a week after Marja arrives, Anya followed her from home – mostly because Marja was telling her how wonderful it was. This was when she was still all full of excitement and thinking everything was working out, and now she's blaming herself for Anya getting sucked into it as well. Marja managed to escape, but Anya … She says if we can work out some way to get Anya out as well, then she'll let us tell her story.'

'Right. *Okay.*' Rob sat back, and turned the remaining finger of Twix over in his hand. 'And how exactly are we supposed to do that? Do you have a plan?'

Alix beamed a smile at him. 'No I don't. I have a *master plan.*'

Gerry looked up to find Janine leaning in the doorway of his office. She wasn't looking at him, but through the glass divider into Rob's office. Gerry looked there too and didn't see anything other than Rob and Alix apparently arguing with each other. They were marching about the fairly confined space, waving their hands like they were on a stage, but that was nothing new or remarkable. They were always going at it. But there was always a healthy dose of banter with it, and Gerry liked that. He liked them. He liked all of his staff. He liked his newspaper.

'I was thinking,' said Janine, side profile, emphasizing what he liked to call her fit-for-forty figure.

'That's always dangerous.'

'About who you need to get rid of.'

'Janine, it's nothing to do with you.'

'I know that.'

He blew air out of his cheeks. 'Okay, hit me with it.'

'You need me, that's a given.'

'Apparently.'

'You need Rob because he's doing a good job turning us around. You need Pete because he's the backbone of this place, and besides which his redundancy money would probably bankrupt us. Michael and Sean? They cost hardly anything and they work all hours because they're grateful to have a job.'

'*Mmm-hmmm?*'

'Don't get me wrong, I really like Alix. But you are running a business.'

'Thank you for your input, Janine.'

'Any time.' She gave him a wink and sashayed back to her desk.

Gerry sighed. This wasn't going to be easy.

It was serendipity or fate or the good grace of St Francis de Sales, the patron saint of journalists, that just as Navar's expensive white Land Cruiser pulled away from the kerb and threatened to disappear around the corner of Hamilton Road, Michael turned and was able to hail a passing taxi. This wasn't hectic London or even slightly less hectic Belfast, this was Bangor, which had never knowingly known any form of hectic. But nevertheless, there it was, and Michael climbed into the back, scarcely believing his luck, or the fact that he had for definitely the first and possibly the last time in his life the opportunity to exclaim, 'Follow that car!'

Which is where his luck threatened to run out, because the driver, an elderly man with nicotine-stained fingers and heavy jowls, immediately burst into laughter and then stalled the car. He was thinking it was a wind-up, and it took several long moments for him to be convinced otherwise, during which Navar got further and further away. Finally the engine was started and they took up the pursuit, but their luck was further flummoxed by a series of red lights on Main Street that Navar, with much better timing, managed to avoid. However, his vehicle was big and shiny and hard to miss even in heavy traffic, and once they were out of the main drag, Michael's taxi was finally able to make considerable headway. By the time they reached the end of Dufferin Avenue they were sitting directly behind Navar, and able to see the kids chatting in the back.

Michael expected they would end up in Kilcooley. That was the kind of place that immigrants or those claiming asylum would tend to be sent. He could imagine them all crushed into some dank and damp apartment, the kind that would already have been turned down by a homeless alcoholic because he believed it wasn't fit for human habitation, because first world poverty was a nonsense. The Navars of this world would accept it with good grace in the full knowledge that they would soon work their way out of it.

But, in fact, they didn't get anywhere near Kilcooley – instead they were barely half a mile along the Bryansburn Road before Navar turned off into Maxwell Road, widely regarded as the most salubrious location in town. Michael wondered briefly if Navar and his family had another job as well – they certainly seemed to be a very efficient little taskforce. About half-way along, the Land Cruiser turned into a wide driveway leading up to a large Victorian detached house with an apparently recently built double garage beside it in which sat two expensive-looking cars. The Land Cruiser crunched across gravel and came to a stop by the front door. As Michael's taxi drew up, the family got out and hurried up to the front door. The mother paused to key in an alarm code before inserting a key and leading the way in. Michael sat, quite astonished, for several moments before being prompted by his driver; he quickly scrambled for some change and handed it over; his request for a receipt was denied. A few moments later, he found himself standing on the pavement in the pouring rain looking up at what clearly seemed to be Navar's very impressive house, with not a little modicum of despair. Michael still lived with his parents, and couldn't ever imagine owning something so salubrious. He largely existed in a bedroom that still boasted the posters he had hung when he was fifteen – one for the original version of *Star Wars* and one for Billy Wilder's *The Front Page*. He had accidentally stumbled across the movie on a Sky channel and had watched it a hundred times; the farce and the fun and the drama of it had lured him towards journalism, though he had quickly discovered that life on the *Chicago Examiner* was nothing like that on the *Bangor Express*, that Pete was nothing like Jack Lemmon, and Rob the opposite of Walter Matthau.

'Excuse me – can I help you?'

Michael had zoned out. As he focused back in he saw that Navar was back at the Land Cruiser, with the rear door open and a plastic Tesco bag in his hand, and looking at him with a mixture of curiosity and suspicion.

'I—'

'I know who you are, but what are you doing here at my home?'

'I was doing a story … on the accident and thought…'

'You followed me to my home?'

'No … yes … I was just wondering…' Navar moved closer. He looked quite young, maybe still in his thirties, and his demeanour wasn't exactly stern, and definitely wasn't threatening. He was no Crilly, that was for sure. 'I was just … well, to tell you the truth, yes, I am doing an article on the accident, but also my boss thought there might be a story in you as well.'

'In me?'

'Yes, I mean – he saw that your whole family seems to be working at the car wash, and he was worried that you were being exploited by Mr Crilly.'

Navar nodded his head slowly. 'I see,' he said. 'Well, ahm…?' He raised an eyebrow.

'Oh – Michael, I'm Michael.'

'Well, Michael, perhaps you would like to come in and have a cup of tea?'

Without waiting for a response, Navar turned back to his house. After just a moment's hesitation Michael followed. He was led along a tiled hall that gave him glimpses of large family rooms on either side, both with impressively huge televisions, and into an equally spacious and modern kitchen, which they had to themselves. He could hear footsteps above and the sound of water running. Navar indicated for him to take a seat at the long wooden bench-style table and then set about filling the kettle.

Michael said, 'This is … lovely. But I have to ask – if you live here, why are you working for Mr Crilly in his car wash?'

Navar smiled round at him: 'And what makes you think it's his car wash?'

'I, uh, just presumed. And the way he orders you about and he collects the money and seems to come and go as he pleases…'

As he waited for the kettle to boil, Navar stood against the sink with his arms folded. He had a slight smile on his face. 'I'm afraid, Michael, that you have the wrong end of the stick. *I* own the car wash. Mr Crilly works for me.'

'He … are you sure? I mean, it doesn't look like—'

'And that's deliberate. He talks to the customers and he collects the money – you see, in towns like this, people are not comfortable talking to foreigners. They're not – racist, if you understand, they're just … shy, perhaps? Afraid of the unfamiliar, even in this day and age. It is not a problem, it is what it is.'

'But your whole family is working there, even your little children…'

'It is good for them to learn the family business.'

'But shouldn't they be in school or…?'

'They are home-schooled. And they are doing extremely well. We can set our own hours, it works well for us.'

'Gosh. Well. I hadn't thought of that. And, and, the car wash … pays for all of this?' Michael waved his arm around the kitchen, but meant the house and the car and the big televisions.

The kettle had boiled and Navar slipped two teabags into sturdy mugs. 'Michael – people here will not wash their own cars. If they are willing to throw their money around, it would be remiss of me not to catch it. But – to answer your question – does that car wash pay for all of this? No, it does not. It pays for some of it.'

'And if you don't mind me asking…?'

'Where does the rest come from? Not at all. I am not hiding anything or doing anything illegal. It comes from the other twelve car washes I own, in towns all over your beautiful country. All of them employing local people, I might add, and all of them – very successful.'

Navar brought the tea across to the table, then returned for milk from the fridge and a small bowl of sugar. As he set them down, Michael said, 'You know, this is wonderful, and it's exactly the kind of story my boss would love to run. A real good-news story. He's always banging on about us sending out a positive message, this'll be right up his street. Do you think you would—?'

Navar gave a little shrug. 'I do not think it will do any harm. But tell me, this newspaper of yours ... Is it lucrative?'

Michael gave an involuntary laugh. 'You joking? It's dying on its feet!'

Right up until five minutes before Alix's master plan swung into action Rob was still saying no, no, no, there was no way on earth he was doing that. It was ridiculous.

'There's no one else, Rob. You think Pete would do it...?'

'No, of course he wouldn't because he's not a mug like—'

'I wouldn't even ask him because, for one, he'd have a hernia if he ever had to move out from behind his desk, and for two, he's a big chicken, we both know that. He's not a reporter like you, he's a desk jockey. This is your chance to get back out there, to bring this story home. You'll be the one picking up the awards for this, not me.'

They were in Alix's car, parked about fifty metres down from the house of sin. Sean was in the back.

'Thanks for the pep talk, Alix,' said Rob. 'But you forget, I'm the editor of the paper, if anyone's going to be a desk jockey, then it's me, I'm not supposed to—'

'Supposed to? Is there a book of rules? Seriously, Rob – it's not asking that much. I know you can do it. Come on.

I'd suggest Michael but he's too young, he melts when ordinary women talk to him, he'd disappear completely if he was put in there with—'

'I'd go,' said Sean, 'but you know…' and he held up his camera.

Alix suddenly pointed up the road ahead of them. 'And there he is…!'

There was a run-down terraced house about a hundred metres away, which Marja had identified as the latest incarnation of Rory's brothel. They only had his forename, and without a surname even Pete was a bit stuck. Now he was standing just outside the closed front door, talking on his phone. He was a tall man with long curly hair and a goatee beard. According to Marja, Rory ran his business from a similar series of largely anonymous houses across the country that he rented out on short leases. He constantly moved location so that neighbours wouldn't become overly suspicious and call in the law. This latest house, and where they were parked, was on Victoria Road, overlooking the harbour. It was close to but just outside the town centre. There was a car park about fifty metres away, which meant there wasn't a constant stream of cars stopping outside.

'You're sure it's—?' Rob asked.

'The hair and beard, I'd say he fits Marja's description. And I'd say *that* looks like a punter.'

There was a second man, this one sandy-haired, somewhat rotund and wearing a smart-looking black business suit, walking briskly along Victoria Road, but he slowed as he approached the brothel. He nervously touched his tie, and then checked his back pocket, presumably for his wallet, before peering more closely at the numbers on the houses. He actually walked past the brothel, perhaps unnerved by

Rory standing outside, but then he turned, clearly took a deep breath, literally girded his loins and marched back towards the front door. He reached for the doorbell, but before he could press it Rory spoke to him. There was a brief exchange, and then they both stepped inside. Rory reappeared less than a minute later, closing the door after him and taking up the same position.

'See,' said Alix, 'easy as that.'

'That's easy for you to say.'

Rob took a deep breath. 'I can't believe I'm doing this.' He swallowed. 'Who am I again?'

'You're John Grant. All set up by text. You're booked in at 6 p.m., so you better get your skates on. And don't forget your money, all nicely pilfered from petty cash. You can ask for a receipt if you like ... What can possibly go wrong?'

'Don't even say that. We don't even know for sure, she's in there.'

'We're pretty sure, and even if she isn't, you're still getting to see the inside of a brothel. Unless of course you already—'

'No, I don't...'

'Single man...'

'Please...'

'I'm not the one with a red face.'

'I can't help having a red face. It's blood pressure.'

'Or guilt...'

'Alix, I—'

'Relax, I'm only winding you up.'

'Okay, well, it's not—'

'Unless I'm not, and you really do...'

'Oh, for Christ sake ... Right, here I go...'

And he was out of the car then and striding towards Rory's brothel, which, for at least the first few paces, seemed like the more comfortable option. It wasn't that he had actually been to one before – he really hadn't – he just hated looking so guilty in front of Alix. And Sean, of course. He couldn't help it if he coloured easily. If someone had accused him of assassinating President Kennedy, he would have turned scarlet just as quickly.

Rory was still on the phone, or pretending to be; Rob suspected it was his routine for appraising punters, as if he could somehow check if they were either cops or psychopaths. As he approached the front door Rob deliberately avoided making eye contact, but before he could ring the bell Rory snapped out: 'Help you there, mate?'

'Oh – no, no thanks – I've an ... old friend...'

'I know why you're here.' There was a scowl. Up close he looked to be in his mid-forties, his skin heavily tanned, his brow corrugated. 'What's the name?'

'Rob Cullen...' Rob realized his mistake almost before he said it, but he couldn't stop it from coming out. Rory's eyes flitted down to his phone, and then up again to Rob. '... Sorry, sorry,' Rob said quickly, 'it's John ... John Grant ... Sorry, I was using a...'

Rory didn't look surprised or annoyed. 'Don't worry, everyone does it. This past week alone I've had George Best and Vladimir Putin. It's just a way of keeping the appointments straight, so as long as you have the cash you're good to go.'

'I have the cash okay,' said Rob, reaching into his jacket, 'a hundred and—'

'Not out here.' Rory produced a key and opened the front door. Once inside, in a hall that smelled of Pine Fresh and was bare save for a telephone table stacked with unopened bills, he clicked his fingers and said, 'Now I'll be taking that hundred and fifty.'

Rob handed it over. As he did, and Rory began to count it out, he noticed a faded paramilitary tattoo on the brothel-keeper's forearm.

Satisfied, Rory said: 'The girls are in the lounge at the top of the stairs. You take your pick. You have twenty minutes. Show some respect, no rough stuff, you want longer or any extras, you pay the girl, she knows the prices.' Rory nodded up the stairs. 'So, have a nice day.'

Rob swallowed involuntarily.

'First time?'

'Ahm, yes it is…'

'Well, nothing to worry about. They're very good, and they've seen it all before, whether you're hung like a bull or a squirrel. Relax, enjoy and I guarantee – you'll be back for more.'

He gave Rob a theatrical wink before slipping back outside to resume his role checking on arriving punters. He was also guarding the exit – in case someone tried to rough up a girl or make off without paying for extras, or perhaps, Rob reflected as he hesitated at the bottom of the stairs, he was waiting to hammer any undercover reporter that tried to screw with his lucrative business.

Rob's eyes were drawn to the mail stacked on the telephone stand. The top letter was clearly an electric bill, and addressed to one Rory McBride. Well, if nothing else, at least the mystery of his name was solved. He could back out now and still come out ahead. Minus, of course, the £150 from petty cash. As he began to mount the stairs Rob deliberately flooded his mind with ideas about how he was going to explain the missing money to Gerry, mostly so that he wouldn't have to think about what was waiting at the top. But it was no use. When he stepped out onto the landing and was confronted by three girls sitting on a *chaise longue* and clad only in black lingerie, he was even redder of face and grinning like an idiot.

The girls, blonde-brunette-blonde, all said 'Hi!' together, like the Andrews Sisters, but also, *not* like the Andrews Sisters.

Rob said, 'Hi!' right back at them, although in a voice high-pitched and cracked. The light in the hall was not particularly good, which was probably on purpose. The three girls all stood up, but it was the middle one, with the darker hair, who came forward. Perhaps it was her turn, or she was in charge – the madam, or maybe that was a term he'd picked up from bad TV. He was still grinning, he couldn't help it. His shirt was sticking to his back. She said, 'Hello, sir – you have come for good time?'

Up close, she was forty-five if she was a day. Too old for the girl he was looking for. He glanced over her shoulder at the other two – one looked to be of similar age, buxom, the other, a skinny wee thing with a pockmarked face, who was more likely in her twenties.

'I was – told to ask for Anya.'

There was a slight rolling of the eyes in response – a kind of bored resignation – before she turned on her very high heels and guldered up at the ceiling, 'Anya – another one for you!'

The woman returned to her seat. Out of sight, a door opened above them, there came the *clip-clip* of heels on a bare wooden floor, and then again as they descended a short flight of stairs. Then a small, almost cherubic-looking face peered over a bannister opposite the *chaise longue*, and a single finger indicated for Rob to follow. Rob cleared his throat, then did as he was told. As he walked past the three women, he said 'Ladies', and then began to mount the steps. Looking up, Anya's black lacy bottom was just at his eye level. He swallowed.

There was a door at the top, which led into an attic room with a slanting roof and a foot-square view of the darkening sky. Before him there was a double bed with a quilt hanging off one side. A half bottle of vodka and a saucer brim-full of ash sat on a small locker. There were magazines and assorted shoes and underwear scattered on the floor. Anya was standing in a small *en suite* bathroom, checking herself in the mirror. She was undeniably pretty, with short brown hair. When she stepped back into the room and he saw her properly for the first time, he realized that she didn't look any older than seventeen. She was already reaching to unhook her bra when Rob said 'No – please ... don't...' but it was already too late.

'Maybe it wasn't such a good idea,' said Alix, her fingers drumming on the steering wheel. 'Maybe we should just have walked up and confronted him. Rob's been gone for ever.'

'He's been gone about two minutes,' said Sean.

'Well, it feels like for ever.'

'I know. Imagine sending your boyfriend into a—'

'Shut up! He's not my ... Don't you ever say—'

'All right, keep your hair on...'

'Well, he's absolutely not...'

'Although it is the sort of reaction you'd get if you were trying to keep it secret and he really was...'

'Sean!'

'Just saying...'

'Well, don't.'

'I'm only winding you up.'

'Well, you're not. You're just being annoying.'

'Youse get on very well.'

'I get on very well with you, it doesn't mean—'

273

'Well, I'm open to offers.'

'Oh catch yourself on and concentrate on your job.'

Sean grinned and raised his telephoto lens again, framing Rory perfectly. 'That's the thing about stakeouts,' he said. 'Too much time to kill, gets you thinking about who's doing what to who.'

'To whom.'

'Sure about that?'

'No. Not really. Anyway there's nothing—'

'She ... doth protest too—'

'Shut up!'

He shut up. For about thirty seconds. Then he said, 'Do you watch *Friends*?'

'Everyone watches *Friends*. There isn't anything else on.'

Sean nodded. After another twenty seconds of silence: 'Why do you ask?'

'Chandler and Monica. They were doing it but trying to keep it quiet. But it always comes out.'

'*Jesus.* Give it a—'

'Just saying, like.'

'We are *not* Chandler and Monica.'

'Fair enough.' Another ten seconds. 'Because he's older, Rob would be more like Tom Selleck.'

Alix snorted. 'If he was anything like Tom Selleck, I *would* be shagging him. But as it happens I'm—'

'Christ, here we go!' But Sean wasn't looking at Alix, he was looking at Rob charging down the road towards them.

Alix saw him, too. 'Bloody hell!'

And then Rory in pursuit. He was about twenty metres back, and running with a very strange, staccato gait, almost as if there were weights attached to his ankles. Alix started the engine. Sean flung open the back door. As Rob reached the car he flung himself into the back seat and, without waiting for a bloody obvious instruction, Alix took off, with the back door swinging in the wind and Rory yelling something incomprehensible after them.

They got to the end of the road. Alix stopped, checking for traffic and indicating left. She could see Rory in the mirror, still that weird body movement, but bearing down.

'Just go!' Rob yelled.

Sean cackled as he fired off a stream of photos out of the back window. Just as Rory was about to catch them Alix pulled out of Victoria Road and sped off towards the town centre, leaving the brothel owner flailing in her wake. Rob finally managed to grapple the door shut while shouting, 'Bloody hell! Bloody hell!'

Sean laughed even harder. 'What're we running away for?! There's three of us!'

'That's easy for you to say!' cried Rob. 'He was swearing all kinds of violence! Bloody hell!'

'What happened?' Alix demanded, staring at him in the mirror, 'What bloody happened in there...?!'

Rob placed his hand on his chest. 'Wait ... wait till I get my ... Bloody hell...' And then he too was laughing. 'Bloody hell. I'm too old for this. I was always too old for this! Bloody hell!'

There was a car park at the end of Queen's Parade. Alix threw the car in there, driving to the emptiest part and screeching to a halt. She swivelled in her seat.

Rob shook his head. 'Bloody ... hell. Anyway ... I give your man the money and he sends me up to the girls. I ask for Anya, she comes down from, like, this attic room and takes me back up to it. Then next thing I know she has her bra off...'

'Yeh-hey!' exclaimed Sean.

'Sean!' Alix jabbed a finger at him. 'This girl is trafficked, a *slave*...'

'I withdraw my yeh-hey.'

'And her knickers were half—'

'Yeh-hey!'

'Sean!'

'Sorry...!'

'Anyway—'

'*Anyway*?! She had her clothes off!'

'*Okay*... Keep calm... I was the one in there...'

'I am calm. Now—'

'I stop her. I tell her to put her bra back on. She must have thought it was some kind of kinky request...'

'Yeh...!'

'Sean,' said Rob, 'even I'm saying enough is enough.' Sean playfully put his hands over his ears. 'Right – I say as quickly as I can who I am and what I'm doing there, that Marja has sent me ... and next thing I know she's fled out the door screaming blue murder for Rory...'

'Jesus!' said Alix.

'I know! So I fire my clothes back on...'

'You—'

'Joke ... And because it's at the top of the house there's no other way out, so I run out after her until I'm at the top of the stairs and the front door is already opening and he's coming in and I now know he's an ex-paramilitary so I'm not wanting to tangle with him so I just fire along the hall past the other girls and I dive into the first bedroom I come to ... Fortunately it's empty, and I'm across to the window, pull it up and scramble out ... first floor, but there's a drainpipe there and I just about get hold of it and shimmy down it ... well, *half*-shimmy, I fell most of the way ... but it wasn't that much of a drop so just a couple of grazed knees at worst ... and here we are...'

Alix was looking at him with her mouth half open. 'Bloody hell,' she said.

'I know,' said Rob, 'I feel like lying down in a dark room.'

'So do I,' said Sean. 'Sorry! I can't help it! But well done! Really, seriously. You survived, you escaped by the skin of your teeth, and I've the photos to prove it!'

'I'm not sure I want to see those,' said Rob.

'Why do you think she reacted like—?' Alix asked.

'Well – in the ten seconds I've had to think about it: maybe we forgot to check if her English is up to scratch?'

'God,' said Alix, 'I never thought – because Marja's is so good I just presumed—'

'Or it could be something else. Maybe he's got her so traumatized she panicked, because she knows she'll get a battering if he thinks she's part of it...'

'Either way it's a screw-up, and we've possibly made it worse for Anya as well ... and it's my fault because I came up with the stupid bloody master plan in the first place.'

'No,' said Rob, 'well ... yes, but there was always a chance of it going wrong, and it was as much me just not communicating with her properly.' He rubbed both of his hands hard across his face, as if he was chiselling off a topcoat of grime. 'Christ, what was I thinking? What am I always saying?'

'Don't get involved,' said Alix.

'Don't get involved. I should have stuck to my guns.'

'No, don't say that. We were trying to do something good. You went in there and you did it, and many's a man wouldn't have even tried, so well done you. And you forget one thing, Rob.' She raised an eyebrow.

'What's that?'

277

'There's always Plan B.'

'Yeh-heh,' said Sean from the back.

Rob had asked Alix and Sean to keep his escapade at the brothel on a need-to-know basis – it was an ongoing story that needed to be protected, and clearly nothing to do with the fact that he was deeply embarrassed at basically falling out of a first-floor window and being chased by a pimp with artificial knees. Yes, indeed, as Pete quickly revealed when they returned to the office, several years previously Rory McBride had been shot in both knees by his paramilitary chums for ripping his own comrades off in a drug deal, and now walked with some difficulty, and could hardly run at all. But it became clear the next morning when Rob sauntered into work that his need-to-know basis clearly extended to everyone who worked there, including the cleaner.

'A brothel just round the corner from us,' said Gerry, standing with Pete and Janine, looking in at Rob as he sorted the mail. 'Who knew?!'

Janine gave him a look.

'I really didn't,' said Gerry.

'I don't think that's what you want your editor doing,' said Pete, 'diving out of a brothel window with his pants down…'

'I don't think he actually—'

'I'm imagining him with his pants down,' said Janine.

'Please,' said Gerry, 'that's not an image I want in my head.'

'Oh I don't know,' said Janine, 'there is something quite cute about him, in a dishevelled, slovenly kind of way.'

'You always did like the dishevelled slovenly look,' said Gerry.

'Not in your case,' said Janine.

He gave her a look. She gave him one back. They had history. Modern history that Pete suspected was quite possibly ongoing. Their flirting, and it was definitely flirting, made him feel awkward, so he was quietly relieved when he saw Rob indicating through the glass for him to come in.

'So word continues to spread...' Rob said without looking up.

'Oh yeah, I saw it on Facebook...'

'You—'

'Joking.' He took a seat in front of Rob and crossed his legs. Then he flicked at imaginary dust on his trouser leg and did his usual good job of avoiding direct eye contact. His eyes roved about, as if he was looking for something to be unhappy about. 'But yeah, the general consensus seems to be that you were supposed to make your excuses and leave before she took her clothes—'

'I was in the act of it when she whipped them off.'

'And that's what I've been telling people, but you know what they're like. Wouldn't it be terrible if she turned out to be underage as well?'

'You what...?'

'I heard she looked really young. If she's just a kid, and she was naked with you, that puts a whole different slant on it, that's the kind of thing you don't recover from...'

'I didn't do—'

'I know you didn't, I'm just saying, people get hold of the wrong end of the stick, and before you know it it's the gospel truth and you're on the sex offenders' register.'

Rob gave an exasperated sigh. 'Nothing happened,' he said, 'and she's over age. Anyway – have you been able to turn anything else up about Rory McBride? If anyone has to worry about bloody underage, then he's...' Rob trailed off. He knew Pete was just winding him up, but it was hard not to get riled. He was mortified. He'd gone from life-saving hero to knockabout clown in the space of a few hours.

'Well,' said Pete, 'besides his mobility issues, he has various convictions for violence, so he's not to be treated lightly. It's unlikely he's working alone, so if he's maybe not the fittest, I'm sure he can call on guys who are. You don't think he clocked who you were?'

'Didn't seem to...'

'Well, it's a small town and people talk...'

'Really...'

'So I'd watch your back for a while. I take it we're letting this one slip now? Let the old order return – the police do what they do, and we report on it.'

'Well,' said Rob, 'actually, we may be having another crack at it. I think it's an important story and—'

'Yes, it is. Doesn't mean we have to put ourselves into it...'

'Well, I'll decide that.'

Pete finally focused on Rob, and he looked at him for what felt like a long time before he said, 'You're the boss.'

'Yes, I am.' Pete unfolded his legs and began to stand. Rob said, 'Oh – and while you're here, just wanted to say – best of luck.'

'Luck?'

'Aye – you know, about the redundancy?'

'You what...?'

'Oh sorry – I don't mean it's you, I've no idea who it is – I thought you would have heard. You normally have your ear so close to the ground...'

'No, I—'

'Sorry if I've put my foot in it...'

'No, you ... why, what's happening...?'

Rob lowered his voice, 'I'm not supposed to say anything, but I want everyone to have a fair chance.' He leaned forward on his desk. Pete leaned in too. 'I've to lose someone from editorial. It's not down to me, it's Gerry who'll make the call. But I've an idea how he's thinking – listen, Pete, I know you and I maybe didn't get off on the right foot, but I hope we're fine now...' Pete nodded. '... and I think you're indispensable, but Gerry, well, we both know he doesn't really have much of a clue about journalism, or how this place ticks. He's a businessman, what he'll be looking at is the bottom line. Michael and Sean, I don't think they've much to worry about, they're trainees and they're not costing that much; he's already told me I'm staying, so that leaves you and Alix. Now, you're the senior man, you cost a little bit more, and that might be a problem. See, Alix, she's good too, but she costs less, and ... I hate to say this, and I'm not for one moment saying it's right, but we both know Gerry has an eye for a pretty face and a well turned ankle. I'm just saying.' Rob raised an eyebrow. Pete sat back, looking like he'd been punched in the stomach. 'You're a backroom guy, an unsung hero, maybe – maybe for the next few days, the more you stand out, the more you throw yourself into things, the better Gerry will appreciate what you do. He'll see you're not just a one-trick pony – know what I mean?'

'I ... sort of...'

Rob looked beyond Pete and saw that Gerry was just approaching the door. 'Oh-oh,' he said quickly, 'speak of the Devil.'

Pete glanced back, then he quickly jumped to his feet.

Rob gave him a wink. 'Talk to you later,' he said.

Gerry stepped back to allow Pete out. Then he came in and closed the door. He thumbed after Pete. 'God, the face on him.'

'Gerry, that's his normal face.'

Gerry sat where Pete had been sitting. 'Well, he should do something about it, last thing we need is more misery around here. So, anyway, you were wanting to talk to me?'

'Yes, I was. I need two hundred quid to hire a prostitute, and permission to use the company credit card to book a hotel room to bring her to.'

'O-kay,' said Gerry. 'Do you want four hundred and you can hire two?'

'Gerry, I'm serious.'

'Rob, is there something you want to tell me? Are you getting addicted to—?'

'Gerry, we're going to get Anya. Lure her to a hotel room, then smuggle her out.'

Gerry nodded. 'Who's Anya?'

Rob sighed. 'Anya is Marja's friend.'

'And Marja is...?'

'Do you listen to nothing?'

'Of course I do. But names ... not my strong point. I take it these are the two hookers.'

'These are the two girls who were being held against their will, and forced to sell themselves for sex. This is a major story, right on our doorstep, and I need you to okay the money.'

'Why? As I understand it you took the first lot from petty cash without so much as a by-your-leave.'

'You were out of the office ... and that's not what we're talking about...'

'It's what I'm talking about. You can't just go around spending my money on prostitutes, willy-nilly, so to speak.'

'Gerry...'

'Tell you what, you can have the money and the credit card if you tell me who you've selected for redundancy.'

'I haven't selected anyone, it's not going to happen. Gerry, think of the bigger picture – this is not only going to be a great story for us, but if we pull it off, the nationals are going to be all over it, TV as well. That means money, quite a lot of money.'

'Well, why didn't you say? But still, to be honest, what I'm mainly still hearing is if we pull this off. What if you don't? What if it all goes pear-shaped and you get battered or the girl gets hurt? This isn't the sort of thing you can get insurance for, not to mention the fact that the way we are at the moment we're struggling to pay for third party, fire and theft. But what if?'

'It *will* work,' said Rob.

'I like a confident man,' said Gerry, 'but I also like a back-up plan.'

'This *is* the back-up plan.'

'No, I mean to safeguard my investment. Tell you what, put my money where your mouth is – I'll spring for the girl and the hotel, but if I don't see an immediate return on my investment, then you agree to what I've asked, you get rid of one of your reporters.' Gerry extended his hand. 'Deal?'

Rob took it. 'Deal,' he said.

Gerry smiled widely. 'Now this at least makes it interesting. Good man you are.' He got up and went out. Alix, just passing, said, 'What's he so happy about?' from the doorway.

'He thinks he's making one of you redundant.'

'And is he?'

'Over my dead body. Would you call the rest of them in? We have a plan to discuss.'

Alix went to gather them.

Sean was the first to saunter in. He said, 'Is it true someone's getting the chop?'

'Don't you worry about it,' said Rob, 'it's just Gerry trying to cut costs. The free coffee may not be free anymore, but that's about the extent of it.'

Janine, perched on her desk, drinking some of that free coffee, watched the team troop in, then turned to Gerry, who, with nothing else to do, had begun to water the over-watered office plants.

'Editorial meeting at this time on a Tuesday?' Janine asked. 'What's up?'

'Rob's hiring another hooker. But this time he's looking for a volunteer to take her to a hotel.'

'Same old, same old,' said Janine.

The Royal Hotel was literally just around the corner from Rory McBride's brothel on Victoria Road. Like many of the buildings opposite the promenade on Queen's Parade, it had taken a battering both from the sea air and the failing economy and as a result it was looking a little the worse for wear. But it remained defiantly open. Businessmen of a certain age preferred it to the nearby Marine Court Hotel because it was cheaper and friendlier, even if it didn't have many, or indeed, any of the *mod cons* associated with the newer establishment. Even the fact that they used an out-moded term like mod cons fitted with the Royal's customer profile, not that they would ever have countenanced such a thing. Rob or Alix, given the choice, would have chosen to stay at the Marine Court. Gerry would have stayed at the Marine Court – but he would drink at the Royal. Janine wouldn't have been seen dead at either of them. Pete had the Royal written all over him. So this was where he booked himself in, and Forty-three was the number of the room he gave to Rory McBride when he called to book a prostitute for an out-call visit.

Everyone was stunned when Pete volunteered for the mission.

'You?' said Alix, and then for emphasis added: '*You?*'

'Why not?' said Pete. 'You forget, I was doing stories like this before you were even born.'

'Was this before or after the war?' Sean asked.

'First or Second?' asked Michael.

'Were you actually in the war?' Sean asked.

'First or Second?' asked Michael.

Pete made a face. He wasn't actually *that* old. He maybe had a couple of years on Rob, but he was the kind of man who had always looked older than he was, and his natural conservatism in style and dress and attitude aged him as well. Pete was comfortable and dependable, a worker, a toiler behind the scenes, he believed in family and the church and a quiet life, none of which prevented him from being a two-faced shit-stirrer with a bitter streak; but nobody's perfect. He was definitely the least likely of all of them to volunteer to lure a prostitute to a hotel room, although when they discussed it later, when he was out of the room, Rob said, 'Well, who knows? Maybe he does it all the time. Isn't it usually the quiet ones you have to watch?' Rob was only joking, but they all nodded solemnly.

Pete made the call to Rory from his desk. Rob tried to shepherd the rest of the team away so he could have some privacy, but Pete wasn't the least bit bothered. He spoke with his usual calm efficiency. He asked Rory what girls he had available that evening and took his time before deciding on the one whose description most closely matched what he knew about Anna. Rory then confirmed her name, and as they concluded the details of the coming transaction Pete gave the rest of the team the thumbs-up.

By nine o'clock that night Rob and Alix were in one vehicle, sitting in the car park opposite the Royal – which also gave them a view of Victoria Road, along which Anya and presumably Rory would walk to the appointment, it being only a matter of a few hundred yards away from the brothel. Sean was in one of the few parking spaces immediately in front of the hotel, with his camera surreptitiously mounted on the dash to capture the comings and goings. Gerry, who had nothing to do with any of it, but was nevertheless fascinated by the cloak-and-dagger nature of it, had positioned himself in the hotel bar much earlier than was either necessary or advisable, and was quite drunk by the time Rory and Anya entered through the revolving front doors. He had already seen Sean's photos of Rory, and recognized him immediately, while also having a vague notion that he'd previously noted him as a character about town; Anya, if it was indeed her, was no *Pretty Woman*. There was nothing glamorous about her: she was thin and looked sickly; she was dressed as if she was on a work placement in an accountancy firm rather than for seduction, but maybe that was what was required to blend in. They both looked slightly dishevelled from the sea wind howling outside. Gerry, now on his fourth pint, wondered why the woman on the reception desk, which he had a clear view of, didn't challenge them when they went straight for the lift. It was a small enough hotel, and not exactly busy, so she must have had a good idea who was staying there; instead she exchanged a bored nod with Rory as he waited for the lift to arrive, which made Gerry think that maybe she knew exactly what was going on and that it happened regularly. Small, quiet, seaside town like this.

Out in the car, Rob phoned Pete.

'They're on their way up.'

'Okay.'

'No need to be nervous.'

'I'm not nervous. We need rid of scumbags like Rory McBride.'

'That's the spirit. Good luck.'

Pete cut the line. Of course he was nervous. He stood facing the door. He was wearing his office shirt and tie, open at the collar. His jacket was lying on the bed beside a briefcase he'd brought from home. Pete had been married to Edna for seventeen years. It wasn't a happy marriage. It had sucked the life out of him and made him sour. He was aware of it but couldn't help it.

There was a knock on the door. On a bigger paper there might have been hidden cameras, or a crew listening to everything in the next room, ready to pounce and confront. Pete had a notebook and a pen. The pen was mightier than the sword, though right at that moment it didn't quite feel like it. He'd opened a bottle of beer and poured half of it down the sink, but now he lifted it, took a swallow and went to the door, for all the world the stressed businessman looking for some R&R after a hard day of negotiation.

Rory stood in the open doorway, Anna slightly to one side.

'Mr West?'

'Aye. Bang on time.' He ran what he hoped were lascivious eyes over Anya. She forced a smile for him. 'Do you want to...?'

Rory and Anya stepped into his room. Anya stared at the floor. Rory glanced around, then raised his eyebrows at Pete.

'Of course,' said Pete, 'it's right here...'

He lifted his jacket from the bed and removed his wallet. He quickly counted out the £200 and handed it over.

Rory folded it into a back pocket and said, 'You've thirty minutes, starting now, no rough stuff, show some respect, you want longer or any extras, you pay the girl, she knows the prices. I'll be downstairs in the bar. Enjoy yourself.' He gave Pete a wink, then breezed out of the room.

Pete closed the door after him and stood facing it, listening. Anya started to speak, but he turned and put a finger to his lips. She let out a resigned sigh. Another weirdo.

'He is gone,' she said. 'Like he say. Now...'

She stopped suddenly, because the bathroom door was opening. She took a step away from it, towards the window, suddenly terrified that some other horror was about to befall her, but then, as a familiar figure appeared in the doorway, her face seemed to collapse. 'Marja!' she cried. 'Marja!'

Marja, indeed, stepped into the room. They rushed towards each other, each giving out a little cry, and hugged and kissed, released each other, then embraced again; they spoke excitedly in their mother tongue. Pete gave them their moment. He moved into the bathroom and poured out the rest of his beer. Then he returned to the bed and pulled on his jacket. He took out his phone and called Rob. He said, 'The eagle has landed.'

'Brilliant,' said Rob, and gave Alix the thumbs-up.

It meant that they were now entering the most critical phase of Plan B – getting Anya out of the hotel. There was a back exit, but they could only access it through the hotel kitchen, which was now closed for the night. They would have to go down in the lift, straight out past reception and through the swing doors to a waiting car. That meant that for a brief moment they would be visible from the public bar and therefore of being spotted by Rory.

'So,' Pete asked, 'is everything okay?'

'Well,' said Rob, 'there's good news and there's bad news.'

'Oh shit,' said Pete.

'Don't panic. Good news is we're already parked right outside, about three steps from the doors. Bad news is that Rory isn't alone anymore – two fellas have joined him for a drink and they don't look they're Jehovah's Witnesses. So, if he spots you, you may not be chased by a pimp with gammy knees, but two thugs who look like they're not entirely unfamiliar with the inside of a gym, or a prison, for that matter.'

Pete heard Alix say, 'Stop scaring him...'

'I'm not, I ... Okay, Pete, it's fine, chances are they won't even notice, I can see from here they're facing away from you, they're watching some football on the telly, everything will be fine and dandy. You're good to go. The engine's running, the back doors are open, we'll see you in a minute.'

Pete took a deep breath. 'Okay,' he said.

And everything nearly went like clockwork. Marja explained what they were doing to Anya. Anya, beaming widely, was all for it. Marja, still battered and bruised from the accident, was moving a little too stiffly and slowly for Pete's liking. As they travelled down in the lift, Pete said, 'As soon as the doors open, straight across, don't look anywhere else, just concentrate on getting outside and into the car.'

As they reached the ground, Anya slid her arm around Marja's waist to give her more support. Pete moved to their left, so that he could provide some protection if anyone came at them from the bar.

The doors slid open and they stormed out – three abreast and so intent on making the revolving doors that none of them noticed the waiter coming from the right; as they collided, the drink-laden tray he was carrying flew into the air, almost in slow motion – at least that's how Gerry saw it – before crashing to the ground.

Everyone turned from the bar.

'Run!' Pete yelled.

A moment later the revolving door was spinning and then they were out of it and onto the pavement. They did not hear the cry of rage from the bar; nor, as they rushed towards Alix's car, were they exactly aware that the two thugs, with Rory following behind, were so very close to catching them. The pursuers were in one large compartment of the revolving door and about to explode out onto the pavement when the door stopped its forward progression – because someone else was pushing it the other and completely wrong way, and he was laughing, and he was clearly pissed, and neither party could go forwards or back because they were both pushing so hard. Rory screamed abuse at the drunk and the thugs waved their fists, but it only made Gerry laugh some more. It was only a few seconds before Gerry released his grip and allowed the sudden release of thrust to propel him back into the hotel lobby and the pimp and his thugs outside, but it was long enough; they stood watching helplessly as Alix's car disappeared around the corner onto High Street. Gerry, satisfied that Plan C had worked perfectly, stepped up to the bar and ordered another pint.

Two days later, a cracking paper was out with a front-page story on the girls' flight and Rory's arrest, with Alix's in-depth interview with Marja running across the centre pages. Gerry knew it was a good team effort, and Rob had been right – it did generate a lot of interest from other, bigger, newspapers, and it was carried by all the local radio stations and TV news programmes. None of it translated into cold hard cash, unfortunately. One of the reporters would still have to go. But, on this cold Friday morning, he was no closer to finding out which one. Rob had been avoiding him ever since he came in. Pete, himself a revelation, was beavering away. Alix's story could have graced any national. Michael and Sean were bickering and bantering; they had the enthusiasm of youth, not to mention the attractions of the minimum wage. Gerry had come to the paper almost by accident, but gradually, gradually, he was coming to love it. What it was doing, what it represented, what it was going to do. He loved the people he worked with every day, Rob and Janine, Pete and Alix, Michael and Sean, he loved the cut and thrust of it, the intrigue, the adventure, even the dull bits were less dull than anything else he'd ever worked at. But he *still* had to lose a reporter.

'Mr Gerry, is it?'

Gerry turned to the counter, and saw an Indian man in a smart grey business suit. 'Close enough,' he said. 'What can I do for you?'

'I would like to buy your newspaper.'

Gerry nodded before lifting one from a stack to the left of the till.

Navar smiled. 'No, sir, you do not understand. I want to buy your newspaper.' He lifted his hands and spread them. '*All* of it.'

CHAPTER 7

THE NEXT TO LAST OF THE MOHICANS

There was a burglary on Westmoreland Drive – an opportunistic thief, spotting a downstairs window open, decided to chance his arm, but found more than he bargained for. Probably nobody would have been any the wiser, because he sneaked in and sneaked out, except he felt so badly about it he decided he had to tell someone, but his good breeding wouldn't allow him to call the cops. So Rob, the only one left in the office that morning, took the call. The burglar didn't exactly introduce himself as a burglar, instead dressed it up a bit – he was off-his-head drunk, desperately needed to use a toilet, saw her window open and went in. It was the smell that alerted him – he hadn't even gone into the room, didn't need to see anything to know that someone had died in there, and quite a while ago too. He wanted to make it very clear that it was nothing to do with him, he was only looking for a place to piss, he wasn't going to do it on the street, he wasn't a dog. He hadn't touched anything, done any damage, stolen anything. Rob asked him for a contact number, and the burglar almost fell for it. Then he told Rob to fuck off and hung up.

Rob called the police, and then made sure he was outside the house in time for their arrival. He was on nodding terms with the two constables who turned up. They didn't object to him going up to the front door, but asked him to wait there. Their faces were already grey, their lips turned down at the corners, their noses bunched up trying to repel what they were so bloody obviously about to discover. There was no mistaking it. Death had a distinctive aroma, a pungency that seeped through walls.

Five minutes later one of them came out and was sick on the well-tended rosebushes.

Charlie Harper, the undertaker, arrived not long after. He was all breezy on the way in, but ten minutes later came out for a breather, a sheen of clammy cold sweat on his brow and a shake to his hand as he struggled to light his cigarette.

Rob hadn't been at the paper for very long, but he already knew him pretty well because between the death notices and the obituaries there was a lot of interaction. Rob said, 'I thought you'd be used to it.'

Charlie shook his head. 'My job is to stop them ever getting to that state. She's been there at least a month.'

'Any signs of...?'

'Foul play? No such luck.'

'Any idea who she is?'

'Nobody special, Mr Cullen,' said Charlie. 'Just someone everyone else forgot about.'

And on the walk back to the office, Charlie's words stuck with him. They annoyed him. Nobody special. Someone everyone else forgot about. He repeated them half an hour later at their morning briefing, Alix, Michael, Peter and Sean sprawled out before him, more interested in their coffee and doughnuts, at least until Michael became aware of him

293

glowering in his direction and stopped chewing and said, 'What?'

'How would you like your own mother to end up like that?'

Michael shrugged helplessly. His mother was barely forty. His grandparents were in their sixties. He didn't know anyone who had ever died, had never been to a funeral or seen a dead body.

Rob said, 'Isn't there something special about everyone?'

'Even Peter?' asked Sean.

They started giggling, but Rob's dour face sucked the life out of it.

Alix nodded, lips pursed, hoping it would add the modicum of solemnity or gravitas Rob was clearly aspiring to. 'It's awful that she lay there for so long,' she said, 'but without wishing to speak ill of the dead, maybe nobody found her because ... well, she was probably very old, and most people lead very dull lives and it kind of stands to reason that not everyone does have something special about them ... otherwise the ones that genuinely are special wouldn't be considered special because it would be so ... common...'

Rob didn't look impressed. He said, 'There's a story here. I don't just mean about a body lying undiscovered for so long. There's a story in everyone. I want to know who she was. What she did with her life. The details. The ambitions, the disappointments. She was someone's daughter, someone's mother. She had a job or she raised children or she did both. She was absolutely special to someone, and maybe not in a good way. Let's find out. Let's write honestly about someone's life, warts and all.'

'Maybe it was the warts that killed her,' said Sean.

Rob just looked at him.

Sean held his hands up. 'Sorry.'

294

Rob shook his head. 'Will you handle it?' he said to Alix.
'Me? I've a mountain of—'

But a call came in for him and his taking it signalled that
the meeting was over. As they returned to their desks Pete
said, 'Do you think he's feeling guilty because he hasn't seen
his own mother for a while?'

'Do you know that or are you just bullshitting?' Alix asked.

'Bullshitting. I don't even know if he has one.'

'Everyone has one,' said Michael.

'Except you,' said Pete. 'You came out of a test tube along
with Dolly the Sheep.'

'Dolly the . . . ?'

'Oh youth,' Pete sighed, 'wasted on the young.'

'I've no idea what you're talking about either,' said Alix,
though of course she had. She looked at Rob, through the
glass of his office, now talking animatedly on the phone.
Sometimes Rob had these grand ideas for stories that would
probably have seemed fine on the *Guardian*, where they had
the time and the staff to do them properly, but here . . . it was
hard enough handling the workload as things were without
having to find time to explore their editor's philosophical
whims. But he was the boss. She would look into it. She was
pretty convinced she would end up handing in a traditional
news story anyway. There would literally be nothing to report
about the old woman. Or almost literally. A dull life and a
death that was interesting only because she had lain undiscovered for so long. Alix would get quotes from local politicians
saying that it was a sad reflection of today's society that
someone could drop off the radar like this; she would speak
to the neighbours, who'd say what a sweet old lady she was,
but that she valued her independence and it wasn't unusual
not to see her for several weeks. She might pick up a few

mundane biographical snippets. She was a veteran of hundreds of calls to mourning relatives – obituaries were the bread and butter of local papers – so she knew that 99.9 per cent of people lived dull and uninteresting lives. Rob's determination to make a silk purse out of a sow's ear was doomed to failure. And, anyway, the chances were that by the time she sent the story through he would have forgotten about it because he'd been pretty distracted in the past few days. He was up on his feet now, pacing with his phone. She knew incredibly little about him. Sure, there was the wife and the kids. The job in England and the unexpected return. But he'd started here, he had to have family. Maybe Pete was right – the story wasn't really about the old woman, it was about Rob and his poor relations with the rest of his family.

Pete said, 'Navar's back.'

Alix followed his gaze to Gerry's office, where another earnest conversation was clearly taking place.

'Third time this week,' said Michael.

'What do you think they're up to?' asked Sean.

'Maybe Gerry's thinking about getting into the car-wash business,' said Alix.

'I've been to Navar's house,' said Michael, 'there's definitely money in soapy bubbles.'

They all nodded.

'Chances are,' said Pete, 'Gerry owes him money, or has squirrelled out of a deal.'

'Chances are,' said Alix.

They all nodded. They loved Gerry. But they knew what he was like.

Janine loved him more than they did, and *absolutely* knew what he was like. He was a deeply flawed individual, but she was devoted to him. She was also devoted to his newspaper.

Janine had a simple philosophy that she might have hijacked from the Loyalists: No Surrender was her mantra. The newspaper would not fail on her watch. And, if it did, such failure would never be placed at the feet of the advertising department because she would simply not allow it. She *was* the advertising department. She took it as a personal affront when people refused to bow to her sales pitches. That was quite a pressure to live with. But she didn't let it get to her. Of course she didn't. That morning she was at Alcoholics Anonymous.

There was about a dozen of them, in a church hall on the Groomsport Road. There was tea and coffee and orange juice. A middle-aged man in an expensive-looking suit was on his feet. 'My name is Frank, and I'm a chocoholic,' he said, and half of them didn't know whether to laugh or not because, for all they knew, he really did have that problem. That was the thing, you were very rarely *just* an alcoholic. Maybe this Frank had Easter eggs hidden all around his house. Maybe he shotgunned Smarties before work. Janine, at least, could see the twinkle in his eye. He said, 'And besides that, I'm a bit of an alcho as well. It has been six months since my last drink – unless you count the chocolate liqueurs I had at Christmas, sucked them dry before I realized.' There was at least now some gentle laughter. When Frank was done, Ryan, the group leader, thanked him and then asked them to give a warm welcome to their newest member. She stood up and said, 'My name is Janine...' She nodded around them. 'And I could murder a drink, though I would hope to get off with manslaughter...' This got even fewer laughs, but Frank liked it. He clapped his hands. She got a coffee afterwards, and when she turned from the table, Frank was standing in front of her, beaming. 'Well done,' he said, 'it's always hard the first time.'

'The first time?' said Janine. 'Every time I fall off the wagon I go to a different group. This is the third this month.' His mouth dropped open a little, but then she smiled and said she was only raking him, that she had indeed been unbelievably nervous.

She fixed him with a look and he said, 'What?'

'Do I know you from somewhere?'

'Funnily enough,' said Frank, 'I was going to say the same about you. I know these groups are supposed to be anonymous, but you can't help being curious ... do you mind me asking what line you're in?'

'Advertising,' said Janine. 'I work for the local paper. Or overwork for the local paper – I think that's how I ended up here. You?'

'I'm in property. Commercial. In fact – the new shopping complex down by St Patrick's? I do believe your paper had a go at us a few weeks ago.'

'Ah,' said Janine. 'In that case...' She nodded towards the doors. 'My taxi's here.'

But she smiled with it, and he laughed. They gazed at each other.

Industrial-strength air freshener had clearly been sprayed, but there was still a long way to go. Sean made a barfing sound as soon as he got out of the car. Alix told him to man-up, show some respect, someone had died and he said, 'Really? Hard to tell.' The body had been removed, the undertaker and the police were long gone, but the front door was lying open. Alix rang the bell and then was surprised at who came walking out.

'Irene Bell.'

Irene, hair still dyed the distinctive henna-red she'd adopted in her last year at school, cardboard box under her arm and clad in a blue smock, studied Alix, her brow furrowed at first but then the penny dropped and she said, 'Bell no more, Irene Dunne now ... Alix ...?'

'Oh, still plain old Alix Cross.'

Irene laughed. 'Alix – you were never plain old anything!'

'Well, not so sure about that!' Irene had stopped half-way down the hall – so Alix took advantage of that to thrust her hand out and step into the house. 'So how're you doing anyway?'

'Ah, just the same old.' She thumbed back into the house behind her, 'Haven't won the Lottery yet. What about you? Kids or anything?'

'Nope, not yet – still in the paper ...'

'The—?'

'The *Express*? That's why I'm here ...'

'Oh! Right! Maybe I did know that. You're the journalist. I thought maybe you were a relative ...'

They stood awkwardly for a moment, until Alix remembered to introduce Sean. 'Sean, this is Irene – we went to school together about a hundred years ago. Irene – Sean's our staff photographer.'

Sean held out his camera. 'In case you thought this was just very complicated jewellery.'

Irene's brow furrowed.

'Don't listen to him,' said Alix. She nodded into the house beyond. 'So you're ...?'

'Oh – I was Bertha's health worker.'

'Oh – I see. Bertha. That was her name. Bertha ...?'

'Bertha Malloy. I was only with her this last year or so.'

'All the same, I'm sure it was quite a shock.'

'Tell me about it. She was old as the hills but fit as a fiddle.'

'She was ... dead ... for some time before...'

'She was.' She nodded. Alix nodded. Irene cleared her throat. 'I'm sorry – what is it you say to journalists when you don't want them to report what you're—?'

'You mean, like off the record?'

'Off the record, that's it. Well, *off the record* ... Bertha was bloody hard work, and that's why nobody found her, they were all too scared to go near her, God knows I tried...' Irene sighed. 'Not that anyone deserves ... well, you know what I mean.'

Alix nodded vaguely. 'But if you're her health worker ... then she had been unwell at some point...?'

'Oh, last year she had a bit of a heart thing, but she was fine...'

'Does she have family or...?'

'Not that I'm...' Irene trailed off. 'Tell you the truth, I'm not really supposed to be speaking to you at all. Not *you* you, but the press – do you know what I mean. It's drummed into us. You're supposed to go through the press office. It's nothing personal.'

Alix smiled. 'That's all right, absolutely – I'll give them a bell. But you know how it is, you get through to a bloody computer and it's all, if you want to speak to so-and-so press number three and then you press the wrong one and you're back in the queue again ... do you think you could just give me a few more details about her, it'll give me somewhere to start...?'

Irene made a face. 'I'm sorry, it's more than my job's worth.' *Jobsworth* was indeed the word that echoed through Alix's mind. She just about managed not to say it out loud. It wasn't like Irene was being tempted to divulge state secrets. She tilted the cardboard box towards them. 'I'm really just here to pick up any paperwork, would surprise you the number of people who pass away and they don't have anyone close enough to tidy up their affairs.'

'So sad,' said Alix. She nodded down at an ornate telephone stand. There were a couple of unopened letters sitting there. The top one was clearly stamped with the logo of the Churchill Nursing Home, which was about half a mile away.

Irene, noting her interest, immediately picked them up and dropped them into the cardboard box. 'Listen,' she said, 'I'm going to have to lock up here.'

'Yes, of course,' said Alix. She and Sean began to retreat along a hall that was lined with shelves heavy with china ornaments and decorative plates. 'What'll happen to all this stuff?'

'I imagine if no one claims it, it'll be sold or dumped. Not sure who does that. Council, I expect.'

'And what about the funeral?'

'Pretty much the same.'

'That's terrible,' said Alix.

'It is, but again – you'd be surprised.'

Irene ushered them fully outside and locked the door behind her. She swung the keys round into her hand and told them she had to get going. 'No rest for the wicked,' she said.

As she drove off, Alix shook her head after her, then turned to study the empty house.

Sean fired off a couple of photos. Then he said, 'Yer woman – were you good mates at school?'

'I was head girl and she was captain of the hockey team. We hated each other.'

'But now?'

'Pretty much the same, I imagine.'

'She seemed friendly enough.'

'Two-faced cow.'

Sean nodded. 'You or her?'

Rob was just finishing a call to Rebecca when he realized that Gerry was standing in the doorway, arms folded, apparently listening in. When he cut the line, Gerry shook his head and said, 'You know, I don't pay you to make personal calls.'

'Gerry, you hardly pay me at all.'

Gerry considered that. After a few moments he nodded and said, 'Fair point. Anyhow – can I have a word?'

'Have several.'

'Not here. Walls have ears. How about I buy you lunch?'

'Christ, Gerry, have you taken leave of your senses?'

'Very funny.'

'I'm serious.'

'Yeah, right. Grab your coat before I change my mind.'

Rob grabbed his coat. They went to the Hong Kong Palace. Rob hadn't been there since the furore over the netball story and was somewhat nervous about how Mr Smith would greet him, but he seemed genuinely pleased to welcome him back. He asked after Anna and was told she had reapplied for her student visa and was hopeful of being allowed back into the country. He asked if there'd been any more trouble with the authorities over his staff and he just rolled his eyes. When they were ordering their drinks Gerry asked for tap water. Rob asked for a Ballygowan. 'That's it,' said Gerry, 'go mad for it.' Gerry spent the next twenty minutes beating around the bush. He talked about everything except what was really on his mind. Wind-surfing, volcanoes, suede shoes, the Middle East – basically what'd you'd get studying the average newsfeed on Facebook.

Eventually Rob put down his chopsticks and just said, 'Out with it, Gerry.'

Gerry put down his knife and fork – he was old-school. 'Thing is,' he said, 'I've had an offer to buy the paper. It's not brilliant, but it'll allow me to get out with my trousers on.'

'Do you mean the shirt on your back?'

'You clearly haven't seen my bank statements. No, it's Navar.'

'What's Navar?'

'Who wants to buy me out.'

'Car-wash Navar?'

'Car-wash Navar seems to be rolling in it, not that you could tell that from what he's offering. But at least he's offering. What's so funny?'

'Nothing – just the gossip had it that you were getting into car washes, not the other way round.'

'You think I have the money to get into anything? Apart from jail, that is?'

'Popular opinion would be that you have plenty squirrelled away.'

'Popular opinion is a load of shite. He has plans.'

'I'm listening.'

'Make it a free sheet, boost digital, might have to lose a body or two. But he'd definitely want you to stay. Janine too.'

'Pete? Alix? Michael? Sean?'

'Not my call. I can make all kinds of promises, but they're pretty much worthless once he's the owner.' Gerry took a sip of his water. 'So what do you think?'

'What do I think?'

'What do you think?'

'As if it's not a *fait accompli*.'

'It really isn't. I may yet win the Lottery and save us all.'

'I think…' Rob took a sip of his own water. He set the glass down, deliberately taking his time. 'I think that I have news of my own.'

As Alix had expected, the neighbours were useful only for a few bland and predictable quotes – Bertha had kept herself to herself and didn't like to be fussed over, it wasn't unusual not to see her for weeks at a time, how shocked they were. They didn't know anything about her history or her family. She supposed if they had been terraced houses there would have been more interaction, but Bertha's was a large Georgian house surrounded by unkempt hedges, while the neighbours on either side and across the road were young married couples with kids; they'd enough to be getting on with without worrying about the auld dragon across the way. On a whim, on the way back to the office, with Sean complaining because he still had a stack of photos to process, Alix stopped off at the Churchill Nursing Home and spoke to Sarah Compton, the manager. She knew her from previous stories – three of the home's guests/inmates had made it to a hundred in recent years and received telegrams from the Queen. It had been Alix's job under Billy Maxwell to attempt to interview the poor dears – and it was always the women who seemed to make it to a century not out. It was nearly always a disaster – they might have reached a hundred, but they rarely retained many of their faculties, or, indeed, marbles; their heads would flop down onto their chests and they'd be covered in drool and food and smell of pee and air freshener and mothballs and they would hardly be aware that there was a party going on in their honour or that the Queen had been in touch. But Sarah Compton was always friendly and bubbly and anxious to help whatever way she could. Alix liked her, though the more experienced she became as a journalist the more she understood that you never knew what people were really like, that they presented you with their public face, and it was only later, when they were arrested with a decapitated head in their fridge, that their true selves were revealed. Although, of course, there hadn't been a lot of decapitated heads during her time on the *Express*. That was wishful thinking.

Alix was greeted with a wide smile and the offer of tea and shortbread, which she accepted even though she knew Sean was sulking in the car.

'Oh yes, I remember Bertha all right...' Sarah gave a roll of her eyes.

'Yes, that seems to be the general opinion...'

'Well, to be fair ... she was just ... well, she knew what she wanted. She took no prisoners, but most of the time she was lovely. You know she used to be a union rep at Gallaher's?'

'Galla...?'

'The old cigarette factory in Belfast? In its heyday thousands and thousands worked there.'

'Sorry, I—'

'Well, anyway, Bertha was used to – well, agitating to get what she wanted. She was pretty ill when she first arrived here, so it took a while for her to find her feet, but once she was up and about – well, I think my job became pretty redundant. She thought she was running the ship, and to be frank we did butt heads a few times, but ultimately I think she was just trying to help. She could see things – flaws – from her side of the fence that we, as, like, management, could never really be aware of. So she was brilliant that way and actually we got on like a house on fire – which is quite apt really because the one thing she would not accept was that she couldn't smoke in her room. Oh, the battles we had over that. In the end she signed herself out and went home, and actually she was quite right, there was no reason for her to stay, she'd recovered from her illness and was fighting fit. Sometimes literally. And do you know something? I'll miss the auld bat. I was very sad to hear she'd gone. Do you know when the funeral is? I would like to pop along.'

'Not yet, no – sounds like it might be a council job, don't think anyone's come forward. You wouldn't recall if she had any relatives visit or friends or...?'

'I'm not sure about relatives, but there was someone who...' She was up from her chair then and out of the door and asking one of her staff. She came back with a name and the idea that the visitor sometimes wore a Marks and Spencer uniform. She was all apologies for being so vague, but Alix was more than happy. It was a clue, a lead; she was a dynamic reporter destined for the top.

As she left, Alix started thinking about Rob again, about his instincts for a story and how good they were, and then about why he'd been so distracted over the past few days and what his phone call had been about. She was still thinking about him when she got back in the car, and hardly noticed Sean's glare or the way he tapped his watch face. As she started the engine she said, 'What do you think of Rob?'

'Wah?'

'Rob. What do you think of him?'

'I think he's going to be pissed off because I'm behind in my work.'

'Do you think he's got some dark secret we don't know about?'

She still had it in her head about Sarah having a decapitated head in the fridge.

'No idea. Why, have you heard something?'

'No. Not at all. I was just thinking about how he seemed to turn up out of nowhere. Was just wondering.'

Sean was nodding now. 'Well, Pete always said—'

'Be wary of what Pete—'

'. . . Pete always says that something will come out. Child porn.'

'Child porn! Where the fuck did—?'

'He just said it. And once it's in your head it's hard to—'

'Jesus Christ, Pete has no business—'

'I didn't say it, Pete said it . . .'

'Well Pete's a fucking wanker.'

'You said it . . .'

'And if anyone's going to have child porn on their—'

'And now that's in my head as well!'

Alix nosed the car back out onto the main road. 'Let's forget we ever had this conversation,' she said.

'Agreed,' said Sean.

A hundred yards further along, Alix said, 'Impossible.'

'Absolutely,' said Sean.

Another two minutes passed in silence, and then there was a low growl from Sean. 'This,' he said, 'is not the way back to the office.'

'I know. I just have to pop into Marks and Spencer for something.'

'Christ,' said Sean.

'I know. Tell Rob it's my fault.'

'I'm not talking to that pedo.'

And then they were both laughing.

Rob wasn't laughing, he was genuinely conflicted. Gerry had a dour look on his face, and had switched from tap water to wine. He was saying, 'Jesus Christ, Rob, I wasn't expecting that.'

'Well, it's not like I was hiding it, I only found out this morning.'

'I'd like to say I'm pleased for you. And I kind of am. I never thought phone hacking was your style.'

'Well, it wasn't. As an exhaustive and expensive internal inquiry has found.'

'And now they want you back.'

'They do.'

'The same people who seized your computer and escorted you from the building.'

'They were protecting themselves. Standard practice.'

'Appalling. And you'd go back to that?'

'I have to consider it.'

'*Why?* Don't you like it here?'

'Yes, of course I do, you know that. But ... Gerry, I appreciate everything you've done for me, but my kids are in England ... Not being there for them, it's killing me.'

'I understand that. Yes.'

'And the money.'

'We can't compete with that, obviously. Rob – Navar has made it a condition of buying the paper that you stay on for at least a year.'

'Gerry – there are plenty of editors out there...'

'No, Rob, there aren't.'

Rob sighed. 'Bloody hell,' he said.

★

'Sian, is it?'

She was stacking punnets of strawberries in a busy Marks's aisle. Sian, slight of frame and with her fingers sheathed in blue transparent gloves, had indeed been a regular visitor to the Churchill Nursing Home. She said Bertha was 'quite a character' and 'was always up for a fight'.

Alix smiled and said, 'Yeah – I heard she was a trade union rep at Gallahers.'

Sian's brow furrowed. 'Was she? Didn't know that.' She put her blue hand to her chest and said, 'I feel really bad now. I kept meaning to get round to see her but...' She shrugged helplessly. 'I heard she was ... for a while.'

'Well, we're not really sure how long. How did you know her?'

'I didn't really – what I mean is, I got to know her over this past few years but it was really my mum that knew her. They were great mates. When my mum got sick she made me promise that I'd look in on Bertha to make sure she was okay. My mum always said that someone should have given that woman a medal.'

'Bertha...? Because...?'

'Because of all the good work she did. Civil rights.'

'Civil ... you mean, like in America or...?'

Sian smiled. 'I know, I said the same – I don't know how old you are or where you went to school, but I tell you, when I hear civil rights I'm thinking about Martin Luther King and all that, but no, I'm talking about what went on here, all the stuff they hardly teach you about any more. When all those marches were taking place up in Derry and the like, voting rights and jobs for Catholics, Bloody Sunday and all that...'

'Bloody Sunday, yes, I know about Bloody—'

'And so did I – or I thought I did. You think Bloody Sunday

and you think Derry and marchers getting shot and the IRA really taking off because of it, so we kind of think that everyone involved would have been Nationalist or Republican, right? But actually, it wasn't just in Derry, it was all over, and it wasn't just Catholics, there were stacks of Prods involved as well. And Bertha was one of them. In Belfast. And the way my mum told it, she made a lot of enemies, and she received a lot of threats but she never took a step back. She said Bertha was never one for the limelight, but absolutely she was a driving force. Fearless and passionate, she said.' Sian blew air out of her cheeks. 'Fearless and passionate, yet she was lying there for maybe weeks and nobody cared enough to...'

'It wasn't your fault,' said Alix. 'As far as I can see, it was no one's fault. It just happened.'

Sian looked far from convinced. 'Nice of you to say. But I'm not sure my mum, God rest her soul, would agree with you. But then she was an auld frickin' battle-axe as well.'

Things were going rather well, Janine thought. He was so keen that he met her in the Café Nero for breakfast the next morning. She asked him lots of questions about his property business. He said it had been tough for the past few years, but that the market was starting to pick up.

'Well, for some,' said Janine.

'I thought your paper was doing okay. At least it's coming out every week.'

'Just about. We get plenty of the wee local advertisers – but the big companies, they hardly know we exist. When they've money to spend, they take one look at the circulation figures and then go with one of the big city papers. They really don't understand what we do, how much a paper like ours penetrates the local community, how much…'

Frank held up his hands in surrender. 'Okay, enough, I'm convinced, where do I sign?'

They both laughed.

'But honestly,' said Janine, 'it would drive you to drink.'

'Or at least another cappuccino?'

'Deal. But it's my turn to…'

'Not a bit of it.' He stood – but instead of going immediately to the counter he stopped and leaned on the table. 'It's lovely talking to you,' he said. 'My wife – unless you're an addict yourself, it's very hard for someone else to understand. But you absolutely get it. You've been there.'

She raised her empty cup. 'And not going back.'

He raised his own and they tapped.

She was buzzing from both the caffeine and her breakfast date when she got back to the office. He'd walked her to the corner and they'd chatted for a few minutes, at least until Pete came walking past, his eyes suddenly out on stalks when he saw her up close with Frank. She was hardly at her desk before he was over wanting to know who he was and she responded with, 'None of your beeswax.' Then Alix came in and wanted to know why she was glowing and Pete said, 'She's got a new man,' and Janine responded with, 'Have not. And besides, it's purely business.'

Alix was pretty buzzy herself. She'd taken a drive past Bertha's on her way in and struck lucky – there was a council employee there helping to clear out the perishables who wasn't quite as jobsworth as Irene and didn't object to her poking round the house. She found a goldmine of photos and was surprised when the woman didn't object to her borrowing some of them. The council worker was firmly of the opinion that they'd all end up in a skip anyway – 'If no one comes forward in the first twenty-four hours, then they hardly ever do. Sad but true.' So Alix returned to the office with a cardboard box full of pictures reflecting every stage of Bertha's life – from long-skirted schoolgirl to the factory floor, and from married life to the civil-rights marches and beyond.

'So she was married, then?' Rob asked after she'd excitedly plunked the box down on his desk and they began to search through them.

'Oh yes, but he seems to have died about thirty years ago. The old dear was past ninety, so she was.'

'Any kids?'

'No evidence of.'

'She's like *The Last of the Mohicans*.' Alix looked at him blankly. 'It's a book,' he added. 'A very famous book. And a movie. A very good movie. Daniel Day-Lewis.'

'Oh, I like him.'

'Anyway...' And he lifted another framed photo.

She peered over his shoulder. 'Civil-rights march – that's more your era.'

'Yeah, right. But still – union agitator, civil-rights campaigner...' He raised an eyebrow.

Alix took hold of the box. 'All right smarty-pants,' she said, 'it still doesn't mean there's something special about everyone – you just got lucky.'

She turned for the door, but he said her name – she spun back, still smiling, but something about the set of his face and the way he was rubbing at his chin caused her to drop it and push the door closed behind her. She leaned against it with the box in her arms. And waited.

'I've been offered my old job,' said Rob.

'Oh – right.'

'They want me back in a fortnight.'

'Well. And you're going?'

'My kids.'

'Of course. Ahm. Congratulations. Is this common knowledge?'

He looked slightly hurt. 'No, of course not. I wanted you to know.'

'Now I know.'

'I wanted to ask your opinion.'

'Why?'

'Just because. We're … We're…' He shrugged. He was looking in her general direction, but not actually at her. Every few moments their eyes would make contact, and then his would flit away. She didn't know how she felt. There was a jumble of thoughts. The bottom wasn't dropping out of her world, and she wasn't about to do a Mills & Boon swoon, but her head was definitely confused. There were butterflies in her stomach, but not in a good way. Like before an exam. At the gynaecologists. Or like eating wild mushrooms and not being certain they weren't toadstools. Then she realized that that was rubbish because she'd never eaten a wild mushroom in her life. It was more like taking ecstasy and not knowing whether it was the real deal or something some undertrained Chinese pharmacist had concocted with the aid of rat poison that was going to kill her but not until she'd enjoyed several hours of mesmeric dancing …

Alix tried to focus.

Rob was leaving.

There was a little fluttering angel on her shoulder whispering that she could apply for his job.

'So,' he said, 'what do you think?'

'It sounds like your mind is made up.'

'No – not at all.'

'Your wife is there.'

'My kids are there.'

'Your kids – like you say. Better pay, I'm sure, lifestyle, promotions…'

'Yes, undoubtedly…'

'Although these are the people who thought you were a…' She trailed off. Not brave enough to say it.

His brow furrowed. 'Thought I was a what…?'

'I don't really know – whatever it was they thought you were that caused you to scurry over here to take Billy Maxwell's job before he was cold in his grave.'

Rob laughed suddenly.

She said, 'Sorry, I didn't mean, I just mean…'

'I didn't scurry anywhere.'

'I know that. I said I was—'

'And really, why exactly did you think I left my paper?'

'I have no idea.'

'Well, you clearly have…'

'No, really, but you never said why, so naturally – people speculate.'

'And what did you speculate?'

'I didn't speculate at all.'

'So what did Pete speculate?'

'Pete? I never mentioned Pete.'

'You really don't have to.'

She nodded. He nodded.

She said, 'It's none of my business.'

'What I did or didn't do or me going back to England?'

'Either.'

'Really?'

Alix shrugged. Now she was avoiding his gaze.

'Anyway,' she said. She thumbed behind her. 'Things to do.'

'Okay. Ahm, keep it under your hat for now?'

'Yes, of course.'

She returned to her desk.

Pete said, 'What was that all about?'

'What was what all about?'

'The big powwow?'

'It wasn't a powwow.'

'You okay?' Michael asked. 'You look upset.'

'I'm not upset, why would I be upset?'

'Because he hates your story,' said Pete. 'It's a load of old rubbish.'

'Why would you say that?'

'Because they usually are.'

'You're so inspirational, Pete, that's why I love you.'

'You love me?'

'Take a wild guess.'

Michael began to sing: 'Alix loves Pete, Alix loves Pete...'

'Okay, children,' said Janine, 'I'm going to the bun shop, anyone want anything in the bun shop?' She had her bag on her desk and was rifling through it for her purse. She found it and took out a tenner and tossed it back in. There were no takers. 'Please yourselves,' she said and skipped happily for the door.

'Someone's happy,' said Pete.

'Maybe she's in love,' said Michael, 'like you and Alix.'

'More like Alix and Rob,' said Pete.

'Yeah, right,' said Alix. She turned to study her computer, aware that her face was reddening. She swore to herself and prayed that nobody had noticed. Pete certainly hadn't because he was out from behind his desk and crossing to Janine's: in her hurry out of the office her bag had toppled over and the contents had partially spilled onto the floor. He crouched down and began to pick them up.

'You're such a Good Samaritan,' said Sean.

Alix snorted.

Michael looked round from his computer and said, 'Why the red face?'

'Blood pressure,' said Alix, as she got up and grabbed her coat, before adding, 'and overwork. See you later.' And she was away, her head still a jumble and making a determined effort not to glance towards Rob's office as she left.

Pete returned to his desk, looking thoughtful. Michael turned to him and said, 'Do you think they're doing it?'

'What?'

'Rob and Alix.'

'He's married.'

Michael nodded. 'Well, that rules that out, then.'

But Pete wasn't listening. He was up again and crossing to Gerry's office. He knocked on the glass. Gerry waved him in.

'Any chance of a quiet word?'

'Come in, come in, my door is always open. Except of course when...'

'It's about Janine.'

'What about Janine?'

'Well, I know you two are ... were ... close...'

'Yes, Pete...?'

'And you know I'm not one for gossip...'

'Yes, Pete...?'

'It's just that this ... just fell out of her bag.' He strode across to Gerry's desk and set down the A5 flyer he'd picked up. He tapped it. 'Alcoholics Anonymous.' Gerry's brow furrowed as he studied it. 'Just wondering if ... well, you knew about it ... or if you don't ... if you should know about it ... in case you can ... you know ... help in any way.'

Gerry nodded. 'Thanks, Pete,' he said, 'your concern is noted.'

By now she really had enough information for her story, but she badly needed out of the office. Alix took her iPad, with Bertha's old photos scanned and uploaded, and called in at the Mace/post office on the corner to show them who she was talking about and to ask if they dealt with many older folk in similar situations – their nearest relatives and friends gone and withdrawing from the world to such an extent that they could lie dead for weeks or months without anyone really noticing. And by chance the first woman she spoke to, Agnes Muirhead, remembered Bertha well and got all tearful when Alix showed her some of the wedding photos. 'Gosh,' Agnes said, 'when they come in, they're so old and decrepit you forget that they were young once – she was so gorgeous.'

'So when was the last time you would have served her?'

'Bertha? Oh, it's been a while. More than a year. The grand-daughter comes in on a Thursday and picks up her pension.'

There was a little catch in Alix's breath.

'Her – I wasn't aware there was a granddaughter. Or even a daughter.'

'Oh yes – I always asked after Bertha and I remember because she always used to make that wee face you make when you're trying to sound positive but actually everything is going downhill. Do you know what I mean?'

317

'Of course. I don't suppose you remember her name or know where I might…'

'I do … but I can't tell you. Data protection. They'd have my guts for garters. Is that okay?'

'Yes … of course.'

'It's so sad. She was only in last week picking up the pension, so I suppose it must have been quite sudden in the end?'

And *this*, Alix decided, on the way back to the car, was *exactly* what it must have felt like to be closing in on a Nazi. The granddaughter was still collecting Bertha's pension even though she'd been lying dead for weeks. And if she didn't know she was dead – she might even turn up tomorrow to claim it as normal.

As she pulled out of the car park she jabbed the button to phone Rob.

He said, 'What's got you so excited?'

She told him. He told her to slow down and tell him again.

He said, 'Well that's a turnip for the books.' And she giggled happily. 'So what're you going to do now?'

'See what I can find out about the daughter, then this granddaughter who left her to rot. Maybe try the Public Record Office in Belfast for a start.'

'Okay – very good. But … without raining on your parade, let's not get too carried away. You've other work to do, too.'

'And it will be done.'

'We could put this on the back burner until this week's paper is—'

'Absolutely not! You're the one wanted this done.'

'Okay. All right. See what you can get and let's discuss later.'

'Yes, boss.' He chuckled. She liked the sound of it. She said, 'Oh … and … about earlier.'

'Earlier?'

'Your news. I *am* pleased for you.'

'Oh. Well. Thanks. Nothing decided yet.'

'And very happy that you're not really a pedo.'

Alix cut the line.

There was, hopefully, the news story still to come about the uncaring granddaughter who collected and possibly spent Bertha's pension, but that would depend on tomorrow's events. For now the main feature article about her life and times and the circumstances of her sad demise had to be written, and that meant Alix doing it on her own time if there was to be any chance of it being ready for that week's paper. That also meant switching off the TV, opening a bottle of red and laying out her notes and research material on the kitchen table. She began sifting through it, writing her notes and editing them down. She was about fifteen minutes into it – and, somehow, on her second glass – when the doorbell rang.

Rob was standing there. He held up a bottle of wine. 'I was just at the offie,' he said, 'and passing by here and thinking there's nothing worse than celebrating alone.'

Alix folded her arms. 'What are you celebrating?'

'Apparently I'm not a paedophile. Or, for that matter, a phone hacker.'

'Phone hacking? Was that it?'

'That was it. Or not it, as the case may be.'

She nodded her head slowly. He stood somewhat awkwardly.

'You really haven't lived here for that long, have you?'

'How do you mean?'

'There's no route from any of the local wine shops that would take you past my house on the way back to your house.'

'Sat nav,' said Rob, 'is notorious for this kind of thing. Besides, I meant to ask you to join me when you got back to the office, but you didn't come back.'

'I was working. And actually, I still am.'

'*Okay.*'

'But I suppose you can come in.'

She stepped aside. As he brushed past her she detected Lynx Africa and Polo mints. She directed him to the kitchen table. They finished her bottle off first. Then they opened his. She kept saying she should get on with her story, but somehow she didn't. Their talk didn't flow smoothly. Neither of them knew what *this* was. He could sense a chill when he mentioned his wife or kids. They were on safer ground with music and movies and old boyfriends. They laughed about Pete and what he was like at home, or on holiday, or how he might dance to The Smiths. They talked about Alix and what she wanted to do with her life. They talked about the paper, and she pointed out its many flaws and how she wanted to change it. They talked about Gerry and Janine and whether they were still doing it and what a chancer Gerry was and what a dragon Janine could be and tried to imagine what they'd be like in bed together. Rob said, 'Gerry'll be ducking and diving as usual,' and they got into hysterics over that and then realized that the second bottle was empty and Rob said, 'I suppose I'd better be going.' Alix said he better had because she had a story to write still. And somehow they hadn't addressed any one of the small herd of elephants in the room. Rob pulled on his jacket and she walked him to the door. They stood there, with it half open, and Rob said 'Well...' and she said 'Well...' and he gave her an awkward hug and then he was just pulling away when she caught hold of his lapel and pulled him back and kissed him on the lips, just very briefly and then shoved him out of the door saying, 'Go, go, go…'

She closed it after him and returned to the kitchen muttering, 'Bloody hell, bloody hell, bloody hell…' She stared at her work spread out on the table and knew that nothing more would be written that night.

Rob stood on the doorstep, and said, 'Bloody hell.' He looked at his car, and then looked at his keys. He swore, and started walking, and before he reached the corner the heavens opened. At first it didn't feel too bad, but after a while the cold and the chill began to bite into him and his head started to ache and he wondered what the hell he'd been thinking of, turning up at her house like that – he was her boss, he was married, he had kids and he was going back to his old job.

As Rob was getting drenched, and lurching from happiness to confused despair, Gerry was dashing from his car across to the intercom outside Janine's apartment block. He pressed the button repeatedly until eventually she answered with a gruff, '*What*?'

'Janine, it's me, let me up.'

'Me? Who?'

She sounded half asleep.

'*Gerry*.'

'Gerry? But it's not Tuesday night.'

'Very funny. Let me in.'

'But what if I'm with one of my other lovers?'

'Please. This is serious.'

'What is?'

'Janine!'

'All right – keep your hair on.'

She pressed, and a minute later he stepped out of the lift

and up to her front door, which she'd left open for him. She was standing at the kitchen counter, in her dressing gown, and pouring herself a glass of red. There was a second glass for him, but before she could start to fill it he put his hand over the brim and said, 'Not for me.'

'Christ – it must be serious. Has someone died?'

'No, of course not.'

'Has Rob been arrested for—'

'No. Janine. I'm not going to beat around the bush here.'

Normally she would have made a joke at this point, but Gerry was indeed looking very serious, so instead she just nodded slowly and watched as Gerry reached into his jacket and produced a small printed flyer and set it on the black granite.

'Alcoholics Anonymous,' he read. Then he nodded at her. 'Have you anything to say?'

'Only that I'm very sorry for your troubles.'

'You ... *my* troubles?!'

'Well I know you like a drink but—'

'I'm not talking about me! You Janine, you! We've been close, so incredibly close ... I thought you would have said something ... What?' She was smiling at him over the rim of her glass, which was just caressing her lower lip. 'Do you think you could just put the glass down for a moment so that we can talk about this? It's important.'

His hands were gripping the edge of the counter, and she could see his knuckles almost glowing white because of the pressure he was exerting. Janine set her glass down. She placed one of her hands on top of one of his. She gave it a little squeeze.

'Gerry – don't take this the wrong way, but you are such a fucking halfwit.'

'I...'

322

She tapped the leaflet with her other hand. 'Where did you even get this from?'

'Pete accidentally—'

'Pete! I might have known. Gerry, don't you know me at all?'

'How ... how do you mean?'

'Don't you know how hard I work for this paper, your paper ... ?'

'Yes of course, but if I thought it was driving you to—'

'Gerry, I don't have a drink problem ... !'

'That's what everyone—'

'I'm only going to AA so I can snare some advertising.'

'You *what* ... ?'

'In fact I was going to surprise you with it tomorrow. You know our new shopping centre? How they've given us bugger-all so far and no plans to?'

'Yes ...'

'I knew if I could get to the right guy, if I wasn't being palmed off by their advertising agency, then I knew I could reel him in. It's what I do. Look at a problem and then work out how to solve it. And if it meant standing up at an AA meeting and pretending to have a problem, then I was quite prepared to do it. And, actually, the amount I do drink might qualify for a problem if I wasn't absolutely able to cope with it. In fact, enjoy it. I can drink anyone under the table, you know that, because I do it with you all the time.'

'Yes, you do. You *really* mean this is all ... ?' Janine nodded. 'I ... don't know whether that's incredibly wonderful or deeply, deeply disturbing. Possibly it's both. But either way ...' He pushed his empty glass towards her. 'Now I need a frickin' drink.'

'That's my boy,' said Janine, lifting the bottle.

It wasn't only a fading seaside resort and a dormitory town for Belfast: it also sometimes felt like one vast retirement community, there were so many old folks' homes. This one, Cruickshank Fold, was located behind a barrier of pines so huge that for all of her life Alix had either walked or been driven past without knowing that there was anything at all behind them, let alone an old mansion that five years previously had been turned into a twilight refuge for those who could no longer look after themselves. This was where Alix found Bertha's daughter Grainne – a permanent resident for the past three years. She'd suffered half a dozen strokes and could no longer see or hear or communicate. Her nurse looked like a guard out of *Prisoner: Cell Block H* but was surprisingly softly spoken as she sat with Grainne and gently stroked her hand.

'Poor woman,' said the nurse, 'it's a terrible thing when your own daughter is more infirm than you are. Oh, Bertha was here every day without fail. Grainne's in her seventies, so Bertha must have had her young. She was brilliant with her – Grainne can't really do anything for herself but Bertha picked her up and turned her round and changed her clothes like she was a teenager. Then she just stopped coming a few weeks ago and I supposed she wasn't well again. I asked the manager to make a few calls, but I'm not sure if she got anywhere.' She lowered her voice and leaned closer to Alix. 'You kind of get taken over by events, places like this – hardly a week goes by without one or other of them passing on.'

'It must be very difficult.'

'It was at the start, but now it's like water off a duck's back.'

'What about Grainne's daughter? Does she not lend a—?'

'Tell you the truth, I wasn't aware that she had one. She's

certainly never visited, and Bertha never mentioned her. I mean, there are always family fallouts so you never really know who's who. But that surprises me, Bertha was always so open and chatty.'

'This is such a complete and utter waste of time,' Sean was saying. They'd been sitting in the car for over an hour. He raised a hand and counted off on his fingers: 'One, you don't know if she's turning up. Two, you don't know what she looks like. Three, she might leave it until next week. Or, four, she might have heard her granny's dead and so there's no reason for her to come at all. And five – you've a perfectly good phone you can take a photo with if she does turn up, so that I don't have to sit here all day because I've a hundred and one better things to be doing.'

They were sitting in the car park outside the Mace/post office. They had coffees and doughnuts. It was a stakeout. Alix said, 'I agree with all of the above. But I have a gut feeling she will turn up.' Sean rolled his eyes. '*And* if she does I want to get a proper, professional, action shot of her in the act, and only you, with your consummate skills, can deliver that, not Mr Jobs and his blessed iPhone.'

'Sweet-talker. I'm giving you twenty-six minutes, then I'm out of here.'

'That's very precise.'

'It will take me four minutes to get where I have to be, and I'm due there in thirty minutes. Do the math.'

'Do the math? Did you swallow an American?'

'Not yet,' said Sean.

'Oooh, that's gross.'

'And not how I meant it to come across at all. But you

get my drift. *Do the math* has entered the lexicon of common expressions, you don't have to be American to say, *do the math*.'

'I'm not even sure if *entered the lexicon* has entered the lexicon of common expressions.'

Sean made a face. Alix made one back. Then she said, 'Holy shit...' and nodded across the road to where a woman they both recognized was just entering the shop.

'That's—' said Sean.

'Bingo.'

They hurried across. Alix saw that she was already at the counter and stood watching her get served from behind a carousel of greetings cards. Agnes Muirhead wasn't on duty. The woman taking her place hardly even looked up as she handed over Bertha Malloy's pension. As her target turned away, shuffling the cash into her purse, Alix stepped out in front of her.

'Irene Bell,' she said.

Irene looked up, half-way to a smile that quickly faded when she saw who it was. 'Irene Dunne – remember?'

'Of course. Irene *Dunne* – collecting your pension?'

'Maybe in another thirty years! For one of my ladies. All part of the job. Anyway, gotta run...'

And she brushed past.

As she stepped outside, Sean was waiting. He fired off a dozen rapid shots, one touch of a button.

'What the fuck are you doing?' Irene snapped, while upping her pace.

Alix hurried to catch up. 'Irene ... Irene?' Irene increased her speed again. 'Irene – I know what you're up to. That's Bertha's money. You've been collecting it every week while she's been lying dead and for God knows how long before...'

326

'That's bollocks!' Irene shot back, before darting out into the road. A car skidded to a halt, but she hurried on, head down, determined to escape.

And of course she was going to – it wasn't as if Alix was about to rugby-tackle her or make a citizen's arrest. She was quite happy to watch Irene get into her car and speed away.

Sean came up beside her and saw the look on her face. 'Now, that's what I call a smile. The satisfaction of nailing your story, in the finest traditions of crusading journalism.'

Alix nodded. 'All that, yes. But mostly revenge on that two-faced cow for the hell she put me through in school. What a bitch.'

Sean nodded, too.

'You or her?' he asked.

Rob was looking at Alix through the glass as she worked feverishly to finish the news end of her story before deadline – she'd handed in the feature already – and thinking about the kiss. He knew it was just a daft peck on the lips brought on by too much drink, but there was something about it that . . .

'Penny for them?'

Gerry in the doorway.

'Mmmm what?'

'A million miles away, man.' He came in and closed the door. 'But have to say, that's a fine-looking paper this week.'

Rob nodded warily. 'Gerry, I've had time to—'

But Gerry raised a hand. 'Before you say anything, I thought you should know – I've decided to turn down Navar's offer. Janine's come through with some decent ads that should see us through the next few months – and, to tell you the truth, I just can't bear to sell. He seems like a good bloke, an honest bloke and he's certainly enthusiastic. But he probably shot himself in the foot, because he made me realize what a privilege it is to run this paper, and that actually I quite like the newspaper business. So I've done what all good businessmen do – I've courted his investment and then stolen all of his best ideas and told him to get lost. I'm determined to make a go of it, Rob – now what about you? Does this change anything? Are you going to stick with us or creep back to those scoundrels in England? Is your mind made up?'

'Yes, it is,' said Rob.

CHAPTER 8
DOG DAY
MID-AFTERNOON

As distractions went, it was a pretty big distraction.

Rob arrived late to the office on the Wednesday morning having taken a long weekend off to go and see his kids in England. Pete holding the fort, big decision in the air, speculation rife. When he walked through the door he kept his eyes front, but was aware of everyone and everything: Michael staring at his screen, pen in his mouth, a million miles away, Pete on the phone, Alix typing furiously, Janine at the counter talking to advertising clients, Gerry doing what he did best, watering the plants, but by the time he got to his office door he knew that all eyes were upon him. Even the plants seemed to turn in his direction. A tiny little bit of him was enjoying it, the teasing, being the focus of attention. But his head was still all over the place.

As Rob closed the door Michael spun in his chair to Alix and said, 'Poker face or what?'

'That's his normal face.'

'He's going, isn't he, Gerry?' Janine said as her short-shrifted clients left.

Gerry poured out the final few drops from his plastic watering can before stashing it under the counter and turning to address his staff, Eisenhower on the eve of the invasion. 'I told you,' he said, 'I asked him to take the weekend to think about it. It's a big decision and, as soon as I know for sure, you'll know. But I will say this – no matter what happens we are still a team. There is no "I" in team.'

He nodded at them wisely.

'No, but there is one in bullshit,' said Michael, then immediately regretted it. His face reddened and he deliberately dropped his pen, then bent to hunt around for it as a way of deflecting Gerry's glare.

Pete said, 'He knows fine well. They've clicked their fingers and he's away back to London. He wasn't seeing his kids, he was having his corner office repainted.'

'And what would you know about it?' Alix asked.

'I'm just saying. Or maybe you have the inside track?' He added a suggestive wink. She made a face and was about to respond but Pete's phone began to ring and he held up a hand to stop her. Alix blew air out of her cheeks and returned to her screen. But then immediately spun back as Pete said, 'Seriously? Christ. Okay, much appreciated.' He cut the line, but the receiver remained cradled under his chin with his fingers poised over the buttons. They were all looking at him. 'Someone's tried to rob O'Connor's post office on High Street. Shots fired. Cops all over the place. Caller seems to think Gavin O'Connor's trapped in there with the robber.'

'Like a hostage?!' said Michael. 'Brilliant!'

'It's not *brilliant*, it's the opposite of fucking *brilliant*. I know the O'Connors. Bloody hell.' As Michael held his hands up in apology, Pete nodded at Alix. 'Do you want to find Sean and get down there…?'

'Yes, me too,' said Michael.

'No – you work the phones for now … See if you can track down a photo of Gavin O'Connor, I know we had him at some function a few months back…'

'I'd really rather—'

'Just do it, Michael.'

'Contrary to popular opinion,' Rob said from his doorway, 'I'm still in charge. I presume we're talking about the robbery? Just got a call myself.'

'I was only—'

Michael was smiling.

Rob said, 'Alix see if you can find Sean and get down there. Michael – work the phones for now … and see if you can track down a photo of Gavin O'Connor … I think we had one a few weeks ago … Pete … keep up the good work.' A wink and back into his office.

Pete didn't like being winked at by that patronizing shit. He glanced about him, hoping he hadn't said it out loud. Alix was smirking at him, but that didn't mean anything. She was always smirking. Just once, he'd like to slap her stupid smirking face. Michael was huffing and puffing while he looked up contacts on his phone. Alix grabbed her coat. Sean came sauntering out of the kitchen, coffee in hand, and asked what was up. 'You. Me. Out. Now,' said Alix and thumbed towards the door.

Gerry said, 'I'll be having that, then,' and took Sean's coffee from him and sauntered across to Rob's office. He pushed the door open with his foot. Rob was just settling behind his desk.

'Exciting, eh?' said Gerry. 'This is what it's all about, right?'

'Jesus, Gerry, will you give me a chance? I'm only through the door.'

'No time like the present, chum.'

Rob waved his hand at the door. Gerry back-heeled it shut behind him and sat opposite. He took a sip of his coffee. Nodded. 'So,' he said.

'Gerry, it's not the paper. I love the paper – though I could probably earn more in McDonald's, plus I'd get free chips.'

'You're like one of those overcompensated footballers, always agitating for more. They should concentrate on the game they love.'

'But actually I don't mind the money so much – it's a living wage for me, here, and I do like it here. But it's not a living wage for my kids. Not in London. And, besides that, I miss them. I really miss them.'

Gerry was nodding slowly. He took another sip. 'Tell me, Rob – did I ever tell you about my mate, the Manchester United fan?'

'No, Gerry, you didn't.'

'Well, he lives and breathes them. Goes to every home match.'

'Gerry, what're you—'

'Hear me out. He lives just around the corner from me. He's a teacher, wife, two kids, not a lot of spare money around. Yet somehow he still manages to go to Old Trafford for every home game. That's every other week. You'd say to yourself, that's not cheap, how does he manage that? And do you know how he does it?'

'No, I don't, and I'm not sure I really—'

'Once a year, when the fixtures for the new season come out, he sits down and books his flights, books them so far in advance that he gets them for next to nothing. A couple of pounds, a tenner, sometimes. He loves United, but he knows he can't live there, but he can still see them every other week with a bit of forward planning. And vice versa.'

'You mean Man United come to him? Jesus, Gerry, you love your parables, don't you?'

'It's do-able Rob. Think about it.'

'I have been thinking about it. I'm still...'

'Well, think harder. I need your answer by the end of the day. I've a business to run. When Steve Jobs died, Apple didn't hang around. When Bill Gates died...'

'Bill Gates isn't—'

'It's not an ultimatum. I just need to know.'

'It sounds like an ultimatum.'

Rob's phone rang. Gerry kept eye contact with him as he picked it up. Rob listened for a moment, then said, 'For me? Are you sure?' Listened a bit more then thanked the caller and hung up. He pushed his chair back and stood. He slipped his jacket off the back and began to pull it on. 'It's the police,' he said. 'They need to talk to me.'

'Have they changed their minds? Are they charging you?'

'Funny,' said Rob.

It doesn't happen very often, a small local paper finding a major national news story on its doorstep, but when it does it can have a queer effect – some journalists rise magnificently to the occasion, others disappear into their shells and wait for the fallout. It can have a lot to do with timing. The *Express* is a weekly paper, coming out on a Thursday morning. If this story had broken on a Friday or Saturday it would have been of very little benefit – all the news value sucked out of it by the time the next issue came round. But if it happened on a Wednesday, and concluded fortuitously, say at about midnight, then that's perfect timing – next morning's paper would be bang up to date and sales could be huge. Sales, reputation, pride.

Today is Wednesday.

The function of a local paper when a national story breaks is also to act as the titular fount of all local knowledge for the descending media – the news channels, the daily-paper newshounds, the radio stars, none of whom can be expected to know very much about the little town they're suddenly sent to. A local paper usually provides this assistance free of charge. Usually. It's dressed up as a *quid quo pro* thing, but generally it never works out like that. By the time the visiting press have filed their stories and fired up their satellite trucks for their next destination they've largely forgotten who gave them a hand and who provided that essential local insight. Promises made, promises forgotten, from *High Noon* to tumbleweeds.

Rob, of course, had seen this from both sides, first as a young reporter in a small town, and latterly as a journalist on the *Guardian*. As he drove down, it absolutely crossed his mind that this might be a good way to go out – showing off what he and his team could do, what kind of a paper they could produce, that they could compete with the biggest and the best. But his main concern was how he was going to stop himself from becoming part of the story.

The hostage-taker wouldn't talk directly to the police but somehow he had hold of Rob's name and wanted to negotiate through him. The idea, the chief inspector said, was to listen and not say much – he was basically a Samaritan, and Samaritans got sacked if they started offering advice. Rob asked if they didn't have a trained hostage negotiator for situations like this, and the chief inspector said of course they did, but they were all away on a course. Rob started to laugh. It wasn't reciprocated. The chief inspector said they were flying back from London but it was his responsibility to keep the situation under control until they got there, and Rob was part of that. Pulling on water wings and dipping his feet in the pool till the swimming instructor arrived.

It was a blessing really that the robber had chosen to go into the smaller of the town centre's two post offices. This one was at the top of High Street – O'Connor's was one of the few remaining mom-and-pop operations. If the robbery had happened in Main Street, then many more people would have been at risk.

Rob found a parking spot some distance away – word was out amongst the locals. As he approached he could see at least a dozen police cars, two ambulances, the fire brigade and a chip van. There were camera trucks and photographers and journalists, with more arriving every minute. There was tape at both ends of the street, keeping everyone back. As Rob pressed through the watching crowds he nodded hello-hello-hello to numerous familiar local faces but shrugged away demands for the latest news on the siege. He liked that they presumed he would know. Rob, with his finger on the pulse. Rob, who could barely find the pulse. He spotted Alix and moved up beside her. If anyone had the pulse.

She glanced across. 'Come to check up on us?'

'Yes.'

They were about a hundred yards from the shop. The metal grilles over the display window had been pulled down, but the front door was still accessible. There were police cars immediately opposite, parked in a V shape with several uniformed officers crouching behind. They were armed, but that wasn't unusual for Northern Ireland.

'Where's Sean?' Rob asked.

'Went round the back, see if he could see anything.'

As Rob scanned the crowd, he saw Pete pushing through. And behind him – Michael. He couldn't blame them, really, it wasn't often a story of this magnitude came along. Journalists could be as big rubberneckers as the general public, plus they got paid for it. For today at least, everything else was going to take a back seat.

Alix frowned. 'It's still my story, right?'

'It's our story. The paper's.'

'But I'm, like, the chief reporter on it. Pete's going to try and muscle in, but sure he's not written a story since before the war, and Michael can hardly tie his shoes, so … that would leave you. Maybe this is exactly what you want, Rob Cullen, maybe you've set this all up so you can go out in a blaze of glory.'

'Nice try, but whether I'm going anywhere has nothing to do with this.'

'Then what are you doing here?'

'I'm leading from the front.'

And with that he ducked under the police cordon. Alix's mouth dropped open. He glanced back, giving her a wink. Her mouth remained open. Michael came up beside her and said, 'What the hell's he doing?'

'I don't…'

He'd been stopped by a constable, but instead of chucking him out he was being led forward to where Chief Inspector Clifford was standing talking urgently into his radio. Alix knew Clifford. She knew him to be an uncooperative, bumptious and humourless shit. This wasn't just her opinion, it was the general consensus. She was sure he thought highly of her as well, although realistically he probably didn't think of her at all. He was too self-centred. He had no time for journalists.

Clifford said, 'He's been identified locally as Patrick Casey. Mean anything to you?'

'Not off the top of my head. But he could have been mentioned in a story or something.'

'Well, he seems quite determined to talk to you.' Clifford raised a mobile phone. 'So, for the next few minutes you're not a journalist. You're not interviewing him. Be friendly, be calm, ask after Mr O'Connor, ask if he wants food or water, but don't agree to anything. Don't let him bargain. My people will negotiate when they get here.'

Clifford pressed a button. Rob's throat suddenly felt dry.

'Mr Casey ... Patrick ... I have Rob Cullen for you.'

Clifford handed the phone over. Rob turned it in his sweaty hand and raised it. There was something about the name nagging at him. 'Hi, hello, how're you doing?' he said, and immediately regretted it. Too breezy. Cleared his throat, lowered his voice. Man of authority, respected in the community. 'This is Rob Cullen, I'm the editor of—'

'Rob Cullen – I know who the fuck you are. How's it going, Rob?'

'Ahm – yes. Fine. Better for me than for...' He stopped himself. Clifford was glowering at him. 'What can I do for you Mr Casey?'

'Mr Casey! Would you listen to you! Rob – it's Patrick. From the paper.'

'The...'

'The fucking *News Letter* man! The good old days!'

And with that, the penny dropped. An ancient penny, a penny covered in the dirt and rust of time. Patrick Casey. Rob had just started on the morning paper in Belfast. Billy Maxwell had been his first boss there, but Patrick Casey was his first friend – not a journalist, a typesetter just a year older than him but already a veteran. Boy apprentice when you could still just about be one – been there since he was barely sixteen. So Patrick knew the ropes and went out of his way to show Rob what was what when most of the other editors, subs and reporters had been too busy, or too up their own arses to bother. Sink or swim was the prevailing attitude back then. Patrick was also one of the few Catholics employed on a paper that totally represented the Protestant heartland, and this at a time when the Troubles were still roaring along, so working there wasn't without its risks. They'd somehow become mates, drinking buddies and gotten themselves in and out of a few scrapes. But, as is the way of things, once Rob had properly found his feet the need for Patrick Casey had diminished and they'd hung around less and less. Rob had always felt a little bit bad about that – while doing absolutely nothing about it. Then he'd moved to a new job in England and hadn't given Patrick a second thought, or even a first, in many years. He'd had no idea he was now in Bangor. And now the best he could come up with was: 'Patrick ... fuck sake!'

'Good to hear you, man. Remember back in the day – you were the only one on that whole fucking paper ever called me Patrick. It was always Paddy with everyone else. And you know why.'

'Aye, well, different times.' Paddy was a way of emphasizing that he was different – Patrick could be Protestant or Catholic, but Paddy made him sound properly Irish, properly Catholic. Like a stage-Irish leprechaun. Their way of putting him in his place, or letting him know they knew what he was and that they weren't happy about it. 'So – what the hell's this all about?'

'Don't really know, mate! Whatever it is, it's fucked up. But sure – c'mon in and I'll tell you all about it.'

'Well, I'm not sure I ...'

'Ah, come on, it'll be a bit of crack.'

And then Patrick Casey cut the line, leaving Rob staring wide-eyed at Clifford.

'Well?'

'He wants me to go in.'

'Well, that's not happening.'

Rob nodded. Relief. And then immediately, guilt. Even if he hadn't seen him in years, Patrick was still an old friend. Someone who'd stood up for him and protected him. Something terrible and traumatic must have happened in his life that he could end up like this. And if he was turning to Rob in his time of need, then how could he really say no – particularly as there was a hostage whose life was clearly in danger? Could he really have that on his conscience?

A little bit of him was also thinking about the paper.

And about possibly being a hero.

He couldn't help it. It just flitted through.

And then he was thinking: are you fucking mental? Patrick has a GUN. Shots have been fired.

You have children.

Rob said, 'We're old friends.'

'Does he have a history of...? Have there been mental health issues or...? Did he ask for anything?'

'Don't know, don't know, and all he asked for was me.'

'No demands? Did he say how the hostage was?'

'No, and no.' Rob looked back at the watching crowd. He picked out Alix. He wondered what she would do in this situation. And what she would expect him to do. Would she think him a hero or a fool for going in? And why was he even thinking that – she was just ... Alix. Nothing more. He had family in London, he was getting the hell out of Dodge – wasn't he? It came to him then that, although he'd got on great with Patrick Casey in those first months at the paper, there was always something about him that was a bit ... chippy? That while Patrick had been fairly placid most of the time, when the drink was in, he was easily offended and quick to anger, and this was what had usually gotten them into those scrapes. And that, in fact, now that he thought about it, the *News Letter*, even though it was a Protestant paper for a Protestant people, hadn't actually been a hotbed of bigotry and that what *Paddy* had perceived to have been persecution was just sharp-edged banter. Rob himself had calmed and defused situations where Patrick had gotten hold of the wrong end of the stick. But Patrick had never been violent – angry, yes, but he wouldn't harm a fly. He was sure of it. So maybe the risk wasn't that great. He could talk him down again.

Bloody hell.

Alix couldn't work out what was going on. Even though Rob was involved in an animated conversation with Chief Inspector Clifford, he kept glancing in her direction. She was distracted for a moment by Pete and Michael finally arriving beside her. She looked Pete up and down and said, 'You're out from behind your desk. I didn't think you actually had legs.'

Pete's upper lip curdled up. 'Of course I have. In fact, you can watch them walk into Rob's job when he goes.'

'*Right*,' said Alix. Then couldn't help but add: 'Is he going? You've heard?'

'Not exactly,' said Pete, 'but it's inevitable. We're just waiting for the white smoke to go up.'

'Which means you know nothing and you're just slabbering for the sake of it.'

'Just wait and see. He's just putting his time in.'

Michael nodded forward. 'He doesn't look like someone who's just putting his time in.'

Alix turned. Rob was walking towards the post office.

No police by his side. Just a Tesco bag-for-life in one hand, his phone in the other.

As the crowd began to notice, a hush descended, until the only sound was the distant cry of a seagull high up, and the whirr of cameras as they captured Rob's progress. Alix could feel an almost palpable longing coming from the crowd for something dramatic to happen, a crowd weaned on dramatic twenty-four-hour news channels and *Avengers* movies. They were desperate for an immediate and possibly explosive conclusion.

She whispered, 'What … the fuck … are you doing?'

And as if in response her phone pinged and force of habit just about managed to drag her eyes away from Rob, just for a millisecond to glance at the screen; but then she saw *his* name. She clicked and the text said: 'Close your mouth and go do some work. Gunman is Patrick Casey.'

She looked back up in time to see the front door of the shop open and Rob step inside. Not even a glimpse of the gunman, of Patrick Casey. The door closed and the crowd drew breath again, breath tinged with disappointment and anti-climax.

Alix showed the text message to Pete. He nodded and said, 'It's a start. Go and find out who he is.'

'I'd prefer to stay here.'

'I'm sure you would, but he's just told you what to do, so … ?'

Pete was right, of course. She would achieve nothing by standing staring at the post office. Rob had given her a name that the other media didn't have – so she'd a head start and an opportunity to show them what she was made of. But she couldn't resist saying: 'You know, Pete – you may think you're second in command, but isn't it funny how he chooses to text me rather than you?'

She was already stalking away when he responded with, 'That's coz it's not me he's trying to get into bed with.'

She stopped, gave him a look and said, '*Trying*?'

And a patronizing wink.

She thought this was pretty clever, at least for about twenty seconds, then she decided that actually it made her sound cheap and slutty, but it was too late to take it back, or do anything about the twin red blotches on Pete's face.

Patrick Casey of course looked older. It had been twenty years. But he appeared more like thirty, maybe even forty, years older. Rob didn't know if he'd been sick or it was just bad genes, but he had not aged well. The stress of what was going on now probably didn't help much either. Patrick's eyes were out on sleepless stalks, his skin blotchy, hair clinging to his skull like wisps of wool on a farmer's barbed-wire fence. Rob was through the door, but not yet into the proper body of the shop when Patrick put the gun to the back of his head and snapped out: 'What's in the bag?'

'Patrick – take it easy. Nothing – water, and crisps.'

'Crisps?'

'Just what they had to hand, but they'll send whatever you want, need, within reason.'

Patrick pushed the door closed. 'And you can put your fucking hands down. Unless you're going to jump me.'

'No, I'm not going to…'

'What're they saying about me – all sorts of shit I'll bet?'

'No, not at all, they're just concerned about—'

'Don't give me that crap. We both know what they're like.'

Patrick waved Rob forward with the gun. He immediately saw Gavin O'Connor slumped down on the public side of the post-office counter, clutching his side; blood was soaking through his white shirt; his skin was grey. Rob crouched beside him and asked the stupid but necessary question. 'How're you doing there?'

O'Connor grunted. His eyes stayed on Patrick.

'He should be in a hospital,' said Rob.

'Tell me something I don't know. But if they hadn't shot him in the first place there'd be no need for it.'

'They...?'

'I never did nothing.'

'You were robbing me...' O'Connor rasped.

'And? Did I shoot you? No I did not. My luck there was a passing patrol. My luck they're the only cops in the whole fucking United Kingdom who still carry guns. And your bad luck that they start firing and ask questions later. But I'll bet that's not what they're saying out there, is it, Rob?'

'Well, they—'

'Of course it fucking isn't. They'll say I shot him. That's how they operate. And they'll fix it so that, by the time they drag me into court all the evidence will show it, too. Well, I've news for you, and news for them, I'm not going anywhere till they admit what they've done.' He clicked his fingers suddenly, and it took a moment for Rob to understand that he wanted the bag-for-life. He handed it over and then watched as Patrick greedily snatched out the water, twisted off the cap ... and then hesitated. He handed the bottle across to Rob and said, 'You drink first. At least half of it till I see if they've put something in it...'

'Patrick, it was sealed, and anyway they didn't have time to...'

'Drink it.'

He drank it. 'See, there's—'

'Now him...'

Rob held it to O'Connor's lips. As he did, Patrick moved to the door. He stayed to one side of it and moved his head forward just a fraction to peer out. 'Fucking vultures!'

he hissed. 'They were waiting for me. Or *you*...' He poked a finger back at O'Connor. '... you pushed an alarm or something...'

'I didn't do anything...'

'Well, they didn't just magically appear! Then they start shooting!'

'You had a gun, you were waving it about...'

'Well I wasn't going to rob you with a fucking pea-shooter, was I?'

He turned back, his face inflamed, sweat dripping. His clothes were sticking to him, big damp patches, his hands were slippery with it; he'd one finger curled around the trigger in case of a surprise attack. Rob didn't know much about guns – he didn't know *anything* about guns – but he knew that sweaty fingers and an expectation of attack wasn't a good combination.

Patrick paced about, muttering to himself. Rob screwed the top back on the bottle and said, 'Let's just try and keep things calm.' Patrick stopped and glared. 'Come on, I'm just trying to help. And remember – you asked for me.'

Patrick snorted. 'You didn't know your arse from your elbow, when you started with us. I pulled you out of a few close ones.'

'Yes, you did. And I pulled you out of a few, too. They were good times. Scary, but good.'

'Aye, well, try pulling me out of this one.'

'I'm not sure how I can...'

'You put me on the front of your paper.'

'Well, I'd take that as a given.'

'I mean – you tell everyone that I didn't shoot him. Tell everyone how they trapped me, how they're always after me, will never leave me alone, that they set me up for this...'

'I can certainly put your side of—'

'No! I tell you what to say, you print it. They don't get a fucking look-in.'

'Patrick – it doesn't really work like that. You know that. Everyone gets to have their—'

'No. They've had it their way long enough. This time I'm calling the shots.' For emphasis he waved the gun in Rob's direction. 'All I want you to do is tell the truth, what's so fucking hard about that?!'

'Nothing, Patrick, nothing at all...'

Except that truth, like beauty, is in the eye of the beholder.

Pete was a dick of the highest order, but he knew his stuff. Before Alix got anywhere finding out exactly who Patrick Casey was, Pete was on the phone with an address off the High Donaghadee Road. It was a two-up, two-down terrace that was considered working-class in Bangor but would have passed for middle- twelve miles up the road in Belfast. Pete didn't say where he'd gotten it from – he rarely did – but she knew it wasn't the police, otherwise they would surely have been there already. But as soon as she rang the doorbell and saw the smiling wife, Stephanie, it was clear that she remained in blissful ignorance. She'd a baby in her arms, and was shepherding back two toddlers with her feet as she gave Alix a breezy hello. When she said she was from the paper and asked about the police, she hardly blinked. She said. 'What's he done now?'

Alix asked if she could come in. Stephanie knew it was serious then and ushered her in. She led her down a hall and through the kitchen and out into a small, paved garden sur-rounded by a high wooden fence. There was a plastic slide and various toys littered about. They sat on slightly wonky bench seats on either side of a weather-beaten picnic table. As she lit up, Stephanie offered Alix a cigarette. Alix refused. There was no sign of an ashtray, and the ground was littered with discarded butts. As Alix described what was happening at the post office, Stephanie sat with her eyes closed, nodding slowly, while furiously inhaling and streaming smoke out through her nose. She swore several times. Eventually she said, 'I knew something like this was coming. Yesterday, yesterday I found out he got made redundant three weeks ago. He was working at a meatpacking place in Balloo. Hated it. He's a printer by trade but those jobs have gone to pot. Anyway, he was getting up every morning and pretending to go to work, only he was hitting the boozer instead. Like I say, found out yesterday and I told him to get out, 'cos it's not the first time.' There were tears in her eyes. 'Look, I don't want to sound like some hard cow who doesn't care, but I have these 'uns to be thinking about…' She nodded at her kids, two of them playing with the cigarette butts on the ground and one still on her lap, enjoying the benefits of her habit, 'and he's broken so many promises, been fired from so many … it's really just been a relief to get him out. He's got a heart of gold, love, but no common sense.'

When the moment seemed right, Alix asked if there was a photo of Patrick she could borrow for the paper. At this point she was usually either chased out or presented with hundreds of alternatives. Stephanie asked for a moment and then disappeared inside – she was gone for about five minutes. Alix busied herself picking up as many of the cigarette butts as she could and putting them in the bin. There were hundreds of them. Her hands stank. She was cleaning them with a handy wipe as Stephanie returned, but she didn't comment. She didn't appear to notice the clean-up. She was studying the photo in her hand and looking wistful. 'He was so handsome in his day...' she said, 'and he's still got it...' He did not, at least to Alix, look the slightest bit handsome, but horses for courses. Stephanie held out a small plastic medicine bottle. 'I don't know if there's any point in getting these to him? He has some disorder – doesn't like to talk about it – something that's close to schizophrenia but not as bad, but affects his concentration and moods – Jesus, he can flare up ... you may take these. They don't work like headache pills, two and you're right as rain in half an hour, but can't do any harm. I don't think he's been taking them and maybe that's...?'

'Why don't you bring them, maybe you can coax him into—?'

'No – I'm not going.'

'But he's your—'

'I know what he is. And I told him, if anything else happened I wouldn't go and sort it out, 'cos I'm always doing that. So I'm not going to. I don't need it. The kids don't need it. Christ, if he has a gun – where would he even get one?' Alix nodded, but she knew they weren't that hard to come by, not in an area like this. 'And anyway, what difference will it make? Do you think they're just going to pat him on the head and send him on his way? Armed robbery, Alix, someone's been shot from the sounds of it ... me being there's just going to make matters worse.'

'But you might persuade him to let his hostages go.'

'Hostages? I thought you said there was one...?'

'There was, the post-office guy – but my boss has gone in there too to try and talk to him. And last I heard he hadn't come out, so it looks like he's one too. Please ... you should do what you can to—'

But she shook her head. 'I can't,' she said, 'not this time...'

347

Gerry and Janine arrived together, flustered because they'd very recently been on the verge of having sex, and it not even a Tuesday, when news filtered back about what Rob had done. The boss immediately said, 'What the *fuck* was he thinking of, going in there?'

'Didn't consult us,' said Pete.

'He has no fucking right to ... How long has he been in there now?'

''Bout an hour.'

'Jesus Christ. That's not good, that's not good at all. Someone should tell his next of ... you know, his wife.'

Pete was looking at him. Janine put a hand on his arm. 'Love, that's your job.'

'Bloody hell.' Gerry took his phone out. 'I've no idea how to get in—'

'I'll text you her number,' said Pete.

Gerry stared at him. 'How the hell do you ... Doesn't matter. Send it.' He shook his head at Janine. 'What sort of a bloody idiot walks into a place like—?'

'Would you not do it for me, love, if I was being held hostage?'

'Who would dare take you hostage?'

He stalked away. Pete sent the contact and smiled up at Janine. 'I think we both know what Gerry would do,' he said.

Janine would have responded with something snarky but her eyes were suddenly drawn towards the post office. The front door was opening. As people began to notice, a hush descended. Gavin O'Connor came staggering out. The door shut behind him. He made it about ten yards before collapsing. After a brief hesitation, while they sought the all-clear from Clifford,

348

two policemen hurried forward, grabbed him by the shoulders and dragged him back behind the cover of the parked vehicles.

Inside the post office, Rob turned to Patrick and said, 'Thanks for that.'

'Your call, mate, though I don't know why you done it. You don't even know him.'

'I know him a wee bit. And he was bleeding and ... anyway, it's done.'

'And now for your half of the bargain.'

'Patrick – I said there were no guarantees.'

'You'll find a way.' He nodded down at the counter. He'd foraged a laptop from an office out the back. It was up and running and they'd a Wi-Fi signal. 'Write what you said you'd write. And write it like your life depended on it.'

Pete watched as Gavin O'Connor was loaded into the back of an ambulance. Police and paramedics were doing their best to shield him from view, but they could see he had an oxygen mask clamped over his face, and as the watching crowd broke into spontaneous applause he had enough strength to raise his hand and give them the thumbs-up. Pete watched approvingly as Sean fired off a number of shots. He raised his phone and said to a waiting Michael, 'Doesn't seem to be anyone around here getting in a state about what's happened or getting into the ambulance with him, so maybe he has no family. Have you found the house?'

Michael was three miles away, in the smart car that had once been Janine's, which had then been passed on to Rob and was now increasingly becoming his only choice of transport. As the paper's fortunes had ever so slightly improved – or, at least, Gerry's credit rating was marginally less bad

– they'd been able to lease a couple of contract vehicles for the senior staff. That meant that Michael was lumbered with the embarrassing smart car with the *Express* logo plastered all over it that nobody had ever wanted to be seen dead in. John Travolta had pimped up his car into a 'real pussy wagon' in *Grease*. The *Express* smart car was the exact opposite of whatever the *Grease* vehicle was. It was a repellent. Pete told Michael he should count his blessings, getting the run of a company car at his tender age. And that actually worked for about an hour, or until he drove it home and his mum and dad came out for a look. They weren't the types to beat around the bush. His dad said it looked like something that Benny Hill used to drive around in. 'That's you,' his mum said, 'you're Ernie, the fastest milkman in Bangor West.' Michael had no idea who Benny Hill or Ernie were, but he knew what a milk float was. One had overtaken him on the way home.

Now his pride and joy was humming slowly along past the big houses on Maxwell Road, looking for Gavin O'Connor's house. Pete had given him the number. He found it about half-way along what was commonly known as the most exclusive street in town, three doors up from Navar's, and let out a low whistle. 'Bloody hell,' he said, 'there's money in stamps. Between this and frickin' car washes I'm definitely in the wrong business.'

Pete laughed and said he'd heard there was family money and the house had been inherited. All he wanted Michael to do was fire off a few photographs on his phone, knock on the door and, if there was no reply, call with the neighbours and get a few shocked quotes from them.

'I'll give it a go, though I don't see too many signs of life in any of the houses. They're too busy coining it in. Up the workers, I say ... speaking of which...' A man in tattered blue dungarees guiding an electric lawnmower had just appeared in the front garden of the house directly opposite O'Connor's. 'I'll give you a buzz back if I get anything interesting, and fingers crossed nothing happens with Rob, at least until I get back down there. I mean—'

'I know what you mean, you heartless—'

Michael hung up before Pete could finish. Then he got out of his embarrassing car and hurried across the road. One good thing about the car was that he never really had to prove to anyone who he was. It was taken as read that nobody would volunteer to drive round in a car like that. Its yellow and red livery made it look like something that had been rejected by *The Wizard of Oz* for being too garish.

Michael had to say 'Excuse me?' twice before the guy with the lawnmower realized he was there and switched off. His eyes immediately flitted to the smart car. Michael stood on one side of a low wall and said, 'Sorry to bother you – do you happen to know Mr O'Connor across the road or are you just working here?'

'Do you mean, am I the gardener? Or don't you think I would condescend to cut my own grass?'

'I—'

'Gavin's my neighbour, but he's not here today, you'll more than likely find him—'

'I know exactly where he is.'

Michael quickly told him about the robbery and the hostage situation.

'That's ... terrible.' He stared across the road. He bit on his lower lip. 'I wonder if I should nip across and do their grass, too. Like a gesture of solidarity.'

Michael ignored that. 'Could you tell me what he's like, and how you feel about what—?'

'Oh no – I mean, but I really don't want to be talking to the local rag. No offence.'

Michael's cheeks were reddening. 'Have you actually read it recently? The local rag.'

'No, but I—'

'Well, you should give it a go. Might surprise you.'

He turned away – then right back. 'Sorry – you said, you might pop across and do *their* grass too … is that just a turn of phrase? I was told Mr O'Connor has no family…?'

'Well, yes and no – his wife was Canadian, she passed away five or six years ago now – as I understand it she had a daughter from a previous marriage. She'd be in her twenties now, but she's been back these past couple of months. Think maybe she's been doing something at the university – but I do know she was helping Gavin out in the shop some days. I see them leaving every morning. She wasn't caught up in…?'

Michael got back to the car as quickly as he could. He called Pete and said, 'There may be another hostage.'

And then he was zipping back to the crime scene as fast as his comedy car could take him. First person he saw when he parked up was Sean, standing a fair bit away from the action, talking to another photographer. As Michael jogged up, the other guy nodded and moved off. Michael excitedly told him about the possible second hostage. Sean didn't seem quite as excited. A bit more dour than usual.

'What's up?'

'Nothing.'

'Out with it.'

'Seriously, nothing. Nothing much.'

'Sean…'

'That guy I was talking to, works for a photo agency up in town.'

352

'So?'

'Says my work's been noticed.'

'I'm sure it has, it's hard to get photos so out of focus, particularly with the technology we have these days.'

'Funny.'

'So what'd he say?'

'He said they've seen my work and think it's good. I should think about joining an agency as a freelance – staff jobs are going the way of the dinosaur…'

'You can say that again…'

'And with an agency, big story like this comes along, you syndicate your stuff and you're rolling in it.'

'The man has a point.'

''Cos no matter what I take here, I'm getting my pay and that's it.'

'Likewise. And did he offer to cut you in on any brilliant pics you get and can slip to him on the QT?'

Sean cleared his throat. 'Maybe.'

'I had the same from a guy from a news agency. Bunch of sharks, the lot of them.'

'Aye,' said Sean. 'I suppose.'

'Mate, the grass is always greener.'

'Aye, and sometimes it actually is.'

There was a hole in the shutters, not much more than a pinprick, but enough for Patrick Casey to keep an eye on the activity outside. It was getting into the gloom of early evening now; there were more police, more media. Somewhere in the background Rob could hear the jingle of an ice-cream van. There had been intermittent chats with Chief Inspector Clifford, but Patrick refused to let Rob speak to him directly, instead making him shout across the width of the post office that he was okay. And he was: apart from his racing heart and his banging head and his realization that he was the biggest fool on the planet, walking into a situation like this. He had kids. He had his whole life. And here he was banged up with a nutcase holding a homemade gun.

Homemade. That's what he said. Some old stage gun his dad had owned, his dad who'd worked as a prop guy at the Lyric in Belfast, but Patrick had adapted it in his workshop. Nothing better to be doing with his time. And it clearly worked. Rob wasn't buying for one moment that the police had shot Gavin O'Connor; Patrick had done it, it was written all over him. Yes, he'd pulled Rob out of more than a few scrapes when they'd been young and stupid, but it came to him now that most of the pulling-out had been achieved by acting madder than the next guy. His colleagues had always said that Patrick was a bit of a headless chicken, you just wound him up and he set blindly off, knocking over whatever or whoever got in his path. And now Patrick was standing over him, home-made gun perilously close, watching while Rob typed out his manifesto, his life story, his *raison d'être*, knowing all the while that no one, least of all his own paper, was ever going to publish it, not in this form, and that while he had done the noble thing by bargaining for Gavin O'Connor's release, it left only him as the hostage and victim. Once that would have meant something for about half an hour, but the Internet meant that the stupidity of his death would live for ever.

Patrick was stomping around saying, 'This is nuts! I was only in for fucking stamps!'

'With a gun...'

'Only for insurance ... they were fucking waiting for me ... let me see...'

354

Rob moved to one side, one eye on the door, as Patrick began to read the story. He could make a bolt for it. And get shot in the back. He could just jump him. Punch his lights out. His last fight? Primary seven. And he got hammered. Rob was no man of action. Man of inaction. But the pen was mightier than the sword.

Load of crap.

'Fuck sake!' Patrick swung round, gun up. 'What the fuck is this?'

'It's what you—'

'No, it fucking isn't!' He jabbed the barrel of the gun at the screen. 'He *believes*, he's *convinced*, he *maintains* … you're making it sound like I'm imagining it all! The fucking truth is they ambushed me! They shot the oul' fella and now they want to make it look like it was me! I told you what to write so *just fucking write it …* !'

'Patrick … listen to me … c'mon, you've worked in papers, you know what they're like – if I write it the way you want me to, they'll never print it …'

'It's your paper, they'll do exactly what you—'

'No – I only edit it. If I do it your way, then it's not a balanced story, they just won't let me …'

'Even to save your life?'

'Not even to save my life …'

'You always were a gormless fucking spineless little shit.'

'Thanks.'

'Why do you think I called you, out of all people?'

'Because I'm a gormless fucking … whatever …'

'No, Rob, Jesus, I don't mean any of that, you know me, I always opened my fucking mouth before my brain was in gear. I called you because we go back. Because I trust you. I just need you to put my side of the story across so that those

355

bastards...' And he stopped suddenly – a sound from above. 'Christ, they're...' And he jumped behind Rob and raised the gun to his head. 'Any of you bastards come down those stairs, I'm blowing his fucking head off...!' He pushed Rob forward, behind the counter, towards a set of stairs leading up to God knows what. 'Do youse hear me! You try anything and...'

And then they were both looking up the stairs. There was a girl, nineteen, maybe twenty, cowering there on the top step, summer dress, clasping her red knees, tear-stained face, blonde tangled hair ... 'Please...' she said.

'Who the fuck are you?!'

'I work here...' Accent American. 'My stepfather ... when you ... I was using the—'

'Did they send you in here? Did they fucking—?'

'No...!'

'Patrick,' said Rob, 'look at her, nobody sent her in...'

'Please, I just want to go home...'

Patrick rubbed his gun hand across his brow. 'For fuck sake,' he spat. 'Right – get down here...'

She stood hesitantly and began to move slowly down the stairs, leaning on a chipped wooden bannister for support. As she reached the bottom and Patrick pulled her into the body of the shop she let out a little yelp. Patrick moved the gun from covering Rob to resting it against her neck.

'What've you been doing up there, who've you been talking to...?'

'Nothing! No one!'

'Where's your phone?'

'My bag was down here!' She pointed behind the counter. 'Look, it's in there...'

There was a brown leather handbag resting behind a stool. Patrick looked at it and shook his head. 'What's your name?'

'Lisa…'

'Well, listen, Lisa, you sit the fuck down there…' and he indicated the wall opposite, beneath one of the windows, 'and if you move a muscle I'll fucking shoot you. Because that's what it's come to. Did you see what happened? Did you see the cops shoot your dad?'

'He's not my … and no, I was upstairs, I just heard a shot and—'

'Well, it wasn't me.' He swung round, pointing the gun at Rob once again. 'But this stuck-up shit doesn't want to put that in his precious paper.'

'I'm just trying to—'

'Well, tell you what – if you won't do it for your own life, how about you do it for this wee doll's? For sweet little Lisa here?' The gun ranged back. 'Eh, how's about that, then?'

He said it like Jimmy Savile said it.

Abject fear from Lisa, her eyes huge and wet.

'Patrick, there's no need to—'

'There's every fucking need! Now, write what I told you to write!'

Rob nodded slowly. 'I'll write it. Okay. But just listen to me. I know what I'm talking about, I know what will fly and what won't, that's what I've told you again and again. If we just make it about you blaming the police, then it won't get printed, not in a million years. But if we make it about you, what drove you to this…'

'Nothing drove—'

'Are you married?'

'What the fuck…'

'Kids? Do you have kids?'

'Yes! Three!'

'Then that's what we use, you did this for them. You were

357

driven to it. Patrick, come on, you're not stupid, they're going to throw the book at you for this. But at least we can make your case. Maybe you're Robin Hood, robbing from the rich to give to the poor...'

'I am the fucking poor!'

'Well, there you go! Desperate times call for desperate measures...'

Patrick tapped the barrel of the gun against his cheek. He shook his head. He sighed. 'Fuck sake,' he said, 'it shouldn't have come to this.'

'You can still walk out. I'll walk out with you.'

'No, not now, not till I have my say.'

'Then, have it. Your words, mate, but I write them in a way that people really understand what happened. Then we can all walk out of this.'

Patrick snorted. 'You know something?' Rob shook his head. 'Stamps are really fucking expensive. That's what this is about.'

'How do you mean?'

'I was applying for jobs, needed some stamps, I was like 5p short and that oul' fucker wouldn't let me off with it.'

'And you just happened to have a gun with you.'

'Problem is, I owe 5ps everywhere. I have to watch my back.'

It was dark – or would have been but for the arc lights the police had set up, so that it looked more like a film set than a real-life siege. Gerry said to Michael, 'It's like *Dog Day Afternoon*,' and Michael nodded, not having a clue what he was on about. Gerry said the same to Pete and Pete said, 'Remind me how that ended?' while knowing fine well that one of the hostage-takers took a bullet to the head. Gerry said it to Janine and she went all dreamy-eyed and purred, 'Al Pacino...'

Gerry said, 'He was just a boy then. He must be knockin' seventy now.'

'I'd still do him,' said Janine.

Sean appeared at Michael's shoulder.

'Anything good?' Michael asked.

'There are a limited number of pictures you can take of metal shutters.'

'I was thinking about what you said earlier.'

'About you being a prick?'

'When did—?'

'Only rakin'. About what?'

'About you and the agency fella.'

'Offering me a job?'

'You never said he offered you a job.'

'Aye. Well. He did, kind of. Without actually saying it out loud.'

'Well – like, I didn't mean to rain on your parade. All this…' And he nodded towards the police cordon and the gawping crowd. 'Not the sort of thing that happens here every day, or month, or year, or … What I mean is, with a camera, you can travel anywhere. See the world. Or at least Belfast.'

'I know that. But you had the chance to go to uni. You never took it.'

'Well, I deferred it. I can still go.'

'I thought you turned it down.'

'Well. I might have given that impression.'

'You sneaky fucker.'

'Well, I'd be an unemployed sneaky fucker if this paper goes tits up. So sometimes it's good to keep something in reserve.'

'I don't know. Can't say I'm not tempted. But, you know, it's not like I ever dreamed about doing this in the first place.

I was happy on my skateboard and smoking the odd spliff. Then Rob comes along and tells me I'm a photographer, and next thing you know, I *am* a fucking photographer. And this is, y'know, it's home. I'm comfortable here.'

'Beware of comfortable, or you'll end up like him.' Michael nodded along the line of the cordon towards Pete. 'A prematurely aged gargoyle in corduroy trousers and comfortable shoes.'

'A fate worse than death.'

Pete saw them looking at him. He knew they were talking about him. It didn't worry him in the slightest. The day he took what little shits like them had to say seriously was the day he'd hang up his quill.

Gerry was saying, 'But it makes you think.'

'Sorry, what?'

'How your whole life can change in an instant.'

Pete nodded. After a few moments of appropriate but imaginary contemplation he said, 'So if the worst happens ... I mean, if he goes back to England...'

'The King is dead, long live the King.'

'Meaning?'

'Well, you'll step in.'

'Or some other young hellion with power points and slides and digital dreams will talk the good talk and you'll hire them on the spot because they're new and shiny. And then when they realize they're working in a dump they'll be off in a couple of months, just like yer man in there.'

'Pete, I think we've both learned a lot since Rob came. There's been a bit of an Arab spring.'

'Well, we know how that ended.'

'Fair point. But at least we're still here, and we might not have been. Even you, though you're probably not prepared to admit it, have changed the way you think about things. Some things, anyway. So, if he does go, you'll definitely be in prime position.'

'Prime position.'

'Definitely top five.' Gerry gave him a wink. 'Anyway – talking about leadership qualities, we're going to have to put the guts of this paper to bed in the next hour no matter what goes down here. You can handle that okay?'

'Is the Pope a Catholic?'

'Well, these days it's hard to ... C'mon, I'll give you a lift back, I'll give you a hand where I can ... What about these guys?' He nodded along the line to Michael and Sean, who'd now been joined by Alix.

'They're better off here. Alix'll keep them right.' Then he cleared his throat. 'Not that I think she has any particular talent in that direction.'

'I hear you, Pete, I hear you.'

Janine and Alix watched them go. As if Janine could read her mind, she said, 'The day he becomes editor, is the day hell freezes over.'

'You think?'

'I know. Never underestimate pillow talk.' She gave Alix a theatrical wink. 'Talking of which, what about you and our hostage?'

'Rob?'

'No, the postmaster. *Yes*, Rob.'

'What about him?'

'Alix. C'mon. It's written all over you. You're nuts about him.'

'Yeah, right. I'm not nuts about anyone. Especially—'

'Does he know?'

'Does he know what?'

'How you feel about him?'

'FFS and LOL, Janine.'

'I'm sorry, what?'

'There's nothing going on!'

'Listen, I see the way you look at him. And he, at you.'

'We have a bit of a laugh, that's all.'

'Alix, don't knock it. It's the best feeling in the world.'

'What is?'

'Being in love. I do it all the time. And I've four engage-ment rings the buggers are never getting back and a divorce behind me, so I'm something of an expert. I'm just saying, if there is something there, go for it. Nothing worse than regrets.'

'Why, have you heard he's going, on your famous pillow?'

'Nope, not a dicky bird.'

They nodded, eyes on the post office. After a minute Alix said: 'So what about you and Gerry? Is that love?'

'God, no. We're just fuck buddies.'

Alix snorted. 'I wish I hadn't asked.'

Janine was laughing, too. But then she glanced behind at the sound of a car door slamming and her smile faded. 'Alix – what I said, about being in love and just going for it? Well, you might want to park that for a bit.'

Alix looked where Janine was looking – and there was Rebecca, Rebecca of the thunder thighs and huge ass, Rebecca the ex who wasn't quite an ex, Rebecca just having climbed out of a taxi, immaculately dressed in a black suit, Rebecca looking pale-faced and wide-eyed as she took it all in, the post office, the police cars, the waiting crowds, the ambulance, the fire brigade, all eerily overlit by banks of lights better suited to a movie set, or with nothing at all seemingly happening, a TV drama on pause.

'Fuck,' Alix said under her breath.

'Look at her,' said Janine. 'She looks like she's dressed for a funeral.'

She regretted saying it immediately.

Sort of.

Patrick had Lisa up by the elbow and was now making her stand over the computer where Rob had just finished writing his second draft of the story he wanted printed on the front page of the *Express*. She was to be the man or woman in the street, giving her reaction just like any normal reader. This was quite hard to do, given that she was a hostage with a gun being held on her. But she wasn't stupid – scared shitless, yes, but bright enough to know to play along, to tell him what he wanted to hear.

Patrick said, 'So? What do you think? Does it make me look like an idiot?'

'No … Of course not,' said Lisa, her voice reedy. 'It makes you look like … someone who loves his wife and kids and … resorts to desperate measures to help them…'

Patrick nodded slowly. 'That *is* what it's about. Okay.' He turned to Rob. 'And yet she hasn't come. If she'd come, the cops would be on saying your wife's here and wants to talk to you. She hasn't come because she doesn't care.'

'You don't know that,' said Rob, 'and you haven't asked for her. Maybe they don't even know about her or she doesn't know about you. They won't have given your name out. She might have no idea at all.'

'*Really*?' Thick with sarcasm.

'Really. But, listen, if they're going to run this in time for tomorrow's paper, they're going to need it now. And I'm not saying they will run it, or if they do if they'll run all of it. But unless we send it we'll never know.'

'Send it, then. But I don't want it in tomorrow's paper. I want it in tonight's.'

'We don't come out until—'

'Make an exception. This is important. The story needs out there now.'

'Well – I can ask. It's not up to me.'

'Just fucking do it. And Rob – I was a good printer, you know that, but I was never a big reader. If you've done anything sneaky here, and I haven't spotted it, and you send it off and they find something out which helps them get in here, or it makes me look like a fuckin' eejit, you're the one who'll be getting the bullet in the back of the head. Or maybe even the front. You hear what I'm saying?'

'Maybe I should take one more look at it.' Rob leaned closer to the screen – but then immediately backed up. He smiled. Forced it. Keeping it light. 'Patrick – I wouldn't do that. Just let me send it, okay? But once it's gone, it's out of my hands, it's not my call what they do with it. Okay?'

'Do it,' said Patrick.

Gerry never claimed to know anything about the actual news side of his business – he was more interested in watching the money come rolling in. Or not, as the case often was. Even on the big stories, he tended to leave them to it. This night, however, it was personal. He paid scant attention to the advertising features waiting for his approval and more to what Pete was working on, the story Rob had just sent through, the story that his life probably depended on, a story about which they were intent on making a decision themselves, without involving anyone else, like the police, or psychologists or family members. They were a law unto themselves, and probably foolish with it. He knew it, but couldn't, or wouldn't do anything about it. Pig-headed. Always was. 'Gerry always knows best,' Janine said, 'even when he doesn't.'

Pete said, 'So this goes on the front, and the hostages walk free.'

'So it *is* hostages?'

'Yup. Not sure if the police even know that yet.'

'So we run it, right?'

Pete just stared at the screen.

'Pete?'

'We could.'

'Could?'

'Maybe even should.'

'Pete? What?'

Pete sighed. 'I never thought I'd hear myself say this – but I am. I'm thinking what would Rob do in this situation?'

'Well, he sent you the story so—'

'Under duress.'

'We don't know that.'

'I think we pretty much do.'

'The problem is – it's really not a front-page story. It's a feature article. It's an interview. Lots of background. It's not a news story. *This* is a news story.' He clicked a button and an alternate front page appeared. 'Alix's. Once again, I hate saying it, it's really very good. And exactly what we should be printing. Big story. Dramatic. Well written. Will sell a lot of copies.'

'So we make up a dummy edition tonight, make sure they see that in the post office, and then print the proper edition tomorrow when hopefully this is all over. Might cost me a few extra quid but I'm good for it. I can dock it out of Rob's wages.' Not even the hint of a smile from Pete. 'What's the problem?'

'Problem is that Rob was able to send us his story. So we know they have Internet. Therefore this Patrick Casey can contact anyone he wants to check if the paper is out there, on sale, available. The fact is that he could just put it all up on Facebook or speak directly to every media organization in the world. But he has chosen us. That says something, and it means we have a big responsibility. And it shows how important he thinks our paper is, how we serve our community, how he can trust us to get his message across.'

'Not forgetting that he's a fucking looper.'

'That may be. But he's still picked us. And remember, the story also says he used to be a printer, so he's going to know how easy it is to run off a fake cover.'

'So what the bloody hell are we supposed to do?'

Pete nodded slowly at the screen. Then looked up at Rob: 'It's not *we*, Gerry, it's *you*. The buck stops with you. I don't mean it unkindly, but you're the boss. You can go out there and ask the cops what to do. Or you can run Rob's story, no dummy cover, fully printed and distributed as per instructions. Even if it doesn't ultimately save his life it will definitely buy him some time so that someone who does know what they're doing can try and save him.'

'Tell me again what the downside of printing it is, then?'

'It betrays every journalistic principle we stand for.'

'And should I really give a flying fuck about that when a man's life is at stake? This isn't fucking *Lou Grant*.' Pete nodded. No further explanation necessary. Look it up. 'Do you think a single one of our readers gives a frig about our journalistic principles? They want news and courts and football. They

want badgers and drunks and new jobs. They won't give a shit
if we print a bullshit story for one week to save a man's life.'

'No, they won't.'

'Then, what's the fucking problem!'

'It's the wrong thing to do. It's giving in to his demands.
It's caving in to terrorism.'

Gerry began to nod slowly, but then stopped and his brow
furrowed. 'No, Pete...' he said, 'you're wrong...'

'How? It *is* terrorism. If he was some Islamist nutter about
to cut Rob's...'

'No, I mean you're wrong about it being my decision.'

'How do you—?'

'You've been gagging to be editor all these months, and
now here you are, the man in charge. I always told Rob I
wouldn't interfere in editorial decisions, and I'm not going
to start now. Rob isn't here. He's on his holidays. He's indis-
posed. You're his deputy, you're in charge, Pete. It's your call.
Make the wrong call, and yes, he might die. But you'll still get
to be editor. Make the right call and he walks free, and you'll
be a hero, or more likely no one will thank you for it and
you won't even get a pay rise out of it. But it's still your call.
So make it.' Gerry thumbed behind him. 'Now I'm going to
do what I do best. Water those fucking rubber plants.'

He turned away.

He really did.

He thought he had argued his position expertly.

Though a large part of him knew he was running away
from making a decision. It was the story of his life.

Two hours later, a single light just visible burning inside the
post office, but no other required because of the arc lights,

the police in ever greater numbers, a trained negotiating team finally arrived but having nothing to do because Patrick Casey wasn't taking any calls. The crowds had thinned – the combination of a heavy downpour and early-onset boredom. Nothing was happening, they were tired and hungry and had work the next day and they could watch it on TV. In HD, which was better than real life.

Alix was miserable. They all were. When you're on a story that requires a lot of hanging about, the adrenaline gradually dissipates, or at least morphs into a kind of bone-wearying fatigue. There are only so many notes you can make, people you can call or photographs you can take. Essentially you're waiting around for someone to die or get released. Even if you know them, you just want it over, one way or another.

There was a coffee shop on the corner that agreed to stay open late. Agreed because they were concerned. Possibly for Rob, possibly for their profits, probably a bit of both. Alix joined the queue. There was a deal for a hot chocolate and a muffin. She wasn't much into muffins so asked if she could swap it for one of the cookies stacked right beside them by the till, in the same small display rack. The barista said no. That wasn't the deal. The deal was for the muffin. Alix gave him her sweetest smile and said she didn't like muffins. The barista was unmoved. Alix told him to forget about the muffin and she'd just take the hot chocolate. He went to make it. Alix fumed. She stared out of the window. She could see Rebecca. Standing by herself. Rebecca of the thunder thighs. When the barista came back she ordered a second hot chocolate. When he brought that back she said she'd reconsidered and would take the original deal. She paid. She lifted her two carry-out hot chocolates and one of the muffins and turned for the door. The barista called after her that she'd forgotten one of her muffins.

'No, that one's for you.'

'For me?'

'Yes, I want you to stick it up your hole.'

And then she was outside on the damp pavement, hoping that those behind her in the queue would have found it funny, but realistic enough to realize that they'd probably just think she was a snotty cow. No matter. She girded her loins and headed across to Rebecca. She gave her a breezy-yet-sympathetic *hi* and held out one of the hot chocolates. When Rebecca took it she also handed over the muffin. It was an unspoken peace offering, and also an attempt to further enhance those thighs.

Alix said, 'You looked so alone standing there. We should have come over earlier.'

'You have your jobs to do. I'm sorry, but you're ... Angie ...?'

'Alix ...'

'Alix, of course.' Rebecca took a bite of her muffin, and Alix was partly thinking *I hope you choke on it, you fat bitch* while knowing full well that there was no reason at all why Rebecca should remember her name, particularly at this time, when the man she was still married to was locked up with a crazed gunman. But she couldn't help herself. It was human nature. Or dog eat dog. Or the circle of life.

Alix was staring at the post office, but became aware of Rebecca looking at her – appraising her, probably.

Rebecca said, 'Are you humming "The Circle of Life"?'

'Was I? Sorry. Wasn't even aware of it. Nervous. Tense. I do that. Hum. Or whistle.'

Stop fucking babbling ...

Rob's in there. With a gun to his head.

Rob ... the man I ...

... work for ...

369

Fuck!

She found herself putting her hand on Rebecca's arm. She said, 'I'm sure he'll be fine.' Rebecca nodded. 'The guy with the gun – he's married, but his wife won't even come down. She's that pissed off at him.'

'Well, at least I'm here.'

Yep. His wife. Mother of his kids.

Eat up.

The distraction came in the form of Michael's ridiculous smart car pulling up and him hauling out a tied bundle of the *Express*, fresh off the press. Alix was confused – the paper wasn't due out until the morning, and by then she was certain the siege would be over, one way or the other. It had to be a special edition – but why rush it out long after the shops had shut? She wasn't thinking about the fact that her story would be the lead. Or very little of her was. It was only natural.

Patrick came away from the tiny hole in the shutters and said, 'Papers are here.'

Lisa said, 'Do you want me to go out and get them?'

'You'll do a runner. Rob, you go.'

'How do you know I won't?'

'Because I'll shoot her if you do.'

'I didn't think you shot people.'

Stupid thing to say, but out before he could help himself.

'Seems like as good a time as any to start.' Patrick was smiling, but without even the essence of humour. 'Maybe we should both go, mate. Just charge out. They won't expect that. Be like the end of *Butch Cassidy and the Sundance Kid*.'

'I don't much care for the end of *Butch Cassidy*.'

'*I don't much care.* Listen to you, all airs and graces.

Just go and get them, mate.' He walked Rob to the front door, taking care to stay off to one side, out of sight of the sharp-shooters he was sure were lining the rooftops. The Mexicans with their Gatling guns. As Rob reached up to open it Patrick said, 'And, mate...?' Rob looked back at Patrick's gaunt face, his hooded, desperate eyes. 'I know we go back – but really, don't try anything, okay?'

Rob wasn't going to rush anything. He was going to give them as long as possible to realize something was happening. He blinked against the glare of the arc lights. Then he stepped out with his hands raised. A *whirr* of cameras. A buzz of glad-iatorial anticipation from the crowd. The bundle of papers was sitting tied up about six metres away. One step at a time. He tried to pick out faces in the crowd – but the lights were too bright. He was an actor on stage, a rock star.

A voice said, 'How's it going in there, Rob?'

The chief inspector.

'Fine,' said Rob. 'And dandy.'

From behind, Patrick hissed, 'Shut the fuck up and get them back in here.'

Sean had the perfect picture. In that instant it didn't matter that Rob was his boss, his mentor, the man who'd gotten him into this bloody business, it was all about catching the hostage crouching down by the papers but glancing up, his eyes wide with terror and shock. It would look brilliant in black and white.

Then another movement caught his attention – higher up, above the shop, figures moving in the shadows.

Rob looked down at the front page of the top paper.

At the huge headline: *Siege.*

A sub heading: *Gunman shoots one, takes hostage in post-office drama.*

And beneath that, a familiar by-line: *Exclusive by Alix Cross.*

Rob stared at the cover and tried to think big important thoughts, in case they were his last. About the meaning of life. But the only things that came to mind were his kids, the phrase *this is where the shit hits the fan,* and Alix. He wanted to strangle her. Or kiss her. But beyond everything he wanted to live. He could make a dash for it now. If Patrick wanted to shoot him he'd have to step out from behind the door and expose himself. There would surely be marksmen waiting for just such an opportunity.

But he knew he wouldn't, couldn't do it.

Yes, he might survive. But he'd be like that fella on the *Titanic,* the one who'd slipped or tricked his way onto the lifeboat. The one who couldn't live with the guilt and blew his brains out later.

'Rob!' Patrick hissed.

Now or never – see my kids, people won't blame me.

Patrick's not really that bad. He'll never harm Lisa. She's only a wee girl. American girl. Tom Petty. He wouldn't shoot her. If he shoots her, America will probably invade. It has form.

Fuck!

Rob lifted the papers and turned back to the post office. He stepped inside and the door slammed behind him. He carried the papers across to the counter, Patrick behind him, 'C'mon, c'mon, c'mon, lemme see...'

It was *Dog Day Afternoon.*

Patrick could have demanded helicopters or millions in unmarked notes, instead he wanted Wyoming, or at least the *Bangor Express.*

He stared at the cover – still partially obscured by plastic tape, but the anger was building. He reached across the counter and grabbed a pair of scissors and snapped the binding free, and there it was in all its glory.

'Fuck.'

'Patrick.'

'You fucking fucker.'

'I told you they—'

'This isn't what we sent! This isn't what we agreed!'

'And I did what I could. But I warned you…'

'You fucking stitched me up!' and he snapped the gun right up into Rob's face. 'You lying, cheating, fucking bastard.'

'Please don't,' said Lisa.

'And you shut the fuck up, too!'

'It's okay,' Rob said to her, 'it's going to be—'

'No, it fucking isn't!'

Patrick kept his gun on Rob, but used his free hand to flick open the front page. Rob's article covered the second and third pages. There were photos of Patrick, younger, older – and of his wife and children.

'You fucking—'

'They're just doing their job, Patrick, you know how it works…'

'This one thing I asked! This one thing!' Back to the front page. 'I gave you everything and you turn out this fucking shit!'

And it was an odd thing.

Rob no longer felt scared.

Or, he must have done, but it was masked by something, a sudden dawning of wisdom, something he'd dragged out of his … soul, or heart, or liver … God knows, but enough for him to shake his head and just calmly say: 'You know something, Patrick?'

'*What*?!'

373

'From what I can see, it looks like a pretty good paper. You'd have been proud of putting that together once. I'm proud of it now. What my team has done. We're only a wee paper, but look at it, it looks class.'

'Are you taking the fucking piss?'

'No, Patrick, I'm not.'

Rob took a step back. He beckoned Lisa closer. She hesitated before moving beside him. Maybe whatever he had discovered was catching.

'What the fuck are you doing?'

'Patrick. I did what you asked. I warned you how it might turn out, but I did it. Whatever way you look at it, your story is out there. People will love the front page, and as a journalist that's what you want. You want to capture your reader. Big news, big headlines go on the front. Then they'll look inside for the detail. So they will know your story. And that was my side of the bargain. So now you have to let us go.'

'We didn't have any fucking bargain!'

'Yes, we did.'

Standoff, gun raised, hand shaking.

'Patrick – were you telling me the whole truth? About shooting Mr O'Connor? Was it really the police?'

'Yes!'

'Because you're not the sort to shoot anyone?'

'No!'

'Then you're not going to shoot us, are you?' Rob put his hand out, and Lisa clasped it. 'So we're going to walk out of here now. It's up to you what you do. I'd quite like you to drop the gun and walk out with us. I'll tell them you didn't harm us, it was just a misunderstanding which got out of hand. And if what you say is true, then the forensics will soon prove it, won't they?'

'They can fix forensics so it looks like . . .!'

'Just come with us, Patrick. End this now.'

'No! No fucking way! And you're not going anywhere!'

The gun roving between the two of them now. Rob felt Lisa shaking against him. She could probably feel him, too.

'Yes, we are,' said Rob.

And he turned them for the door.

A single gunshot rang out.

Unmistakable.

An instant, but also an eternity.

There were police on the roof, behind their cars, frozen.

Rebecca holding hands with Alix, involuntarily.

Sean's camera raised, but how do you take a photo of a sound, maybe of an invisible death, except to swing round and capture the faces of those watching, mesmerized, terrified and gloating?

Pete there, Michael, even Gerry and Janine.

And a door opening and Rob coming out with his arm around a stumbling Lisa, and the police, not sure yet what was happening, yelling for them to stop.

And Rob and Lisa on their knees with their hands raised.

And a car pulling up, and Patrick's wife Stephanie guiding her two children out of the back, and then unstrapping the third from the car seat and them all looking towards the lights, and the man and woman on their knees surrounded by armed police and other armed police cautiously approaching the front door of the post office, which was now flapping open and shut in the breeze because there was no one left alive inside to stop it.